THE FROZEN SEA

HEARTLANDS

LIGHTSPIRE

VASTRA

EASTERN
BARONIES

ORLES

MALTHUSIA

ADELPHUS
RIVER

ELARIS

SPARRA

SOUTHLANDS

ANCIENT
SEA

TAU LORREN

TO RED WASTES

ANDREW SHVARTS

HYPERION

Los Angeles   New York

First Edition, May 2017
1 3 5 7 9 10 8 6 4 2
FAC-020093-17104
Printed in the United States of America

This book is set in 12-point Minion Pro, Avenir/Monotype; Amulet/ G-Type Fonts
Designed by Tyler Nevins

Library of Congress Cataloging-in-Publication Data

Names: Shvarts, Andrew, author.
Title: Royal bastards / Andrew Shvarts.
Description: First edition. • Los Angeles ; New York : Hyperion, [2017].
  Series: Royal bastards • Summary: Tilla, the illegitimate daughter of Lord
  Kent, bands together with other outcasts in an attempt to prevent civil
  war and protect Lyriana, a sheltered visiting princess whose life is in
  danger.
Identifiers: LCCN 2016028096 (print) • LCCN 2016055900 (ebook) ISBN
  9781484767658 (hardback) • ISBN 9781484798539 (ebook)
Subjects: CYAC: Fantasy. Adventure and adventurers—Fiction. Fathers
  and daughters—Fiction. Illegitimacy—Fiction. Insurgency—Fiction.
  Princesses—Fiction. Magic—Fiction.
Classification: LCC PZ7.1.S5185 Roy 2017 (print) • LCC PZ7.1.S5185 (ebook)
  DDC [Fic]—dc23
LC record available at https://lccn.loc.gov/2016028096

Reinforced binding
Visit www.hyperionteens.com

For Alex

one

Princess Lyriana came to Castle Waverly two months after I turned sixteen. That meant fall was setting in: the trees were red, the roads were muddy, and when Jax and I sat in the abandoned sentry tower on the eastern wall, passing a skin of wine back and forth, we could just barely see our breath in the air as we talked.

"Well, Tilla? Any sign of them?" Jax asked. He was slumped on the ancient stone of the tower's floor, his back resting against the waist-high wall, while I sat just above him on the edge of the parapet, my bare feet dangling over a hundred-foot drop. It was midafternoon, but the sun was hidden behind a gray blanket of clouds.

I squinted out at the gap in the sea of treetops where the road emerged from the redwood forest. The feast began in just a few hours, and we'd already seen most of the guests arrive: the Lords of all the minor Houses, riding proud amid their hoisted sigils, and the Chieftains of the Zitochi clans, clad in cavebear furs, looking massive on their shaggy, horned horses. There was still no sign of the guests of honor, though, the Princess and her uncle. That seemed right. When you're that important, you make everyone else wait for you. "Just a few more minutes. I promise it'll be worth it."

"Uh-huh," Jax said. "Pass the wine."

I leaned over and dropped the skin into his broad, callused hand. We shared the same mother, a castle servant named Melgara. Neither of us had known her, since she'd died birthing me when Jax was two, but she'd given us the same wavy auburn hair and pale, freckled complexion. But while Jax's father had been a traveling soldier who'd given him a square jaw and a strong, dimpled chin, mine was Lord Elric Kent, head of House Kent, High Lord of the Western Province, Very Important Man. I had his face: lean, pointed, all high cheekbones and sharp angles. And I had his eyes: narrow, bright, sparkling green. A visiting Lady had once called them "aristocratic," and I'd coasted on the happiness of that compliment for weeks. Mostly because I'd thought it meant "pretty."

"So, this Princess." Jax took a swig of wine and passed it back to me. "Think she's good-looking?"

"Oh, I'm sure she's gorgeous." I grinned. "And I'm sure she's just dying to have a roll in the hay with a mop-haired, sweat-smelling stable hand."

Jax turned up his head in mock offense. "I happen to think I'm ruggedly charming."

"And I happen to think you've got horse shit on your boots."

"What? No! That's just . . . That's just mud!" Jax craned

his head down and sniffed. "Oh. Nope. You're right. Horse shit." He rubbed the sole of his boot on the stone wall's edge. "Speaking of which, you gonna come by the stables anytime soon? Lady Dirtmane misses you."

"Her name is Enchantress," I said with a smile, but avoided his real question. Truth is, I hated riding in the fall. It reminded me too much of being a little girl, back when I'd been my father's only child. Fall was when he was home the most, so we'd go riding together all the time, and he'd shown me the fog-shrouded forest and the beautiful black-sand coves and the ruined shrines of the Old Kings, the ones we were supposed to keep secret from the Lightspire priests. Those rides were my best memories of childhood. Possibly my whole life.

Then that beady-eyed wife of his, the one who called me a parasite, had popped out a daughter for him. A *real* daughter, not a bastard like me. We went on rides less and less. And one day we stopped going on rides at all.

Just in time to pull me out of that terrible memory, the trees at the edge of the forest shook with the thunder of dozens of clopping horseshoes. "Hey!" I shouted to Jax. "They're here!"

Jax instantly popped up alongside me, and his spyglass was already in his hand. The big liar was totally still interested.

The first men to step through the trees were royal foot-men. They were even more impressive than I'd imagined: tall and fit, their faces hidden behind shining mirrored masks, their armor covered in intricate silver serpents. They marched in lockstep and held high banners with the sigil of the Volaris Dynasty: a luminescent tower glowing with inner light, with a blackened sword on one side and a blossoming elderbloom on the other. Four ivory white horses trotted after them, their manes billowing softly like fresh snow. They pulled behind them the fanciest carriage I had ever seen, with a rounded canopy and gold inlays on the frame, jostling along the road on polished, gleaming wheels.

"Oh, come on," Jax muttered. "Is the Princess in a carriage? Am I not even going to see her?"

I elbowed him in the ribs and kept staring. What was it like in there? Was she wearing a dress made of glistening silk? Did she get to sit on fluffy pillows and eat bellberries and sip fancy sherry? Did a handsome, shirtless servant fan her with a giant leaf, oil dripping down his chiseled abs?

The carriage kept rolling, its mysteries unanswered. A dozen more footmen marched behind it. And then, once they'd all walked on, a lone horse rode out from the trees, with a single rider on its back.

"Whoa," Jax whispered. "Is that . . ."

"Rolan Volaris," I whispered back. Archmagus of the Royal Mages. The King's brother.

Unlike everything else in the procession, there was nothing ornate about him. His horse was a plain black mare, he rode in a leather saddle, and he wore only a simple gray robe. But I still couldn't take my eyes off him. Rolan's skin was a pure, rich black, darker than anyone I'd ever seen. His gray hair was shaved close to his scalp, and a neat silver beard framed his mouth. Even in the hazy light, I could make out at least a half-dozen Titan Rings on each of his hands, gold bands with ancient gems set in them, glistening like a rainbow.

More amazing than anything else, though, were his eyes.

They burned turquoise, impossibly bright, like they weren't just reflecting light but making it, two smoldering stars set into his face. He looked like something ancient and powerful, hiding in a person's skin.

"Bow to the King or die by the Ring," Jax muttered.

I scowled back at him. Since when did Jax quote the rebels? "You shouldn't talk like that," I said. "Not when he's here."

"It's not like he can hear me," Jax said. "Wait. Can he hear me? Is that a mage thing?"

"If it is, I'll make sure to speak at your funeral. 'Here lies Jax the stable hand. The only surprise is that it took seventeen years for his big mouth to get him killed.'" I stretched out my arms, and the muscles in my lower back flared with pain. That was probably my fault: I'd spent the last three nights sleeping on the hard wooden floor of Jax's room. Not a great idea, I know, but it's such a hassle to sneak back into my room after a night partying with Jax's friends.

"Hey," Jax said, glancing up at the sky. "It's the first night of fall. Sky should be clear tonight. When you're all done fancy-pantsing it up at the feast, you wanna head down to Whitesand Beach and do our thing?"

"Sure." I smiled. According to Jax, he only had one memory of our mother: sitting by her side on a white beach, gazing up at the sparkling Coastal Lights in the night sky. One year when I was five or six and feeling exceptionally sad, Jax snuck me down to the beach, and we hung out there all night, looking up at the Lights together. We'd lain there, side by side in that soft, shimmering sand, and he'd sung me the lullaby she'd always sung him, "The Mother Bear's Kiss," and promised me that as long as those pretty green ribbons twisted in the stars, everything would be okay. Ever since then, going to the beach when the Lights came out had been our little tradition, our way to remember our mother. It was silly and sentimental, especially since I'd never even met her, but hey, it was what we had.

The tower bells clanged five times in the distance, and my smile curdled. "Ugh. I gotta get going. I've only got a few hours to get ready for the feast."

"I'll walk with you. We've got a few good sips of wine left." Jax glanced down at the stairway leading to the tower's base. "Tunnels?"

"Tunnels."

The tunnels were our not-so-secret secret. Everyone at Castle Waverly knew that during the Golden Age, when the West had been its own Kingdom and not just an occupied Province, the Old Kings had built a network of hidden passages underneath the castle, connecting the various quarters; my ancestors used them to hide from Zitochi raiders, and later, during the Great War, to ambush invaders from Lightspire. Most people thought the tunnels had long collapsed or been filled in. When Jax and I were little kids playing hide-and-seek, we'd stumbled upon a cracked hexagonal tile in a larder in the Servants' Quarters, and discovered that a handful of the tunnels were still around. Well, still around in the loosest sense. They were dark and dusty and filled with rubble, and most of them led to dead ends. But there were still a few that went to hidden exits, like the heavy hexagonal stone that slid aside at the base of the eastern watchtower. The tunnels were perfect for sneaking out to see Jax and his friends in the middle of the night, or for getting lost whenever Head-maiden Morga decided I was overdue for an etiquette lesson.

Besides. Why would I ever walk across the courtyard like a sucker when there was an awesome hidden tunnel I could sneak through?

A few minutes later, Jax and I walked side by side through the narrow corridor, its earthen walls lined with jutting tree roots. Jax, one of the tallest guys in the stables, had to duck low to keep his shaggy head from bumping into the ceiling's lower jags. I held my Sunstone, a gift from my father, and its soft white light lit our way. My ancestors, the hardened Kents of yore, would've made their way through by flickering torchlight, but who was I to turn my nose up at the latest and greatest in Western innovation?

"So. You're really going to that feast tonight," Jax said as he tossed me the wine skin. "I bet that'll be fun. Putting on a fancy dress . . . having your hair braided . . . whispering 'Thank you, m'lord' when Miles kisses your hand . . ."

I sighed. Kissing Miles, the bastard of House Hampst-edt, had stopped being a fantasy ever since we turned twelve and he tried to woo me with a sonnet, got an asthma attack, and threw up on himself. The fact that I'd just sprouted a good head taller than him didn't help. "Maybe he'll stay away from my hand this year. . . ."

"Are you kidding? That guy loves kissing your hand! I'm pretty sure that's the only reason he comes to these things!" Jax stiffened his neck and put on a prim, nasal voice. "'Oh, I so can't wait for the festivities this evening! Perhaps my good Tillandra will let me caress her knuckles with my warm, wet tongue!'"

"Shut up!" I shoved him in the shoulder and he stumbled forward, tripping over a loose slab. *Good.* "At least I have standards. As opposed to, you know, giving every visiting miller's daughter your world-famous 'tour of the haystacks.'"

"Millers' daughters love haystacks. Who am I to deny them?"

We came to a fork in the tunnels where a small path branched off; it was mostly collapsed, but you could crawl through a narrow gap in the rubble to make it to an exit in the Servants' Quarters. Jax split off to walk through it, bracing for the usual (and hilarious) ritual of squeezing his brawny frame through the crack, but then he turned back to me, an unusually serious look on his face. "Honest question, sis. Why do you do it?"

"Do what? Go to the feast?"

"The feast, the dress, the whole thing. Why do you keep putting yourself through this?"

I turned away from my half brother. "I'm Lord Elric Kent's daughter, Jax. I might be a bastard, but I still have my duties."

"Come on, you know that's not true," Jax replied. "You already sleep out in the Servants' Quarters every night. You don't even bother heading in for your lessons anymore. And Lord Kent has three real daughters already. It's not like he's going to legitimize you. I'm sure if you went to him and said you didn't want to go to these things anymore, he wouldn't even care."

I didn't say anything, just stared out silently at the dark passage in front of me. Jax had no idea, no idea at all, how much his words cut. He couldn't. He just saw the side of me that I showed him, the side that didn't mind sleeping in the rafters of the stables or wearing the same pair of dirt-crusted trousers three days in a row. He didn't know how much I secretly liked the fancy dresses and the formal dances, how often I still closed my eyes and imagined myself being a noblewoman, how much I envied those three little girls.

He didn't know how desperately I still wanted my father's love.

"Tilla?" Jax asked.

I lifted the skin to my lips and swallowed the last of the wine, let its warmth slide down my throat and into my belly. Then I turned and tossed it to Jax, forcing a smile. "Free wine and free food. How could I pass that up?"

He caught the skin, shrugged, and turned to the gap in the wall. "Can't argue with that. See you after the feast, sis." And then he was gone.

I walked the rest of the way on my own. A cold draft blew in from somewhere, swaying the cobwebs. I closed my eyes and savored its feeling on my skin, even as it made all my hair stand on end. It felt better than the sting of Jax's words.

TWO

THE TUNNELS' EXIT IN THE CASTLE WAS IN A STEAM chamber in the lower baths. I waited in the dark passageway under the tile for a good few minutes, making absolutely sure it was empty; once I had started to open it when Headmaiden Morga was inside, and I saw way too much of her colossal, naked ass. As soon as I could see it was clear, I shoved the hexagonal tile aside and pulled myself up, scrambling my feet against the tunnel wall, and then closed the passageway off after myself as quietly as I could.

The bathing lobby was empty, thank the Old Kings. I needed to get cleaned up before the feast. And by "get cleaned up," I meant soak in a hot tub for a good hour.

By that point in my life, I could honestly have gone on just fine without most of the comforts of the Nobles' Quarters. I didn't need the fancy stuffed quails they served in the Great Hall; the brown goat stew they cooked up in the Servants' Quarters tasted just fine. I didn't need to sleep in my canopy bed with its fluffy pillows and soft sheets; as much as the floor of Jax's room made my back ache, I felt safer sleeping down there, with people I liked, than alone in a cold, stone room. And I sure as hell didn't need to sit around trying to memorize the Kent family tree for Headmaiden Morga, not when I could be out hiking through the woods or lounging on the beach or playing Drinking Truths with Jax's friends.

But hot baths? I couldn't live without long, hot baths.

I reached for the handle of the door to the Lord's Bath, and that was when I heard it. The splashing of water. The squeal of three giggling voices. The hushing of a stern, older one.

Evelyn Kent and her daughters. My half sisters. House Kent's rightful heirs. Playing and enjoying their bath before the feast while their doting servants scrubbed them clean. Getting ready to sit at the head of the room, by my father's side, while I had to sit all the way in the back.

So I wouldn't be getting my bath after all. The real daughters got first dibs. As always.

I stormed out of the bath, spun a corner, and stalked toward my room. A familiar bitterness soured in me. Maybe Jax was right. Maybe it was time to give up on this childish fantasy of my father deciding to legitimize me, this idea that I'd be a real noblewoman with a castle to call her own and a last name to answer to. Maybe it was time to stop dreaming about being Lady Tillandra Kent and embrace just being Tilla of the tunnels, who sleeps on the floor and has mud on her pants. Maybe it was time to tell my father good-bye.

With every step I took, I became more and more certain. I was going to do it, and do it tonight. Screw this feast, screw braiding my hair, and especially screw that fancy teal dress with the beaded collar and the flowing train. I'd blow it all off. Instead, I'd spend the night hanging out in the Servants' Quarters with Jax's crew, dancing and laughing and getting the best pick of the feast's leftovers. Maybe I'd even make out with that hot, broad-shouldered blacksmith's apprentice. And when my father came to look for me tomorrow morning, I would tell him I was done with this and done with him. I'd embrace the commoner side of me, and be as happy and content as Jax. This was it. This was the last straw.

Then I threw open my door and found my father in my room, staring silently out my window, his thin hands folded neatly behind his back.

"Ah!" I startled, then pulled the door shut behind me. "Father! I didn't . . . I wasn't expecting . . ."

He turned to me, his head cocked slightly to the side. He was already dressed for the feast, wearing a black tunic that clung to his tall, narrow frame. His brown hair hung straight at his shoulders, and you could only make out the faintest silver strands starting to appear in his neat beard. A narrow gold chain lay across his collarbone with clasps on each shoulder, and at the center of it dangled a golden medallion with an eagle emblazoned on it: the crest of the High Lord of the Western Province. "Hello, Tillandra," he said.

"Hi!" I blurted out, my eyes darting wildly around the room. If I'd known he was going to come by, I would have at least gotten it ready. It wasn't just that my bed was unmade or that my clothes were all over the floor. It was how obvious it was that I didn't spend any time here. My desk was a mess of dusty papers, stacks of uncompleted assignments for Headmaiden Morga. The walls were covered with keepsakes

I hadn't touched in years: a wooden mask from the time my father took me to Bridgetown, a pinwheel from a harvest festival three years ago, a wooden sword from back when Jax and I would play Warriors and Zitochi with the Dolan brothers. It looked like a child's room. A child who'd forgotten it.

"You were out," my father said drily. "I was waiting for you."

"I was . . . um . . ." I scrambled for a plausible excuse. Bathing? I was too dry. Riding? I was too clean. Studying? No one would ever believe that.

"You were out getting into trouble with that half brother of yours," my father said, his disdain for Jax barely concealed.

I looked down at my feet, cheeks burning. "What can I help you with?"

He walked toward me slowly, stiffly, his face unreadable. My father was always a calm, serious man, never rising to anger or showing any fear. I'd spent hours trying to analyze a memory of his face, trying to find the real expression behind the stern front, hoping to crack it for just one smile. "I know that you have been removing yourself from courtly life lately. That you have become distant here, preferring the company of the servants."

"I . . . I may have skipped a few lessons here and there, but—"

"I'm not chastising you, Tilla," he said sharply, and I decided it'd be best to shut up and let him talk. "I'm saying I don't blame you. I know you and I were once much closer. And I know you're smart enough to understand why that had to end. You know our laws."

I nodded. I'd heard that in the other Provinces of Noveris,

bastards were treated differently, but out in the West, the laws were clear. Each Lord could take exactly one unlawfully born child as the House bastard. This child would be raised in the castle but separate from the other children, alongside the family, but not part of it. At any moment, the Lord could legitimize the bastard as a rightful child, or disown them altogether. The reasons for this were coldly practical: kids died, wombs went barren, and a Lord always needed an heir. Jax liked to call us "noble spares."

"I married Lady Evelyn Yrenwood because I needed her father's armies to keep the peace," my father continued. "I had heard it said she could never have children, but those rumors were wrong. The laws of the Old Kings dictate that her daughters are my rightful heirs. The laws dictate that you must always come after them. The High Lord of the West must uphold the old laws, even when he would choose not to. That's the cost of power. That's the burden. We're all bound by our roles."

I nodded again, but less certainly. What was he saying? That he only married Lady Evelyn because he had to? That he wanted to legitimize me but couldn't because of the laws? That he really did love me as a daughter?

No. Couldn't be.

"Do you know why the royal family is visiting us?" he asked. That was a subject change if I'd ever heard one. I struggled to keep up.

"As part of her education, Princess Lyriana must visit all four Provinces," I said, happy to know the answer to this one. Like everyone else in the castle, I'd been gossiping about the Princess's visit for months. "She grew up in the city of

Lightspire, so she knows the Heartlands, obviously, and she's already visited the Eastern Baronies and the Southlands. That just leaves us."

"That's why the Princess is here, yes," my father said. "But why is the Archmagus here with her?"

I stared at him blankly. To protect the Princess? To tour the land? Something about taxes?

"He's here as a show of force. To remind us of our place. He's here so we know just how quickly the King could tighten his grip on us, if we so much as threatened to wriggle out."

"Oh," I said. I knew plenty of Westerners were unhappy with being part of the Kingdom, of course. Once the old-timers down in the Servants' Quarters got a few pints of beer in them, they'd start cursing the royal tax collectors and singing ballads about the Golden Age and telling dirty jokes about Lightspire priests. And I heard the stories that came in, about those rebels who called themselves Rattlesnakes, ambushing caravans from the Heartlands and smashing the Titan shrines dotting the roads. But I'd never thought that was a big deal, just some angry people and the grumblings of old fogeys. I'd always thought most people in the West had accepted King Leopold Volaris of Lightspire as our rightful ruler. Was I just sheltered? Were things much worse than I'd thought?

"I found this on your desk," my father said. He reached into a pocket in his tunic and held something out, something small and golden that sparkled in the sunlight. My stomach plunged with embarrassment as I recognized it: a thin golden necklace with a pendant of an elderbloom blossom. I'd bought it from a traveling Heartlands merchant a week ago, who swore up and down they were all the rage in Lightspire. I never bought fancy jewelry, but that stupid merchant had put the idea in my head that I'd be meeting the Princess, after all, and if she saw my necklace and liked it, well, that was the first step to becoming friends, and could I imagine being *friends* with the *Princess*?

It had seemed so plausible then. But now, staring at the necklace in his hands, my cheeks burned. "I just . . . I thought . . . This merchant, he was really . . ."

My father spared me any further blubbering by ignoring me altogether. "Have I ever told you the story my grandfather told me? About the day the Great War ended? The day we surrendered?" I shook my head, because of course he hadn't. My father never told me anything. "My grandfather was just a little boy, five years old. And his father, Albion Kent, was the King of the West. The last of the Old Kings." His voice was strange, distant. "It was right here, in the Great Hall of Castle Waverly, where Albion Kent bent the knee to the King of Lightspire, where he tossed off his crown and put on the chains of the High Lord. My grandfather was there, hiding behind my mother's skirt, watching his own father destroy the Kingdom our family had ruled for centuries. There were riots that night, riots all across the West, angry mobs that attacked the castle and had to be put down by the King's mages, our new protectors. 'The West will never forget,' the people yelled as they died. 'The West will never bow.' When my grandfather told me this story, there were tears in his eyes." My father tossed the necklace back onto my desk. "And now my own daughter wears the Volaris sigil."

No words came to me, partially because I was so mortified, but mostly because I couldn't understand what was happening. My father was talking like one of those old-timers, but nothing he'd ever said before had even hinted he felt this way. He defended the king's tax collectors and quelled any talk of rebellion. He made sure all captured Rattlesnakes were publicly hanged. He even let a visiting Lightspire priest set up a Titan shrine in the old crypts, something that I knew made many of the servants unhappy. Had I been that wrong about him?

"The West has never fit well in the Kingdom. We were the last Province to bow, and the one that went down fighting. Our people are proud and free. We don't sit well beneath a gilded throne. We never will." My father let out the softest chuckle. "You might even say we're the Kingdom's bastard. Do you understand?"

"Of course," I replied.

"The next few days will be incredibly important, Tilla. Change is coming. Tremendous change. And with it, tremendous danger." He turned back to me, his stern green eyes piercing mine, like he was trying to see right through me. "When the time comes, I'd like you to help me. I'd like you to stand by my side, no matter what happens. Can I count on you?"

"Of course, Father," I said, and meant it with every bit of my heart.

He took a step toward me, and I thought he might actually embrace me, or kiss me on the forehead like he used to when I was a little girl. Then he hesitated, stopped himself, and with a sad nod, turned to the door. "I'll see you at the feast?"

"Definitely."

I swear, for one second, the corners of his mouth twitched, giving just the barest hint of a smile. "Good," he said.

He shut the door. I stared at it for a moment, then collapsed onto my bed.

What in the frozen hell had that been about? My father had actually seemed to be saying he cared about me? And then all that stuff about the West and change and standing by his side? What did he know that he wasn't telling me? The way he'd talked, it was almost like he was sympathetic to the Rattlesnakes . . . but that couldn't be right. The rebels hated him. They called him the King's lapdog. They—

I squished the thought. I wasn't going to let myself get caught up speculating about the real meaning of my father's words. I didn't have time for that.

I had a dress to get into.

THREE

CASTLE WAVERLY HAD ONE OF THE MOST BEAUTIFUL GREAT Halls in all the West, a cavernous stone chamber bigger than some Houses' whole keeps, and tonight it looked better than ever. Dozens of chandeliers sparkled overhead, their multi-colored inlaid Sunstones casting the whole room in a rainbow of light. The tables were covered in imported silk cloths, far too fancy for the drunken Lords spilling wine on them, and the redwood floor was so polished you could do your hair in it. Oil paintings hung on the walls in golden frames, depicting generations of the Kent family, from my father and his father through all the Old Kings, all the way back to the grizzled pioneers who'd first crossed the Frostkiss Mountains to settle this wild land.

Getting dressed had taken me forever, so I got to the feast a good half hour late. This was the most full I'd ever seen the Great Hall. The Western Province was divided among fifty Houses, and it looked like all their Lords and Ladies were here with their retinues, the tables packed shoulder-to-shoulder, and the party was already in full swing. A quartet of singers stood on a rounded platform, their joyful voices belting the bouncy (and surprisingly filthy) "Lady Doxley's Garland." Servants roamed among the tables, carrying glistening silver trays with rows of spiced oysters and braised salmon and minced lamb wrapped in spinach leaves. At all the tables, the Lords of the West drank and shouted. Amazingly, Lord Collinwood was already passed out, his bushy beard soaking in his beet soup.

The biggest surprise was at the very front of the room, near the entrance. There, on the inset stone shelf that normally housed the crowns of the Old Kings, sat twelve golden statues with blank smiling faces and glistening jewels for eyes. They were from the Titan shrine the priests had set up, and they'd been moved here to, I don't know, make them seem more important, I guess?

I would've loved to sneak in through the back, but courtly etiquette demanded all guests, even bastards, enter through the Great Hall's main entrance, to pay their respects to the host's table. There was my father, seated at the center, with Archmagus Rolan seated opposite him. There was no sign of the Princess, which was weird, but Lady Evelyn was on my father's right and my three half sisters on his left. They looked absolutely adorable, their blond hair curled, their little dresses sparkling. What I'd give to be sitting in their place.

I made my way across the Hall, squeezing past servants and guests. The Lords of the West had mostly seated themselves by region. One table had the pale, dark-haired Lords of the swamps along the southern coast; another had the Lords of the northern quarries, ruddy-faced and bearded; a third sat the coastal Houses that ran along the shore to the south of Castle Waverly, their wealthy Lords looking decadent in striped furs from the K'olali Isles. A squire from one of those Houses tried to grab my ass as I walked by his table, so I gave him a swift kick in the shins; that got a big laugh from everyone at his table, including the triple-chinned Lord Darren. As their laughter shook the Hall, I shoved past the last gaggle of guests. There, at the very back of the room—out of sight, out of mind—was the Bastard Table.

As always, it was underwhelming. There was no fancy tablecloth here, just hard, bare wood. This far from the front, the singers' voices were a distant warble. The food laid out was obviously scraps, butts of bread and trimmings of meat. Worst of all, though, were the other bastards. It was rare in the West to see a bastard older than ten. By then, the Lord had usually decided to legitimize or disown. So this table, this table where I was expected to sit the whole feast, was packed tight with squabbling, screaming, snot-nosed brats.

There was just one bastard there my age: Miles of House Hampstedt.

"Tillandra!" he exclaimed, lunging out of his seat as he saw me. "You look absolutely beautiful!"

I could tell he meant it. His big gray eyes looked ready to burst out of his head. He had a round, gentle face with permanently ruddy cheeks, framed by loose ringlets of curly blond hair. He wore expensive tunics, imported from the Heartlands, but they never quite sat right on him, too tight in the chest and too loose in the sleeves.

"Miles," I said. He reached for my hand. With Jax's words

echoing in my ears, I feigned a warm smile and gave it to him, and he lifted it to his lips.

He didn't do anything gross like Jax had joked, just gave a soft, courtly kiss. It was a bit outdated, maybe, but mostly nice. I felt a twinge of guilt for having made fun of him earlier.

I shoved aside Lord Hyatt's redheaded bastard, who'd somehow managed to get a chicken bone wedged up his nose, and took a seat opposite Miles. "So. How're things at Port Hammil?"

Miles shrugged. "Oh, same old hassle. I thought I could take it easy this month because we had an exceptionally good haul from the iron mines, but the caravans got raided by bandits, and we lost half. Then my mother made this deal with the merchants from the K'olali Isles to buy up some dwarf goats to see if they could flourish here, I guess, but with the shortfall caused by the iron loss, we . . ." He stopped. "Oh hell. I'm boring you to death, aren't I?"

"Those dwarf goats sound kind of cute?" I shrugged apologetically. "Any way to get some real food here? I'm starving."

Miles squinted across the room. "I could probably flag down a servant next time one comes by us. Though at the rate they're moving, that'll be next winter, and I'll have a full beard." He slumped back down, food obviously way less important to him than it was to me. "Not that I blame the servants, of course. They've got their work cut out for them. This is the most packed I've ever seen this place."

"Well, it's not every day the Princess herself visits." I glanced back around the room. "Speaking of which . . . where is she?"

"Oh right, you missed all the drama. She hasn't shown up

yet. The Archmagus said she was still getting ready and that we should just start the feast. Your father tried to wait, but the Archmagus insisted. It was all very tense." Miles reached across the table for a butt of bread. "Like things weren't tense enough already, right? My mother was telling me this whole feast is just a cover for the Archmagus to snoop around the West about those missing mages."

"Missing mages?"

"You haven't heard?" Miles seemed incredulous. "Six mages have gone missing from the West in the last three months. And not just some lowly Artificers, either. One of them was a captain in the Knights of Lazan."

"Who took them?"

Miles shrugged. "No idea. My mother doesn't know, either."

If Miles's mom didn't know, no one else had a chance, because she was, more or less, the smartest person in the Kingdom. Lady Robin Hampstedt sat at the table just next to my father's, an older woman with a severe look and a pair of gold-rimmed glasses. She was my father's closest friend and one of the very few women to be the head of a House, inheriting it after her brothers died of frostkiss fever. She'd insisted on remaining the head even after her oh-so-scandalous romance with Miles's father, a lowborn blacksmith, and she'd refused to get married since, despite the dozens of highborn suitors who came calling after her brilliant inventions made House Hampstedt the wealthiest in the West. The Sunstones currently bedazzling the room? All her.

"So." Miles awkwardly cleared his throat. "Are you, um, doing anything after the feast?"

I thanked the Old Kings I had a legitimate excuse. "Actually, yeah. Jax and I have this tradition where we head down to Whitesand Beach to see the Coastal Lights and—"

Before I could finish, the Hall doors flew open with a crash. The conversations in the room stopped at once, and even the singers went quiet. Incredibly heavy footsteps plodded in.

"Oh boy," Miles whispered. "Here come the Zitochi."

I craned around. Three men entered the room silently, wearing bulky black cloaks lined with gray fur. Most of the Zitochi visiting were still camped out in the courtyard, but my father had made an exception for their highest leader, the Chief of Clans. That was the man in the middle, Grezza Gaul, and he was, bar none, the biggest person I'd ever seen. He stood nearly seven foot tall and was built like an anvil. His brown skin looked as weathered as the leather across his chest, and his face looked like it had been hacked from a block of cold stone. Four deep rifts, obviously from a very big claw, were scarred into his left cheek. On each of his shoulders was the top half of a cavebear skull, and two huge nightglass axes formed an *X* across his back.

Flanking him were his two sons. I didn't know their names. The one on his right, the older one, was the spitting image of his father, but the one on the left looked different. He was my age, and he was skinnier than the other, his frame fit but wiry. A long, thin sword in a plain black sheath hung across his back, its unadorned pommel peeking out over his shoulder. While his father and brother had their black hair up in the traditional Zitochi topknots, his hung low and messy around his shoulders.

"Who's that on the left?" I asked Miles.

"Grezza's younger son," he whispered back. "Zin? Zayne? Zobbo?"

"You're just making sounds."

The three Zitochi walked into the hall and stopped just short of my father's table. All around the room, I could see Lords tensing up, their backs stiffening, their fists clenching. The Zitochi were a hard people who lived in the frozen tundra north of our lands. They'd been our enemies for centuries. Many of the men here had lost brothers and fathers battling them. It had been ten years since my father had brokered the truce with the Zitochi, ten almost-peaceful years. But it was one thing to buy nightglass from traveling Zitochi merchants and keep our settlers away from their territories. It was another to invite them into our Hall. This was the first time in history it had happened. I suspected it might be the last.

My father nodded toward a nearby table with three empty seats. Grezza and his sons strode toward it, but then Grezza shook his head. He said something in Zitochi, a grunt of a command. The older son laughed, and the younger son started walking toward us instead.

"What's happening?" I whispered. "Is he . . . a bastard?"

"I don't know. Maybe? I don't think so. Could be?" I could practically see the gears in Miles's head whirring. "Do the Zitochi have a practice of bastardom? Do they even understand what this table is? I mean, I never thought to ask, but I suppose I assumed that—"

"Just stay cool," I said. I was feeling a little excited. I'd never talked to a Zitochi before, not really. And yes, I'll admit it. He was hot. Not in that sweaty, broad-shouldered way like the blacksmith's apprentice, but more of a cold, quiet smolder, like the kind of guy who would sit quietly next to you all night and then suddenly grab you up in a heart-pounding kiss.

Maybe I was imagining things. Maybe I just really needed to make out with someone.

"I'm cool," Miles muttered, obviously on a different wavelength. "It's just . . . you and I don't get to see each other that often, so I was hoping we'd get a chance to talk and . . ."

Miles trailed off because the Zitochi was already at the table. The younger bastards all scattered to the other end, terrified. The Zitochi watched them go, not betraying even a hint of emotion, and then took a seat next to Miles, grabbed a hunk of bread, and began cutting it with his dagger. I got an even better look at his face now. It was as rough-hewn as his father's, his chin as hard, but his cheekbones were higher and his nose sharper. Up close, his eyes were mesmerizing, a deep, luscious brown.

The three of us sat in awkward silence. I realized I was staring. "Um. Hi," I stammered out.

He glanced up at me, then without a word, turned back to his bread.

That stung, just a little. The Zitochi had a reputation as being loud, boisterous people. Was this guy the one exception? Or did he really just not want to talk to me? "I said hi."

This time he didn't even look up.

"Maybe he doesn't speak the Common Tongue," Miles speculated. "I speak a little Zitochi. Um, *vartok slavh kon tonki? Vartok slavh kon tonki?*"

The corner of the Zitochi's mouth twitched. "I speak the Common Tongue just fine." His voice was low and husky, tinged by a soft Zitochi accent. "And you just asked me if I wanted to rub your grandmother."

Miles's cheeks flushed a bright pink. "I did? No, I . . . I thought I got it right. . . ."

I shot my hand across the table. "I'm Tilla of House Kent. And Rubby Grandmas here is Miles of House Hampstedt."

The Zitochi looked down at my hand as if I'd shoved him a vomiting frog. "I'm Zell," he said. "Son of Grezza Gaul." Then he turned right back down to his bread.

I pulled back my hand. I might be a bastard, but he was still a guest in my father's house, and that meant paying me the bare minimum of respect. "Hey! I'm trying to have a conversation."

Zell paused, his dagger halfway through the loaf, and let out a long, slow exhale, like he was just so annoyed at having to put up with this. I was getting ready to smack him with his own bread. "What would you like to converse about?"

"Well, um, maybe you could tell us why you're here," Miles tried. "At the table, I mean. Tilla and I are here because we're bastards—that is, children of Lords born outside the vows of their marriage. That's where you're sitting, see, at the Bastard's Table. So I was wondering, well, if you were . . ."

I was cringing so hard it hurt, but Zell didn't seem fazed. "If I was a bastard?" he asked. "Yes. I'm a bastard. And a failure. And a disgrace."

Miles had no response, so he just made a weird humming noise.

"Should I go get us some wine?" I said. "I feel like we could maybe use some wine."

"I don't drink wine," Zell said. He reached into his cloak

and took out a curved ram's horn, nearly the length of my forearm, with a tin plug at the base. He flicked the plug open, pressed the horn to his lips, and took a swig.

"What is that?" I asked.

"We call it stone milk," Zell said. "You couldn't handle it."

"Why? Because I'm a woman?"

Zell blinked, genuinely surprised. "What? No. Our women drink it more than we do. You couldn't handle it because you're a soft, smooth-skinned, southern-born castle rat."

"Oh," I said, and for some reason, that actually was better.

But still way too insulting. I shot out my hand, grabbed the horn, and took a swig.

Instant regret. Whatever this stuff was, it burned like a gulp of molten iron, and somehow had the alcohol content of a full bottle of wine. I lurched forward, gasping. A dozen heads at nearby tables turned to stare.

"What have you done to her?" Miles rushed over to help me.

"I'm fine," I coughed out. "Really." Already, the burning in my throat was passing, replaced by a warmth in my belly. "It's not half bad."

Zell cocked an eyebrow. It seemed like, for the first time, he was actually paying attention to me. And maybe, just maybe, he was a little impressed. "I'll take that back."

He reached across the table to take the horn. My hand brushed against his as it passed, and I felt something odd, not warm skin, but cold, smooth stone. At the base of each of his fingers, in place of the knuckle, was a small pointed slab of nightglass, glistening darkly in the candlelight. It wasn't jewelry. The slabs were coming out of his skin, growing like thorns out of the bones of his hand.

Zell pulled his hand back. "Never seen nightglass before?"

I'd seen it, of course, on arrows and blades and axes. Nightglass was the northern tundra's chief export, a beautiful black metal that looked as fragile as glass and was harder than steel. But I'd never seen it like this.

Miles was equally captivated. "Fascinating. A living metal that fuses to bone." He circled over to look more closely. "I'd always heard that nightglass could do that. But I'd never seen it in practice. Will it continue to grow? Is the density compromised at all?"

Miles was somehow avoiding the most important question. "Why?" I asked.

Zell folded his hands together, hiding his knuckles. "A disarmed warrior is easily dishonored. This way, I'll never be disarmed again."

I jerked away. I'd let Zell's pretty eyes distract me from what he really was. A Zitochi. A brutal warrior. A hardened killer. Those nightglass knuckles that sparkled like the prettiest jewels? He'd probably used them to bash in someone's skull.

Zell saw my reaction. "Do I repulse you?"

"No," I replied. "You scare me."

"Uh, guys?" Miles had turned toward the front of the room. "Something's happening."

Miles was right. The room had once again fallen silent. The entire hall was staring toward the front, where Archmagus Rolan had taken to his feet. It was like every light had dimmed except the ones on him. For all I knew, they actually had.

"Assembled guests," he said, and I startled. It wasn't that his voice boomed. It was that it somehow carried through the air, as if he were standing right next to me when he spoke. "It is my great honor to present to you . . . my niece . . . the daughter of our beloved King . . . Princess of the Kingdom of Noveris . . . Lyriana Ellaria Volaris!"

The Hall's heavy wooden doors were still shut, but Rolan hurled back one hand toward them. The air crackled with the electric pulse of magic, and a plume of purple smoke and pulsing yellow light burst from his palm, enveloping the entryway. The sound of thunder shook the walls. The room gasped as one. Zell's brother reached for his sword.

Then the single most beautiful girl I had ever seen emerged from the smoke.

Princess Lyriana was fifteen, but she managed to somehow look both older and younger. She was tall for a girl, a little taller than me, with a slender, elegant frame. Her white dress clung to her body like a second skin, adorned with what had to be thousands of beautifully sparkling diamonds, a dazzling ocean of stars. Long white gloves, a style I'd never seen before, covered her hands and arms halfway to the elbow. She had the most perfectly symmetrical face I'd ever seen, like something out of a painting, with big round eyes and full lips, framed by wavy black hair. She was clearly a Volaris like her uncle: her skin was as dark as his, and her eyes burned a warm, brilliant gold.

You could feel the air get sucked out of the room as she walked in. The servants froze in place. Every young man (and many old) perked up, mesmerized, probably playing out some impossible fantasy where she fell into their beds. Next to me, Miles's jaw hung open. Even Zell sat alert.

I'd never felt more frumpy in my life.

My father was the first to rise. "Your Majesty," he said, his head bowed low. "It is my great honor to welcome you to my home. Will you join me at my table?"

She turned toward him, and then something strange happened. She hesitated. She stared out, at the dozens of faces staring at her, at all the hungry eyes. Her perfectly serene expression cracked with what looked like curiosity, maybe even excitement.

Somehow, across that entire crowd, past all the Lords and knights and squires, she saw our table. She saw me. Our gazes locked across the Hall, her beautiful, blinding gold eyes staring right into mine.

"My apologies, Lord Kent," she said. "But actually, I would prefer to sit back there."

FOUR

You know that awkward silence where someone has committed a horrible social blunder, but no one knows how to react, so everyone is just staring at their feet? Imagine that, but in a hall with two hundred people.

My father spoke at last. "Your Majesty, I'm afraid you misunderstand. The guest of honor sits with the host."

"The Princess has made her wishes clear," Archmagus Rolan said, and his voice was as hard as Zell's knuckles. "She will sit where she pleases."

"Ah." I'd never seen my father look flustered before. I didn't like it. "The thing is . . . in our custom, you see, that table is for b—"

"I know who the table is for, Lord Kent," Rolan cut in. "And I repeat that the Princess has made her wishes clear. Do you have difficulty obeying royal commands?"

My father stepped back, biting his lip. A suffocating tension hung over the room, every eye on him. I felt my hands clench into fists. Archmagus or not, Rolan was still a guest in our home, and he had no right to challenge my father like that. But what could he do? Everyone knew how the Kingdom worked. Peasants bowed to their Lords. The Lords bowed to the High Lord. And the High Lord bowed to the King . . . and his enforcers.

I hadn't understood what my father meant earlier, when he'd called this visit a show of force. Now it was perfectly clear. On Rolan's hands, I swear, all his Rings pulsed a bloody red.

"This is an outrage! An outrage!" a rumbling voice bellowed from the middle of the Hall. It was Lord Collinwood, apparently roused by the commotion from his drunken slumber. The red-faced man staggered to his feet, his beard dripping soup down his ample belly, and it would've been absolutely hilarious if I weren't genuinely worried about his safety. "I don't care who the hell you are! No fancy-assed spice-licker gets to come in here and talk to us like that!" He reached down for the dagger sheathed at his hip.

Without even glancing his way, Archmagus Rolan flicked his left hand at Lord Collinwood. The Rings flared an icy, frigid blue. All the light in the room seemed to dim for a second, and the air sizzled with the pulse of magic. Princess Lyriana jerked back, startled, and clenched a hand over her mouth. My eyes burned, and I tasted frost and dirt and rain.

Lord Collinwood stood, frozen in place, his eyes wide with terror, his mouth opening and closing wordlessly. A thick, shimmering block of ice had formed around his pudgy hand, trapping it and the dagger he was gripping firmly in place. He yanked his shoulder a few times, uselessly, then crumpled back into his seat.

"It'll thaw by morning," the Archmagus said dismissively. "Treat the hand tomorrow with a warm compress and some meyberry cream. And thank the Titans above I was feeling merciful."

The room was silent. The message was clear.

Bow to the King or die by the Ring.

My father broke the tension. "I do believe it's time you retired to your chambers, Lord Collinwood. You've made enough fool of yourself for one night." He turned back to Rolan, a polite smile forced on his face. "My humblest apologies, Archmagus, for my own rudeness and that of my guest." He bowed his head before the Princess. "And you, Your Majesty. You may sit wherever you like."

"Thank you, Lord Kent!" Princess Lyriana's face lit up with a radiant smile, even as Lord Collinwood's squires shuffled him out of the room. Did she have any idea what she'd just done? Was this all a game to her? "I apologize for any trouble I may have caused, and I deeply appreciate your hospitality."

"I hope tonight is everything you want it to be," my father replied. "Please. Enjoy yourself. My daughter Tillandra will keep you company."

My heart stopped. All the blood drained from my face. My stomach tied itself into a triple-bound bow. I'd been so focused on the slight to my father I'd somehow failed to think through the consequences. She was coming to *my* table. To sit with me.

My father had just assigned me to entertain the Princess of the whole damn Kingdom.

Lyriana gave her uncle a hug, then started walking the long walk toward us. The room was still quiet, and as she passed each table, every head turned to stare at her.

Next to me, Miles tugged frantically at his collar. "This is happening. This is really happening. She's coming right at us. She's coming *right at us*."

"She's not a wild boar, boy," Zell said dismissively. "All I see is an even fancier castle rat."

"Both of you, shut up," I hissed. I had no idea what I was going to say when she got here, but I was going to try my damned hardest to not embarrass us. At least, not instantly.

Lyriana cleared the last gauntlet of gawking Lords and stepped up to our table, where she stood awkwardly. Miles sat frozen, Zell leaned back amused, and a servant quickly herded all the little bastards away. That left it up to me.

"Your Majesty." I rose to my feet and gave what I really, really hoped was a passable curtsy. "Welcome to our table. I'm Tillandra of House Kent. This gentleman is Miles of House Hampstedt. And this is Zell, of House . . . uh . . . Zell the Zitochi."

"It is my greatest honor to meet all of you." Lyriana bowed her head ever so slightly. Her perfume smelled amazing, like cinnamon and roses and sweetwine all mixed together. I stepped aside, and she took a seat next to mine, folding her hands carefully across her lap. "I do hope I didn't cause too much trouble asking to sit with you. I had no idea it would cause such a scene!"

"Don't concern yourself with it too much, Your Majesty," Miles said. "Lord Collinwood makes a drunken spectacle of himself at every feast. It was only a matter of time."

"That does make me feel better," she said sincerely. "The truth is, I still can't believe I'm really doing this. I'm sitting at an actual Bastards' Table! With actual bastards!"

"Yeah . . . that you are." I forced a smile. If I didn't know better, I would've sworn she was making fun of us, but she seemed so utterly sincere that she had to mean it. Lyriana Volaris, Princess of Noveris, was genuinely excited to sit with a bunch of bastards. I sat down next to her, next to the Princess herself, and tried to look like my mind wasn't reeling. "I just don't think anyone expected you to sit back here."

"I know it's unconventional," Lyriana explained, "but the entire purpose of my journey is to see the breadth of my Kingdom and its people. I have spent my whole life sitting at the front of feasts with nobles and dignitaries, with High Lords and mages. I know your father's kind as well as I know myself. But I don't know the smallfolk, the commoners, the . . . well, the bastards. I don't know the very people I'm supposed to rule. That's why I just had to sit back here. When else am I going to get an opportunity like this?"

Was that what this was about? What we were to her? An opportunity to dip her feet in the commoners' pool, to study us as if we were insects under a glass, so she could rule better from her glistening Lightspire tower?

I shot Miles a glance, hoping for some solidarity, but he was just staring at her with wide, awestruck eyes, like . . . well, like a guy looking at the prettiest, richest, most powerful girl in the Kingdom, I guessed.

"I like to sit in the back as well." Zell barely glanced up. "We Zitochi have a saying: 'The wise man eats with his back to the wall. The fool eats a blade through the back of his skull.'"

Lyriana clasped a gloved hand over her mouth. "That is remarkable! May I write that down?"

Zell blinked. "Why would you write it down?"

"I am so sorry about him, Your Majesty," Miles cut in.

"We don't normally talk like that at the dinner table, or, you know, at all. It's just that Zell is a Zitochi, see, so there's a whole cultural barrier at play, and, well, different etiquette standards. I'm sure you understand. . . ."

Zell crossed his arms over his chest. "I think it's a good saying."

A bustle from the rest of the Hall saved us from the conversation. The servants had gotten the message that the Princess was back here now, and they rushed over, crowding around us with their trays and carafes.

"Your Majesty," said Garreth, head of the kitchen. "May I offer you some wine?"

"Oh, no thank you, kind sir," she replied. "I do not drink. It dulls the senses. And I'm afraid I won't be able to eat much of this food, either. I do not consume the flesh of any beast or bird. But I will be happy to eat more bread, if you happen to have any!"

The servants looked at each other, bewildered. "I'll see what I can do," Garreth replied, then gestured to the others. "We'll leave our trays here. In case you change your mind."

They left, and Zell immediately reached across the table, grabbing a turkey leg. "At least we have food now. Thanks, castle rat."

Lyriana clapped her hands, delighted. "Of course! It is my greatest honor to serve and help you." She looked around the table, her golden eyes wide with wonder, as if we were the most exotic creatures she'd ever seen.

"You don't have bastards in Lightspire, do you?" Miles asked. I couldn't tell if he was being polite or genuinely curious.

"Oh, Titans' blessings, no," Lyriana exclaimed. "It's purely a Western custom. We consider it provincial. Barbaric, even. I mean, to think, you have to sit here, isolated from your families, given only scraps, purely by virtue of your lineage. . . ." She shook her head. "It's monstrous."

It wasn't great, that was true. I'd spent my whole lifetime resenting being seated at the Bastards' Table. But somehow, her saying it like that, her voice oozing pity, made it seem worse than it ever had.

"That's why I'm sitting here with you, seeing your world, experiencing your lives." Lyriana took a bite of the bread, crinkled her nose, and set it down. "My family means well. But too many of them live in sheltered luxury, cut off from the real world, from the people they're meant to rule. I used to be just like that, too, I'll admit. Then I . . . saw something." For one moment, she glanced away. "I started talking to my servants. I left the Nobles' Circle and ventured into the Commons, even into the Sprawl. I saw the beggars and the orphans and the lost soldiers. And I realized how little of the world I had really seen. How little of the world my family cared about."

"Well, we're deeply honored you've chosen to share this with us," Miles said. "Anything you want to see or do, just let us know!"

Lyriana smiled politely. I knew I should be smiling with her. But all I could feel were the nails of my fingers digging into my palm. Of course this was a great experience for her. Because that was all it was: an experience, a vacation, a quick, thrilling taste of a life she'd never have to live. She got to sit with us and marvel at our meager lives, and then she got to go back to Lightspire, to her glistening dresses and her gilded carriage and her loving father and her wonderful, perfect future. And the rest of us, well, we were stuck with our stale bread and our lonely table.

After months of dreaming about it, I was finally sitting next to the Princess of Noveris. And I kind of wanted to slap her.

I looked across the room, to the host's table. The Archmagus was saying something, and everyone at the table was laughing as if it were the most hilarious thing in the world. Well, except for my father, who was just smiling, which was as close to laughing as he got. I could see now just how forced it was, how hard he was working just to look happy. His words from earlier echoed in my ears, his talk of the King's grip and the whispers of rebellion, the story of his great-grandfather's surrender. In that moment, looking at him across a crowded room, I felt like I understood him for the first time, understood the burden of his title. If the West had won the Great War, he'd be a King. Instead, he had to kneel before one, and act like he was grateful.

I remembered the last thing my father had said. Where he'd asked me to help him. To stand by his side.

If he could pretend, I could, too.

"So!" I twisted my face into what I hoped was a decent replica of a smile. "How are you enjoying our Province?"

"Oh, it's absolutely wonderful!" Lyriana beamed. "This journey isn't my first time out of the Heartlands, you know, away from those stuffy cities and those endless, endless plains. After the villas of the Eastern Baronies, nestled into those white cliffs, I was sure I'd seen the most beautiful place in the Kingdom . . . but I think the West might be my true favorite. The trees that reach all the way up into the skies and the fog rolling in from the sea and those gorgeous frost-tipped mountains . . ." She actually sighed wistfully. "And these castles! With their stone walls and their pioneer tapestries . . . It's just all so wonderful, so truly enchanting. Like something out of a storybook!"

"You must be easily impressed," Zell said.

Lyriana nodded thoughtfully, not offended at all. "I suppose that's true, certainly compared to someone so worldly. I can only imagine the life experiences you've had to leave you so jaded." Zell blinked, trying to figure out if he'd just been insulted or complimented. "I just wish I could stay longer and see more. There's one thing that I . . . Well, no. Never mind."

"What is it?" Miles pried, like he was actively trying to ruin my night.

Lyriana glanced down, embarrassed. "It's silly. An old Volaris superstition. They say that great luck will come to a person who dips one foot in the Ancient Sea and the other in the Endless Ocean. I visited the Ancient Sea in the Baronies at the start of my journey, and I thought I might get to stop by one of your beaches . . . but my uncle says we must ride back first thing in the morning." She shook her head. "It doesn't matter. It's just a silly old thing."

I saw Miles's eyes light up with an idea, and my stomach plunged as I realized exactly what he was thinking right before he said it. "We could take you! Couldn't we, Tilla? You said you and Jax were planning to go to the beach tonight anyway, right?"

It took every ounce of restraint not to kick him in the shins. "We . . . I . . . well, Jax and I . . ." I tried, before hitting on a reasonable excuse. "Please, Miles. I'm sure the Princess's uncle wouldn't approve of her sneaking out at night with a bunch of bastards."

"No. He wouldn't," Lyriana said, a sudden hard edge in her voice. "And that's exactly the problem. He keeps me locked away, sheltered from the real world, like some dainty bird in a gilded cage. . . ."

"You gild your birdcages?" Zell asked.

"I'm sick of it," Lyriana said, and I realized my ploy had totally backfired. Bringing up her uncle hadn't discouraged her. It just got her riled up. "Seeing both oceans was the one thing I wanted on this trip, the one thing!" she said, pouting. "And you know what? I'm tired of being sheltered from everything. I'm tired of being protected. If you're going to the beach tonight . . . I would be honored to go with you!"

"The honor is all ours!" Miles swiveled toward me. "Tilla! We can take those tunnels under the castle, couldn't we? The ones you and your brother showed me? They lead to Whitesand Beach, right?"

Forget kicking him in the shins. I was ready to hit him over the head with a leg of lamb. We'd shown him the tunnels once, *once*, and he'd spent the whole time terrified of spiders. And suddenly he was the expert? "Well, yeah, they do, but . . ."

Lyriana turned toward me, gently touching my shoulder with a single gloved hand. I almost flinched. "I assure you, Tillandra, I will be so, so grateful for this. I'll never forget it."

And that was it, wasn't it? No matter how badly I didn't want to spend a minute longer than I had to with this girl, I was trapped. If I said no now, I'd disappoint her. And that disappointment would ripple up, to her uncle, to my father. It didn't matter that tonight was special for me and Jax, or that the last people I wanted to spend it with were Miles and Lyriana. My father was counting on me to entertain her. Or sure as hell not let her down.

Burden of power, I thought. Burden of power.

"Hell yeah," I said. "You want to dip a foot in the Endless Ocean, Your Majesty? I say we go for a swim in it!"

I worried I'd laid it on too thick, but Lyriana ate it right up. "I can't believe this is happening. This is exactly—*exactly*— what I wanted! It's like a dream come true!"

And basically my worst nightmare.

"I'd like to come as well," Zell said, abruptly reentering the conversation.

"What? Why?" I asked. I saw Zell's gaze flit over my shoulder, toward the front of the room where his father was sitting. What was Zell thinking? Why would he suddenly care?

"I don't think that would be appropriate," Miles replied. "I mean, no disrespect, but I just don't think it would be proper for the Princess of Noveris to be out with a Zitochi she just met. . . ."

"Nonsense," Lyriana said. "The proper thing is for a Princess to be educated in the ways of the world. And while the Zitochi may not be my formal citizens, they are my neighbors, and I should learn of them as well." She nodded politely at Zell. "I would be honored by your company."

What was going on? Why was this happening?

"Good. I'll see you there," Zell said, and not a moment too soon, because my father and Lyriana's uncle came striding up to our table. Archmagus Rolan and I locked gazes for just one second, his turquoise eyes scorching through mine. A chill ran down my spine.

"Your Majesty," my father said, "I hope I'm not intruding."

"Oh, no, of course not!" Lyriana smiled. "Your daughter has been a most gracious host!"

My father glanced at me, and I really, really hoped that was gratitude I saw in his eyes. "If you don't mind parting ways with her, some of the other Lords would love the pleasure of making your acquaintance."

"Of course," Lyriana said, and even I could read between the lines. Whatever game Rolan had played by letting her sit with us was up. Lyriana was going to be toured around the various tables until the end of the feast, so this was it. She stared at me with obvious, expectant eyes, so as she got up to go, I rose with her and gave her an almost certainly inappropriate hug. I pressed my face to her ear and whispered, "Lower baths. Second steam room. Loose tile, shaped like a hexagon."

She smiled at me and winked, actually, for real, winked. Then she turned back to the Hall and was off.

I sat back down at the Bastard Table. Zell was leaning back against the wall with a look of bored amusement, while Miles sat up, arms folded across his chest, proud as a pig in a mud puddle. "Well?" he said. "How about that, huh? Can you believe it? We're all legitimately in with the Princess!"

I closed my eyes and sighed. "Hey, Zell."

"Yes?"

"Think I could get some more of that stone milk?"

FIVE

I SPENT THE FIRST FIVE MINUTES AFTER THE FEAST SPRINTING
to the stables to tell Jax what had happened. I spent the next
two hours convincing him that I wasn't making it all up.

"This is insane, Tilla!" he said as we stood side by side in
the tunnels beneath the baths, illuminated only by the dim
glow of the Sunstone hanging by a leather band around my
neck. "Even for you! And that's saying something!"

"Oh, I know," I replied. "Believe me, this is not how I
wanted my night to go, either. But I don't have a choice, Jax.
She's the Princess. We have to do what she says. And you and
I were planning to go to Whitesand Beach tonight. . . ."

"Yeah, so we could do the one tradition we have and toast
our mother's memory. Not so I could sneak out the Princess
of the whole damn Kingdom!" Jax was eating a peach, and he
took mammoth bites out of it as he talked. "I mean, you do
understand how badly this could all go down, right? What
could happen if we got caught?"

"I think you're being overly pessimistic, Jax," Miles said. He was hunched against the crumbling tunnel wall, hands in his pockets. "Perhaps you just don't understand the enormous upsides at play."

"Oh, am I not smart enough to get it? Is it something a simple stable hand couldn't understand?" Jax scowled at him. This was familiar ground; Jax was always insecure about the fact that he wasn't really educated, and Miles had a way of sticking a thumb right into that wound. "You don't have to be a boy genius to understand this. Tilla and I had plans tonight. And you screwed them up."

"For the fifth time, I'm sorry," Miles said, clearly not sorry. "I didn't know the two of you had this tradition. But try to just step back and see the bigger picture. This is the Princess of Noveris herself, and we have an opportunity to get in her good graces! Do you understand what a rare opportunity this is?" He pulled out one hand, jabbing a finger emphatically in the air. "I mean, just think about it. Five years from now, she's reigning. She wants to improve relations with the West. Who will she reach out to? Why, the people she just so happened to have an amazing night with! And what if she wants to bring someone in, to serve as a new ambassador? Are you not getting this, Tilla? This could be our ticket to Lightspire!"

He'd been going on like this the whole time, and I hated to admit that it was starting to work. Not that I thought it was likely or anything. Of course not. And I was still really pissed at him for ruining my tradition with Jax. But I couldn't help starting to picture myself all dressed up in a sparkling dress like Lyriana's, strolling across some glimmering Lightspire pavilion, arm in arm with some gorgeous Volaris Prince. . . .

"And what about me?" Jax asked. "Where exactly do I fit into this scenario?"

"You could come as Tilla's servant?" Miles tried.

"That's right!" I leaned up and ruffled Jax's messy hair. "You'll be my manservant! You'll fetch me wine and wash my clothes and carry me around when I feel tired. But don't worry, dear servant. I'll make sure to put in a good word with all those pretty Lightspire girls."

"I've heard they're *really* pretty," Jax sighed.

A barely muffled chuckle echoed from down the tunnel. Zell was leaning against a wall, cloaked in shadow, but I could still make out his long hair, and glinting through the darkness, his brown eyes. He'd gone back to his father after the feast, and I'd assumed he'd just ditch us, but then I found him patiently waiting for us down in the tunnels, even though I hadn't told him how to get in. A rational part of my brain was still kind of afraid of him; the Zitochi had been our mortal enemies just a few years ago. But for whatever reason, I didn't think he'd hurt us. There was just something . . . honorable about him, even when he seemed dangerous—like the kind of guy who wouldn't hesitate to kill you in a fight but wouldn't dare stab you in the back.

Jax obviously didn't see it. "You think something's funny?" He spat out the pit of his peach, and it bounced off the wall with a clatter. "Hey! I'm talking to you, *glassie!*"

I winced. Some of the more enlightened Western Lords, my father included, had come to believe the Zitochi were a proud and complex culture, worthy of our respect. They avoided outdated slurs like "glassie" and "snowsucker."

It wasn't a popular view around the stables. "What are you even doing here?" Jax demanded.

"I thought we were going to the Endless Ocean." Zell shrugged, but his eyes weren't smiling. "Or did that invitation not extend to 'glassies'?"

"Why would you care about the ocean?" Jax asked. "I mean, you do know you can't kill it or eat it, right?"

"Oh, really? That's a shame." Zell stepped forward, his brow furrowed, and there was something terrifyingly untamed about him. I wondered just how quickly he could pull that sword out of the sheath across his back. "I was in such a mood to kill something tonight."

"No one's killing anything." I tried to push my way forward so I could get between them. "Both of you, calm down!" But neither one of them seemed to hear me because they were already doing that stupid lock-on-each-other thing guys do when they're about to fight. Jax rolled up his sleeves. Zell bounced lightly on the balls of his feet.

"Excuse me?" a thin voice called from right above us. "Could someone possibly help me down, please?"

I looked up. The tile overhead had been pulled aside, and there was Princess Lyriana's head, poking down through the hexagonal hole in the tunnels' roof. "Please? I think someone's coming! I need to get down now!"

"Uh, sure!" Jax rushed under her, even as Zell slunk back into the shadows. "Just come down slowly . . . one foot first, and then—"

Before he could finish, Lyriana tumbled down through the hole. For someone so beautiful, it was probably the least graceful fall I'd ever seen. She hurtled head over heels with a squeak and landed upside down, right in Jax's arms. Her gorgeous white dress, which she was still for some reason wearing, flopped up over her head, leaving her skinny legs kicking in the air and her gloved hands flailing. Jax froze in place, his arms stiff, as if he were holding the world's most precious sack of potatoes. "What do I do?"

"Put her down, you idiot!" Miles yelled. Jax flipped Lyriana over, setting her down gently so she was standing on the cold, dusty ground. She beamed at me with the biggest smile I'd ever seen.

"I did it! Titans' blessing, I actually did it!" She bounced up and down. "I didn't think I would because my uncle left a guard by my door, but he left to relieve himself, and when he did, I snuck out and I ran to the baths and I even hid some clothes in my bed to make it look like I was still there!" She clapped her hands together. "I've never done anything like this before! This is so amazing!"

I looked at Miles, and he shot back a wide grin. This was actually working. Against all odds, somehow his ridiculous plan was actually paying off.

"Oh, I'm so glad to see you again, Miles of House Hampstedt!" Lyriana went on. "And you! Zell of the Zitochi! And you!" She turned to Jax. "Thank you for catching me, kind sir. To whom do I owe the pleasure?"

"I'm Jax," he stammered. "Jax of House . . . Stable . . . Hand."

"Really?"

Jax looked down. "No. Not really. I made that up. I'm just Tilla's half brother who works in the stables. I'll be your guide, I guess."

"And I am deeply honored for your service. Anything I can offer you in return, please, just let me know." She turned to stare down the tunnels. "Now, let's get going! We only have so long before my uncle realizes I'm missing."

I started to ask what exactly he'd do to us if that happened, but decided it was probably better not to know.

Most of the tunnels leading out of the castle had collapsed, but there still was one that led to Whitesand Beach. Unfortunately, getting there meant navigating a labyrinth of tight corridors and crumbling dead ends. Jax led the way, Lyriana followed, and Miles trailed after them, spouting Western history to no one in particular. Zell, though, lagged behind, walking alone. I didn't feel like listening to Miles's rambling or Lyriana's coos of interest, so I fell back with him.

"You seem awfully comfortable down here," I said.

Zell arched an eyebrow at me. "I grew up in Zhal Korso, a city carved into the side of a mountain. I've spent my entire life in caves and passageways."

"Right. Zhal Korso. Makes sense," I said, even though I'm pretty sure that was the first time I heard that the Zitochi even had cities. "I'm sure it's very nice. . . ."

Zell didn't seem to be listening. "Your magical stone. May I borrow it?"

"Magical . . . Oh, my Sunstone. Sure, I guess." I reached up to the band around my neck and unclasped it. "It's not magic, though. Or a stone. Miles's mom invented them, and my dad got me this fancy one." I handed it to Zell, a round leather disk that looked like a compass, except with a hot white fire burning behind its glass face. "It's full of gas from this mine, special gas that makes the fire burn like that. You push that little lever on the side to spark it, and then you can twist it more to make it brighter."

"Clever," Zell said, barely glancing at it. The Sunstones were a symbol of Western pride, a local invention that held its own against the fanciest magic lamps of Lightspire's Artificers. I kind of expected Zell to be blown away, or at least impressed, but he seemed far less interested in the Sunstone than he was in the wall. He held the Sunstone up and reached out with one hand, and his nightglass knuckles sparkled in its light. With the tips of his fingers, he traced three weathered rifts in the wall.

"What are they?" I asked.

"Scars," he replied, reverent. "From ancient battles, long forgotten. Lifetimes ago, your great-grandfather and mine fought in tunnels just like these."

I stepped close to him and reached out, tracing my fingers after his through the long, horizontal scars. He smelled like winter frost on crumbling leaves, like earth and rain. My heart quickened. "Maybe they fought each other."

Zell turned back to me. "What would they think of us now?"

"Hey!" Jax called from around a corner. "Everything okay back there? He's not trying anything, is he?"

"We're fine, Jax!" I shouted back. My cheeks were burning. Why were my cheeks burning? "Come on," I said to Zell. "Let's catch up."

Jax led us through a massive chamber, the single widest room I'd ever seen in the tunnels; the walls here had once been painted, but had long since faded away, leaving just the faintest ghosts of the murals that once had been. As a kid, I'd stared at them for hours, but the most I could make out was a big bear in the left corner, some stars along the ceiling, and a pale crowned figure with a long white beard. Even I knew who that was: Tenebrous Kent, the first of the Old Kings, who united all the pilgrims and settlers east of the Frostkiss Mountains and founded the Kingdom of the West, which his line would rule for the next five hundred years.

My gaze flitted to Lyriana, and I felt a surprising pang of anger. *Until the Volaris came along.*

We left the room with the murals via a narrow passage behind a pile of rubble and through a hallway with holes in the floor, where we could hear the rumbling of an underground river. We eventually came to a tight corridor we had to squeeze through one by one, and when we emerged on the other side, I could smell the softest hint of a salty breeze.

Zell's brow furrowed. "I hear voices. Is someone at the beach?"

"After a feast? Doesn't surprise me." Jax shrugged. "I mean, Whitesand Beach is the perfect place to bring a girl if you're looking to get laid." Lyriana gasped. "Or . . . so I've heard some of the guys say. I, uh, wouldn't know anything about that."

I let out an amused snort. Zell just shook his head.

We rounded the last corner of the tunnels, revealing a jagged opening in the stone wall. Through it, I could see the night sky. And it wasn't cloudy, like I'd worried, but beautifully, wonderfully clear. The stars twinkled white, and the moon hung overhead like a pearl on a strand. An unseasonably warm breeze swept over us. Best of all, I could see the flicker of a gentle green glow, the telltale sign of the Coastal Lights. "Come on!"

The exit from the tunnels let out on a high ledge of a cliff overlooking Whitesand Beach; a barrier of sandstone boulders and twisting vines hid it from view, but if you looked just right, you could make out a small path of loose rocks leading down. I stepped out onto the ledge and shoved a few vines aside. There they were, out in the distant sky: three brilliant emerald ribbons, dancing and twisting like serpents amid the stars, their length stretching as far as the eye could see. The Coastal Lights, the wonder of the West, with the wide Endless Ocean stretching out into the night and beyond. I turned to Lyriana.

But, for some reason, she was looking down at the beach itself. "Is that my uncle?" she whispered.

Yep, sure enough, there he was, standing barefoot in the center of the sandy cove: Archmagus Rolan himself. Dark waves lapped at the shoreline just past him. Two of his bodyguards flanked him, scimitars sheathed at their hips. We were maybe thirty feet above them, but I could still make out their faces. No one looked happy.

Three people stood opposite them. I'd recognize Grezza Gaul's hulking shape anywhere, not to mention the two massive axes strapped across his back. Next to him was Lady Robin Hampstedt, Miles's mom, the night wind rippling through her straight blond hair. And between the two of them was none other than my own father. There was something off about him, something I couldn't quite put my finger on. Something that set my teeth on edge.

"What in the frozen hell?" I turned back to Zell and Miles. "Do you know what they're doing out here?"

Miles shrugged helplessly, and Zell just shook his head.

"Listen!" Lyriana pressed herself against the boulders. "You can hear them!"

We all leaned up against the rocks on the cliff's edge. Lyriana wasn't wrong. The walls of the cove were curved just right, so the sound of voices at its heart carried up the cliffs. Rolan was speaking, and his booming voice betrayed just a hint of anger. "I tire of your riddles, Lord Kent. Why drag me out here in the middle of the night? Do you know where my missing mages are or not?"

My father stepped forward, and I saw a pair of daggers sheathed on his hips. That's what was off about him. My father never went out armed.

Why was he armed?

"My apologies, Archmagus," he said. "With matters this sensitive, I thought it best to talk far from inquisitive ears." He gestured with one hand, and Lady Hampstedt stepped forward. She was a thin, severe woman with a judgmental frown that seemed permanently carved into her face. She held in her arms a small, undecorated chest, just bigger than a jewelry box. Next to me, Miles stiffened, tightening his grip on the stone. "Lady Hampstedt, would you please inform the Archmagus where his mages are?"

"Dead," she said coldly, and I winced. Lady Hampstedt was famous for her lack of tact, but come on, lady!

"Dead how?" Rolan demanded, but his eyes were trained on that little lead chest. What the hell was in it? And why was just looking at it making the hairs on my neck stand on end?

"The Zitochi have a most unusual torture practice," Lady Hampstedt replied, as if that were an answer, "reserved for only their most terrible and hated criminals. They call it '*khai khal zhan*.'"

"*Khai khal zhen*," Grezza corrected.

"*Khai khal zhen*. It means 'the breaking of the mind.' There is a weed that grows in their lands, a brittle black flower that, when chewed, causes a person to experience intense and often terrifying hallucinations, not to mention a complete disconnect with reality. Zitochi shamans chew a single leaf and then commune with their spirits for days." I was getting the feeling she really liked lecturing. "In the *khai khal zhen*, a prisoner is forced to eat fifteen leaves. And then, as they lose their mind, they're slowly and methodically tortured to death."

"The Zitochi killed my men?" Rolan's gaze narrowed at Grezza. "They performed this . . . this barbaric ritual?"

"Well, it had never been done on a mage before, not as far as I can tell. And it made for a truly fascinating experiment." Lady Hampstedt's mouth twitched, giving just the hint of a smile. "A mage's Ring is the source of his power, but the mage's mind is what gives the Ring's magic shape and direction. Destroy the Ring, and you destroy the mage's power. But what would happen to the Ring if you destroyed the mage's mind?" Her tone was chilling, even for her, like she was talking about a funny story she'd overheard in the market.

I was breathing fast. A drop of sweat streaked down my face. Something bad was going to happen. I knew it. I could taste it. I suddenly wanted very badly to go, to be back in the castle, to run into the tunnels, to be anywhere but here, on this beach, about to witness whatever this was. But my stupid legs didn't move.

"What I'm about to show you, Archmagus, will change the course of history." Lady Hampstedt knelt, setting the chest down in the sand. She snapped off the two latches on the front and cracked the lid, just a bit. An eerie light glowed out, impossibly bright, flickering red, then yellow, then blue. "The incredible thing isn't what the *khai khal zhen* did to the mages. It's what it did to their Rings."

She threw open the lid to the chest all the way, and that bright, pulsing light lit up the beach, brighter even than the dancing green bands overhead. Lying in the center of the chest on a padded cloth was a leather disk, just like a Sunstone. But behind the glass face wasn't the usual clockwork mechanism but something else, a thin multicolored gemstone that was the source of all that light.

The gem from a mage's Ring. A Titan stone. But what had they done to it? It pulsed and flared, changing colors almost violently, and in its sleek surface I could see swirling bands of gold and crimson. It was beautiful, insanely beautiful, and terrifying, like someone had bottled a hurricane or chipped a sliver off the sun.

All the power of a mage. Trapped in a tiny little stone.

The reaction from the others was instantaneous. Archmagus Rolan jerked back in horror, as if the box contained a hissing serpent, and his own Rings flared up a searing red. His guardsmen's hands jerked to their hilts. Grezza Gaul wrapped his massive hands around the bases of his axes, and my father just smiled.

Next to me, Lyriana gasped, and Miles staggered back, the blood draining from his face. "Oh no," he whispered. "No, no, no . . ."

"This is blasphemy!" Archmagus Rolan bellowed, his voice booming like a thunderclap.

"No." Lady Hampstedt stood up and lifted the disk up from the chest. She flicked a little lever on its side, the same one I would use to turn on my Sunstone, the one that made a little electric spark. "This is the future."

Then she tossed the disk at the Archmagus, and the gemstone inside sizzled and cracked.

Lady Hampstedt and my father dove away. The Archmagus screamed and threw up his left hand, and the Rings on it flared a vibrant purple. A glowing curtain of light seeped out from his fingers, billowing back to wrap around him like a cloak. A magic shield. But it was too little, too late.

Before the shield could even get halfway around him, the disk hit its shimmering surface, and it exploded.

No. "Exploded" doesn't do it justice. It blew the hell up.

There was a deafening blast that shook the cliff face and sent Miles and Jax tumbling onto their backs. I threw up a hand to shield my eyes from the blinding burst of light that scorched up from the beach like an exploding comet, one that flared gold and crimson and a horrifying, sleek black. The taste of copper flooded my mouth. I could hear ice crackling and flames scorching, earth rumbling and glass shattering. This wasn't just an explosion of force and fire, like the bombs used to clear rubble down in the mines. This was a blast of raw, untamed magic, and it tore through the night and trembled the earth.

I managed to stay upright, even though my whole body was shaking, and blinked the colors out of my eyes. The cove below was a mess. A crater smoked where the Archmagus had been standing, the white sand scorched black, with a half-dozen tiny fires still smoldering around it, alongside a dozen glistening icicles and a few stony crags that poked out of the ground like probing fingers.

The royal guardsman who had been standing to Rolan's left, near where the gem had exploded, was completely gone, just a few scraps of bloody cloth scattered across the beach. The one who had been on Rolan's right had been protected by the shield, so there was a little more of him left, a moaning, blackened husk in the sand, reaching up to the sky with a mangled hand. Grezza Gaul stepped toward him and brought down one of his massive axes in a brutal chop. The guardsman didn't moan anymore.

Behind me, Miles had his hands clasped over his eyes, and Jax was still lying on his back with surprise. Zell sucked in his breath, digging his fingers into the stone. Lyriana started to shriek, and, moving on pure impulse, I clasped a hand over her mouth and trapped the scream.

Time seemed to slow down. My ears were ringing, either from the blast or from the rush of blood. My heart thundered in my chest so hard it felt like it was going to explode. And the truth tightened around me like a clenching fist.

Change is coming, my father had said, *and with it, tremendous danger.*

He hadn't been talking about negotiating with Archmagus Rolan. He'd been talking about killing him.

Farther down the beach, something was moving, something ragged and bloody and gasping. I could barely believe it, but it was Archmagus Rolan. And he looked *terrible*. The explosion had thrown him back at least two dozen feet. He lay on his back in the sand, gurgling red foam from broken lips. His left arm was gone completely. Half his face was scorched raw, and his left eye was a dripping socket. A few bright blue crystals poked out through his skin.

And yet despite all that, he was still moving. With a throaty gasp, he lurched up and threw out his right hand, the one that was still there, the one still covered in Rings. They flickered a bright, hot white, and the air crackled with the electric pulse of magic. A scorching bolt of lightning burst out of Rolan's hand and struck Grezza's shoulder, hurling the Zitochi backward across the cove. He slid across the sand, leaving a long, broad streak in his wake. Rolan turned his arm toward a cowering Lady Hampstedt, a second bolt charging between his fingers. She threw up her hands in terror. . . .

And then my father sprang to his feet and sprinted across the beach. The Archmagus swiveled his hand and let out another blast of lighting, but my father veered to the left, dodging it, and then suddenly he was right at Rolan's side. In one seamless motion, my father whipped his dagger out of the sheath on his belt and sliced it through the air. Rolan's fingers came off his hand, tumbling into the sand, and the bolt of lightning vanished with them. My father slammed his knee into Rolan's face, knocked him onto his back, twirled the dagger, and then plunged it down through his wrist, nailing it into the blackened sand.

It was over. What good were Rings if you didn't have hands?

Lyriana squirmed, but I held her tight, refusing to release my grip on her mouth. Tears streaked down her cheeks, hot against my hand. I didn't know much. But I knew I didn't want our parents seeing us up here.

"Grezza! Robin!" my father shouted. "Are you hurt?"

"I'm fine," Lady Hampstedt replied, and Grezza pulled himself out of the sand with a grunt. His armor was scorched through on his shoulder, and smoke billowed off the burned and bubbling skin exposed. He didn't seem to care.

"You swore your mage-killer would end him." My father stood tall over Rolan's form. "And yet he still breathes."

"I hadn't counted on him casting his shield. It absorbed too much of the blast." Lady Hampstedt looked the giddiest I'd ever seen her. "But think! Think! That was the weakest gem with the lightest charge, and it still was enough to shatter the Archmagus's own shield! Think of the power at our hands!"

"I don't know . . . what madness this is . . ." Rolan gasped out. "But please. Please. Don't hurt Lyriana."

"Your niece?" Grezza walked over to my father's side, collecting his bloodied axes out of the sand. "My elder son, Razz, is in her room now. Slitting her pretty little throat."

Lyriana trembled in my arms, and I felt her heart pounding in her chest, her breath against my hand.

"It's true." My father's teeth sparkled bone white as he hunkered down by Rolan's side. "An unfortunate necessity, Archmagus. Your niece is already dead."

"No!" Rolan moaned, and for the first time, his voice sounded pained.

Behind me, Jax leaned against the wall, pale and distant. Miles sat in a quivering ball, his face hidden in his hands. Zell had turned away, disgusted. And I just stood frozen in place, holding Lyriana tight against me, hoping, wishing, begging, that this wasn't happening. It couldn't be true. My father would never kill an innocent girl. He was a good Lord. A good man!

Yet there he was, hands dripping blood.

"You will pay for this," Rolan whispered. "All of you. The King will come for you! He'll send an army!"

"The King will know only what I tell him. And I'll tell him the Zitochi did it," my father said. He leaned over Rolan, his face just inches away. "You've figured it out, haven't you? You see where this is going?" My father drew his second dagger from his sheath. "Your mages will die. Lightspire will burn. And the Kingdom of the West will rise again."

He plunged the dagger up to the hilt into Rolan's left eye.

At last, I turned away. It wasn't the blood welling out or the wet crunch or the way Rolan twitched as he died. It was the look on my father's face, wild and unhinged and happy. All my life, I'd dreamed of cracking his stern facade and seeing the real man underneath. I'd dreamed of seeing a smile. Now I had. And I never, ever wanted to see it again.

"Congratulations, my friends," I heard him say. "Ten years we've waited for this moment. At long last, our liberation begins."

"The great mage dies like a man." Grezza laughed. "Weak and begging."

"Most men wouldn't have summoned lightning from their damn hands," Lady Hampstedt replied, and when I looked back, she had her palm on Grezza's shoulder, a little too tenderly. "How many of his Rings are still intact? We'll need every one we can get."

"I see three. Maybe four." Grezza knelt down, plucked a loose finger out of the sand. "Weak little man. I could have taken him alone, easily," he grumbled, and pulled the Ring off with a hearty yank. It flew through the air, sparkling like a star. . . .

And landed right in the pile of rubble that led up to our ledge.

Oh shit.

Grezza walked toward the Ring. I looked back at the others, desperate, but none of us knew how to react. We stood there, frozen, as Grezza strode to the rubble and picked up the Ring. And we stood there, frozen, as he glanced idly up the cliff face and saw us.

Grezza didn't freeze. He reached for his ax.

I turned back to the others. And I screamed.

"Run!"

SIX

I expected Grezza to come charging up the hill, ax held high. I didn't expect him to just throw the damn thing.

It left his massive hand way too lightly and came hurtling at my head, a whirling, glistening discus of razor-sharp nightglass. I couldn't move. Not fast enough.

Zell tackled me from behind and shoved me to the ground, just as the ax whistled by overhead. It bounced off the stone of the outcropping with a shower of sparks, flying into the night.

I lay there for just a fraction of a second, the weight of Zell's body on top of me, the cold stone pressed against my face, gasping in the night air. Grezza Gaul, Chief of Clans of the Zitochi, had just attempted to murder me. And his own son had saved my life. This couldn't be happening. This couldn't be real.

Then I heard Grezza's thundering footsteps charging up the pile of rubble and decided it was probably real enough. Zell shoved off me and I lunged to my feet. In front of me,

Miles and Jax were already rushing into the tunnels. Lyriana wasn't with them, though. She was sitting on the ground, trembling, her hands clenched over her mouth, her eyes wide with shock. I reached down, grabbed her hand, and jerked her up to her feet. "Come on!"

She might've been in shock, but at least she moved when I pulled her. The two of us rushed through the opening in the cliff's wall, back into the darkness of the tunnels, and Zell raced alongside us. Luckily, I hadn't bothered to turn off my Sunstone, and it lit our path, its circle of light weaving wildly as it swung by the band around on my neck. I could just barely see the light of Miles's Sunstone ahead, ducking around a corner, and I chased after it.

"They killed him," Lyriana said as we rounded the corner, her voice hollow and broken. "They killed my uncle. And they wanted to kill me."

"If my father catches us, he will kill us all," Zell replied. "Keep running! Now!"

We had one obvious advantage: Jax knew the tunnels and exactly which way to go, how to avoid the loops and dead ends. But walking through the tunnels was one thing. Running was entirely another. I tripped over loose stones and bounced off tight corners with my shoulders. Lyriana's beautiful white dress, now torn and stained, kept getting caught around her feet, and I kept having to catch her as she fell. But still I ran, following Miles and Jax, ignoring the pain, pushing away the fear. I could be scared and upset later. Right now I needed to survive.

Voices sounded from behind us, echoes bouncing off the wall. Our parents were in the tunnels. Grezza shouted something, a furious, muffled growl, and my father yelled back in reply. I couldn't make out his words, but I swear he sounded upset. Maybe this was all a misunderstanding. Maybe if I just turned around and went back to him, he'd protect me. He'd wanted me by his side, after all. He'd wanted me to stand by him through whatever danger came next. Maybe it wasn't too late to still join him.

Next to me, Lyriana cried as she tripped, her foot caught in a hole in the ground. Could I just abandon her? Let my father kill her? The thought was horrible. But so was the thought of going on the run from my own father, of throwing away everything I'd ever dreamed about, especially when it was so close. I mean, hell, I didn't even really like Lyriana. I still kind of wanted to slap her. Was I about to give it all up, to ruin my life for the sake of some entitled, sheltered brat from Lightspire?

"Tilla!" Jax shouted from somewhere nearby. I turned to see him leaning against a narrow passage hidden behind some rubble, the light from Miles's Sunstone shining distantly through. My stomach plunged at the sight of him as I realized the much more awful truth. Because this wasn't just about Lyriana, not anymore. It was about Jax. Even if my father could be persuaded to spare me, even if I still had a chance at joining him, even if I could stomach letting Lyriana die . . . he'd never let some scruffy stable hand live knowing all about his terrible secret treason. I didn't know who my father was, not anymore, but that grinning, dagger-wielding murderer down on the beach? He'd slit Jax's throat in a heartbeat.

I had to run. For him.

"Over here!" Jax shouted. "We might be able to lose them!"

I knelt down to help Lyriana through the passage, and Zell followed after. As I went to go through, Jax grabbed my shoulder. His face was pale, drenched in sweat. I'd never seen him look so scared. I think he understood. I think he knew what I knew. "What the hell is happening, Tilla? What did your father just do?"

"I don't know," I said. "I'm sorry." For what? For getting Jax involved? For what my father had done? For being his daughter in the first place?

I didn't have time to think about it. "Keep moving," I said, and the two of us pushed through the passage.

The chamber we stepped into was familiar: the wide, empty room with the faded murals on the walls. Zell, Miles, and Lyriana stood in front of us, frozen in place for some reason. I was about to yell at them to get moving, and then I saw the flames flickering beyond and realized the room was already occupied.

A dozen Zitochi men stood opposite us, looking just as surprised as we were. I could tell they were warriors: they wore dark leather armor and had their black hair up in topknots. Two held torches, casting dancing shadows along the chamber's walls. The others wielded weapons: nightglass daggers and hand axes, even a full-length broadsword.

"Oh no," Zell whispered.

"'Oh no,'" one of the Zitochi repeated in a high-pitched voice, and stepped forward. I recognized him from the feast: Zell's older brother, Razz. The one who had been sent to kill Lyriana. "I've been looking for you, Princess," he said, and his voice almost sounded flirtatious. "Too bad my baby brother found you first. Guess we've always had the same taste in girls."

Our group pushed together instinctively, Zell and Jax stepping to the front. Miles was visibly trembling, and Lyriana didn't look much better. I pushed myself in front of them, even as I knew I couldn't do any good.

"Brother." Zell stepped forward, raising his empty hands. "Let's talk about this. You don't understand what's happening here."

"Oh, shut up, Zell," Razz said. I got a good look at him for the first time, and I didn't like what I saw. He had the same handsome features as his brother, but on him they looked wrong, twisted somehow. A thin scar in the shape of a fishhook cut up his right cheek. His bloodshot eyes looked blank, empty. Everyone else in the room was tense, but he was grinning, and there was something very wrong with his smile, like his teeth were there but also not, flickering white and black in the torchlight.

Then I realized it. They were flickering because they weren't teeth at all, but pointed nightglass, fused to his gums the way Zell's blades grew from his knuckles.

He'd had his canines replaced with nightglass fangs.

I stepped back involuntarily. I needed to get as far from him as I could.

"When we found the Princess missing from her room, I wondered if we were dealing with a traitor," Razz said. "And when we followed that reeking perfume of hers to these tunnels, well, I knew it had to be an inside job." He reached behind his back and jerked his weapons out of their scabbards: a pair of curved daggers, razor-sharp on one end, jagged and serrated on the other. They didn't just look designed to kill. They look designed to hurt. "But to think! It was you! My pathetic, snow-cub brother! Is this seriously where you found your balls? This is how you finally get your revenge?"

Even with his accent, the tone sounded familiar. He reminded me of Val, a butcher's son who'd laughed as he made me watch him drown a piglet. It wasn't just the emptiness in his eyes or the cruel curl of his mouth. It was the tension oozing off him, the nervousness, the way his hatred and aggression seemed forced, like he had to constantly hurt others just to keep his own thoughts at bay. Zitochi or Westerner, all bullies were the same.

"This isn't about us, Razz," Zell said. "This is bigger. More important. This is about our people. Our future! Our father has sold us out, all of us. He's conspiring with the Lord of this House to bring a war to our lands!"

The other warriors looked toward Razz, who just shook his head. "Did you hear that, men?" he shouted. "Because I know what I heard. 'Wah wah wah, my feelings got hurt. Wah wah wah, my daddy is so mean!'" He laughed, and his men laughed with him. A few tightened their grips on their weapons. Zell stepped back, sucking in his breath. He must have finally realized just how screwed we were.

"Kill them all," Razz said. "Leave the snow cub for me."

The warriors advanced. Zell whipped his sword out of its sheath, its thin, delicately curved blade sparkling dangerously. Miles let out a pitiful wail, and Jax stepped up to Zell's side. My hands clenched into fists. I didn't know what was going to happen or what I could do. But I knew I would go down fighting.

A hand pressed against my back. Lyriana stepped forward, pushing past me and Zell and Jax to stand in the front.

I was going to pull her back, but there was something different about her. Her cheeks were still slick with tears, but her eyes didn't look hopeless anymore. They looked hard, focused, furious. The air around her crackled as she walked. The taste of snow and frost filled my mouth. A cold wind swirled around her.

"You were going to kill me," she said, and her voice was impossibly deep and unearthly, the rumblings of mountains grinding together. "I came here as a guest . . . and you were going to kill me."

She reached out her hand, extending her long, elegant fingers. She'd finally taken off her gloves.

And for the first time, I saw her Rings.

A concussive blast of force burst out of her hand, hitting the Zitochi warriors like a focused hurricane. They flew off their feet, slamming into the walls of the cavern, their weapons shattering, their torches flying away. Deep rifts spiderwebbed out in the walls behind them, like cracks in a pane of glass. The ground shook beneath our feet. Dust rained down from the ceiling.

"You killed my uncle!" Lyriana screamed, and the air sucked in around her hand, gathering for another blast.

Razz, lying in a heap on the ground, was the first to respond. "She's a gods-damned witch!" he screamed, and hurled one of his daggers.

It grazed Lyriana's shoulder, barely cutting her, but it was still enough to throw her off balance. She jerked to the side, and the blast ripped out of her hand straight into the side of the chamber, blasting a hole through the wall with an explosive spray of dirt and stone. The tunnels trembled. Chunks rained down from the ceiling, not just dust, but whole, fist-size slabs of stone. One of the Zitochi screamed in pain. Jax tumbled over into the dirt.

The ground lurched hard beneath me, like a horse bolting. I fell onto one knee and found myself staring into the hole Lyriana had blown through the wall. Cold, stale air gusted through the darkness, and I could hear the sound of rushing water. The underground river, the one we'd heard earlier. It was nearby, much closer than I'd thought.

"Kill them!" Razz yelled, and a few of his men staggered up to their feet. The walls of the chamber buckled and groaned.

Even as my heart thundered in my chest, even with dirt blinding my eyes, I realized one thing with absolute clarity: if we stayed here, we'd die.

I grabbed Lyriana and lunged forward, through the hole in the wall, into the darkness.

I'd expected solid ground, but instead my feet hit a steep, crumbling slope. I managed to get out the very beginning of a scream before plunging down in a fumbling, painful roll. I immediately lost my grip on Lyriana. My Sunstone jostled around wildly, illuminating the barest glimpses of where I was: a weathered stone ceiling, jutting stalagmites, scattered piles of stone. The tunnels must have been built into a natural cave system, and I was hurtling through it head over heels, falling down this hill to who knows where. I could hear Lyriana screaming, and other voices following after, maybe Miles and Jax, maybe Razz and his men.

The slope ended, and I fell off it. For a horrible five seconds, I was in free fall, flailing through the air, waiting for impact. Then I hit water, stunningly cold, like being shoved into a bucket of ice—a bucket of ice with a raging current. I was underwater, choking, wrenched along by a force far too strong to swim against. The roar of the river drowned out the world. I went under, then out, then under, then out. When Jax and I were kids, we played a game when we went swimming where we'd try to dunk each other below the water. This was like that, except horrible and terrifying. I gasped and gagged, flailing as the river's current hurled me downstream.

I pushed above the surface just in time to see the ceiling of the cave vanish, replaced by the twinkling stars of the night sky, zooming by as if they were all falling. I could even make out the green glow of the Coastal Lights. The river must have exited the cave, which was good, except that meant it was carrying us out to sea. I twisted around and could just barely make out a sandy shore, but I was being pulled away from it far too quickly.

A chunk of debris slammed hard into my back. Pain flared through my side, so severe I felt it tingling through my fingers. I whipped around the debris and went back under, but now I didn't have the strength to fight. The current dragged me down. I gasped, and water flooded my lungs, dank and foul. My eyes burned. My side ached. I felt the water plunge me down into the depths. I was scared, so scared I'd crossed into a strange, shocked calm.

I was going to die here. I was going to drown in the current and be carried out to sea, my bones forgotten like so many others'. I was going to die a sixteen-year-old virgin without a last name, who never got to become a Lady or travel to Lightspire or even fall in love. I was going to die.

Then something grabbed me. It wasn't a hand, not quite.

It felt like I was suddenly wrapped up in something warm and glowing and safe. It was like being draped in a snug blanket after coming in from the rain, like being hugged by your father after you'd just been crying. It wasn't just physically warm. It was comforting, loving, reassuring. This warm something, whatever it was, grabbed me as I sank and lifted me up, gently, tenderly, out of the depths.

I gasped after breaching the surface and spat out murky black water. The force that held me lifted me up into the air, so I was floating a good foot above the ocean. A yellow light enveloped me in its soft glow, and I knew that was what was holding me up, where that feeling of safety and warmth was coming from. Droplets of water floated off my skin and hovered impossibly in front of me, like snowflakes dancing at winter's first fall.

I heard a gasp, so I craned my head as much as I could. There were more yellow lights behind me, and in them, more people: Miles, Zell, and Jax, all hanging above the water in glowing bubbles, all looking as stunned as I was. I tried to shout out to them, but my lungs still hurt too much, so I just made a soft grunt, one that sounded happier than it should have. I couldn't help myself. I was just so, so safe.

I felt a jerking motion and realized we weren't just hovering anymore, but moving. That same force that was holding the bubbles pulled us through the darkness, away from the ocean crashing behind us. Now that I wasn't sinking, I could see the cave's exit, a gaping maw in the side of a stony cliff face, the river rushing out like a flickering tongue. But we weren't being carried back into the cave. We were pulled instead to the side, toward a long, white-sand beach just by the river's edge, laid out under the cliff side. There was one more light on this beach, this one tall and thin and stationary. A figure stood at the heart of it, arms raised up, head cocked back, hands glowing bright.

I couldn't tell where the light ended and where Lyriana began. Her hair had streaks of gold running through it, pulsing like rivulets of molten metal. The Rings on her fingers were burning so brightly I couldn't even see her hands. Her pupils and irises were completely gone; her eyes were all yellow, twin suns bursting with light in the middle of her face.

She waved her hands forward, and we all drifted toward her, onto the shore. I felt my feet touch solid ground. The warm glow released me, and I tumbled down. I'd never been so happy to get a faceful of sand. I spat out the last of the water with a hacking cough, even as I heard the impacts of the three guys hitting the ground around me. Zell landed in a neat crouch, bracing himself with one hand. Miles fell straight into the sand. Jax collapsed into a heap, panting and gasping.

"Lyriana?" I looked up at her, shielding my eyes with one hand, squinting through her unearthly glow.

"Tillandra," she said, and her voice still had that rumble to it, like it was coming from the heart of a thunderstorm. "You're safe."

The light around her snuffed out like a candle. Her Rings flickered and went dark. She blinked, and her eyes had pupils again. "I did it," she said, her voice her own, as bubbly as it had been when she'd first come tumbling into the tunnels. "I really did it!"

Then she keeled over face-first into the sand and lay still.

seven

"Lyriana!" I screamed. I tried to get up and run to her, but my legs betrayed me. They were no longer magical, floaty, feel-good legs, but real legs, legs that had just slid down a jagged hill and been immersed in freezing water, legs that exploded with pain and sent me collapsing into the sand.

Jax, snapping out of his daze and scrambling over, was the first to her side. He turned her over onto her back. A minute ago Lyriana had looked like the Titans on the murals in the castle's shrine, a glowing being of light and power. Now she looked terrifyingly small and broken. Her beautiful dress was torn in dozens of places. Her bare feet were bloody and swollen. Jax pushed aside the wet hair clinging to her face and pressed his ear to her lips.

"She's breathing!" he shouted, and my stomach unclenched with a surge of relief. "She's breathing. I think she just . . . she just magicked herself out."

I didn't know you could magic yourself out, but I suppose

I also hadn't known Lyriana was a mage in the first place. I didn't think anyone had known that, not even my father. The royal family must have wanted it kept a secret.

"She saved our lives," Zell said softly. Through the dim light, I could only see his silhouette on the shore's edge, facing the dark ocean beyond. "She saved all of us."

"Well, pardon me if I'm not ready to play the trumpets and break out the cake," Miles replied, his voice hoarse and scratchy. He squatted on all fours in the sand, head bowed low, his wet curls wrapped like tendrils around his ears. "We might be safe from the ocean. But what do we do when those Zitochi lunatics come tearing out after us?"

"They won't," Jax grunted. "The cave collapsed after we went through. And even if they followed, they'd be swept out to sea. We never would've made it without the Princess. She saved us from Zell's psycho crew."

Earlier tonight, an eternity ago, I might've scolded Jax for being offensive. But now I was just too exhausted, too sore, too broken. I just wanted to collapse into the sand and pass out. I just wanted it all to go away.

Zell turned to Jax, just the barest hint of anger dancing in his eyes. "That wasn't *my* crew," he said. "And even if it was, they're not the ones to worry about. It's your people we should be scared of."

"*My* people?" Jax lurched to his feet, and not very gracefully. "*My* people are passed out drunk in the stables right now! That wasn't *my* father going berserk up there with an ax or *my* mother blowing up the Archmagus with some crazy-ass magic bomb!"

"My—my mother was obviously coerced," Miles

stammered. "She just built the weapon. It was the others' scheme."

"My father is a warrior, not a schemer," Zell said. "If anything, your mother was the one who seduced him into it. . . ."

"My mother would never—"

"It was my father," I said, and the night went silent. "He's the one behind this all. He's the traitor."

Zell, Miles, and Jax turned to stare at me. "Tilla," Jax said, "you don't know. . . . I mean . . ."

"No, Jax. I do know. We all know it. This was all his plan." I think I said it just to shut them up, but now that the words were out, they had the unmistakable weight of truth. "My father is a traitor. My father is a killer. And now my father probably wants me dead." The words felt like a knife, scraping me hollow. I wished Lyriana had just let the current take me away.

There was nothing else to say after that. Zell turned back to the ocean, and Miles slumped into the sand. Jax ran his hands through his messy, wet hair, craning his face up to the sky. I closed my eyes and drowned out the voices in my head. I focused on the wet sand in my hands, the breeze on my skin. I felt the weight of my soaking clothes for the first time, felt their chill against me.

"It just doesn't make sense," Miles muttered, still trying to somehow think his way out of this. "None of it. Even if . . . even if our parents are secretly Western radicals . . . what in the frozen hell are they trying to accomplish? What does killing the Archmagus and blaming the Zitochi gain them?"

I hadn't even stopped to think about this yet. "It . . . lures more mages into the West," I speculated. "Sets them up for an ambush."

"Right, but with what? That mage-killer bomb my mother had was powerful, but how many more could they have? Your average mage has, what, three, four Rings? Multiply that by six missing mages and that's twenty-five bombs, tops. Nowhere near enough to hold back even a single company of mages." Miles shook his head. "There must be something we're not understanding here. There has to be a reasonable explanation. We just need to talk to them and find out what's going on."

"Are you kidding me?" Jax demanded.

"My mother is very reasonable," Miles pressed. "If I could just talk to her, I could find out what really happened and make sure she understood we didn't mean any harm. I'm sure I could persuade her to give us a second chance."

"For you and me, maybe," I said, unable to keep my mouth shut any further. "But what about Jax? What about the Princess? There's no way our parents would let them live, not with everything they know." I didn't mention Zell, but I didn't have to; I think all of us got the picture about what his family would do to him if he went back.

Miles cradled his head in his hands, his voice trembling. I could tell he was crying. "But what . . . what's the alternative, Tilla? Running away? Turning our backs on our homes? On our lives? On our own parents?"

I didn't even know how to answer that. Could I really do it? Just run away and never set foot in Castle Waverly again, never lie down on Whitesand Beach, never see my father again? I thought of his face down at the beach, that wild, gleeful bloodlust that had made me want to scream. Could I go back to him, even if I wanted to? Would I ever look at him the same way? Even if he forgave me, could I ever forgive him?

Of course, a little voice inside me whispered. *He's your father. And you love him.*

"Look," Jax said, mercifully pulling me out of my thoughts. "We don't need to answer the big questions right now. What we need is food and shelter and some clothes that aren't ripped to shreds."

"And how do you propose we get those?" Zell asked.

Jax craned his head down the beach. "I don't know how far that river took us, but we're still obviously on the Western Shore. I've got friends up and down this coast. I say we sit tight till morning, and then when the sun's out, I'll get us somewhere safe, somewhere we'll be taken care of. We can figure it out from there."

"Won't our parents look for us?" Miles asked. "Tonight, I mean?"

Zell shook his head. "Right now, anyone after us is trapped in the tunnels. It'll take them hours to get out, and even longer to get together a half-decent tracking party. Besides, they have no idea where we went." He jerked his head toward a pile of driftwood lying under an outcropping at the base of the cliff, near the cave's entrance. "We can make camp there. Get a small fire going. Stay warm." He turned to gaze back out at the ocean. "I'll take first watch."

A part of me wondered why we needed a first watch if we'd be safe until sunrise, but I didn't question it. It wasn't just that Zell was the only one among us who had even half a clue how to get by in a situation like this. It was his manner: cool, confident, collected, like this was just the same old shit he always had to deal with, like this was nowhere near the worst day of his life. His own father and brother had straight up tried to kill him, but he still didn't let any emotion break through, no fear or sadness or anything. I couldn't tell if his stoic facade was just that or if he really was that jaded. Some distant part of me knew that probably wasn't healthy, but right then I didn't care. In that moment, on that beach, Zell's calm was pretty much the only thing that made me feel safe.

He had lost that pretty sword of his in the cave, so he pulled the sheath off his back and tossed it into the sand, followed by his soaked leather and furs. Miles paced back toward the outcropping, gathering hunks of wood. And Jax knelt down by Lyriana, lifting her up in his broad arms, and then we all walked toward the cliff face. She looked so small and fragile now.

"You think she's okay?" I asked.

Jax sighed. "I hope so. I hope we're all okay."

My heart sank. I felt guilty, as if this were all my fault. In a way, it was. If it hadn't been for me, Jax would still be happily drinking with his buddies in the stables. If it hadn't been for me, he'd still have a nice, safe life ahead of him. "Jax," I said softly, "I'm so sorry. . . ."

He glanced at me, one eyebrow cocked, the same sweet, goofy brother I'd loved my whole life. "Shut your face, sis," he said, and walked off toward the outcropping.

I smiled despite myself and walked after him.

EIGHT

AN HOUR LATER, I WAS LYING ON MY BACK IN THE SAND, EYES shut, trying to fall asleep.

Ten minutes after that, I was sitting up, wide awake, and knew there was no way in hell it was happening.

I stood up on the beach, my back aching, my legs still sore. I was near a surprisingly well-made fire gently flickering in a pit that Jax and Miles had dug. Miles lay on his side nearby, deeply asleep, twitching and whimpering. It was, just maybe, the saddest thing I'd ever seen. Jax was a few feet away, asleep half upright against the cliff wall, with Lyriana lying beside him. The two of them looked almost peaceful, if you ignored the rips in their clothes and the bruises blossoming on their skin.

I couldn't believe they were able to sleep. My mind was still racing, a million thoughts colliding. I had to take a walk. Or a run. Or maybe just wade into the ocean and scream into the night sky. But I had to do something.

I walked out from under the outcropping, toward the dark, lapping waves. The Coastal Lights hung in the sky above, soft and faded now, flickering away into nothingness.

I made it maybe two steps before I heard Zell's voice. "Still awake?" he asked from behind me.

I spun around. Zell was sitting on a driftwood log just past the outcropping's entrance, facing out at the ocean. He was almost totally hidden in shadow; if he hadn't spoken up, I wouldn't have noticed him at all. "I was just going to go for a walk. I need to clear my thoughts."

He shrugged. "I doubt a walk will help with that. It's never helped me." An awkward silence lingered in the night air between us. "You can . . . join me. If you'd like."

Why the hell not, right? Not like my night could get any worse. Zell slid over, and I sat down on the log next to him. He had stripped down to a thin, sleeveless undershirt that clung to him like a second skin. I tried hard not to glance at his toned, lean arms; at his broad, bare shoulders; at the firm muscle where his neck met his back, just barely visible through his flowing hair. "How's your watch going? Any sign of them?" I asked.

Zell shook his head. "None. I haven't heard anything but the crashing of the waves and the whistling of the wind." He had this funny way of talking, like he was being poetic without even remotely realizing it. He craned his head up to the sky. I couldn't read his expression. Sad? Worried? Longing? "Can I . . . ask you something?"

"Sure."

"I don't understand what happened tonight," he said. Was that a hint of embarrassment in his voice? "I mean, I can understand some of it. I understand why my father did what he did. His reign as Chief of Clans is crumbling. He has promised our people great prosperity and glory, neither of which he has delivered. If your father offered him gold and grain, perhaps even the return of some of the Borderlands . . . I can see why he would offer his ax in return." Zell closed his eyes, his brow furrowed. "But it's your father I don't understand. Aren't the Princess and the mage his rulers? Doesn't he bow before them?" He finally turned to look at me, his eyes shining bright in the moonlight. "Why did he do it? Why would he want to kill the family he swore to serve?"

"It's . . . it's complicated," I said. "Your father, he's the Chief of Clans, right? Are there other Chiefs who oppose him? Who want to be the Chief themselves?"

"Of course. The Conclave this year was brutal."

"Conclave?"

Zell arched an eyebrow, like he really expected me to know this. "Every three years, all the Chieftains of all the Clans gather at Zhal Korso for a great Conclave. After four days of games and feasting and drinking, the Chieftains who would wish to lead present their arguments in the Hall of Bones. Then all the *zhindain*, the clanless women, vote on who they believe will be best. And that man is the Chief of Clans."

"Oh," I said, even though I didn't really understand at all. "So, the Chief changes, then? Often?"

"Of course."

"Well . . . that's not how we do it," I said. "The Volaris family rules us. They have for one hundred and twenty years, since the Great War. When the King . . . Right now, that's

Leopold Volaris. . . . When he dies, his oldest child, Lyriana, takes over. And then she'll be the Queen until she dies."

"But that makes no sense." Zell stared at me skeptically, like I was pulling some kind of trick on him. "What if your King's child is a fool? What if she leads your people to ruin?"

"We don't have a choice, Zell. They have the power. The magic. All the men of the West couldn't stand against the mages."

"Magic. Like what your Princess did earlier tonight, when she pulled us out of the water." Zell was obviously still a little in awe. "I've never seen anything like it."

"What she did was amazing," I admitted. "But it's just a fraction of what the mages can do." I hadn't paid much attention to Headmaiden Morga's history lessons, but I remembered vividly all her accounts of the battles of the Great War, all the gory details. "They can turn men inside out from a mile away. They can rain down fire and lightning from the skies. They can rip the earth out from under a battlefield and turn rocks into monsters that battle for them."

"How did they come by such power?"

"From the Titans. Well, from their Rings." Zell stared at me blankly, as if I were saying total gibberish. He really didn't know any of it, did he? "Your people . . . the Zitochi . . . you don't have any stories about Titans, do you? Giant men who came from the heavens, who transformed the world with their amazing magical powers?"

Zell furrowed his brow. "There are ancient legends about great monsters from the South, huge pale men who came from the sky with hands of fire. The shamans say the first Zitochi, who used to live down in the forests you call home, fled these

monsters into the frozen tundra, where we've lived ever since."
He stroked his chin. "Could these monsters be your Titans?"

"I don't know," I said, more surprised that the Zitochi had apparently once lived in the West. "All I really know is what Headmaiden Morga taught me."

"Which is?"

I sighed. Why was I, of all people, the one teaching a history class? I could barely remember half this stuff! "A thousand years ago, my ancestors were simple folk scattered in tribes across the plains of the Heartlands, wearing animal furs, living off the land, that sort of thing. Then the Titans came down from the heavens. To them, doing magic was as natural as breathing. They settled among the tribes and taught them all kinds of things, like farming and medicine and how to build castles."

"Why?"

"The Lightspire priests say it was because they were angels, beings of pure kindness, come to better our kind and save us from ourselves. That's why they worship them."

Zell's eyes flickered with curiosity. "But you don't."

"No. I mean, not really. I don't know." I'd been brought up to respect the religion of Titan-worship, if only because it was the religion of our King in Lightspire. But a few years ago, when I was going through my question-everything phase, I'd gone asking around and found out what they'd believed in the days of the Old Kings, before we'd been conquered. "Some people say the Titans weren't angels but demons. That they brutally conquered our ancestors, used them as slaves to build their cities and plow their fields. That they used magic to oppress the entire continent."

"I find that easier to believe," Zell said. Honestly, I did, too. I remembered the tapestries in my father's archives, hundreds of years old, drawn by men who'd seen Titans in the flesh. They showed terrifying creatures, hulking giants that stood twice as tall as any man, their heads bald, their eyes glowing white, their beardless faces identical and beautiful and always smiling, like porcelain masks. They sure didn't look like angels. "But the Titans are gone now."

I nodded. "No one knows why. Just a hundred years after they came, they disappeared overnight, leaving behind only the empty cities they'd built. The priests say it was because they were leaving the world in our hands now and testing us to see if we could rise to their level or whatever." I shrugged. "With the Titans gone, my people . . . my ancestors . . . were free to settle this new world. All kinds of little Kingdoms sprang up over the continent. There were the Baronies of the Eastern Shore, the Dynasty of Hao in the Southlands, those weird little Kingdoms in the swamps whose names I can never remember . . . and there was the Kingdom of the West."

"That was here," Zell said, understanding.

"Yup," I said. "After the Titans vanished, a bunch of my ancestors finally braved the Frostkiss Mountains and discovered these big old forests on the other side of them. Those pilgrims settled this land, and eventually one family came to rule over all of them. My family. The Old Kings. The Kents."

"But they didn't have magic," Zell said.

"No. No one did, not for a long time. See, most of the Titan cities collapsed when they vanished, but one of them—the biggest, Lightspire—kept standing. For a long time, it was just a powerful trade city, nothing more. But then the family that ruled it uncovered the secrets of Titan magic, hidden in some buried libraries or whatever. They learned how to use the Titans' weapons, their Rings, and that was how the first mages came about. The Volaris founded the School of Mages, and created an unstoppable army. One by one, they conquered all their neighbors, turning Kingdoms into Provinces and making their Kings bow. And finally, they came for us. The Kingdom of the West." I let out a deep exhale. "That was the Great War. A hundred and twenty years ago, after their mages killed almost half the men of the West, my great-great-grandfather Albion Kent surrendered. And the Kingdom of the West became the Western Province, just another territory of the great Kingdom of Noveris."

Zell was quiet for a while, thinking. "It sounds like your people have often been slaves," he said at last. "First to the Titans. Then to this Lightspire King. Your father, then . . . he did what he did so your people could be free. There's honor in that."

"I . . . I guess so," I said, looking up at him. In the flickering orange light of the dying fire, his face looked serene, as calm and thoughtful as the statues of the Old Kings. But there was something else in his eyes, something that seemed almost gentle. Was Zell . . . trying to make me feel better?

And was it actually working?

Something rustled and flickered overhead. I looked up to see a dozen streaks of sparkling light cut through the night sky, zipping past us like blue-and-yellow shooting stars. Zell startled, but I held out a hand to calm him. "They're just Whispers."

"Whispers?"

"Magical little birds. We buy them from the Artificers Guild in Lightspire," I explained. I'd spent hours as a girl gazing into the straw-lined cages in Castle Waverly's Whisper roost, because how could I not? They were so damn cute, tiny little owls no bigger than your thumb, with big glistening eyes that looked like galaxies. A lot less cute was how they crumbled into bone and dust after they'd delivered too many messages, but I made sure to not be around for that part. "Most of our towns have Whisper roosts. You tell a message to a bird and which roost to fly to, and then it'll go there and pass your message along, speaking your words in your voice. It's how we communicate."

"Those came from your father's Castle," Zell mused. "He's sending the word out."

"Yeah," I said, but which word? That the Zitochi had killed the Archmagus, and, what, kidnapped the Princess? What was his plan now? Why had he done any of this?

I thought again of the beach, of the crunch as my father drove the dagger into Rolan's eye, his vicious grin. The Whispers vanished, leaving us in the dark. "My father was ready to kill an innocent girl in her sleep," I said. "Where's the honor in that?"

"Honor," Zell repeated, as if tasting the word in his mouth. "I suppose honor can mean whatever we twist it to mean." He paused for a full minute before speaking again. "Do you know why I went with you tonight? To spy on you. To spy on your Princess. I thought that if I brought my father details of your castle's weak points or some secret about the Princess, he might soften toward me."

I reeled at that. Before, Zell admitting that he just saw us as enemies to spy on would have gotten my blood boiling. But he sounded so lost it was impossible to feel anything but sympathy. "I pretended to be your friend so I could betray you," he said. "And I didn't do it for my people or my family's honor. I did it because I wanted my father to be proud of me again. I did it for the man who threw an ax at my skull. So what does that make me?"

"A bastard," I said. "Same as me."

Neither of us said anything after that. The waves crashed in the darkness, and a light breeze tinged with their salty spray swept over us. Zell's hair ruffled gently behind him. I shivered but hid it well. I tried to think of something to say, but nothing came to mind, nothing that could make sense in this impossible moment. There weren't words for what I was feeling, for the knowledge that my entire world had crumbled in the space of one night, for the understanding that nothing would ever be right again. I looked at Zell, and he looked at me. I could tell he was thinking the same thing.

So we sat there together in silence on the log, listening to the waves, staring out at the night.

And I felt the tiniest bit of comfort that at least I wasn't alone.

NINE

THE NEXT THING I KNEW, I WAS WAKING UP AND IT WAS midmorning. "Whu . . . ?" I grumbled, blinking into the light. I felt like it had just been the middle of the night minutes ago, but now the hot sun hung overhead. My throat was so dry it felt like I'd swallowed a bag of sand. I jerked up, my back incredibly unhappy that I'd been sleeping against the log for hours. "What's going on?"

"Very little," Zell replied. He was sitting cross-legged in the sand just a few feet away, facing the ocean. I had a feeling he'd been there for a while. Miles was standing next to him, his hair a frazzled mess, his hands in his pockets. Looking back at the camp, I could make out Lyriana's silhouette by the gently smoldering fire pit, huddled in the shadow against the cliff's wall. But where was . . . ?

"Jax went off to scout the area," Miles said. "We're just sitting tight until he gets back."

"Right. That makes sense." I stood up with a stretch. Zell

seemed to be in his own world, doing whatever weird thing Zitochi do in the morning. I felt a sudden flash of embarrassment. What had last night been about? What was that moment we'd shared? I didn't want to think about it, so I turned to Miles. "You holding up okay?"

"About as well as I can be," he replied. "I keep racking my brain, trying to figure this all out. I'm sure if I could just sit somewhere quiet and concentrate, I could come up with something, a plan to fix everything, without anyone else getting hurt."

"How's it looking?"

"All I've got is step one," Miles sighed. "Find somewhere quiet to sit and concentrate."

I looked back at the fire pit, where we'd set up camp. Lyriana wasn't just sitting there. She was hunched with her face in her hands, crying, almost shaking with grief. Even from across the beach, I could make out her muffled wails, her despairing sobs.

"She's been like that all morning," Miles said. "Jax and I tried to talk to her, but it . . . it didn't help. Maybe you could try? I'm sure you'd do better than we did."

Why? Because I'm a girl? I bristled a little at that, especially since I probably had more in common with Zell than I did with a sheltered butterfly like Lyriana. But then she let out another heaving, shuddering sob, and I turned to head her way. I'd be a terrible person if I didn't even try.

Lyriana heard me approach. She glanced up sniffling, as I came over, and she looked even worse than I'd imagined. Her cheeks were stained with tears, and her eyes were bloodshot and weary. Her hair hung in tangled clumps around her face.

A dark bruise had blossomed around her jawline, probably from the fall through the caves, and her lip was split open and bloody. She didn't look like the Princess who had stunned everyone at the feast or the mage who had saved our lives. She just looked like a girl who'd been through hell.

She sobbed again, a full-body wail, like a widow at a funeral. And maybe it made me a bitch, but I couldn't help but feel kind of annoyed with her. We'd *all* had a bad night. We were *all* in huge trouble. But the rest of us were holding it together and not having full-on meltdowns. So why couldn't she?

"They killed Uncle Rolan," she muttered softly. "They killed him like he was nothing."

That feeling of annoyance curdled instantly into guilt. *Right.* She hadn't just had a bad night. She'd watched her uncle get slaughtered before her eyes. She had every right in the world to melt down. Hell, she had every right to punch me in the face.

"I'm sorry," I said, sitting down next to her. "It was terrible." I desperately wished I could think of something better to say, something that wasn't so trite or obvious or hollow. But what could I say? I hadn't paid much attention to my etiquette lessons, but I was pretty sure there wasn't a standard expression for *Sorry my dad killed your uncle.*

"He told me it'd be dangerous. He said people would want to hurt us. But I didn't believe him. I didn't listen." Lyriana's voice quivered. "I don't want this anymore. I don't want to experience the world. I don't want any of it. I just want to go home."

"We all do," I said, and my chest ached. I felt terrible for having judged her so much the night before, terrible for all the misfortune my family had brought down on her. I reached out to hold her, pulled my hand back when I realized I shouldn't touch the Princess, and then decided that we were well past the point of respecting those sorts of boundaries. I wrapped my arm around Lyriana and pulled her close and held her against me as she cried, as her tears soaked my shirt. Her body racked against mine, heaving with her wails, but I held her firm.

That seemed to help, just a little. She stopped crying and turned back to me with a sniffle, her head cocked to the side as if really looking at me for the first time. "You betrayed your own father to protect me," she said. "You could have handed me over, but you didn't. You saved my life."

"Yeah, well, you saved us all from drowning," I replied. "So I guess we're even. And hey. You got to dip that foot in the Endless Ocean after all."

"I dipped a lot more than a foot." She gave just the faintest hint of a smile. "If you can get me home, I promise you'll be safe. I swear by the Titans, I'll make sure no harm comes your way."

And what about my father? Would any harm come his way? I didn't dare ask, because I already knew the answer.

"Hey!" Jax's voice shouted from up the beach. "I'm back!"

I tried to help Lyriana up so we could see what was happening, but she didn't budge. "Please," she said. "I don't want to talk to anyone else. Just leave me here for now. I'd like to grieve alone."

There wasn't much I could say to that. I gave her shoulder a gentle pat and then headed back up the beach. I could make out Jax's figure, his bounding strides recognizable even that far away. "I've got great news," he huffed as he came to a stop next to us. "Really great news. Turns out we are insanely lucky!"

"I'm going to have to disagree with that," Miles muttered.

Jax ignored him. "I figured out where we are! We're in Beggar's Reach, the stretch past the old quarry, through the thick old woods. That must be why this cove's so hard to find. That river carried us even farther north than it seemed."

"How is that great news?" I asked.

"Because you know who lives nearby?" Jax's cheeks crinkled with a big ear-to-ear grin. "Tannyn and Markos!"

"No way," I smiled. Tannyn and Markos Dolan were a pair of brothers who Jax and I had grown up with. Their father had been the official vintner of Castle Waverly, and as kids, the four of us had been inseparable, tearing around the courtyard, splashing in the creek, pranking the visiting merchants, and hiding from Headmaiden Morga. Tannyn had been Jax's best friend, a good-natured athletic boy who'd always been down for a race or a dare. And Markos . . .

Markos was a year younger than me. He wasn't the smartest boy, and certainly not the most handsome, and he stuttered when he got nervous. But he was sweet and gentle, and a lifetime ago, he'd been my first kiss.

"They're old friends of ours," Jax explained. "Their dad used to work in the castle, and when he retired, Lord Kent gave him this vineyard out on the coast. He died a couple of years ago, but his boys inherited the place. And guess what? They're just a few hours' walk from here!"

"Tannyn and Markos. Wonderful," Miles grumbled. He'd never gotten along with the brothers. Once, when we were little, Tannyn had pushed Miles into a creek, and Miles had run crying to his mom. Both brothers caught a whipping for that, something they never forgave him for.

"And what will these old friends do for us?" Zell asked.

"They're good guys," Jax said. "Tannyn's practically a brother to me. They'll give us food, clean clothes, a place to lie low while we figure this all out."

My stomach rumbled audibly. I realized suddenly just how hungry I was. "It's a good idea. Better than staying on this beach all day. And I can vouch for the guys."

"Oh, I'm sure you can," Jax said, his smirk barely concealed. He never got over the fact that Markos and I had made out.

Zell didn't seem to pick up on it. "If you both trust them, then it's good enough for me. We should leave now and travel along the coast as far as we can, staying hidden in the cliff's shadow—"

"Wait," Miles interrupted. He rubbed the bridge of his nose with his eyes shut, the way he always did when he was thinking. "Wait, wait, wait. We have to split up."

Jax spun toward him. "What? Why would we possibly do that?"

"Look, for all we know, every soldier in the West is out there looking for us. What happens if we all get caught together?" None of us answered. "Right. I don't know, either. But I don't think it'll be good."

"And we'll be better off if we split up?"

Miles sighed. "Look around, Jax. What do you see? Because I see three worthless bastards, a worthless stable hand, and one absolutely priceless Princess."

Jax didn't seem to get it, but I did. "Lyriana's the one our parents really want. Until they capture her, the rest of us, well, we still have value to them. . . ."

"Because we know where she is," Zell finished, then cocked his head at Miles. "Smart."

From there, it was just a matter of deciding who stayed and who went. Jax insisted he had to go, because Tannyn would be most likely to listen to him. Miles tried to insist I should stay, because I'd be safest with the Princess, and yeah, that kind of pissed me off. I pointed out that I had history with the guys, too, and that just made Jax snicker. Zell offered to stay back, but Jax didn't trust him with Lyriana. In the end, despite Miles's stammering protests, we decided that Jax, Zell and I would go, and Miles would stay back with Lyriana. They'd be safe, hidden here in the shadow of the cliffs. Safe as they could be.

We gathered our stuff and prepared to set out. I checked one last time on Lyriana to make sure she knew what was happening and was okay with it; she let out a few soft *meep*s that I think meant yes. As I headed out to join Jax and Zell, though, Miles stopped me halfway up the beach. "Tilla, wait. Can I talk to you for a moment?"

"Miles, I know you don't want to stay behind," I began. "But it just makes the most sense, okay?"

"That's . . . that's not what this is about." Miles stared down intensely at his bare feet. "I just . . . I wanted to give you something. Just in case." He reached into his coat and took something out, a small leather disk.

"Your Sunstone?" I asked. "I already have one. . . ."

"I was thinking we could trade. See, I modified mine this

94

morning." He turned it over in his hands. "I was thinking about what my mom did with that mage-killer, so I ended up tinkering around. Normally, there's a safety that immediately vents the gas if the glass facade is compromised, so I used a hairpin to disable it and . . ." He must have noticed the glazed look on my face. "If you break the glass while it's on, it'll go boom. Not like the mage-killer or anything, but enough to start a fire and scare off anyone coming at you."

"Oh." That did sound kind of useful, actually. I took the Sunstone and turned it over. It was fancy, one of the really nice ones they sold in the upscale shops of Port Hammil. The lining of the disk was gold, inlaid with tiny sparkling rubies, and the back had an engraving of an owl, the sigil of House Hampstedt. Below was their House motto, *Minds Before Might*. I remembered this Sunstone: Miles's mom had given it to him as a present for his thirteenth birthday. He'd been so proud of it he'd spent his entire visit to Castle Waverly showing it to anyone who'd pay attention.

And now he'd turned it into a bomb. For me. "Miles . . ."

"Just take it." He closed my hand around it and pushed it away before I could change his mind. I awkwardly pulled my Sunstone off my neck and gave it to him, and he looked down at it thoughtfully. "Listen," he said. "In case . . . in case this is the last time I see you . . . there's something I should tell you. Something I should have told you a long time ago."

Oh no. Not an awkward declaration of love. That was the absolute last thing I wanted to deal with. "I'm coming back, Miles," I said. "That's a promise. Whatever it is, you can tell me then."

He nodded. "Yeah. You're right. I'll tell you then."

It was better that way. Way, way better. I left him back at the fire pit with Lyriana and caught up with Zell and Jax. "What was that about?" my brother asked.

"Nothing," I replied, heading up the coast as briskly as I could. "Now, come on, boys. Let's get walking."

TEN

IT WASN'T THE WORST HIKE I EVER TOOK, BUT IT WAS definitely up there. Jax led us along the beach for an eternity, until my feet ached from walking in the shifting sand. After that, it was just a climb up a steep, crumbling slope, and then a slog through some overgrown forest. If it were anyone else leading us, I'd be sure we were lost. But Jax knew the Western Coast like the back of his hand and could navigate a maze at night blindfolded. So I followed him, shoving past the rustling oak trees, tromping over crackling leaves, trying (and failing) to avoid muddy puddles.

We got to the Dolan estate around midafternoon. An hour's ride from the town of Hale, this was probably as far north as Western vineyards could go; any farther north and you'd start encountering the frosty Borderlands and the Zitochi tundra beyond them. A thin veil of clouds hid the sun, casting the world in a gloomy gray light. We stepped out of the forest and onto some gently sloping hills dotted with rows and rows of barren white posts, their grapes already harvested. Another day, I might've thought it looked pretty. But right now they looked way too much like graves.

"I don't like it," Zell muttered. "Too exposed. Anyone could see us here."

"Right. Which is why we're headed toward the house." Jax jerked his head down the vineyard. A country estate lay at the end, a beautiful two-story manor with a painted stone front and a red-shingled roof and pretty arched windows with carved wooden panels. A stable sat to the side, and an exceptionally cute herb garden sprawled out alongside it. It was a hell of a place for an old vintner, even one who'd served Castle Waverly for thirty years.

How did the old saying go? *A Kent will reward loyalty a hundred times over, but punish betrayal just once.*

We were halfway across the vineyard when Tannyn stepped out of the house, carrying an empty tin pail. He was stout and handsome, with toned biceps and neatly combed brown hair. I hadn't seen him in a couple of years, but they'd obviously been good to him: his arms were bigger and muscular like Jax's, and a sandy beard dotted his dimpled chin.

"Hey!" Jax shouted.

Tannyn looked up and saw us. His jaw dropped, and his eyes went wide. Did we really look *that* bad? "Jax! Tilla!" he shouted.

Jax let out a booming laugh. "Come on, Tannyn! Is that any way to greet your old friends?" He glanced back at Zell and me. "Oh. Right. It's not every day your friends show up with a glassie warrior."

Tannyn rubbed his eye with the back of his big ruddy hand. "Forget him. What are you doing here?"

I stopped moving, uncertain, but Jax pushed toward the house. "I'm gonna level with you, Tannyn. We're in trouble. Big trouble. We need your help."

"My . . . my help?" Tannyn asked, and then blinked, as if he suddenly understood. "Right. Okay. Yeah. Of course! Whatever you need! Why don't you come on in and tell me what's going on?"

"That's my boy!" Jax beamed and broke into a sprint. I wanted to rush after him, but for some weird reason, my legs held firm. An unpleasant truth twisted my stomach. We'd come all the way out here because we desperately needed help . . . but if we went in there, we'd be pulling two more people into this mess. If my father got word that they'd sheltered us . . . they'd be just as screwed as we were. I looked to Zell, and he was standing firm, too, his brow furrowed, his gaze intense. Was he feeling guilty, too? Or was this something else entirely?

"Jax," I called out. "Maybe we should—"

"Markos!" Tannyn yelled, cutting me off. "Get out here! You're not going to believe it! Tilla and Jax are here . . . and they need our help!"

The door to the stables swung open. A tall, thin young man stepped out, jaw hanging open in disbelief. Markos Dolan had barely changed. Messy blond hair hung down around his shoulders, and even in the shadow of his hand, I could make out his crooked nose and freckled cheeks. From across the vineyard, his pale green eyes found mine. "T-T-Tilla!" he stammered.

I remembered that night, three years ago, after the Summer's Bounty feast. The adults were all drunk, either passed out around the Castle or singing dirty ballads in the Hall. Jax and Tannyn had stolen a whole skin of wine and snuck off to drink it. Markos and I had found ourselves hiding out in the hayloft above the stables, lying together in a big, soft pile of hay, laughing about the ridiculous things we'd seen the Lords doing below. Then the conversation had lulled, and he'd kissed me, or maybe I'd kissed him, but either way we were kissing, soft but frantic, my hands around his shoulders, his gently holding my waist. I still remembered so clearly the way he'd nuzzled the side of my neck, leaving a little trail of little fluttering kisses down to my collarbone. I remembered how he'd held me close afterward, my back pressed against his chest, feeling his heart, how he'd somehow known just how far I'd wanted to go and stopped there.

"W-why . . . why are you here?" he said now, the color draining from his already pale face. "Why are you—"

"I'm sure they'll tell us all about it, Markos," Tannyn cut in. "But let's get them cleaned up and fed first! They look like they just came from a war!" He shot his brother an intense glare. "Get in there and get some water ready, man!"

"Right. Yeah. Water." Markos broke his gaze away from mine, rushing into the house. I wanted to call out something, to warn him, to turn back. . . .

Jax stepped past Tannyn and vanished into the estate's doorway. It was too late, wasn't it? He was in. There was no turning back now. One way or another, Tannyn and Markos had tied their fates to ours. I wanted to throw up.

"Then, let's go," Zell said, and marched forward.

Tannyn knelt down and picked up his pail. Zell and I made our way toward him, and he stood back up. "Tilla," he said. "And . . . well, someone I don't know."

"This is Zell," I explained. "He's with us. He's . . . he's in the same mess we are."

"Right." Tannyn looked him up and down, his gaze lingering on the long dagger sheathed at his waist. "Look, I don't know what kind of trouble you're in. And I can't even begin to imagine why you're showing up at our house with a gla—with a Zitochi. I want to help. I do. But . . ."

"But you won't let me in your house," Zell said coolly, and Tannyn didn't reply.

"He's a good guy," I explained. "Really. And he needs help, too. I'll vouch for him, okay? He won't cause any trouble."

Tannyn sighed. I could tell he was just putting on a friendly front for Jax, that inside he was worried, trying to figure out just how badly this could all end for him. He wouldn't like the answer. "At least leave the weapons outside, okay? For my peace of mind?"

Zell glanced at me, and I nodded. "Do it, Zell."

He shrugged, unlatched the belt holding the sheath at his waist, and tossed the dagger down by the entryway. Then he pulled a second knife out of a sheath under his shirt, and a third one from a strap on his boot. He threw them on top of the dagger. "Satisfied?"

"Not the word I'd use," Tannyn replied, and stepped back into the house. "Come on in."

We followed him inside, and even as sore and hungry and unhappy as I was, I couldn't help but admire the place. Jax had visited them before, but this was my first time. The floor was smooth tile, and nice tapestries hung down the walls, showing pictures of humble farmers and vintners at work in the field, alongside a beautiful, hand-drawn map of the Western Province. A winding stairway led up toward the bedrooms. There was a big fireplace on the opposite end of the room with a pair of elegant swords mounted on the wall above it. A long wooden table sat in the middle of the room, and on it, a bowl of the most succulent, ripe, juicy raspberries I'd ever seen. Jax had already slumped down into a chair and was busy shoveling them into his mouth.

Tannyn must have seen my hungry stare. "Pull up a chair, too," he said. "Have some food. You look like you could use it."

I crossed the room in record speed to plop down next to Jax before he could polish off all the berries. My stomach practically roared with hunger. I had no time to worry about looking ladylike, not today. I wolfed down a handful of berries, and they were, no joke, the most delicious thing I'd ever tasted.

A pair of doors at the room's end swung open, and Markos hurried out from the kitchen, holding three carved wooden cups with water. "Here!" he handed them out. Jax grabbed one so eagerly he spilled half of it over the table. Zell declined. I reached out to take mine, and my fingertips brushed with Markos's. He pulled back his hand, and his cheeks flushed a tiny bit.

"Markos," I said, "it's been a while." He and his brother had moved out of the castle just a week after that fateful night, and we'd barely spoken since. This certainly wasn't the reunion I'd imagined. "You're looking good."

"Th-thanks," he said. "You look really good, too." He must have seen me glance down skeptically at my frayed sleeves and mud-caked pants, because his flush deepened to a full scarlet. "I mean . . . not your clothes, but you . . . your looks . . . I . . . That is . . ."

"It's okay, Markos. I get it," I replied. Jax was grinning ear to ear. I kicked him under the table.

Markos turned away, unable to keep my gaze. "Tannyn, listen . . . maybe we should . . ."

"Get them some food!" Tannyn finished. "That's a great idea. Why don't you go into the kitchen and get something ready? Maybe a stew with that rabbit I brought in yesterday?"

"I . . ." Markos tried, and then looked down. "Right. Okay. A stew. I'll get right on that."

Markos shuffled off into the kitchen. Jax shot up out of his chair and hurried after him. "I can help with that!"

"He's just going to eat half the ingredients before they go in the pot!" I called after him, even as he vanished around the corner. "Watch out!"

I'd thought that might even elicit a smile from Zell, but he just stiffened in his chair, a tense look on his face. What was wrong with him? Why was he so on edge?

"Hey. What do you think of these?" Tannyn asked. He was standing by the fireplace and idly reached up to take one of the swords off its mount. It had a thin, flat blade, shorter than most Western swords, maybe the length of my arm. The cross guard looked like it was made from some kind of a bony shell, and the pommel held a gleaming purple stone. "Markos bought them off a merchant from the South. I thought he wasted his money, but, well, you know Markos."

"It's nice." I forced a smile. "Very elegant."

Zell's hands clenched around the arms of his chair, the nightglass shards on his knuckles jutting out. I wasn't imagining it. He was tense. And I felt myself starting to get tense, too. There was something off here, something I couldn't quite put my finger on, something just out of sight. My heart started to quicken.

"So," Tannyn said. He leaned back against the fireplace, the sword still in his hand. It was like he was trying to look casual holding it but didn't know how. Why was he still holding it? Why had he taken it down in the first place? "Want to tell me what's going on?"

"We saw something," I said. "Something we shouldn't have. And some . . . some people are really mad at what we saw, and they're after us, and . . . and we just need to figure out what we're going to do." I sighed. "I'm sorry. I think that's all I can tell you."

"It's fine. Totally fine. Don't worry about it. Honestly, I don't even want to know more." Tannyn turned the blade over in his hand. "Just relax. We'll get you some stew and something to drink, and maybe a nice bed to sleep in. You guys can figure it all out then." He was being friendly, so friendly, but was this weird? Should he have been asking more questions? Or was I just reading too much into it? Was I losing my mind? Why were my knees shaking so much?

"And horses," Zell finally spoke up. "Could you get us horses? If we needed them?"

"That might be a little tougher, but . . . but yeah. We've got enough." Tannyn nodded.

"For all of us?" Zell pried.

"Yeah. We've got five horses to spare."

Zell let out a sharp exhale.

Tannyn froze in place.

Five horses to spare, Tannyn had said. But we hadn't said a word about there being five of us. As far as he knew, it was just me, Zell, and Jax. So how did he . . . ? How could he . . . ?

Oh no.

The room exploded into a flurry of motion. With a roar, Tannyn lunged toward us, the sword in his hands plunging right at me like an arrow. But Zell was faster. He hurled himself back in his chair, shoved one hand out to take me with him, and kicked the bottom of the table up with his feet. Zell and I fell to the ground onto our backs, and the table flipped over, acting like a shield between us and Tannyn, whose sword drove into the wood with a shower of splinters and stuck, its razor-sharp point just a few inches from my face.

He'd tried to kill me. Tannyn Dolan, the boy I'd grown up with, had just tried to kill me.

I lay there, stunned, but Zell moved. He kicked up off his back and pounced like a cat, clearing the table in a single stride to drive his fist right into Tannyn's neck . . . and plunge his nightglass knuckles straight into his throat.

The two fell back against the fireplace. Tannyn's eyes went wide with pain and horror. Blood bubbled up from his lips, even as his hands twitched at his sides, and he let out a terrible, rasping gurgle. Zell jerked his hand aside, tearing what was left of Tannyn's throat open, and Tannyn's life shot out of him in a hot red spray.

There was a commotion from the kitchen, the clatter of dishes and the impact of bodies hitting the ground. Jax's scream cut through the house. Now I moved, jerking up to my feet and sprinting around the corner.

Jax lay on the floor, with Markos on top of him, surrounded by shards of a shattered plate. Markos was holding a knife, a long, sharp butcher knife, and Jax's hand on his wrist was the only thing stopping him from plunging it into Jax's chest. Markos pressed down, overcoming Jax's struggles, bringing the blade closer and closer. "I'm sorry!" he stammered. "I'm so sorry!"

I acted on pure instinct. I crossed the room, grabbed a heavy iron frying pan off a rack, and swung it in a hard, vertical arc that caught Markos right on the side of the head.

When I was a little girl, one of my favorite books was *Muriel Vagabond*, a funny little story about a girl in a theater troupe who fought off robbers. She'd hit them with a frying pan, and it made a hilarious WHOMP sound as she bopped them out cold.

There was no hilarious WHOMP sound here, just the sickening wet crack of the pan fracturing Markos's skull. He tumbled off Jax with a yelp and fell onto his side, twitching, moaning, blood pooling around his head like tea spilled from a cracked cup.

My stomach turned on me. A hot wave of bile shot up my throat, and I just barely kept myself from throwing up. On the ground, Jax gasped for air. "What . . . ? what . . . ? Why . . . ?"

I tried to lean down to help him, but I almost fell over. My legs were made of water. I slumped to the floor, my head spinning, desperate to find the words. "They . . . they tried . . ." But nothing came out, nothing that could make what had just happened make sense.

Jax sat up and wailed as he looked through the kitchen's doorway back into the main room. Tannyn lay against the fireplace, his face slack and pallid, his hands limp at his sides, his shirt soaked red from the ragged ruin that was his throat. "No," Jax moaned. "No, Tannyn, no . . . Oh no, why . . . ?"

"He tried to kill us." Zell stepped around the corner into the kitchen. His voice was flat, his face blank, emotionless. You'd never guess he'd just murdered a man with his bare hands. How could he be so cold, so calm? "I didn't have a choice."

"He . . . he . . ." Jax's eyes glistened with tears as he crawled forward. His pain cut me worse than all the falls and scrapes of last night. "Why? Why would they . . . ? How could they . . . ? Why?"

"That's what I'd like to find out," Zell replied. He stepped past Jax, past me, over to where Markos was moaning. Zell kicked him in the side, rolled him onto his back, and then knelt over him, driving his knee down into Markos's chest. Markos let out a howl, eyes wide with pain.

My impulse was to shove Zell, to protect Markos, to stop this. But I held back and did nothing.

"How did you know?" Zell demanded. "Why did you try to kill us? Why?"

"W-w-whisper," Markos choked out. "Flew into town. This morning. R-r-roost master wrote it up." He reached into his jacket with a trembling hand, his fingers twitching. I hoped that was just from fear, but I knew it was probably the concussion. He pulled out a crumpled brown parchment, and I reached over, took it, unfolded it. . . .

"Oh no," I whispered.

I'd seen parchments like this before, of course, plenty of times, big printed flyers with the word WANTED at the top and a bounty at the bottom, usually with a description of some scruffy brute wanted for rape or murder or theft. I'd never thought I'd see one with my own name.

"What does it say?" Jax demanded. "Please. Read what it says!"

"'Wanted dead . . . for murder and treason,'" I read. "'In an act of savagery that will forever shame our great Province, these three West-born youth, along with a Zitochi exile and a servant girl from Lightspire, murdered the visiting Princess Lyriana Volaris and Archmagus Rolan Volaris in cold blood. They committed this grave act at the behest of the Zitochi tribes and should be considered traitors to the Kingdom of Noveris. They are extremely dangerous, and may spread seditious lies, including passing the Lightspire servant off as the Princess. Anyone aiding them will be found guilty of treason and executed without mercy.'" I reached the bottom of the paper and realized how badly my hands were shaking. "'Lord Kent has authorized the people of the West to kill these five on sight. The bounty for their bodies is ten thousand Golden Eagles each.'"

Below were our names and the descriptions of the five of us, written up in shockingly precise detail. I didn't need to read them out loud, and I didn't need to know that the best word to describe me was apparently "plain." Any other time, that would've stung. Now, it was the least of my issues.

"They framed us," Jax muttered, slumping back onto the floor. "Those sons of bitches, they . . . they . . ."

"They marked us for death," I said. The paper fluttered out

of my hands. I didn't realize I'd had any hope left, but I must have, because my chest tightened with the horrible feeling of it draining away. Because that was the terrible truth, the one I hated to admit, that all this time, even with everything that had happened, I'd still thought maybe there was some way out. Maybe, if we just lay low and bided our time, there'd be no need to keep this secret and Jax wouldn't be in danger. Maybe, just maybe, my father and I could work this out, and things could go back to how they were.

No. My father wanted me dead. My own father wanted me dead.

My eyes burned. I held my head in my hands. I'd been so close, closer to his trust than I'd ever been in my life, so close to finally earning his love. . . .

And now he'd just ordered the entire Province to kill me.

Zell alone seemed unfazed. "Last question," he said to Markos, still holding him down with a knee to his chest. "Is anyone coming here soon? Are you expecting any visitors tonight?"

"No," Markos said.

"Good," Zell replied.

Then he reached down, took Markos's head in his hands, and snapped his neck with a loud, brittle crack.

I clenched back a gasp between my teeth. Jax screamed and dove across the room, tackling Zell and slamming him back into the floor. "What the hell? You just killed him!"

"He tried to kill you!" Zell shouted back. He effortlessly slid out of Jax's grip and flipped him over, sending him sliding across the kitchen. "Or did you somehow miss that part?"

"He was down . . . wounded . . . beaten!" Jax hissed. "You didn't have to kill him!"

"Are you really that much of an idiot?" Zell stood up and turned away. "He would have gotten help and told everyone what happened. Then they'd know we were still alive, that we were here! We'd lose the one advantage we have!"

"But . . . but . . ." Jax stammered. "We could have taken him with us! As a prisoner!"

"A useless oaf with a collapsed skull, bleating away to anyone in earshot, dying slowly, painfully, and loudly!"

"You didn't have to kill him!"

They kept arguing, but I'd stopped listening. It was like the weight of the world had drowned them out. I couldn't move. I couldn't breathe. All I could do was stare at Markos's face, turned sideways on the tile floor, his eyes still glistening with his last, drying tears. The eyes I'd stared into so longingly that night in the hayloft, the eyes I'd been sure I'd look into for the rest of my life. Markos wouldn't have a rest of his life. Not anymore.

I forced myself to look away, to Jax sprawled on the floor, sobbing, and then to Zell, his face hard and cold. Blood trickled down from the nightglass blades on his knuckles, streaming along his pale fingers, along his killing hands. I'd thought they'd be still, like the rest of him, but they were trembling, just barely, a tiny shudder he couldn't conceal, and he was trying. That coldness, that calm, was a mask, I realized, a mask for something terrible raging inside him. And it was starting to slip.

It'd be so easy to blame this all on him.

So easy. And so unfair.

"We all killed them," I said. Jax turned to stare at me, stunned, and Zell's eyes flitted my way. I caught a glimpse of whatever was behind that mask, something raw and aching. "We killed them the minute we showed up here, asking for their help. We killed them the minute we made them choose between their lives and ours. There was no other way this could have ended." I stared at the floor. "All Zell did was make sure we were the ones who got to walk away."

"But . . . he . . . It just . . ." Jax ran his fingers nervously through his hair. "Shit! What do we do now?"

"What we came here to do," I said. "We grab food, clothes, weapons. Anything we can get our hands on. We take their horses. We go back for Miles and Lyriana. And we run like hell."

Zell nodded. "That's the best plan anyone's had all day."

Jax stared at us in disbelief. "Tilla, how can you be like that? How can you be so cold? I mean, this is Tannyn and Markos we're talking about! This is—"

"I know who we're talking about, Jax. And I'm being like this because I have to." Because the only other option would be to completely lose my mind. "Please, Jax. Don't make this any worse than it is."

Jax let out a shaky breath and pulled himself up to his feet. "Fine. You're right. Let's just . . . let's just go." He walked out of the kitchen and back into the main room, where he stood for a moment over Tannyn's limp body. It seemed like he wanted to say something, some kind of apology or good-bye, but he couldn't manage to choke out any words. He just stood there, tears streaming down his cheeks, then took a single sharp breath and turned to go upstairs.

Zell walked after him but stopped right as he passed me. He knelt down, rested one hand on my shoulder. "You acted fast and protected your brother," he said softly, his lips almost touching my ear. "You did the right thing." He squeezed my shoulder gently, warmly. "Thank you."

Then it was just me alone in the kitchen, alone with Markos's body, alone with the silence. I knew that I should get up. That I should get moving. That I should start rummaging through the drawers, looking for food that wouldn't go bad, for sacks to carry it in.

But first I leaned over to Markos and ran my hand along his face, gently closing his eyes. He looked a little better. Peaceful, maybe.

"I'm sorry," I whispered to his still, broken frame. "I'm so sorry."

I got up and got moving.

ELEVEN

"No way," Miles said, his soft hands shaking as they held the crumpled WANTED poster. "No . . . they wouldn't. . . . Mother wouldn't. . . ."

"She did, Miles," I replied. "She did." We were all huddled together back at the beach camp, the sky overhead just starting to darken. When Zell, Jax, and I had returned, we must have been a hell of a sight: riding along the beach on horses laden down with bags bursting with supplies. Miles had lunged up, cheering, and even Lyriana had cracked a smile. Then we got closer, and they saw the grim looks on our faces.

Zell and Jax had hung back to lay down some posts to tie up the horses. That left me to break the bad news.

"This is an order of execution." Miles shoved the paper back into my hands. "My mother wouldn't. . . . I mean, she must not have known. . . . Because this is . . . This means . . ."
But even as he stammered, I could see the truth settle in his

eyes. "Titans' breath. This means they want us dead. Mother wants me dead."

"I know how you feel," I said, even as I realized I kind of didn't. I'd always been distant with my father, so the pain I was feeling was that of a dream destroyed, the loss of something I'd never get to have. But Miles and his mother had always been inseparable. He'd always been loved, really loved, way more than any bastard I'd known. So for him this had to be so, so much worse. "I'm sorry, Miles."

Miles turned away. "We're so screwed."

"Are we?" Lyriana asked. She was looking way better than she had this morning; I guess she'd managed to get the grief out of her system. She sat on a driftwood log, nibbling on some hard cheese from one of my bags, her golden eyes sparkling in the fire's flickering light. She wasn't quite as impressive as she'd been in the Great Hall, not with her hair a mess and her dress in tatters, but at least she didn't look like a drowned kitten anymore, either. "Will the people of the West be foolish enough to believe such a flimsy tale? Would they ever mistake me for some servant girl impostor?"

I decided to ignore her weirdly condescending tone. "For ten thousand Eagles? I think they'd believe you were a Titan."

"It's brilliant, really," Miles muttered. "They've turned every single person in the Province against us with one simple decree." He didn't say what he was thinking, and he didn't have to: only his mother would have come up with such an elegant, calculating scheme.

"My uncle warned me about rebels in the West, about those who would try to harm us. But he said they were cowardly, craven fools." Lyriana shook her head. "I see now he was wrong. He hadn't counted on your parents' cunning, on the depth of their hatred and evil."

"Hey, now, my mother's not evil," Miles tried. "It's more complicated than that. . . ."

"You defend her? Even after what she did to my uncle? Even after what she's done to you?"

"I said it's complicated. . . ."

"I'm sure it is," Jax said as he strolled over, and not a moment too soon. "But right now no one gives a shit about your feelings, Boy Genius. So let's cut the moping and focus on what actually matters." Jax had never exactly been nice to Miles, but this was harsh, even for him. I'd never seen Jax so sad and angry. He'd barely spoken the whole ride back, much less cracked a smile or a joke. It made my heart ache.

Jax knelt down and unfurled a long parchment over the ground: the map of the Western Province from the Dolan brothers' wall. It showed all the major villages, castles, and landmarks, not to mention dozens of sharp lines indicating mountains and forests. The Province was roughly a square. To the north were the Borderlands to the Zitochi tundra. To the east, cutting the Province off from the rest of Noveris, were the Frostkiss Mountains, a massive sprawl of jutting, icy peaks made of jagged granite and crawling with ice apes.

"Any ideas where we should go?"

"Do we have to go anywhere?" I asked, looking at a big round dot on the map's northwestern coast. Castle Waverly. "I mean, this cove seems pretty safe. Couldn't we stay here until we figure out a way to get help?"

"If I know my father, he sent my brother and his men to hunt us." Zell walked over to join our group, two heavy bags of supplies slung over his shoulders. "Razz is one of the best trackers Clan Gaul has ever produced. I've seen him hunt a wounded elk thirty miles through a snowstorm. Every minute we spend near the castle is a minute he draws closer to finding us." Zell looked away. "You won't like what happens if he does."

"Great. That's just great," Jax grumbled. "Then where do we run? North?"

"We don't flee Zitochi by running into Zitochi lands. Don't be so stupid," Miles replied. He was staring so intently at the map he didn't even notice that I had to throw up a hand to keep Jax from slugging him. Miles jabbed his finger at a dot halfway down the Western Coast, a place I'd never heard of called Port Lorrent. "There. We could go there."

"And what's at Port Lorrent?"

"It's a trading post, one with a distinctly unsavory reputation," Miles answered, as if this were common knowledge. "My mother used to do business there, with some . . . importers. It's a really rough place. Smugglers, fugitives, outlaws. The kind of people who don't give half a damn what you've done or who you killed, so long as you've got coin."

Lyriana scowled. "And you'd . . . what? Have us join these people?"

"No, of course not. But if we got in touch with them, I bet they could get us on a ship and smuggle us out of here. They could get us somewhere safe, somewhere far away. The K'olali Isles, maybe. Even the King's forces wouldn't find us there."

"The K'olali Isles," I said. They were an independent island nation way out in the Endless Ocean, a tropical paradise as far as I knew. I'd heard of towering lush mountains and jungles full of strange creatures and sprawling coastal cities where laid-back sailors drank rum out of coconuts in the shade. I could think of a lot worse options.

"I've always wanted to go to the K'olali Isles," Jax said. "That's the best thing I've heard all day. If you're serious about this . . . I'm in."

"Me too," I said, then turned to Zell, who was staring at us quizzically. "You'd like this place, Zell. Might have to get used to wearing less fur."

"I will wear whatever is regionally appropriate," he replied.

Miles let out an amused snort. "Okay, then. I'll need some time to figure out how to do this and draft up a list of contacts. We'll need to plan a route as well, not to mention scrounge up some money. . . ."

"I'm not going," Lyriana said.

We all turned to stare at her. "Um," Jax said. "Maybe you missed the part where Zell said his psycho brother was going to skin us alive if he caught us here. . . ."

"I never said that specifically," Zell said. "Though it's not implausible."

"I don't care," Lyriana insisted. "I'm not fleeing. Not when the fate of the Kingdom depends on me." She shook her head angrily. "This isn't just about me, about us. Killing me was always just a means to an end. Your father has a plan, Tillandra." She gestured to the WANTED poster lying in the sand. "I'm sure Whispers have already reached Lightspire with news of the so-called murders. When word of this reaches my father, he'll lose all sense and reason. He'll send out whole companies of mages to avenge me."

"They'll blame the Zitochi," Miles mused. "And if they're going into the northern tundra, they'll stop by Castle Waverly. . . ."

"Where my father's men will ambush them while they rest," I finished. "That's got to be it."

Lyriana nodded. "I suspect so. Lord Kent aims to restart the Great War . . . and he'll do it by slaughtering mages in cold blood."

The rest of us looked at one another. Jax cleared his throat awkwardly. "Well, if no one else is going to say it, I will. Who cares? Why the hell would I risk my life to save a bunch of mages?"

Lyriana shot him a glare that could freeze molten ore. "It's not just about the mages, you boor. Can you imagine what a second Great War would look like? Thousands of people would die, Heartlanders and Westerners alike. Villages would be razed. Men, women, and children would be slaughtered. And our hands would be stained with their blood."

Jax's mouth opened and closed wordlessly. He looked to me for help, but I couldn't meet his gaze. I thought of Markos on that floor, dead because of me, never to kiss anyone again. I thought of Zell's nightglass barbs, dripping crimson.

"Dammit," I said. "Fine. So we can't just run. What do we do, then?"

"These mages," Miles said, still hunched over the map. "Would they recognize you if they saw you, Your Majesty?"

"Of course," Lyriana replied. "In my uncle's absence, they'll be led by my cousin Ellarion." Her voice choked for a second. "He's Rolan's son."

"Then maybe what we need to do is meet up with them."

Miles pointed to a dot at the southeastern corner of the map, and this one I recognized: Pioneer's Pass, a narrow passage through the Frostkiss Mountains. It was the only way to get anything wider than an oxcart into the West.

"The mages will have to come through the Pass," I said. "If we can get there first, we can meet up with them."

Jax wasn't buying it. "So what's the plan, then? Ride all the way to the southeastern corner of the Province and sit in the middle of the road, waiting for some mages to come by?"

"As a matter of fact, that is not the plan." Lyriana bristled. She sat down next to Miles and pointed to a large black castle just next to the Pass. The Nest. Home of House Reza. "My uncle and I stayed there on our journey up, as guests. Lord Reza was a very gracious host, and is a good friend of the Volaris family. I'm certain his loyalty lies with the King. He'll give us shelter and protect us until the mages arrive."

"Isn't Lord Reza up here?" Jax asked. "At the feast."

I shook my head. "The feast was only for Western Houses. And House Reza is . . . special." After the Great War, the Volaris King had deemed Pioneer's Pass too tactically important to be trusted to Westerners, so the lands around it had been given to a powerful House from Lightspire: House Reza. They were hated by most of the Western Houses, who saw them as parasites who got to profit off the very lucrative trade passage. I'd only heard my father swear once, and that was when he called Lord Galen Reza *an arrogant brat with his lips stuck to the King's ass.*

Hard to imagine that he was my best shot at living to see seventeen.

"What do you think, Jax? How long would it take us to get to the Nest?"

Jax knelt over the map, using the side of his big hand to measure out distances. "Twelve days?"

"Riding on back roads?" Zell asked. "Traveling under the cover of night?"

"Twenty days. Maybe twenty-five."

"Then it's a plan," Lyriana declared. "We ride south and east toward the Nest, and take shelter with Lord Reza until the mages arrive."

Jax sighed. "So that's a definite no on the K'olali Isles, huh?"

He was joking, but Lyriana turned to him seriously. "I know this is a grave risk I am asking you to undertake. And I promise, it will not be forgotten. The Volaris Dynasty rewards those who help it in its hour of greatest need. You will be heroes of the Kingdom."

Miles shot me a weak smile. "Guess we'll get to Lightspire after all, huh?"

I smiled back. It was stupid, but just having a plan made me feel a little better. And if we did end up stopping a war, saving lives . . .

It wouldn't bring Markos back. But maybe it would make that horrible guilt in my stomach weigh a little less.

TWELVE

It took, oh, ten minutes for me to start having serious doubts about us pulling this off. That was when I opened the sack of clothes we'd taken from the Dolan house and Lyriana stared incredulously at the pair of Markos's pants I'd tossed her way.

"I know they're not as nice as what you're used to wearing," I explained. "But, well, it's all the guys had, and you'll be a lot better off in them than in that ripped dress. . . ."

"I'm not judging the quality. I appreciate the offer." Lyriana looked down, embarrassed. "It's just that . . . I don't know how to put them on."

I blinked. "You don't know how to put on pants."

"I've never had to. No woman in Lightspire would!"

Jax snorted. "Yeah, I bet. You probably got shoved into a solid-gold dress the moment you popped out from between your mother's thighs."

Lyriana shot him a withering glare. "I can tell that you're

trying to offend me with your coarse humor, and I assure you it won't work. I'll have you know I made it a point to speak openly with my servants, and I've already heard all of my coachmen's bawdy jokes. I'm sure they'd put yours to shame."

"You've heard bawdy jokes? Really?" Jax asked. "Like what?"

"Like . . ." Lyriana thought for a moment, then snapped her fingers. "Like the one about the priest's daughter and the stable hand!"

Jax shrugged. "I don't know that one."

I elbowed him. "Yes, you do. You told it to me. The daughter ends up having sex with the stallion."

"What? No! That's not the joke! The joke is that she . . ." Lyriana trailed off as awareness dawned in her eyes, then looked down at her feet, mortified. "I seem to have misunderstood the punch line."

Jax let out a braying laugh. Zell nodded thoughtfully. "I believe the Zitochi have a similar joke, except it's a priestess and an elk—"

"Somehow, I don't think this conversation is going to make any of us look good, so maybe we could just move on," Miles cut in. "Tilla, would you please help the Princess get her pants on?"

Despite myself, I laughed out loud. That was a sentence I never imagined hearing. And I had to fight back an even bigger laugh a few minutes later, when I stood with Lyriana behind a boulder near the cove. She and Markos were roughly the same build, so I'd thought his clothes might fit her, but she was drowning in his rumpled gray work shirt. His pants had turned out to be too loose, so I'd had to tie them around

Lyriana's waist with a bit of cord. They were still too long, scrunched up around her ankles. She looked ridiculous, like a little girl who had somehow gotten into her dad's closet. And her regal features, her perfect skin, her glowing golden eyes all just made it so much worse.

"Well?" she asked timidly. "How is it?"

"I'll put it this way. You were right earlier. No one's going to believe you could be a servant girl."

We packed up our camp, but then, of course, we had to argue for a while about who got to ride which horse. With three horses and five of us, there would have to be some sharing involved. There was no question that Lyriana couldn't ride alone: it turned out she'd never actually been on a horse, just had horses pull her carriage, and was actually somewhat afraid of them. Miles offered to ride with her, but she'd looked down and stammered, deeply embarrassed at the apparent impropriety of touching a boy. I'll give her this: it took a lot of prudishness to make Miles look like the worldly one. That meant that I'd ride with Lyriana, and, after only twenty more minutes of arguing, that Zell would ride alone while Jax and Miles would share the third horse.

We left just after sundown. Jax led the way, guiding us down the beach and up into the forest. I knew that the farther we got from Castle Waverly, the less we could rely on his knowledge of the land, but here, at least, he was still an expert. Just to be safe, we decided to take a longer route, arcing far east around Castle Waverly before plunging south; we didn't dare try any roads. Instead, we tromped along an overgrown trail, our horses gamely stepping across tangled roots and slippery stones, treading lightly through the dark water of barely flowing creeks. I'd offered to use Miles's Sunstone, which he'd refused to take back, but Zell said it would give our position away. So we rode instead by the light of the stars and the moon, which half the time were hidden by the canopy of leaves overhead.

I was scared. No, I'll admit it. I was terrified. I'd never been out in the woods at night, not without a bunch of friends and a campfire and a half skin of wine in my belly. I flinched at every passing shadow, jumped every time the moon drifted behind a cloud, and saw tangled, grasping hands in the branches of every distant tree. Lyriana held me close, her face pressed into my back, her breath fast and scared. Sparkling eyes glinted at us occasionally from the branches: owls, I hoped, or raccoons or something. I thought of all the dangerous animals that lived out here: bears and wolves and skarrlings. And I thought of all the stories I'd loved as a kid, which of course were all about the terrible things that children encountered in the woods at night: gibbering mudmen, crones with stone teeth, and ghosts of lovers long dead, their cheeks slick with bloody tears.

Why the frozen hell had I liked scary stories so much? Why couldn't I have just wanted to read about princesses and ball gowns?

It seemed like the night would never end. But then the first rays of light crept over the horizon and the sky began to turn a soft pink, and it dawned on me that we'd made it after all. Jax led us off the trail, and we settled down in a mossy grove of redwood trees. The grass was soft and wet, but that didn't stop me from sprawling on it. My thighs hurt so bad I never wanted to get up again.

We tied up our horses and set up camp as the sun rose. I was more than happy to lie in the grass, eat a loaf of bread, and then fall deeply asleep, but Zell insisted on going out to hunt. Jax went with him, either because he genuinely wanted to or because he felt like he had to prove his manhood, I don't know. But the two of them went off and left me, Miles, and Lyriana to settle in.

A gentle fog rolled in over the glade. One of the trees had a recess in its bough, like a big, welcoming mouth, and I crawled inside. Tiny mushrooms grew off the slick bark, and I could hear a loon calling out in the distance. Lyriana curled up with me, her head on my shoulder; I was getting the impression she wasn't going to give me a whole lot of space. Miles sat on a stump nearby. Out of all of us, he looked the most changed, like two days roughing it had already kicked the soft out of him. His eyes were sunken, tired, and his curly hair hung tangled around his face.

"Your Majesty," he said, breaking the silence, "may I ask a question?"

Lyriana arched her head up toward him. "Of course."

"What's it like in Lightspire? I mean, I've read plenty of books and accounts and all that, but I've never talked to anyone from there." He looked off into the distance. I couldn't tell what his deal was. Was he genuinely curious? Or was he just trying to say something, anything, to distract himself?

"It's very different," Lyriana replied. She stared out at the grove, shrouded in fog, the ground glistening with dew. "It's hot there, hot most of the year, and so flat you can see for miles if you stand in the right place. And these woods here . . . there's nothing like this. In the city, the only trees we have are those in planters, arranged by the City Beautification Council. And even outside of it, the land is tamed, refined, perfectly sculpted. There is nothing this wild. This beautiful." She let out a slow sigh. "This dangerous."

Miles started to say something, but then the bushes rustled at the far end of the grove. The three of us went silent as they parted to reveal an elegant brown doe, on her own, her back speckled with white spots like a spattering of snowflakes. Maybe she didn't see us, or maybe she wasn't afraid. But either way, she walked straight into the heart of the grove and grazed there, still and beautiful.

"Should we . . . should we do something?" Miles whispered. "The guys went off to hunt, right? I mean, wouldn't they want us to get this deer?"

"What do you want to do?" I replied. "Because I didn't exactly bring my bow and arrow. . . ."

Miles turned to Lyriana. "Can you do something? You know, with your magic?"

"Of course not." Lyriana said. "I swore a sacred oath, Miles Hampstedt. To never kill. To never harm. To only use my magic to help and nourish. I would never hurt a living creature. Especially not one so beautiful." Miles turned away guiltily, and Lyriana looked down at the Rings on her hands. "Besides. I don't know any violent arts. I couldn't kill it if I wanted to."

"What *can* you do?" I asked. I knew the mages kept the secrets of their power deeply guarded, but I was starting to realize just how little I knew about how magic even worked. I didn't realize there were different "arts" that mages knew. I just figured it was all, you know, magic.

Lyriana shrugged. "I can Lift," she said, and flattened her

hand, raising it as if lifting an invisible plate. She had three Rings, two on one hand, one on the other, and they all pulsed a delicate yellow. At the heart of the grove, a stone lifted up, floating into the air exactly in line with Lyriana's hand. The doe looked up, startled. "I can Light," Lyriana said, snapping her fingers. The Rings turned white. The stone fell to the ground, but a gentle ball of soft light danced out of her fingers, hovering in the air right in front of us, like a tiny star. The doe took off running. Miles and I stared in wonder.

"And I can Grow," Lyriana said. She reached up with her other hand and twisted her fingers in a circle, as if tightening a screw. Now her Rings glowed green, a gentle, flourishing green, like a field of grass. The bark of the tree above us rumbled, and the tiny mushrooms sprouting from it expanded, puffing out like they were being blown full of air. Before my eyes, they grew and grew, from just barely bigger than my thumbnail to nearly the size of my hand, suddenly the fluffiest and most appetizing mushrooms I'd ever seen.

I reached out and plucked them. "It's not fresh venison, but I could probably get by with a mushroom soup."

Lyriana laughed. "I'm glad I'm good for something." She held out her hands so we could see her Rings, and I noticed for the first time how much smaller and simpler they were than her uncle's. "I'm just a novice, I'm afraid. I can't do much more than that."

"Don't be modest," I said. "We saw what you did on the beach and in the tunnels. When you saved our lives. That was a lot more than lifting a stone and growing some mushrooms."

Lyriana turned away, embarrassed. "That was . . .

Heartmagic. It happens sometimes, when a mage loses control, when the emotions they're feeling overwhelm the restrictions of the Rings. It's extremely draining, extremely dangerous. I could easily have died. I should never let it happen again."

"Right. Of course," I said, though if we found ourselves in that situation again, I was kind of counting on it. "I still don't really get it, though. You said you couldn't use your magic to harm. But mages use their magic to harm all the time. I mean, they fight wars and stuff."

Lyriana sighed, and Miles look embarrassed, like this was something I ought to know. It probably was. "The School of Mages has twelve orders, each with its own purpose and vows. The Knights of Lazan, the warriors, are the largest order and the one you're likely most familiar with. They, of course, may use force as they see fit, to enforce the will of the King."

"But there are others," Miles cut in, never one to miss an opportunity to show off his knowledge. "There's the Gazala Guild, you know, the Artificers. There's the Brotherhood of Lo, who handle the bestiaries, and the Maids of Alleja and . . ." He paused, blinking at Lyriana. "Wait, which order do you belong to?"

She smiled slightly and rolled up her sleeve, revealing her slender arm. There, just above her wrist, was a tattooed sigil. It looked like a tiny flowering blossom, glowing a faint, pleasant green.

"The Sisterhood of Kaia?" Miles gawked. "You're kidding!"

"It caused quite the stir in my family when I declared," Lyriana said. "It's the reason my father wanted me to conceal my Rings and my magical aptitude. He's worried about how the other Houses will react."

I felt like a little kid at the grown-ups' table. "Sorry, back up. What's so special about this Sisterhood of Kaia?"

"They're the most controversial of the twelve orders," Lyriana explained. "Their focus is on charity, healing, and compassion."

"That doesn't sound very controversial."

"While the other eleven orders are sworn to serve the will of the King, the Sisterhood of Kaia believes its calling is to serve the people of Noveris . . . even those the King opposes," Miles said. "During the Great War, many of them disobeyed a direct order from the King and crossed the battle lines to heal the wounded, Heartlanders and Westerners alike. It was a big deal. There was talk of disbanding them, hanging them for treason, all kinds of stuff." He turned back to Lyriana. "I apologize if I'm prying, but I have to know. How does the Princess, the Queen-to-Be, end up declaring herself a Sister of Kaia?"

"It's a long story," Lyriana said. "As a child, I never even considered the Sisterhood. I'd assumed I'd be a Maid of Alleja, an enchantress, gifted at glamour and illusion. It's the traditional order for female mages from the great Houses."

"Sounds boring," I said.

"Women in Lightspire do not have quite as many options as they do out here, Tillandra," Lyriana replied, a slight scold in her tone. "The truth is, I loved enchantment as a child. I used to think that's all that being a Queen was: glamorous masquerades and beautiful dresses and the endless wonder of the court. And then . . ."

She paused, like she wasn't sure if she wanted to say more, then sighed and went on. "It happened a year ago. Lady Ella was throwing her birthday party, one of the most important social events of the year. I was late because I took too long to get ready, and by the time we got out, the King's Road was a mess of slow-moving carriages. I didn't want to miss the first dance, so I asked . . . no, I ordered my driver to take a shortcut through the center of the city." She sighed. "He'd been drinking. He made a wrong turn. And we ended up in Ragtown."

"That's the poor part of Lightspire," Miles explained.

"Yeah, I got that from 'Ragtown.'" I shot him an annoyed look. "What happened?"

"I'd never been there before. I couldn't believe it. I'd always known there were disadvantaged people in the Kingdom, but I'd imagined hardworking farmers or tanned, rough sailors. But what I saw in Ragtown . . . people living in crumbling shacks, sprawled out in the streets in tattered clothes, the stench of excrement, naked children so thin you could see their ribs, their faces marred by pox . . ." Her voice trembled. "I could not bear it. I ordered my driver to turn around, but it was too late. A mob rallied at the sight of my golden carriage and swarmed us. I had two bodyguards with me, Knights of Lazan, who began attacking the mob, but there were just so many of them. And . . ."

She closed her eyes. I could feel her heart pounding. She clearly did not want to relive this part of the memory. "When the smoke cleared, my guards were dead. My driver was dead. I was trapped under my crushed carriage. And all around me were bodies. So many dead. And so many wounded. These thin, fragile, diseased people, desperate for even a crumb of bread, and my guards had attacked them without a thought.

"Then the Sisters came. There was a temple of Kaia in Ragtown, the only mage-ministered temple in the neighborhood. They rushed to the scene, before even my father's men could arrive. They pulled me out of the rubble, mended my leg, and treated my burns with their healing arts."

"That's why you joined them," Miles said.

"No. I joined them because they helped everyone else," Lyriana said. "There is a term we use, 'willstruck.' It means when you feel the Titans' guidance most clearly, when you understand exactly what it is they want you to do. In that moment, watching the Sisters tend to these starving, wounded men, these men who had attacked me, who my father would have put to death in a heartbeat . . . I was willstruck. I understood that this was my purpose as Queen, why I was put on this earth. My father is a good King, but his care is for politics, for preserving the family, for building the Kingdom. He does great works. But my purpose is to help all those he missed."

"How'd your father react when you told him you wanted to join the Sisterhood?"

Lyriana looked down, embarrassed, and turned away her wrist. "I didn't tell him. I snuck out as soon as I was better, and pledged myself. I've never seen him angrier than the day he saw my mark."

"Huh," I said. I hated to admit it, but I'd misjudged the Princess. I'd written her off as annoying and sheltered, and, okay, that was still true. But behind that, there was something I'd missed, something I had to respect. I'd spent my whole life torn between two worlds because of my birth, craving the comforts of one while living the reality of the other. Lyriana was torn, too, but she was torn by choice, throwing away one world because she felt a duty to the other.

We sat in silence. Lyriana dozed off. And half an hour later, the bushes at the edge of the grove parted again, now giving way to Jax and Zell.

"Say what you will about the Zitochi"—Jax laid down a half-dozen rabbit carcasses at the heart of the grove—"but this guy can hunt like nothing I've ever seen."

I looked to Zell, who didn't say anything. He had something wet and heavy slung over his shoulders. He knelt down and laid it out on the grass: a doe's body, its neck snapped, its limbs limp. I could make out the familiar white speckles on her back.

I'd eaten meat all my life. Hell, I was ready to eat meat right then. Yet I still felt a weird pang of sadness. I didn't mind eating a doe. But did it have to be that one?

Lyriana felt more than a pang. "You killed her." She scowled at Jax as she stood up. "You killed that beautiful, free creature."

Jax looked confused. "Well, technically, Zell killed her. I just chased her to him, and he caught her and—BAM— snapped her neck with his bare hands and . . ." He finally noticed Lyriana's furious look of disgust. "Did I miss something? Why are you acting so crazy about this? Did they teach about hunting the same day they taught pants?"

Lyriana turned away with a snort. "You're an insensitive boor, and you don't understand anything."

"Really? Because I think I'm the insensitive boor who just killed our dinner, while you sat around here moping!"

"I thought you said Zell killed our dinner," Miles interjected. Jax shot him a menacing look.

"Maybe in fancy-pants Lightspire, you can eat your truffled scones with gold-flecked sauce," he said. "But here, in the West, you eat what you have to! And that means killing meat!"

"You didn't have to kill *her*," Lyriana insisted. "And to be so callous, to boast of snapping her neck like it was sport, like she meant nothing at all, like she was just a—"

"We thank you, Mother," Zell spoke, cutting Lyriana off. We all turned to look at him. He sat cross-legged by the doe's body, his eyes shut, and spoke in the tone of someone repeating something he'd said a thousand times. "We thank you for the bounty of your flesh, that it may sustain us through our hunger. We thank you for the gift of your fur, that it may protect us from the cold. We thank you for the gift of your life, that ours may go on."

We all stood silent. I looked from Lyriana to Jax, but neither had anything to say. Zell's words had taken the fight right out of all us. Zell tossed Jax a skinning knife, and Lyriana turned away. As Jax hunkered over the doe and set to work, Zell stood up and walked off toward the thick trees at the edge of the camp. And I couldn't help myself in following him.

"Was that a Zitochi prayer?" I asked. "Something to honor your Gods before you eat?" I was trying to impress him. Why was I trying to impress him?

Zell glanced back at me. "No. I just made it up because it sounded like the kind of thing you'd want to hear." I saw something in his face I'd never seen before, a knowing glint in his eyes and the tiniest hint of a playful smirk. Then he stalked off into the trees.

I watched him go, wordless, and felt my cheeks burn and my heart quicken, like it had down in the tunnels. What was it with me and this guy? How did I keep being so wrong about him? And why did I even care?

Zell hopped nimbly over a log and vanished into the mist. I shook my head, let out a deep breath, and turned back to the camp.

"Come on, Miles," I said. "Let's get a fire going."

THIRTEEN

My STOMACH FULL, I SLEPT THROUGH THE DAY LIKE A BABY and only woke up around sunset. I shifted from my huddled ball on the grass and sat up, blinking in the grove. The sky was a dull orange, the sun almost out of sight, coloring the whole world as if we were looking at it through a pane of stained glass. Jax was off by the horses, setting up our bags. Lyriana was still asleep in the hollow of the tree.

But it was Zell who caught my eye, which, given that he was shirtless, was not all that surprising. He stood in the center of the grove, and my eyes wandered over his toned back, his lean and sinewy arms, his taut stomach with just a few dark hairs trailing down to his pelvis. But it wasn't how he looked that had caught my attention (just most of it). It was how he moved.

Zell had his eyes shut and a look of perfect, serene calm on his face. In his left hand, he held one of the swords we'd taken from the Dolan brothers, the one with the purple stone in its pommel. In his right, he held a dagger, and its sleek metal sparkled in the orange light. He breathed in slowly and deeply, his whole chest rising. Then he moved, and it was more graceful than anything I'd ever seen. His eyes still shut, he weaved around the grove, his sword spinning in a blur of motion, his stance constantly shifting and adjusting. He would turn to strike behind, then duck low, then thrust his back out, angling himself so flat at the waist he almost bent in half. It was like he was fighting a dozen invisible enemies, sure, but it somehow seemed effortless, elegant, like a river flowing against rocks. This was a practiced series of movements, almost like a dance, and it was just as captivating to watch. In Castle Waverly, everyone always said the Zitochi were simple, crude warriors who had no technique and couldn't appreciate beauty. But this most definitely had technique, more technique than I'd ever seen our soldiers use, and a hell of a lot of beauty, too.

Zell finished with a lunge, a roll, and a graceful spin that left both blades outstretched. He stood there like that, eyes still shut, sweat trickling down his heaving shoulders and chest. Then he shifted back to the original position and started again.

"He's been doing this for an hour now," Miles said. I turned back to see him squatted behind me, a handful of mushrooms in his hand. "What do you make of it?"

"It's really beautiful."

Miles shifted, uncomfortable. "It looks nice, yeah. But would all those fancy twirls and spins really do him that much good against a six-foot knight in full armor coming at him with a broadsword?"

"Or against your mom with one of the mage-killers," I said, and Miles was silent.

"Hey!" Jax shouted from across the glade. "Quit gawking at the Zitochi, and come get saddled up!"

Lyriana stirred in her tree, grumbling in a distinctly non-Princess-like manner. "I'd like another hour of sleep, please. . . ."

"And I'd like to not get killed by Zell's psycho brother when he catches up to us." Jax clapped his hands loudly, startling Lyriana awake. "We ride. Now!"

The ride through the second night was a little better than the ride through the first one, if only because I knew it was possible to do it without dying. I could feel my night vision improving, and I was doing a better job identifying trees as trees and not as looming skeletal monsters ready to kill me. I still didn't like all the eyes glinting at me, especially the ones that came in sets of three, two big and one little: death's eyes, those birds were called, and the name didn't do anything for their reputation. Sometime around the middle of the night, we came upon a slow-moving creek and had to cross it, pushing our horses knee-deep in the dark, still water. Lyriana hung on tightly to my back, her eyes shut. I put on a brave face, but my mind was spinning with images of every terrible thing that could be lurking in the water: eels or skuttlers or bonecrabs, primed and ready to attack Muriel's legs and send us tumbling into the creek.

Oh, I'd named our horse Muriel. That'd happened, too.

There was nothing lurking in the water, or nothing that wanted to mess with us, at least. We crossed the creek without incident and pushed forward. That gave me the most confidence of all. Maybe the forest wasn't that scary at night.

Maybe the wolves and skuttlers and skarrlings were all in my head. Maybe this whole journey wouldn't be that bad.

Then we came upon the cottage.

It was almost morning. We were all feeling tired, swaying on our horses, aching like we'd been put through a grinder. I was already imagining how good it would feel to lie down on some grass and eat some venison, when Zell abruptly jerked his horse to a stop. He threw up his hand, clenched tight into a fist, and even though he'd never taught us any codes, it was clear it meant "STOP." We reared our horses behind him. My heart quickened. What did Zell see out there? What was about to attack us?

Then nothing attacked, and I realized Zell wasn't looking—he was sniffing. I smelled the air, and then I got it, too, the faint but undeniable scent of smoke. Something was burning nearby, smoldering maybe, like a bonfire that had just been put out.

"A campsite, maybe?" Jax whispered. "Should we check it out?"

Behind him, Miles shook his head wildly. "Are you kidding? No, absolutely no! We should get the hell out of here!"

"Shhhh!" Zell hissed. Whatever else was going on, he clearly had a plan of his own. He slid off his horse and took a few steps forward, pushing through a large bush. He gazed out for a moment. Then he gestured for us to come join him. I looked to Jax, who just shrugged, and so we dismounted and went Zell's way.

When we pushed through the bushes, we saw that we were up on a small hill. Down at the base of it was a wooden cottage, or at least what was left of it. It wasn't on fire anymore, but it had been quite recently. The frame was a charred ruin, with thin columns of black smoke reaching up toward the sky like grasping fingers. Two of the walls had collapsed. Bricks were scattered everywhere. The ceiling had fallen in, giving us an eerie view in from above, like a dollhouse from a nightmare. There had been some kind of a battle here: deep rifts were cut into the standing sides of the cottage, and a pitchfork jutted out of a nearby tree.

A man lay on his stomach just behind the cottage. He was wearing a tan work shirt and had a bushy beard. Exactly the kind of stocky woodsman you'd imagine would live out here in the forest. I couldn't make out much of his face, though, because his head had been split completely in half. Another man . . . no, just a boy, lay a few feet away at the base of the hill. A woodcutter's ax was embedded in his back, just below the shoulder blades. The boy must have been trying to run away when someone threw it.

"Shit," I whispered. Lyriana gasped. Miles turned away, looking sick.

"Bandits?" Jax whispered.

"Maybe," Zell said, but he didn't sound like he believed it. "I need a closer look."

"You what?" I asked, not like it mattered. Zell was already sliding down the hill toward the ruined cottage. Before I could think better of it, I went after him, and Jax followed, despite Miles's protests. There was something here Zell was after, something he wanted to find. And I needed to understand what it was.

From the distance, we'd only smelled smoke, but now that

we were down at the cottage, there were far worse scents to deal with: blood, rot, bile, and shit. Flies buzzed around the two bodies in thick black swarms. I pulled my shirt over my nose. Jax just shook his head. "What the hell?"

I couldn't find words for a response. I'd been to funerals, of course, but I'd never seen a body like this, all raw and bloated and rotting. It took every ounce of strength I had not to throw up everywhere.

"They were a family," Lyriana said, her voice flat and hollow. I turned back, surprised to see her standing behind me, but there she was. She stared at the carnage with a distant look, and I could see her hands trembling. "A father and son, living out here. Chopping wood, probably to sell in town. Growing their own crops. Taking care of each other. A good life."

I wanted to tell her to head back up the hill, but then Miles let out a horrified cry from the other side of the house. I rushed over to him, and then really wished I hadn't. There was a woman there, the mother, and she . . .

She . . .

I turned away, my stomach roiling, my eyes burning. It was bad. Let's leave it at that.

Lyriana stood behind me, one hand over her mouth. Zell stood next to her, and I could see the exact moment he saw the woman's body. Something in him changed instantly. His eyes went distant for a moment, and then they lit up with fury. His nostrils flared, and he gripped the side of the house so tight that the charred wood crumbled in his fist. "That *khenzar . . .*" he snarled, and then more in Zitochi, words I couldn't understand but I could tell weren't good.

"Zell?" I took a step toward him. "What's wrong?"

"My brother did this," he hissed, as if he could barely get the words out. He was shaking, actually shaking. "He and his men. This is their work."

"How do you know?"

He glanced up at me, and his eyes were so furious that I actually jerked back. "I just do."

"But why?" Lyriana asked. "Why would he do this?"

"Because they defied him. Because they lied to him. Because he was bored," Zell said through gritted teeth. "We have to go. Now. These people were killed no more than a day ago, which means my brother and his men are still nearby. We need to get into hiding and th—"

"Hey!" Jax yelled from inside the cottage. "This one's still alive!"

We all spun his way. My brother came stumbling out through the cottage's ruined wall, holding a young girl in his arms, maybe five or six years old. Her black hair was matted to her face with dried blood, and her clothes were soaked crimson. Jax staggered onto the grass and lay her down, and if it hadn't been for his shouting, I would've thought she was dead, too. Her eyes were empty and distant, and her breath came in the weakest, tiniest gasps.

"Titans' breath," Lyriana whispered, and rushed over. She cradled the girl's head in her arms and delicately lifted her shirt to see the wounds. Based on her reaction, it wasn't good. With a sharp hiss, Lyriana began turning her hands over, clenching and unclenching her fists. Her Rings flickered green, but didn't quite glow, like a candle failing to light in a strong wind. "I'd barely begun studying healing . . ." she muttered. "Come on, come on. . . ."

Zell's expression had shifted. He didn't just look angry anymore. There was something else, a barely controlled panic behind his eyes. "Leave her. We have to ride. Now."

"We can't just let her die," Jax said, and Lyriana didn't even respond, just kept turning her hands and clenching her fists, over and over in desperation. Her Rings kept flickering . . . but they never quite glowed.

"She'll die no matter what," Zell barked. He was afraid now, afraid for the first time since I'd met him, and that terrified me. "And we'll all be dead, too, if we don't go now!"

I stepped toward him, cautiously. "Zell," I said softly, "we have to try. . . ."

His hand shot out and grabbed my arm, and he began pulling me back toward the hill. "No!" he screamed, and suddenly his hard, cold front cracked open, and I saw what was underneath. It wasn't brutality or viciousness he kept buried, but fear and pain, a pain I couldn't even begin to understand, a pain he had to fight every second to keep down or else he'd explode. He was just like the mage-killer, a tempest trapped, raging behind a calm front.

"Zell!" I shouted, as loud as I could, straight into his face. I dug in my heels and pulled my arm out of his grasp. He froze, staring at me with wild eyes. I reached out and took his hand; it was shaking in mine. "Zell," I repeated, softer. "We can't leave her. We just can't."

We stood there for a moment, his eyes blazing into mine, and I wondered if he was going to force us all back onto the road at sword-point. Then he breathed in deep and turned away without a word. He unsheathed his blades, facing the road like a vigilant statue. The message was clear.

Something split in my heart in that moment. I didn't quite understand why, but I could tell that this was one of the hardest things he'd ever had to do. I reached out and squeezed his shoulder, just once, then turned back to the others.

The girl died half an hour later.

Lyriana had done everything she could. She'd tried dozens of different magical forms, her Rings flickering, flickering, but never glowing. After that, she'd gotten desperate and tried to do a medic's work, cleaning the girl's wounds and even forcing breath into her lungs. But none of it worked. Soon the girl lay there, as cold and still as the rest of her family.

Lyriana cradled her, and her arms were stained red up to the elbow. Miles and Jax stood uselessly beside the Princess, a limp bandage dangling in Miles's hands. Lyriana was silent, breathless. Everything suddenly got much colder, and a light frost crept into the dirt by her feet. The air around her crackled and pulsed with tiny charges of magic, like we were at the heart of a lightning storm. That hot, electric smell filled the air. Her Rings pulsed a hard, icy blue.

Was this more Heartmagic? Was she about to lose control?

Lyriana turned away. The pulsing feeling vanished, and the air went back to normal. "I'm fine," she said, forcing her voice to harden. "We bury them. With respect."

I'd thought Zell might object to another delay, but he didn't say a word. He was still standing guard in the road, and I'm pretty sure he hadn't moved a muscle. So the rest of us found some shovels and dug side by side in the soft dirt. A light rain began to pour, unusually warm, and the ground steamed as the droplets hit it. Once we'd had four graves dug, Jax went to carry the bodies, but Lyriana didn't let him. Instead, she used her Rings, gently Lifting and carrying them toward the graves, before delicately lowering them in. They almost looked peaceful, like they were floating down a river, eyes shut, soaking in the sun. After the bodies were down in their graves, Lyriana snapped her fingers together, creating four little glowing orbs of Light that hovered above the graves and then gently drifted up, over our heads, into the stars. "May they light your journey to the heavens," Lyriana said, "where the Titans will greet you with open arms."

I'd thought she might cry or break down again, but now she held firm, her voice just barely wavering.

I walked over to stand next to her and then, impulsively, I took her hand. Jax tossed his shovel aside and joined us, throwing his arm around my shoulders, and Miles stood awkwardly next to him until Jax threw an arm around him, too. I breathed in deep, feeling the warm rain against my skin, watching as the raindrops sparkled white in the light of the orbs above. Footsteps sounded behind me, soft and meticulous, and I glanced back to see Zell. He'd finally left his guard, I guess, and was standing right behind me, gazing up at the lights with an unreadable expression. He whispered something under his breath. I didn't have to ask this time if it was a Zitochi prayer.

We stood there like that, the five of us, gazing up at Lyriana's orbs as if they were the Coastal Lights. Here we were, standing by this ruined cottage, wanted dead by the entire Province, a band of brutal mercenaries after us, and yet, in that moment, I felt . . . safe? Protected? Loved? I felt like

I'd been out in the cold my entire life and had just for the first time stepped into a warm house with a crackling fire.

I looked around, from face to face. We all knew the same thing. We were in this together.

Until the very end.

FOURTEEN

WE RODE HARD FOR A FEW HOURS TO MAKE SURE WE WERE clear, before settling down in an overgrown, abandoned quarry. We built a weak fire in a stone pit, burning lichens and old dry twigs, and sat around it in a circle, quietly eating our venison. No one really wanted to talk, not after that. So I took the lead.

"I think it's time you told us about your brother, Zell."

Zell looked up. "What's there to tell?"

"Uh, let's start with, what in the frozen hell is wrong with him?" Jax said. "I mean, he is evil, right? You know that?"

When Zell finally responded, he spoke slowly, as if carefully selecting every word. "My brother is . . . different. Even as a child. We'd chase each other around the halls, like all brothers, but when he caught me, he'd always want to hit, to bite, to hurt. Then there were the animals he'd get his hands on, the dogs and cats and the rabbits. And then there was . . . there was . . ." He trailed off, swallowing hard. Did this have something to do with his reaction back at the cottage, with that panic in his eyes? What had Razz done to him?

"Zell," I started, but he shook his head and cut me off.

"Our father is one of the greatest warriors in the history of our people. I always wanted to be like him: to vanquish my enemies, to bring glory to the Clan. But that's what it was always about for me. Honor. Razz, though . . . Razz just liked to watch things suffer, to watch people bleed. The more innocent and vulnerable, the better."

"Like I said. Evil," Jax replied. "And I can't wait until he's in charge of all the Zitochi when your dad bites it. . . ."

"That's not how it works," I jumped in. "They hold a Conclave, and all the Chiefs make their pitch and . . ." I realized the others were staring at me. "It doesn't matter."

"I worried about Razz," Zell went on. "So did our mother. He was dangerous, unhinged. And he sought out men like himself for his mercenary band, men with the same appetites. We tried to convince my father, but he . . . he . . ."

"Wait. Your mother?" Miles chimed in. "You and Razz have the same mother and the same father? So how are you a bastard?"

Zell looked at his feet. The whole time I'd known him, I hadn't seen him express anything resembling embarrassment, but now his cheeks flushed with shame. "With my people, a bastard isn't born. He's made. He's made when he disgraces his family, when he shames his Clan. I'm a bastard because I . . . I . . ." He sighed. "I don't want to talk about it."

"Damn, Miles," Jax said. "You just made Zell uncomfortable. That takes skill."

I turned my head sideways, trying to understand Zell's

expression. I couldn't. What was it that he had done? I'd known him less than a month, but I was sure he couldn't have done anything worse than Razz. Something had happened, something to cause all that fear and pain inside him, and that *something* had led to his disgrace . . . but what?

I didn't know. I couldn't know.

The conversation had nowhere to go after that, so we ate in silence, then went to sleep. I rested badly; it wasn't exactly easy to sleep on a bed of sharp pebbles, in the heat of the sun. But I didn't mind, because it made sure that I woke up early, just as the sun was setting, just as Zell was starting his training/prayer/whatever.

I found him at the center of the quarry, practicing. He was doing a slightly different routine this time: fewer twirls and rolls, more stabs and blocks. But he still had the same precise focus, the same rhythmic, graceful moves. He barely looked up as I approached him, and only really stopped when I stood right in his path.

"Hey," I said. "I'd like you to teach me to fight."

Zell blinked at me, perplexed, as if I'd just asked him to teach me to fly. "Why?"

"Because I don't want your brother to kill me. So teach me how to fight him."

"My brother is second only to my father in skill. You wouldn't have a chance against him."

"Fine. Then he'll win. But I want to at least go down with a fight."

Zell stared at me curiously, and I met his gaze. I could tell we were thinking about the same thing. That cottage we'd passed. The woman behind it. The girl in Lyriana's arms. The unspoken weight of that morning hung over us, binding us, and it was enough.

"All right," Zell said. "I suppose this could work. I've been watching you move for some time, and you do have a natural grace."

I raised an eyebrow. "You've been watching me move?"

"I . . . I mean, I did watch you as a . . . There's a way that you move that . . ." He gave up and shook his head. "It doesn't matter. Do you want me to train you or not?"

"I do."

Zell nodded and walked off to go root around in a pile of debris at the quarry's edge. He returned a minute later and tossed me a long oak branch.

"What is this?"

"It's a stick."

Right. Should've seen that coming. I sighed. "Why am I holding a stick?"

"If you want to learn to fight with a sword, you have to learn to fight with a stick." Zell stepped back, then assumed the grounded position he always began his routine with: legs apart, feet planted, knees slightly bent. His hands were empty, though; the sword and dagger lay in the dirt. "Assume this stance."

"Um. Okay." I tried as hard as I could to copy his position, but felt awkward doing it, like the first time I took a dance lesson. Or, really, any time I took a dance lesson. "How's this?"

Zell could barely hide his disappointment. "Know how most warriors die?"

"With . . . honor?"

"No. On their backs." Zell darted toward me, cleared the

gap between us in one stride, and kicked me in the back of my ankle. My legs flew out from under me, and with an incredibly ungraceful flailing of my arms, I fell hard on my ass in the hard dirt. It hurt. A lot.

"What the hell?" I heard Jax yell from back in the camp, and I struggled to turn myself around.

"It's fine, Jax!" I shouted back. "He's just teaching me how to fight!"

Pushing myself up with my arms, I could see Jax back by the fire pit. He stared at me, tried to say something, then threw up his hands in defeat.

I hoisted myself and turned back to Zell. He had his head cocked to the side, scrutinizing me. I could tell what he was thinking: was I going to give up now? My back flared with pain, probably from where I'd landed on an exceptionally pointy stone. My thighs hurt from the riding, and from the anticipation of the more riding we'd have to do. It was starting to dawn on me just how hard learning to fight would be, and how outmatched I'd be even if I tried. And I desperately wanted to go lie down for a short, sweet nap.

But I thought of that family again. And I wondered how many cottages like that Zell had seen, how many of his brother's victims he'd been forced to bury.

"Let's try again," I said to Zell, and planted my feet firmly in the dirt.

FIFTEEN

Not much happened over the next few days.

Well, that's not true. Plenty of things happened. To avoid Razz and his men, we rode even farther away from the main roads, pushing through woods so deep we had to ride our horses in single file just to make it through the dense trees. Sometimes we had to hop off and hack through the bushes to clear a path. Once, while descending a steep, crumbling slope, Jax's horse tripped and Miles tumbled off; it was only Lyriana's quick reflexes with her Lift magic that stopped him from plunging to his death. Another time, after we'd made camp in a sunken ravine, a trio of wolves came upon us. We sat there, tense, weapons in our hands, as they glared at us with their yellow eyes and their bared teeth, but after what felt like an eternity, they ran back off the way they'd come. Miles started joining Zell and Jax on the hunt, and while I don't think he ever caught anything, he seemed damn proud of himself for participating. We had a terrifyingly close encounter with a group of men, bandits probably, stalking through the woods at night with torches held high; we hid from them in a damp grotto, holding our breaths, and they came within twenty feet of stumbling upon us.

What I mean, though, is that things settled into a routine. I'd wake up in the early evening and train with Zell for an hour, slowly learning the khel zhan, his flowing, dance-like fighting style. This training consisted a lot of me falling down, flipping over, or getting hit with a stick when I failed to block one of his attacks. It left me bruised, bleeding, and aching with every muscle in my body. But even after just a few days, I could feel myself starting to improve, could feel my reflexes sharpening and my body hardening. The hurt started to feel good, in a weird way, the hurt of progress, the hurt of growth.

I started to like it. And maybe I was just imagining it, but I think Zell was starting to like teaching, too. He smiled at me more, and laughed more, and I could see a real pride in his eyes when I mastered one of his stances or blocked one of his jabs. Maybe he was a natural teacher. Or maybe, maybe, he just liked spending time with me.

We kept up our push southeast, riding through the nights and camping through the day. Between the guys' hunting and Lyriana's Growing, we were never hard up for food. Zell even killed a woodsram and fashioned us capes from its shaggy gray fur to keep us warm. Lyriana objected for about ten minutes, but put hers on as soon as a cold night wind blew in. The landscape began to change as we moved farther and farther from the coast, the redwoods giving way to more oaks and firs, the roads getting rarer and the forest growing quieter. We could now see the Frostkiss Mountains in the distance, massive blue jags looming toward the sky, the barrier that blocked off the West from the rest of Noveris.

And despite a few setbacks and scares, we began to travel more confidently, more capably. It wasn't just our comfort on the road, though that helped. It was our comfort with one another. We started talking more as we rode and spending more time together in the camps. Lyriana told us about growing up in Lightspire, about her cousin Ellarion, about how she never even stepped outside the palace until she was six years old. Miles and Jax invented a game where they tried to make each other guess things they were thinking of by describing them in rhymes, and while Miles always won by crafting elegant stanzas, Jax did a surprisingly impressive job of finding new rhymes for "ass" and "tits." Even Zell and Jax started to thaw toward each other; Jax taught Zell about all the beasts of the West, and Zell taught Jax how to hunt them. Best of all, there had been no more signs of Razz and his men, and that cottage and the poor family started to fade into memory.

Twelve days after we left the beach, we reached the banks of the Markson River, and I realized the biggest change in our group's mood: we were starting to have hope.

We made a camp on the river's west bank, settling down in a cluster of trees while the current roared next to us. The Markson was the largest and longest river in the West, running south from the Zitochi tundra before arching west to meet the ocean at the bottom of the coast. Most travelers crossed it by passing through Bridgetown, a legendary hub of trade that spanned the Markson's narrowest point. That was a no-go for us, obviously. We'd have to head north, toward some of the fishing villages, and hope to cross using one of their bridges when no one was looking. I didn't mind. Camping alongside the river meant fresh fish, not to mention a place to wash off the dirt and grime. Zell even shaved, scraping the edge of his dagger along his face until it was bare. Miles and Jax passed. I think they were starting to like their scruffy, stubbly beards.

There was another reason this place made me emotional, one I didn't share with the others. The Markson River was the farthest I'd ever been from home. When I was eight, my father and I had ridden out to Bridgetown for their famous Festival of Masks. We'd stayed in the estate of Lord Collinwood, whose House governed the town, and at night my father and I had walked through the festival hand in hand. I remember being transfixed by it all: the floating lanterns, the musicians playing in the streets, the people in masks, some scary, some beautiful, dancing and drinking and singing all around us. I remember so clearly when, at the festival's climax, they set a giant effigy in the river and lit him aflame. I was so scared, but my father comforted me, let me hide behind his legs and told me it was just a big wooden scarecrow, nothing more.

I didn't like that memory anymore. Or at least I didn't want to like that memory anymore. I blinked the tears out of my eyes and turned back to our camp. Lyriana and I sat together on a log, and Miles was on his knees in front of us, blowing on a pathetic campfire to try to get it to catch. Jax and Zell were down by the river's edge, gutting some fish they'd caught. I could just barely hear snippets of their conversation over the river's roar.

"I don't see the problem," Zell said. "A beast with claws and great brown hair; I'm thinking of a big cavebear."

"You can't . . . you can't tell me what you're thinking of,"

Jax replied, exasperated. "You make up the rhyme, and I guess what it's talking about. If you tell me it's a bear, there's nothing for me to guess."

"Is the point not to make a rhyme?"

"Well, that's . . . that's part of the point, but . . ."

"Damn!" Miles pounded his fist into the dirt by the campfire's edge. It looked like he'd just barely gotten the kindling alight, but the logs lying over it weren't giving. "Sorry. Sorry. Just dealing with this."

"May I try?" Lyriana offered.

"Well, sure, I suppose, but the branches are really damp, so I don't know if you'll—"

Before Miles could finish, Lyriana raised her hand and twisted her fingers in the air, the gesture I recognized as Grow. The fire instantly caught, bursting up from the branches as if oil had been tossed on it. Miles tumbled onto his back in surprise. "How did you . . . ?"

Lyriana shrugged. "Fire grows, same as anything else."

"That's incredible." Miles picked himself up and took a seat opposite us. He had a pensive expression, like he was debating whether or not to speak, and then went for it. "Your Majesty, is . . . is it true that only people born in Lightspire can be mages? I mean, I know most are, but I am a really quick study, and I'd do anything, anything I had to . . ."

"Ah," Lyriana said as if she'd been dreading this question. "You speak the truth, Miles. The Titans blessed Lightspire and Lightspire alone with the gift of magic. That's the Heavenly Mandate, the entire basis for the Volaris Dynasty's rule. No soul born outside the city has ever possessed magic, and none ever will."

"Oh." Miles tried, and failed, to hide his disappointment.

"But . . . there are many other things you could do! For every mage, there are a dozen scholars, studying the lore of the Titans, deciphering their buried secrets and searching ancient barrows for more Rings . . ." Lyriana said. "I think you'd be great at that."

"Professional bookworm. Yeah, that's right up his alley," Jax said. He and Zell had walked over while we were talking, and settled down with us. Jax rested on the log next to Miles while Zell set up skewers for the fish. "How about me? Is there a perfect job in Lightspire just waiting for me to come along?"

"Well, that depends," Lyriana replied. "What do you want to do?"

Jax blinked, unprepared to be taken seriously. "Well, I . . . I guess I hadn't really thought about it. I mean, I was raised to be a stable hand. Figured one day, maybe I could be a stable master, something like that."

"Is that what you want?"

"I don't know." Jax blinked. "Maybe? Not really, I guess? I don't think I really had much of a choice."

"You do now." Lyriana smiled. "*When* we reach Lightspire, you'll all be rewarded with wealth, status, land. You'll have servants of your own, and you'll be able to do whatever you want to. When we get there, you can put your old lives completely behind you. You'll be starting anew."

We all looked around at one another, letting the gravity of her words sink in. Jax let out a long, slow whistle, then snapped his fingers. "I've got it! Do they have brothels in Lightspire? Because I always thought it'd be fun to run a brothel!"

"Must you ruin every single conversation with a crude

joke?" Lyriana crossed her arms. "Can you not be serious about anything?"

Jax grinned. "On the contrary! I'm very serious when it comes to brothels! There's one in Millerton. Whew, you should see these girls. . . ."

Lyriana turned away with a sniff of disgust. Just then, Zell perked up, apparently joining the conversation for the first time. "I've got it! Whether man or fish or ram or deer, a bear is the beast that all should fear!"

Jax let out a groan and cradled his head in his hands. "I hate this guy. I hate him so much."

Everyone laughed, including Zell, who I'm pretty sure was just messing with Jax at this point. But I felt distracted. Back on that beach, the idea of actually reaching Lightspire and reaping the royal benefits had seemed like an absurd fantasy, the sort of lie people tell themselves to keep moving; sure, sure, we'd get our happily-ever-after. But now, halfway to safety, it was dawning on me that it might actually happen. *Holy shit.* I might actually get to Lightspire. I might be . . . well, if not a noble, then as close as can be, and certainly more well-off and wealthy and powerful than I'd ever be in the West. I'd have all the dresses and carriages and dashing suitors I'd ever want. The thought was incredible. Amazing. Overwhelming.

So why did it make me feel so sad?

That night, we looked for a bridge to cross the Markson. We didn't dare risk riding out in the open, not until we were sure we had a clear run, so Zell and Jax went off to scout the way, arguing about who'd win a fight, a Western greatcat or a Zitochi cavebear. They took Lyriana with them this time;

her glowing balls of Light were proving increasingly useful at navigating, and were safer than Sunstones, given how quickly she could snuff them out. Miles and I stayed back to watch the horses and our supplies. I didn't mind. My body was aching even more than usual. Training with Zell that day had consisted of him honing my reflexes by having me attempt to catch rocks.

Mostly I just got hit with rocks.

I sat by the water's edge, staring into the river. A thin veil of clouds blocked out the sky overhead, but they'd part just long enough for a beam of moonlight to light up the rushing water. If I squinted and stared way, way down, I could see the faintest light in the distance: Bridgetown, shining like a candle in the dark.

"Hey," Miles's voice said from behind me. "Tilla, I found something for you."

I glanced back as Miles walked out of the forest brush. To be honest, I hadn't noticed he'd been gone. He plopped down next to me and extended his hand, revealing a palm full of green speckled berries shaped like little bells.

"No way," I beamed. "Bellberries! Where did you find them?"

"Well, they tend to grow along the Markson, and I remembered they were your favorite, so I just went scrounging, and you know, got lucky." Miles blushed a tiny bit. "Go ahead. Have some."

He dumped a few into my hand, and I popped one into my mouth. It was perfect: tart but sweet, with just a tiny sour hint. I savored the taste, letting the juices melt into my tongue. "Mmmm . . . so good," I said, and waited until the taste had completely faded before opening my eyes. "How did you know they're my favorite?"

"Don't you remember?" Miles asked. "It was at the Harvest Feast, when we were, what, seven years old? My mother and I were visiting Castle Waverly, and you'd had this big fight with your Headmaiden, so we decided to run away. We snuck out the South Gate and made it all the way to Harken's Beach with a knapsack full of bellberries and scones." He paused, waiting to see if I'd remember. "We hid on the beach all day, talking about how we were gonna be vagabonds and travel around robbing people and never have to have parents again. It was such a good day." He looked out at the water, a wistful glaze in his eyes. "But then you ate all the bellberries and wanted more, and we ended up just going back. Our parents hadn't even noticed we were gone. You remember that, right?"

Kind of, sort of, maybe? Not really? But obviously this was like a hugely significant memory for Miles, so I felt guilty and nodded. "Oh yeah. Yeah. That day. That was great."

"Yeah, it was," Miles said, still staring out. Maybe it was the moonlight, but he looked totally different, nothing like the soft, chubby boy who'd sat down opposite me at the Bastard Table. Our time on the road had changed him. His features looked harder, stronger, and I had to admit the layer of blond stubble lining his chin looked pretty good on him. He looked like he'd lost ten pounds. "You think about what Lyriana said? About the new lives we'd have in Lightspire?"

"Thinking about nothing else," I replied, trying to sound more upbeat than I really was. "It's like a fairy tale, right? You save the Princess, and then she takes you to her castle, and then you never have to worry about anything again."

"Yeah, it is." Miles sighed. "I just wish this were the other kind of fairy tale, the one where everything went back to normal at the end."

I cocked my head to the side. It was weird to hear him say it out loud, the thought my conscious brain beat down every time it dared surface. What if my father took me back? What if he forgave me? What if my life could just go back to the way it was?

I shoved the thought down, deep in the ocean of my consciousness. I didn't want to think about it. I turned to Miles to chastise him, but then I saw how exhausted his eyes looked, how worn and broken. He wasn't as sad as I was. He was way worse.

"Miles." I reached out and put my hand on his shoulder, giving him a light squeeze. He actually startled. I guess it was weird for us to touch, not something that happened often, but he just looked so broken. "I'm sorry. I wasn't being sensitive. You lost so much more than I did. . . ."

"Did I?"

"Well, yeah. I mean, you were actually close with your mother. And she was going to legitimize you at some point, right? You were going to be the Lord of House Hampstedt. That's a hell of a thing to look forward to." I shrugged. "What did I have to look forward to? That great rainy day when my father finally decided to disown me, so I could accept my lot in life as a servant once and for all?"

A silence hung over us. Miles looked at me with an odd expression. "You don't know," he said softly. "You really have no idea."

"Don't know what?"

Miles shook his head. He looked sad still, but it was a different kind of sad, one I couldn't read. "You weren't going to be a servant, Tilla. That was never their plan for you."

I pulled my hand back. The mood had changed in an instant. "What are you talking about, Miles? Whose plan? Our parents'?"

Miles closed his eyes. When he spoke, it was stilted, choppy, like he was struggling with each word. "I heard them talking. A few years ago. Mother made me swear not to tell a soul. She said it would jeopardize everything if I did."

I could tell this was hard for him, like he was on the cusp of revealing something that had been eating at him for ages. But I was impatient, and his slow roll was pissing me off. "Miles, what the hell are you talking about?"

"No point keeping a secret for a woman who wants me dead, right?" Miles laughed, a brittle, bitter laugh that sounded wrong coming from him. "You're right, Tilla. I *was* going to get legitimized. But Mother got tremendous leverage out of not having an heir, of men thinking they actually had a shot at wooing her and fathering the child who would lead the House. It was politics, plain and simple. On the day before my eighteenth birthday, I was to become the heir to House Hampstedt." He paused for an intolerably long time before finally getting it out. "And you were to be my wife."

"What?" I jerked away. "Don't screw with me, Miles. Don't make things up."

"I'm not making anything up." He actually sounded kind of indignant. "Our parents had it all planned out. Your father cared about you, Tilla. He couldn't legitimize you, of course, not without causing a huge scandal. But this way, he'd ensure you were the Lady of a noble House, his most loyal ally. And I'd be with someone my mother trusted." He said it so casually, like this was no big deal, just some business thing, and not the most important turning point of our whole damn lives. "It was their way of merging our families, I guess. Looking out for both of us."

"Looking out for us." I stood up and turned away. My stomach roiled. I felt like I was going to pass out. Too many thoughts spun through my head at once, colliding against one another. This was proof of what I'd hoped for so desperately all along: that my father actually cared about me, that he thought about me, that he wanted me to stay in his life, one way or another, even after I turned eighteen. He'd had a plan for me, and that plan was giving me exactly what I wanted. I was going to be a noblewoman, officially, with a title and a castle and a last name. . . .

Except that name was going to be Hampstedt, not Kent. And I'd be with Miles—Miles, of all people—forever, as his wife. Second to him. Sleeping with him. Having his kids. And my father had apparently just decided this years ago, and hadn't ever bothered to tell me. Like my thoughts on it didn't matter? Like I was just a pawn, to be handed off to another House? And how much of this was just politics, anyway, a handy way of keeping our two Houses together? Was this even about me at all?

"Tilla," Miles called out, "I . . . I didn't mean to upset you. I just . . . I thought you should know. . . ."

"And my father?" I shot back. "When the hell was he planning to tell me? Did I even get a say in this?"

Miles looked stunned, like the thought of having a say never even occurred to him. "Would it have mattered?" A familiar hurt look settled on his face. "Am I that pathetic to you? That you'd sooner stay a bastard than marry me?"

"What? No! It has nothing to do with that!" I felt bad for insulting him, because, yeah, that was kind of a harsh blow. But then that just made me madder. Of all things right now, with this insane revelation dropped on me, I was supposed to worry about *his* feelings?

Then it hit me. Miles had known about this. All this time we'd spent together over the last few years, he'd known this, had this secret hidden away like a card up his sleeve. I'd known he had a crush on me, of course. But I'd thought it was harmless, a childhood puppy-dog crush that never went away. But that wasn't it at all. All this time, he'd just been . . . what? Biding his time? Waiting patiently? Like I was the dessert he got for finishing his vegetables? "You knew. . . . You knew all along, and you didn't tell me anything?"

The color drained from Miles's face. "I just assumed that you knew, too . . . that it was, I don't know, an open secret. . . ." He took a step toward me, and I sharply pulled away. "I'm so sorry. I shouldn't have said anything."

"No, Miles. You should have said something. A long time ago." I stomped off down the coast, not even caring where I was going. "You can keep your stupid berries."

My head spun as I walked. I could hear Miles behind me, calling himself stupid, clasping his head in his hands. And honestly? I didn't give a shit. He deserved to feel bad, at least for a little while. I kicked at a stone in my way, knocking it into the river, and for some reason, that made me angry, too.

"Tilla!" a voice called from somewhere ahead. I jerked up to see Jax, Miles, and Lyriana creeping on foot from the forest. Jax led the way. "We found an abandoned bridge, perfect to cross. Go get the horses, and we'll . . ." He stopped, seeing my expression. "Are you okay?"

I didn't even begin to know how to answer, how to sum up everything that had happened into one emotion. But before I could try, Zell stepped in front of Jax and flicked his arm toward me in an impossibly fast blur.

I acted on pure instinct. My hand jerked up in front of my face, even as I ducked back and winced. I felt a hard impact. But nothing hit me. I opened my eyes, just barely, and realized there was a smooth, round rock clenched in my hand.

"What is wrong with you?" Jax yelled.

"She caught it, didn't she?" Zell shrugged. "I knew she would."

I had. A Zitochi warrior had just hurled a rock at my head. . . .

And I'd caught it midair. Me. I'd just done that. Something totally badass and amazing.

You know what? Screw Miles and my father and their plans. Screw Lightspire and titles and being a noblewoman. Right now the only thing I cared about was the stone in my hand.

"Are you okay?" Jax asked.

"Yeah," I replied, and I couldn't hold back my smile. "I'm just fine."

SIXTEEN

OUR LUCK RAN OUT THE NEXT DAY.

We'd crossed the Markson via a rickety, half-collapsed bridge and rode hard to get south the next day. We were starting to brush up against the foothills of the Frostkiss Mountains, and the terrain here was rockier, hillier, than on the other side. Trees and grass gave way to stony pits and sheer cliffs. Riding out here was riskier: the steep hills meant we couldn't get as far from the big roads as we were used to. That meant we had to ride quietly, no games or jokes now. I didn't mind. It was as good an excuse as any to avoid talking to Miles.

That morning, when the very first rays of the sun started painting the sky a rosy hue, we were in a narrow valley between two sloping hills. Right as we wove between a pair of oak trees, Zell sharply reared his horse and raised his fist in the air. The rest of us froze behind him. I tightened my grip on my reins. Zell looked back up the hill intently, his eyes narrowed.

There was a distant twang and a whooshing sound, and

then the shaft of an arrow appeared in the trunk of a tree a few inches from Zell's head.

"Ride!" he screamed.

After that, it was all chaos.

I spurred Muriel as hard as I could, and she took off in a bolt, galloping through the dim light, leaping over stones and roots. Lyriana clutched me, shrieking, as our horse jostled us painfully up and down. Branches whipped by our heads. We were moving too fast to see clearly, but I could hear the thundering of hooves around me and make out the faintest glimpses of the other horses. I heard Miles cry out and Zell scream to keep riding. And I heard more hooves behind us, closing in fast, and the hard, guttural barking of Zitochi.

They'd found us. Razz and his men. And they were hot on our heels.

Muriel raced forward, rounding the valley's corner, nearly tripping. Something whistled right by my ear. An arrow. Lyriana gasped. The world was a dark blur. I knew this was dangerous, that my horse could trip and fall, that I could fly off and break my neck. That'd probably be a hundred times better than getting caught.

"There!" Zell yelled from just ahead of me. He was pointing toward something in the cliff wall: wooden posts framing a dark opening. A mineshaft's narrow entrance. I had no idea why this would be good for us, but I didn't have time to think. Zell rode right up to it, effortlessly hopped off his horse, hit the ground with a roll, and ran in. I glanced to the side to see where Miles and Jax were, and then all at once Muriel let out an agonized whinny and tripped, flying forward and hitting the ground on her side.

The world spun. My body screamed. I flew off the saddle and slid hard across the stony dirt. I felt my sleeve tear, and my skin underneath it scraping open along the ground. Lyriana slid with me, too shocked to even scream, rolling like a hurled doll. A thick cloud of dust kicked up around us, but I could see my horse through the dust, flailing her legs. The shaft of an arrow jutted out of her flank. And our pursuers thundered toward us, louder and louder.

"Come on!" Jax yelled, and I felt his firm hands jerk me to my feet. He was off his horse, apparently, and so was Miles, who helped Lyriana up in front of me. She was breathing, thank the Old Kings, and didn't look to have anything broken, but her eyes were glazed and distant, a thousand miles away. In front of me, the dust cleared, and now I got my first good look at the men chasing us: three Zitochi mercenaries, astride dark stallions, streaking down the valley. A scouting patrol. Razz wasn't with them, but that was a small comfort. The two men on the sides had axes out, and the one in the middle held a bow even as he rode, sliding another arrow into the string.

"Into the shaft! Go!" Zell yelled.

"Muriel!" Lyriana cried, but Miles and Jax were on her and pulled her into the dark opening. They vanished instantly in the shadows, but Zell stayed just past the entrance, his sword unsheathed. I stopped by him. He whipped his shoulder to the side, and an arrow whistled by right where he'd been standing. Was he going to fight? Was this some doomed last-stand sort of thing?

Then Zell turned and slammed his sword into the wooden post holding up the shaft's entrance, like a lumberjack felling a tree. It cut through and stuck halfway. The post was rotten, crumbling. This mine must have been abandoned a long time ago. Up ahead, the mercenaries were almost upon us, and I could see the one in front slide both legs to one side of his horse, preparing to jump.

Zell hacked at the post again, and it buckled, cracking in half. I helped as much as I could, giving it a few hard kicks. That was enough. The post split in the middle and fell over, blocking the entrance behind us, and taking chunks of the rocky ceiling down with it. A blast of dust sprayed in my face. I coughed and gasped, even as Zell grabbed my arm and pulled me along. "That bought us a minute, maybe two," he said as we ran into the dark shaft. "We need to move!"

We only made it a few steps in before rounding a corner and losing even the slightest hints of the sunlight peeking in from the outside. Total blackness enveloped us. The ground felt broken and uneven under my feet. Thick cobwebs clung to my face. I ran into one wall, then another. I could hear the others running, breathing, stumbling through the dark.

My Sunstone! I had a sudden moment of panic that I'd left it in my pack on the horse, but then I felt it in the pocket of my pants. I fumbled it out, my fingers confused for a moment by the engraved casing before I remembered it was the one Miles had given me. I flicked the little lever, the fire inside sparked to life, and then there was light all around us, bright and warm. I could see where we were now, a tight, claustrophobic shaft barely wide enough for two people shoulder-to-shoulder. Under our feet lay a track, the kind mine carts rolled on, but it was worn and broken. The walls were crumbling and forgotten. In front of me, the shaft stretched out into the distance, with no exit in sight. I could hear a commotion from behind us, men grunting as they shoved at the post and rocks blocking their path. Zell had been right. They'd be through in a minute.

"In here!" he whispered from just up ahead, then disappeared seemingly into the wall. He'd found a passage, a narrow doorway leading to a side room. The four of us sprinted after him, pushing through the doorway single file. This room was wider than the shaft, at least a little, a circular stone chamber maybe the size of my bedroom. It was empty, cold, with a hole carved in the middle of the floor encircled by stones, like a well, but draped in a shroud of yellowing cobwebs. Some broken mining equipment lay next to it: they must have raised the ore up through the hole from the lower floors. Lyriana collapsed, gasping against the back wall, while the rest of us spread out.

"It's a dead end!" Jax yelled. "We're trapped!"

"It's not a dead end," Zell replied. In the hot white light of the Sunstone, I could see that his face was slick with sweat, but he still somehow sounded calm, calmer than the rest of us, at least. He turned to the doorway, the glistening tip of his sword leveled at the darkness. "It's where we make our stand."

"What?" Miles panted. "No. No, no, no. We can't . . . There's no way . . ."

"If we run, they'll get us," Zell said. "Here, we've got strength in numbers. We've got the element of surprise. And we've got a good room to fight in. This is our only chance."

My heart was thundering in my chest, and my arm hurt like hell. I was in terrible shape to fight, but Zell was right. We didn't have a choice. I looked across the room and my eyes met his. They looked hard, strong, determined. They made me feel ready. "Give me a knife," I said.

He nodded and tossed me the dagger on his sheath, which I caught with my spare hand. "I'll draw them in here. You get against the wall by the doorway," Zell barked like a seasoned general. I listened. "When they come in, stab them in the back." He pulled the dagger out of his boot and threw it to Miles, who fumbled it, then picked it up off the ground. "You get on the other side of the doorway and do the same thing."

"I don't have a weapon," Jax said.

"You're built like an ox. Fight with your hands. And you! Princess! Use your magic to hurl them into that pit!"

Lyriana looked up, as if snapping out of the trance she'd been in ever since our horse had gone down. "I can't," she said. "I'm a Sister of Kaia. I cannot use my magic to take a life."

"Are you out of your damn mind?" Jax spun to her in disbelief. "Those men are going to kill us! You need to fight!"

"I took a sacred vow!" Lyriana yelled back, and before the two could argue anymore, there was a loud crash from the entrance of the shaft, the sound of splintering wood and tumbling stone.

The mercenaries were in.

I twisted my Sunstone to kill the flame, and we waited in the dark. I could feel my heart thundering, my breath fast and tense. The dagger trembled in my hands. I struggled to remember my training, the things Zell had taught me, but my mind was a blur. I was about to kill. Or be killed. This was going to happen.

I closed my eyes and strained my ears, trying desperately

to hear any sign of the mercenaries. I could just barely make them out: footsteps, padding softly toward us down the shaft. No Sunstone for them. The mercenaries were coming in the dark, or with what little light was filtering through the reopened entrance. I tightened my grip on the dagger and steadied my hands. . . .

Only to hear a sudden commotion. One of the mercenaries cried out. There was a thumping sound, like something heavy hitting the ground. A scream, then another, then a choked gasp. Feet scrambling. Sizzling liquid splattering on stone. And a strange clicking, a sound I couldn't explain, like a dozen fingernails drumming on glass.

Then there was only silence.

"What was that?" Jax whispered.

"Shut up!" Zell whispered back. I didn't like this. I mean, I hadn't liked waiting in the dark for them to walk in, but at least I'd known what was coming. Now I had no idea. I felt a sudden cold chill, a dry sweat. I had missed something, I realized, something very important.

"Maybe they're messing with us," Miles chimed in. "Or maybe they turned on each other. That sounded like a scuffle."

"I said shut up!" Zell replied, but there was a hint of confusion in his voice. He didn't get it, either. That worried me more than anything else.

A dusty wind blew in from the well in the middle of the room. The air was musty, thick, but there was something else in it, too, a smell of rot. I shivered. This was bad. Very bad. Something was wrong here, something even worse than Zitochi mercenaries. What was this place? Who abandons a perfectly good mine shaft, anyway?

I backed up, and my foot kicked something hard and round, the size of a ball. It rolled against the wall with a brittle scrape. I twisted my Sunstone on for just the tiniest bit of light and found myself staring into the hollow eye sockets of a pockmarked human skull.

"Tilla!" Zell hissed. "Turn off that . . ." But he trailed off midphrase, as his eyes went wide with horror. As badly as I didn't want to, I followed his gaze, toward the well at the center of the room. A sound was coming out of it, a skittering, clicking sound, like someone running their nails on a pane of glass.

The cobwebs draped over the well shuddered and rose, not from the wind but from something pushing up on them from below. Lyriana let out a shriek and clasped a hand over her mouth. A single limb broke through the cobwebs first, a skinny, fleshy leg that looked just like a human finger, except it was a foot long, with five barbed knuckles and a sharp, dirty nail at the end. It hooked around the side of the well, its nail digging into the cracks between the stone, and tensed as the rest of its body pulled up through: five more finger-legs, clutching at the edges, and a flat, round head on top of them, like two fleshy dinner plates stacked together. It lifted up, maybe as tall my knee, and stood over the well, its head rotating slowly as it scanned the room.

"What. Is. That?" Zell asked.

"Skarrling," I choked out, though technically, it had many names. Skin-spider. Cave-biter. Miner's bane. Every child in the West grew up hearing stories about the clicking, venomous monstrosities that lurked deep in our caves and mountains. I'd never actually seen one before, of course. No one I knew had. Some people thought they were just a fairy tale, something adults made up to give kids nightmares.

Well, the thing standing right in front of me was sure as hell real, though I'd still probably call it a nightmare. It reminded me of the jellyfish that sometimes washed up on Harken's Beach, but instead of being soft and translucent, this thing was hard, covered in a leathery gray skin pulled taut over its bony frame. Its head spun around in a full circle while the legs held still, and it made a wet, mashing noise, like an old man smacking on his porridge. As the back of it spun toward me, I saw where the sound was coming from: the thing had just one hole in its head, a nasty-looking round orifice framed by bristly black hairs. It suckled the air, in and out, like a baby's lip crying for a nipple.

The old rhyme popped into my head: *Children, children, fear the cave / Or a skarrling's kiss will be your grave.*

I'd been afraid of the mercenaries, but now I was absolutely terrified. I wanted to run, to scream, but my legs stayed planted, too scared to listen. Jax and Miles had pressed themselves against the room's walls, as far from the skarrling as possible. Only Zell stood in the middle, his sword now pointed at the creature. I don't think he had any idea what he was dealing with.

"Nobody. Move," Miles whispered. "Skarrlings are blind and have basically no hearing, but they see with an evolved sensor in their skin that lets them detect any kinetic activity."

"Can you speak like a person?" Jax hissed. "Just this once?"

Miles closed his eyes. "We run, it strikes."

With a particularly mushy smack, the orifice in the center of the skarrling's head puckered open, drooling a yellowish gunk that sizzled against the stone. Four spindly tendrils shot out. They were thin, transparent tubes, no wider than my pinkie, but impossibly long, spindling out of its hole like unfurling intestines. The tendrils slid out across the floor like serpents, tapping along with glistening, jagged barbs at their ends as they searched for prey. The very tips were slick with a liquid as blue as the ocean on a clear day. Their venom.

A skarrling's claws might scratch you red / But its fangs' prick will kill you dead.

Zell was the closest. He stood firm, not moving, even as one of the tendrils probed the ground near his boot. "I can kill it," he said. "I can kill it in one strike."

"Maybe," Lyriana whispered. She looked absolutely terrified. "But can you kill those?"

She pointed up, her finger trembling, her Rings burning yellow. We all looked up. There they were, at least a dozen more of them, clinging upside down to the ceiling ten feet above us in a huddled mass. Now it was my turn to grab my mouth, silencing a scream. That was too much motion. The skarrling over the well swiveled toward me with a throaty, rasping click.

The ones above us had been dormant, sleeping or whatever the hell skarrlings do. But now they stirred, twitching, shoving, chittering softly among themselves. One of them, a big reddish one in the middle, started descending, its knuckles cracking as it crawled over the others. It reached the wall just between Lyriana and Miles and, with a slurping suck, opened its hole, drooling more of that steaming yellow ooze. It hit the stone between them with a sizzle, and a rank, acidic steam bubbled up.

"The skarrling uses its venomous tendrils to paralyze its prey," Miles recited. His face was white, his eyes wider than I'd ever seen them. His chest heaved with every breath. "It immobilizes the body, then slowly dissolves it with its acidic bile, before absorbing the nutrients of the liquefied flesh."

"We have to run." Jax eyed the door.

"We move, we're dead," Miles repeated.

"Well, we sure as hell can't stay!"

The skarrling at the center of the room, meanwhile, still had its sights set on me. Its tendrils slithered away from Zell, probing at the floors and wall around me. I sucked in my breath. Could that barb poke through my boot? It could almost certainly go through my pant leg.

Above us, more and more skarrlings were stirring, slowly creeping down the walls. A few let out their tendrils, and they dangled loosely down the wall, like twitching, poisonous streamers. One of them touched the tip of Zell's sword and began slowly wrapping around it, the venomous barb sliding down the shaft toward his unwavering hands. The big red skarrling had made its way over to Lyriana, and one of its fingertips was hooked through her hair, its dank, puckering orifice pointed right at her head. Her eyes were shut, her lips pursed, her hands clenched tightly together. The center one's tendril was now right along my foot.

And should you earn a skarrling's ire / Hide fast, hide fast, behind the fire.

Fire.

Holy shit.

Fire!

"I know what to do," I whispered. Maybe it was the

insanity of desperation, or maybe I was so scared I'd some-how crossed back over into brave. In that moment, the only thing I felt was clear, focused resolve. "Skarrlings hate fire. That's what the old rhyme says. So we're going to give them the biggest fire they've ever seen." I turned my hand around, just the tiniest bit, showing the others the Sunstone Miles had given me. The one he'd turned into a bomb. "Miles. You sure this thing will work?"

He stared at it, then nodded as he realized what I was planning. "Yeah. It should. Just crank up the gas and break the glass."

"Good. I'm going to throw this at the one in the middle, so it breaks on the edge of the well. Lyriana, I want you to Grow that flame as big and tall as you can. These things should scatter like a startled flock of birds."

"And then?" Jax asked.

"Then we run."

There was no time to discuss the plan, no time to argue over it. This was what we were doing. I tightened my grip on the Sunstone and ignored the scratching of the tendril against the side of my boot. "We go on three. One . . . two . . ."

Lyriana screamed as the red skarrling lunged forward and scraped its dirty nail along her cheek.

I twisted the Sunstone all the way, bathing the room in hot white light. The skarrlings jerked back with a collective hiss, and then I threw it, in a perfect arc, right into the stone lining on the side of the well. It shattered explosively, glass and leather flying in all directions, and a burst of white fire blossomed out.

Lyriana didn't hesitate. She shot out both hands and

twisted them up, Growing the tiny ball of fire into a massive pillar of white flame that shot down the well and up along the ceiling. We all jerked back from the heat. My face burned. Zell hurtled himself to the ground, the ends of his long hair sizzling.

The skarrlings all scattered, moving so much faster than they had before, shrieking as they scrambled up to the farthest corners of the room. "Now!" I screamed. We sprinted out the doorway and stumbled into the shaft. Zell, Miles, and I burst out first, then Jax, and then Lyriana, bringing up the rear, her hands still circling as they kept the fire roaring.

The shaft was bright now, between the daylight flooding in from the entryway and the white fire raging behind us. There was something in the way of the exit, though, something on the floor at about knee-height, moving and clicking. . . .

More skarrlings! Two of them, it looked like, their backs turned toward us. But these seemed different, distracted, hunched over some gooey wet shapes on the floor and making sick retching sounds. My stomach roiled as I realized what the shapes were: the bodies of two of the mercenaries, halfway liquefied, like people who'd been jellied and melted. They smelled horrible, vomit and blood and sickly sweet citrus.

There was no time to think, just act. Behind us, the fire was dying, and the skarrlings were scrambling back down. Zell raced forward, let out a rumbling war cry, and swung his sword in a low, horizontal arc. He caught one of the skarrlings right in the side of the head and sliced clean through it, severing the disk from the legs and sending it flying across the room. The other skarrling turned toward him with a throaty rasp, and he kicked it to the side, crushing it against the wall with the sole of his boot. Its carapace cracked, like the shell of a crab, and meaty brown gunk sprayed out.

The path was clear. The mine's entryway never looked more inviting. I sprinted harder than I've ever sprinted, bounding over the mercenaries' gooey remains. Zell, Miles, and I hit the doorway first, bursting out into the light of the day, the warm, safe, wonderful light of day. I turned back to see Jax tearing after us, and Lyriana just behind him.

Then Lyriana slipped, her foot sliding on a bloody stretch of mercenary, and she fell to her hands and knees.

"Lyriana!" I yelled, but it was too late. That big red skarrling lurched out from behind her. Its maw puckered wide open, and four glistening tendrils shot out, aimed right at Lyriana's back.

"No!" Jax roared. He spun around and dove back into the shaft, back toward the monsters chasing us. Right as the tendrils were about to strike the Princess, he grabbed her up and jerked her to the side, blocking her with his body. One grazed off his shoulder, not breaking through his heavy fur coat, and the other three slashed harmlessly by, scraping off the walls. Behind them, the red skarrling let out a phlegmatic, wet roar and lurched forward, but Jax dove down and grabbed something off the ground, something long and sharp with a black tip: the mercenary's arrow, straight out of his quiver. Jax thrust forward just as the skarrling lunged, and he plunged the arrow right in its orifice, up to the tip, with a slick crunch. The skarrling gurgled and rasped, its limbs and tendrils flailing wildly, then crumpled and lay still.

The two of them rushed out of the shaft, just as the rest of the skarrlings dared to peer around the corner after us. They'd go no farther; skarrlings feared sunlight almost as much as they feared flame. We all staggered out into the sloping valley, gasping, panting, and laughing. I'd never felt so exhilarated in my life.

"Holy shit!" Jax screamed at the top of his lungs. "That was . . . that was . . ."

Zell kept his calm, like always, but even he was breathing a little heavy, and had a smile.

"I think I found our third mercenary," Miles said. We followed his gaze toward a body lying facedown just a few feet outside the mine's entrance. The back of his shirt was torn open, and his bare skin was marked with three round holes, the veins around them pulsing an icy blue. A bloody foam stained his gaping mouth. The skarrling's kiss.

"Damn." Jax shook his head. "Not that I had much love for those guys, but it's a hell of a way to go. Makes you almost feel bad for them."

"I don't," Zell said.

"Yeah, well, you basically don't have emotions between 'gotta kill' and 'yay, I killed,' so that's not really a surprise." Jax laughed. "Still, though. That move with the sword and the kick . . . taking out two of 'em . . . Pretty badass, Zell. Pretty badass."

"You didn't do so bad yourself, stable hand," Zell replied. "It was very brave to run back for the Princess . . . and then with the arrow . . ."

"Let's all give credit where credit's due." I grinned. "We wouldn't be here if it wasn't for Miles's amazing exploding Sunstone. Right, Miles?" He didn't reply. "Miles?"

"Uh, guys," Miles said, but his voice was all wrong. He didn't sound happy or excited. He sounded terrified. We all turned back to him, but he was staring at Lyriana, who stood bolt upright just outside the mine's entryway. There was something off about her: she looked too stiff, frozen, only her hands shaking at her sides. Tears streaked down her cheeks.

"Lyriana?" I asked.

"I'm sorry, Tilla," she replied, then crumpled down in the dirt. Even from a distance, I could see it: her pant leg was torn, ripped off in the chase, and there was something sticking out of the back of her left calf, a black stinger in her skin, the veins around it throbbing a haunting, unmistakable blue.

SEVENTEEN

"SHE'S HOT," I SAID, MY HAND PRESSED TO LYRIANA'S sweat-slick forehead. "She's burning up."

"Her body's fighting off the venom," Miles muttered. He was sitting on a mossy log, his head resting in his hands. "Or doing the best it can."

We were in a small, damp grotto a ways off the Markson, hidden behind tall reeds and the canopy of a majestic willow tree. After Lyriana collapsed, our first priority had been to get the hell out of that valley, to find somewhere safe to regroup. Our horses had run off and Muriel had died, poor thing, but the mercenaries' three horses were still there, so we were able to ride fast. I'd held Lyriana the whole time, pressing her between my body and our horse's neck. She'd at least been lucid for most of the ride: whispering softly that she was sorry, telling me that she felt cold, smiling weakly at my reassurances that she'd be okay.

That was an hour ago. Now she lay on a bed of mossy grass

in front of me, shivering and writhing, unable to even speak. Her eyes were shut tight, her mouth locked in a pained frown. Every now and again, she let out a horrible, weak whimper, and I don't know if that was better or worse than the silence.

I did know one thing. I would lose my mind if Lyriana died. She deserved so much better than this. I thought of her holding that girl in the cottage, arms slick with blood, trying so hard to keep her alive, working and praying even as life left the girl's eyes. Lyriana would fight to her last breath to help a person in need.

I couldn't let her die here. I wouldn't.

The canopy of the willow tree parted, and Jax came in, carrying a leather flask plucked from one of the mercenaries' bags. "I've got some clean water for her. Like you said." He knelt down next to me and pressed it to Lyriana's lips. They parted for just a moment, swallowing a single sip, and then she spat it all back up with a hacking gag. Jax turned away, like he didn't want me to see the pain on his face. "She's getting worse, isn't she?"

"Yes," Miles said. "Rapidly."

"Is she going to die?" I'd known Jax my whole life, but I swear I'd never heard him sound so young, so scared.

Miles hesitated, but only for a moment. "I think so."

"Dammit!" Jax slammed his boot into a nearby stump. I could tell it hurt him, and that he didn't care. "If I'd just moved a little faster . . . I could've gotten to her in time. . . ."

"It's not your fault, Jax," I said softly. I didn't share his anger or his guilt. Looking at Lyriana, I just felt a horrible, numb ache. It was just so unfair, so wrong. This couldn't be happening. Not when we'd gone so far. Not after everything we'd been through. Not to her. "How long does she have?"

Miles walked over to us. He crouched by Lyriana's leg and turned it over very carefully so he could see where she'd been pricked. Back at the mine, the ring of blue infection under her skin had been just an inch or so in length. It had doubled since, her veins pulsing blue halfway to her ankle and her knee. "I don't know," Miles said. "Normally, an untreated skarrling sting will kill a person in six hours, tops. But the venom usually spreads through the body much faster, like it did with the mercenary back there. She's really fighting it." He glanced at her hands, where her Rings were all glowing a vibrant green. "Maybe her magic is somehow helping her."

I thought of Archmagus Rolan, still fighting even after he'd been blown up. "How long, Miles?"

He sighed. "I don't know. A day, maybe? If that?"

"Untreated," Zell said, and we all turned to look at him. He was standing against the base of the tree, his eyes closed. It was the first thing he'd said since we'd gotten here. "You said 'an untreated sting.' Does that mean there's a way to treat it? A cure?"

"Well, no, not a cure, but there are some medicines that can help the body slow down or even fight it off, if you can get them in time," Miles said. "I believe the best-known antidote is a tonic of crushed embrium root, Orlesian ash, and a dilution of—"

"We don't need the details, Miles," Jax interrupted. "Where do we get these things? Can we find them here?"

Miles looked at him like this was the single most ridiculous idea he'd ever heard. "No, of course not. These ingredients are rare, valuable, hard to get. Orlesian ash is imported from

Orles, all the way on the Eastern Shore. To get the kind of medicine Lyriana needs, we'd have to buy it from an apothecary."

"Like in Bridgetown," I said. I almost didn't want to, because having even a glimmer of hope felt like a setup for disappointment, but I couldn't not. "They'd have it there, right?"

The others turned to look at me. I could tell we were all thinking the same thing. "Well, yes," Miles said. "Given how close Bridgetown is to so many mining communities, they'd likely have some skarrling antidote."

"Bridgetown is just a few hours away," Jax said. "We could be there and back before morning."

"Miles said Lyriana could last a whole day." I started walking toward the horses. "If we can get her that antidote in time, she might have a shot."

"What are you all talking about?" Miles cut in, obviously not on the same page at all. "Sure, Bridgetown has the antidote, and it might help Lyriana . . . but so what? We have no way of getting it. We're the most wanted fugitives in the whole Province, remember? We can't just stroll in there, find the nearest apothecary, and buy some medicine. There'll be City Watchmen on the lookout for us, WANTED posters with our faces, maybe even soldiers from Castle Waverly. Riding in there would be suicide!"

"So what?" Jax spun on him. "We just let her die? Is that what you're saying?"

"No, of course not. But we can't throw our own lives away to save hers!"

"If she dies, we die," I said. "The only shot we have at getting out of this is to reunite Lyriana with the mages, remember?

What do you think will happen if she dies? They'll just take us at our word?" I shook my head. "We have to try to save her. It's our only chance."

"I understand that, but what do you want to actually do?" Miles demanded. "We'll be arrested the moment we cross the city gates!"

"Will we?" Jax asked. "Because I'm not so sure."

"What are you talking about? That WANTED poster with our descriptions is probably hanging on every corner in the town!"

"I know, but . . ." Jax hesitated, suddenly insecure, the way he only got when he was afraid he was about to say something stupid. "Look. This has been bugging me the whole time. It might be dumb, but it's not like we have another option, right?" Jax knelt down and dug in his pack until he found the WANTED poster and unfurled it on the ground.

"What about it?" Miles asked skeptically.

"Well, it tells people what we look like, right?" He read it aloud, slowly and choppily—Jax had never been much of a reader. "'A Zitochi male, age sixteen, with black hair down to his shoulders . . . a pale-skinned male, age sixteen, with blond curls framing a smooth, round face . . .'"

"What's your point?"

"Well," Jax said, "what if we just didn't look like that? You know, we cut our hair, put on an eye patch, that kind of thing. Hell, you've got a beard already, Boy Genius. That's half a disguise right there."

"You're right," I said, and Zell nodded. Jax was onto something, and even in this tense moment, I felt a small surge of pride for him. "That could work."

"Maybe," Miles said at last. "You might be right. But what are you proposing? We put on disguises, ride straight into Bridgetown, and try to buy the antidote before anyone recognizes us? That's our plan?"

"You have a better one?" Jax replied. "Because I don't know if you've noticed, but we're kind of running out of time."

We all stared at Miles. He thought wordlessly for a while, then let out a long, deep sigh. "All right. Let's do this."

This time around, we didn't have to debate who was going. Miles was obviously in, since he was the only one who had any idea what medicine we were supposed to be getting. Zell was going, too; if the disguises didn't work, he was the only shot we'd have at fighting our way out. Jax, on the other hand, would have to stay back. If our little camp here got found, Lyriana would have to be with someone who could pick her up and move her in a hurry.

That just left me. And without hesitating, I volunteered to go into town. I said it was because it was better to send more people, to increase the chances one of us got back with the medicine. But that was just an excuse. The truth was, I would've done absolutely anything rather than sit around and watch Lyriana die.

We didn't have much in the way of disguises, but we did what we could. Zell and Miles headed into the river, where Zell shaved Miles's head with one of his daggers. With his distinctive curls gone and that stubbly beard lining his chin, Miles looked nothing like the boy we'd set out with. He looked like a man now, and a weirdly tough man, like a guy who'd spent the last decade hungover in a gutter.

Zell was next. I cut his hair, slicing off all those long black locks with his dagger. We decided to cut it short on the sides and back, a little longer on the top but parted to the side, a look common among Western soldiers and mercenaries. As we sat together in the shallow waters at the river's edge, avoiding each other's eyes as his hair floated in the water around us, I remembered when I first saw him across the Hall at the feast. How could I have possibly imagined where we'd end up? I'd thought he was beautiful, dangerous. But I hadn't known a thing about him, really. Did I know him now?

A few wisps of hair clung to the side of his head, just above his ear, so I reached over and brushed them off, and as my fingertips grazed the soft skin, I realized my hand was trembling. What was this? Why did I feel so nervous, my breath sucked tight in my chest? It's not like we were strangers to contact. Hell, we spent two hours a day grappling in the dirt. But there was something different to this touch, something that made my heart race. There was a tension in the air, a hunger, so thick you could taste it.

Zell must have noticed, because he glanced back over his shoulder. With his hair cut so short, his eyes were even more striking, but there was something new in them, a vulnerability, a hint at a tenderness inside him that I was just beginning to see.

It scared me.

"Here," I said, handing him back the dagger. "It's a little better than the last time I cut someone's hair, but that was when I was seven and ended up nearly shaving Jax bald." It was a joke, a dumb one, to try to break that tension. It failed. Something had changed, something I didn't have the time or emotional energy to fully consider right now.

Then it was my turn to get disguised. I couldn't just cut off my hair without drawing more attention, but Zell had an idea. He got a small leather kit out of one of the mercenaries' packs and opened it, revealing a half-dozen vials full of multicolored powders. He mixed them together in the water, the reds and blues and yellow swirling like magic around his fingertips, and then, very gently, rubbed it on my face, squinting the whole time, like a painter working on a masterpiece. I had no idea what he was doing, and I was kind of afraid I'd come out looking like a clown from a vagabond troupe. But his touch was soft and delicate, and that made me trust him. In the waning pink light, he ran his fingertips along my face, and the nightglass shards on his knuckles sparkled like stars. It was hard to believe these were the same hands that killed so readily.

Then he finished, slapping his palms together with satisfaction, and I took a look at my reflection. I didn't know how he'd done it, but Zell had worked a miracle. He'd added thin black lines, like wrinkles, that aged me a good decade, and made my normally thin eyebrows dark and full. He'd reddened my lips, filled out the bags under my eyes, and given me a distinctive mole on my right cheek.

"Wow," I said. "Good work. I look totally gross."

"You're welcome," Zell replied sincerely. "I think this might be some of my finest work."

"Do I even want to know where you learned to do this?"

"My mother was a *zhantaren*, a . . . How do I say this? Your closest word is 'actress,' but she was much more than that. At every feast, there would be plays telling of our Clan's history, going back to the Era of Legends, when men and Gods lived as one. My mother led these plays and performed the most important parts. She had to know how to change her face, to look like Khellza, the Great Mother, or Rhikura, the crone queen of the Underworld." He got that distant look on his face again, the one where he looked peaceful and lost.

"You and your mother are close?" Zell seemed like such an outsider that it hadn't even occurred to me that he had loved ones left back among his Clan. It made me feel that much worse about him running off with us.

Zell nodded. "As the elder, Razz was always my father's favorite. He was his spitting image . . . aggressive, loud, full of boasts. My father didn't share his cruelty, but Razz could always hide it when he was around. I am much more like my mother. It is seen as unbecoming, weak, for Zitochi men to be quiet, to hide their passions, but I always preferred it. And so does she." He sighed, a tiny little smile on his face, and looked down at his dye-stained hands. "When I was little, she taught me the art of face-painting. It was a game for us, seeing how different we could make ourselves look. I always wanted to be a zhantaren. But, of course, only women were allowed."

I cocked my head to the side. "I'm starting to realize there's a lot I don't know about Zitochi."

Zell nodded. "I've known that for some time."

We made our way back to the willow tree. Jax was kneeling by Lyriana's side, holding a damp cloth to her forehead, and he looked up as we approached. "Wow," he said. "Miles looks like a deranged hermit. Tilla looks like a middle-aged spinster. And Zell looks like . . . well, like Zell with a haircut."

Zell let out a tiny sigh. "I was worried about that."

Lyriana arched up and let out a horrific gasping cough,

one that sounded like it scraped all the way up from her diaphragm, taking most of her lungs on the way. Jax held her until her hacking died down. "It's okay," he whispered. "It's okay, it's okay, it's okay." Then he wiped his hand along her chin, and when he turned it over, the back of it was stained red. "Ah shit," he muttered, and he looked like he'd never tell another joke in his life. "You guys gotta go. You gotta go now."

Mile and Zell took off, leaving me alone with Jax. He sat there on the ground, Lyriana sprawled across his lap, and his hand shook just a tiny bit as he pressed the damp cloth to her head. I'd seen him sad and I'd seen him angry, but I'd never seen him like this before, so tender and nurturing.

"Jax . . ." I struggled to find the words. "This isn't your fault. It really isn't."

He shook his head. "You can say that, Tilla. Doesn't make it true." He gently ran the cloth along Lyriana's cheek. She shivered. "I gave her so much shit. So much shit. And for what? To get a laugh?" He let out a long exhale. "If she dies . . ."

"She won't." I knelt down, wrapped my arm around his big shoulders, and gave him a hug. For a moment, I saw the gravity of the situation, like glimpsing a huge shadow under you when you're swimming. This might well be the last time I hugged my brother, the last time I talked to him, the last time we ever saw each other. This could be the end.

I blinked the thought away. I didn't have time for it. "I love you, big brother," I said, and pressed my forehead to his. He closed his eyes and hugged me back. "We'll get through this. We'll save her."

"We'd better."

EIGHTEEN

"So, I've been thinking about our cover story," Miles said, maybe ten minutes after we rode out from the camp.

"Our what?" I asked. We were still in the woods, trotting our horses through increasingly thin undergrowth as we made our way toward a main road. Walking this slow felt wasteful; I wanted to gallop toward Bridgetown. But of course that would draw attention, especially this early in the day and this close to civilization. So instead we trotted along, edging forward while Lyriana lay dying back under that willow tree.

"Our cover story," Miles repeated. "I mean, what are we going to say if anyone asks who we are or why we're in town? We'll need to be able to say something believable."

I glanced at Zell, and he shrugged. "We don't need to make up something fancy, Miles," I said. "Why can't we just be three friends traveling together?"

"Because we're buying skarrling antidote?" Miles replied, as if this were incredibly obvious. Which, okay, maybe it was.

"That's not exactly a common purchase. It's going to raise questions. Questions we need to be ready to answer."

"Fine. It sounds like you've already got something planned out."

Miles nodded. "I've been thinking about it, yes. What do you think of this? Tilla, you and I are newlyweds from Malbrec, a small town just outside Port Hammil."

"We're what now?"

"Newlyweds," Miles repeated, and could he actually be oblivious to why that was weird? "Our families are well-off, though not wealthy. Yours runs the local inn, while mine provides protection to merchants traveling around the North. As the second son, I find myself trapped in the shadow of my successful brother, desperate to prove myself, especially to my father before his ailing health fails him."

"How long have you been thinking about this?" Zell asked. "And how does it actually help us get the antidote?"

"I'm getting there!" Miles grumbled. "As a wedding present, a distant uncle of mine gifted me several acres of land up in the Northwest, past the Morning Lakes, but just shy of the Borderlands. This is barren frostland, unfarmable, mostly worthless . . . except my uncle swears up and down that the hills there are rich with gold, just waiting to be mined. While most think it's a fool's errand, I'm convinced there's truth in his words, so I'm setting out, along with my new wife, to inspect the territory for myself. And given that we'll likely be venturing into caves and scouting for mines . . ."

"You'll want the antidote on hand, just to be safe." Zell nodded. "Clever. But how do I fit in?"

"You are the Zitochi bodyguard and guide we've hired

to show us the way!" Miles exclaimed. "After all, who would know the land better?"

Zell nodded again and actually seemed a little impressed. I had to admit, it wasn't a bad cover story, but part of it didn't sit right with me. It's not hard to guess which. "Uh, do we have to be newlyweds?" I asked. "I mean, can't we be siblings?"

Zell shook his head. "That's harder to believe. You look nothing alike."

Thanks, Zell.

"Plus, we lose the whole element of the wedding gift, which the story hinges on," Miles complained. "I've thought about this a lot. This is the story that makes the most sense."

"Yeah, but it . . . it just seems weird. . . ."

"What's weird about it?" Zell asked.

I tried to think of a way to answer his question without just telling him the whole truth, and came up with nothing. Miles guided his horse toward mine ever so slightly, and my gaze met his. I could tell that we were both thinking the same thing, wanting to address the issue hanging in the air, the tension we'd been avoiding ever since his ill-advised confession. I kind of hated him for bringing it up like this.

Then I glanced at Zell, at the grave look on his face, and I thought of Lyriana back there in the grove, shivering and trembling in Jax's arms. I saw it again, the sheer gravity of the moment, the shadow lurking beneath the water. The entire Kingdom was at stake, but more than that, my friend's life was at stake. Was I seriously going to make a big deal out of some stupid fake identity?

"No, it's fine." I sighed. "I'm just being prickly. I'll go with it. I'll be . . . pretend to be . . . Miles's wife."

Miles nodded, and at least he didn't seem overly happy about it. "We'll need fake names. Easy ones that we can remember. I'll be Anders Tonnin."

"Muriel," I said. "Muriel Tonnin."

"Zenn," Zell said.

Miles and I both turned to him. "That's a little obvious, isn't it?"

"It's a common Zitochi name." He shrugged and didn't seem interested in discussing it any further.

An hour of silent riding later, we emerged out onto the wide dirt road that led into Bridgetown, its bright lights visible through the night even this far away. At first, it felt deeply wrong to be here; we'd spent so much effort avoiding main roads that riding on one now seemed horribly exposed, like walking into a great feast naked. As we trotted side by side down the road, I held my breath, and when we came upon our first fellow travelers, an ox-drawn wagon laden down with golden Heartlander grain, I felt my heart start to race. But then the husky, bearded man driving the wagon didn't even look up as we passed him, and neither did the young couple walking on the side of the road or the old man riding on the back of a fly-mottled donkey. No one noticed. No one cared.

I shot Miles a confused look, and he threw back a shrug. When we'd set out from the grove, I'd worried this was a suicide mission, that Jax was wrong about the poster, that we'd be recognized immediately, and we were throwing our lives away. But now I couldn't help but wonder if we'd been wrong about the risk all along. Were our disguises that good? Or did we not even need them?

The lights of Bridgetown grew brighter and brighter, and

soon we were coming up on the town itself. I could make out the rickety buildings of East Bridgetown, densely clustered wooden houses with cracked roofs and peeling paint. The story went that Bridgetown had once been two completely different villages, one on each side of the Markson, connected by a single long wooden bridge. Then another bridge had been added, and another, and another, and soon an entire mile-long stretch of river had been built over, and the two towns had become one, with a sprawling night market, the biggest in the West, set up on the bridges in the middle. I still remembered it so clearly from when I was a little girl: rows and rows of stands that went on forever, packed tight on the elevated wooden platforms, open all night under the flickering light of hundreds of mounted torches. I remembered the noisy shouts of the vendors, the smells of fruit and spice and roasting meat, the barely audible river rushing underneath. I remembered my father's firm hand holding mine as he guided me along.

We wouldn't be going to the market tonight, of course. It would be too risky to go somewhere that crowded. All we needed to do was ride into the Common Quarter of East Bridgetown (basically a slum), find the first apothecary we could, buy the antidote, and bail before anyone had a chance at identifying us. Still, as we got closer and closer to the entrance, I could hear the sounds of the market's commotion, distant voices shouting and the faintest notes of music. I felt a sudden, unexpected pang of sadness. I'd always planned on coming back to Bridgetown's night market as an adult, trying on dresses and sampling wines and dancing with some fancy mask on. No matter how tonight went, I was pretty sure that was never going to happen.

If we'd gone in through the nicer, richer West Bridgetown,

we'd have ridden in through a big fancy gate, and probably had to pass an inspection by the City Watch. But in East Bridgetown, we just rode right in, the trees at our sides replaced with crumbling houses, the dirt underfoot by chipped paving stone. From a distance, it looked like any of the poorer villages near Castle Waverly, but once inside, it was stranger, more cluttered, more foreign. If West Bridgetown was where merchants from all over the Kingdom came to sell their goods, East Bridgetown was where they ended up when they went broke. I passed a tavern with four flags hanging over the door, one for each of the Provinces, and the drunks inside were dancing to some strange warbly instrument I'd never heard before. Nearby, just past a pen of squealing pigs, lay a drunk from the Southlands, his head bald, his skin bronze, one chubby hand resting on a strange animal that looked like a lanky gray dog in a bristly shell. A Westerner, a Heartlander, and a Zitochi huddled together in an alley, smoking grief-weed as they rolled nine-sided Devil's Dice. The air smelled like sweat and beer and the unmistakable tang of piss.

Next to me, Zell shifted on his horse uncomfortably. Only City Watchmen were allowed to openly wear weapons in Bridgetown, so Zell had left his sword back at the camp and hidden a pair of daggers under his cloak. He looked around with what I think was curiosity, like he was trying to drink it all in with his eyes.

"It's not all like this," I explained to him, weirdly apologetic. "There are nice parts."

"It reminds me of the Steps in Zhal Korso," Zell replied, and he actually seemed kind of wistful. "Drinking . . . gambling . . . feasting . . ."

"Not to mention whoring," Miles muttered, his gaze stuck on a nearby brothel. Or, more specifically, on the topless women leaning out its upper windows.

"Hey! We're married, remember? There'll be no whoring on my watch," I said, and okay, yes, it was kind of funny. "Now, hurry up and find us that apothecary. Husband."

It took Miles a minute, but he spotted one, a squat one-story building with a pole out front painted white and green: the colors of a meyberry leaf, the universal symbol for healing. We tied our horses to a hitch outside and walked toward its closed wooden door. I worried no one was there, but then I saw some faint candlelight through the shuttered window, and a hint of movement.

Which, of course, made me start to panic. We weren't just riding alongside people anymore. We were going to speak to them.

"I'll do the talking," Miles whispered urgently, obviously feeling the same stress. "We'll just go in, get the antidote, and get out. Don't say anything unless you have to."

"Wasn't planning on it," Zell replied.

"Well. Good, then." Miles reached the door first, then hesitated and took a deep breath. "No way out. No other choice, is there? No. There isn't. Let's do it."

He threw open the door, and we stepped in. The only apothecary I'd been to before was the one in Millerton, which was clean and nicely organized, like the pantry at Castle Waverly. This one was the exact opposite of that. Massive shelves sat behind a cluttered counter, and they were messy with loose herbs, vials, and bags of powders. Yellowed books and crumpled papers littered every single surface. The whole room was lit by a single candelabra on the counter, and there was no sign of an owner, save for some shuffling noises coming from a closed door behind the counter.

"You sure this place will have what we need?" I asked.

"It wouldn't be my first choice." Miles picked a heavy tome off the floor and turned it over in his hands. "But beggars, choosers, all that."

"All that indeed," a dry, accented voice replied. The door behind the counter swung open, and a stocky older man hobbled in, reeking of sweat and cheap booze. He was wearing a rumpled tunic that hung too tight around his heavy gut, and his thinning gray hair had the tips died gold. He wore makeup, but strangely, with thick purple shadows under his eyes and his lips painted bright orange. "My name is Timofei Lorrin Khell-vin-Khorrin, and I hail from Malthusia, the greatest and most wondrous of all the Eastern Baronies," he said. "Apothecary, scholar, and, right now, a man who'd hoped to shut down his shop for the night. Let's make this quick, shall we? What can I do for you?"

Miles cleared his throat and stepped forward. "Well. You see. It's quite a remarkable story. My name is Anders Tonnin. This is my beautiful wife, Muriel. We were married one month ago, down in Malbrec, where a most curious event occurred. You see—"

Timofei interrupted Miles with a rumbling, phlegmatic sigh. "Titans' tits, boy. Can you skip the life story and just tell me what you want to buy?"

"Oh. Well. Right, then." Miles blinked. "We'll need a tonic made. A single vial. Mixed embrium root, Orlesian ash, and skarrling venom, in a solution of—"

"Distilled alcohol and meyberry juice." The apothecary let out a weary sigh. "You could have just said you need some skarrling antidote." There was no sign at all that he recognized us, but given how bleary his eyes looked, I didn't think he would have recognized himself. "Right. One vial will be twenty-five Eagles."

"Twenty-five Eagles," I repeated. "No problem!" I reached for the coin purse on my hip.

There was no coin purse on my hip.

I froze, my empty hand hovering over my side. On a normal ride out to town, that was where I would've kept it. But this wasn't a normal ride out to town. My coin purse was back in my room at Castle Waverly, a million miles away, where I'd left it before sneaking out to Whitesand Beach. I looked back at Miles and Zell, and their faces were just as blank.

Holy. Shit. We'd been so focused on our disguises and backstories, we'd completely forgotten about money.

We had to be the dumbest fugitives who'd ever lived.

Timofei stared at us. "Well? Where's the money?"

"It's . . . um . . . it's a funny story," I said, with absolutely no idea what sentence came after that. How in the frozen hell had Miles managed to come up with a novel-length backstory but hadn't remembered that buying things costs money?

"What's going on here?" Timofei arched a bristly eyebrow. "You do have money, don't you? How could you not?"

He was about to recognize us. I could see it now, that moment of realization, when he'd yell for the City Watch, when everything would come crumbling down. Zell must have seen it, too, because he stepped forward, sliding a hand into his coat to grab his dagger. I shot him a hard look, desperately trying to scream *NO*, because even if it meant our lives, I wasn't ready to just kill an innocent man. My mind spun with other possibilities. Was there something we could bribe him with? Was there a way to just knock him out? Did we have to run?

We had to run.

I sucked in my breath and turned to the door. . . .

Miles stepped forward, a wild-eyed look on his face. He threw out his arms wide and yelled at the top of his lungs, "I offered my love a purse of coin. . . ."

He'd lost it. He'd actually lost his mind. After years and years of nervous anxiety, Miles had finally snapped, and at the worst possible moment, too.

But Timofei didn't seem alarmed or even confused. He stared at Miles, head cocked to the side, mouth crinkling into a giddy smile. "And prayed she'd offer sight of loin!"

"'A Stanza to a Summer Love,'" Miles proudly replied. "Mercanto Oriole. One of his ten best, I'd say."

"One of his top five!" Timofei hustled around the counter, the stack of papers totally forgotten. "Titans' tits! You know the works of Mercanto Oriole?"

"Of course," Miles replied. What the hell was happening here? "He's my favorite classical poet. Maybe my favorite poet of all." He leaned over and picked up a heavy leather-bound tome, the one he'd been looking at earlier. "It is so rare to meet another Mercanto fan. . . ."

"In this dump of a city? You're lucky to find a man who can read!" Timofei rushed across the room and grabbed Miles by the shoulders, clasping him in his broad, sweaty arms, embracing him like a long-lost son. "My boy! Tell me you've also read Mercanto's plays. . . ."

200

"Of course! I read *The Tragedy of Ostrapos* once a year!"

Timofei let out a delighted laugh, and I'm pretty sure this was the happiest he'd been in a decade. "Just when you think your life has hit its absolute bottom, you meet a Mercanto fan!" He slapped his forehead, and his sweaty hand made a smacking sound. "But what am I saying? Here I am, going on and on about Mercanto, when you came in here on business! Let me get you that antidote right away!" He spun toward the shelf of ingredients and sprang to work, grabbing one thing after another. "And don't even dream of money! No fans of the great Mercanto Oriole will ever pay a single brass Eagle in my shop!"

I turned to Miles, mouth agape, and he just shrugged. It was amazing. It was like his whole life, all those years spent with his nose wedged deep in a book, all those times he'd been mocked or ignored or shunned, had built up for this one moment. He was validated. We'd never hear the end of it.

I turned the other way to check on Zell. Given how confused he looked, we might as well have all grown wings.

A few minutes later, Timofei bumbled out of his backroom, a clear glass vial in his hands. A wooden stopper sealed it, and a pale blue liquid sloshed around inside. We were getting the antidote, and getting it for free. At this rate, I'd bake Miles a cake, and I didn't even know how to bake. I reached for the vial, but just as my fingers touched it, Timofei jerked it back. "I said you wouldn't have to spend an Eagle, and I meant it. I would, however, ask you pay a different price."

"A different price?"

He grinned ear to ear, and half his teeth sparkled gold. "Have a drink with me! The three of you! I'll buy a round, and we can all talk of Mercanto and Varleson and the other greats!"

I looked to Miles and Zell for help, but none of us had anything. This was very much not a situation we'd planned for. "Well, we'd love to," Miles tried, "but we, well, you know, were hoping to go to sleep soon. My wife and I, we need to get up very early, you see. . . ."

"Oh, I understand. Say no more," Timofei said with an all-too-knowing wink. "As Mercanto wrote . . . 'A woman wants so far to be / from men who talk of poetry.'" I was starting to get the feeling I wouldn't like this Mercanto guy, but that wasn't really relevant. "One drink. Just one drink. Give a broken old man that much."

I stared at the vial dancing between Timofei's fingers, so close but so far away. I wanted to just grab it and run, to get back to Lyriana and Jax, but that would probably end in Timofei calling the City Watch after us. I couldn't see a way out. We had to play along. "One drink is fine, my love." I patted Miles's shoulder, trying to put on my best loving-wife voice. "But just one. And then we must return to the inn."

"Splendid!" Timofei slapped a hand on the table, almost dropping the vial and giving me a heart attack. I hoped he'd give it to us and we could sneak away, but he opened his coat, revealing a dozen little pockets sewn into the inside, and tucked the vial into one of them. "Follow me! I know of the most charming tavern. Well, it's acceptable. Well, it's a bit of a dump. But the beer is cheap, and the first bowl of nuts is free!"

He led us outside and back the way we'd come before ducking onto a side street. The tavern he brought us to was called the Stumbling Sally, and it was just what you'd expect

Timofei's favorite tavern to be: a run-down two-story shanty with smelly drunks sleeping against the walls and an off-key ballad warbling out the windows. Timofei threw open the swinging front doors and led us into a messy hall packed tight with people drinking and dancing, playing cards, and, in the case of a couple against the far wall, going at it. Three girls, musicians, stood on a small stage in the middle; one strummed a lyre, one played some weird three-pronged flute, and the third sang a song about a drunk who mistook a bear for his wife (guess where it went). Timofei cheerfully led the way in, but next to me, Miles was sweating and Zell's hand stayed inside his coat. Every step we took, I got more and more scared. We might have fooled Timofei, but what were the odds that we'd fool every single person here, too?

I tried to whisper something to Miles about getting out of here, but he couldn't hear me over the room's din, and when I turned around, I bumped right into a firm, broad chest. I stumbled back. The man in front of me was tall and bulky, built like a bull, but more important, was wearing a blue-and-green uniform. The colors of House Collinwood, the ruling House of Bridgetown; a man of the City Watch. A droopy black mustache framed his scowl, and a sheathed sword hung at his hip. He glared down at me with two beady eyes.

This was it. We'd been made. Time to run.

But he just grumbled, "Watch where you're going, girl," and turned back to the bar, leaving me standing there having a panic attack.

"There! A table!" Timofei exclaimed like a giddy little kid. He guided us up the tavern's rickety stairs toward a small table against the second floor's balcony, overlooking the noisy scene below. He plopped himself down in a chair, waved at a passing barmaid, and ordered four tall goblets of "the cheap stuff." I got the feeling he did this a lot.

The table only had three chairs, so Miles and I sat down opposite Timofei, while Zell stood watch. The barmaid set down four dented goblets full of piss-looking beer, and I made a polite gesture of sipping mine. It actually didn't taste half bad. Maybe I just really needed a drink.

Timofei clearly did, too, because he downed half his goblet in one swig and slammed it on the table, a mustache of foam on his upper lip. "Now, then! I must ask . . . what's your favorite Mercanto comedy? And please don't say *The Lady-Mage of Mellinmor. . . .*"

"Of course not!" Miles beamed, and I couldn't tell for the life of me if he was just acting well or if he was really into this shit. "*Lady-Mage* might have its moments, but it's nothing compared to *Comforting a Widow* or *A Woman's Warmest Place!*"

"Just one drink, remember," I scolded Miles. Every second we spent here was a second we risked getting caught. But also I really didn't think I could take much more talk about this Mercanto asshole.

There was a bit of commotion from the tavern's entrance, so I leaned over the balcony to see what was happening. The wooden doors swung open.

Razz walked in.

nineteen

I SUCKED IN MY BREATH AND SPUN BACK TO THE TABLE, straining every muscle in my face to communicate utter terror. Zell understood it immediately, his hand dropping into his jacket, while Miles looked mostly confused. Razz hadn't seen us, though, not yet. That meant we still had time to get out of here before—

"Titans' tits!" Timofei exclaimed, stepping right up to the edge of the balcony. "Look at this rabble! They'll let anyone into Bridgetown these days!"

And of course, Razz heard him. His eyes flicked up to the balcony, past Timofei, and even across the crowded room, his gaze met mine. He saw right through my disguise. His eyes lit up with excitement, and his mouth curled into a grin. His nightglass fangs sparkled darkly in the torchlight.

What was he doing here? How had he found us? And what the hell were we going to do now?

Razz turned around and barked something in Zitochi,

and I could see more men behind him, his mercenaries, hulking figures in black leather armor, swords and axes strapped to their sides. They strode into the tavern like they owned it, shoving their way toward the stairs leading up to us. Razz's hungry eyes never left mine. The tavern went quiet and the music stopped as everyone pushed back to get out of the way of these obvious madmen.

I sprang up, searching for another way out. But there was nothing; only the rickety stairs led down to the first floor, and the mercenaries were already halfway to them. Miles clasped a hand over his mouth. Zell already had a dagger out, somehow.

"What's happening?" Timofei demanded. "What is this?"

Razz and his men had cleared most of the room now and were almost to the stairs when another man stepped in front of them: the City Watchman from earlier, with the droopy mustache. He looked weary and agitated, like this was the last thing he wanted to deal with, but he still blocked Razz's path. "Look here," he grumbled. "Weapons are forbidden to citizens within Bridgetown limits. And it looks to me like you and your boys are packing more than your fair share. Now, I don't want any trouble here. I just want to finish my beer in peace. So why don't you turn around and walk back out of here, and we'll pretend this never happened?"

A slow, easy smile crossed Razz's face. Zell stiffened beside me. "Not a problem," he said to the Watchman. "I'll certainly pretend this never happened when I report back to High Lord Kent. But I have some very important fugitives to kill. So why don't you sit down, have another beer, and get your grizzly old ass out of my way?" He shoved the Watchman aside and took another step toward the stairs.

The Watchman was having none of it. He reached out and grabbed Razz's shoulder with one meaty hand, stopping him in place. "I don't care if you're High Lord Kent himself. No one disrespects me like that. Now, get the hell out of my tavern!"

Razz didn't turn around. His eyes still locked on mine, he made a bored, irritated face, like a child exasperated at having to do his chores. Then he pulled a curved dagger out of its sheath, spun around, and slammed it into the underside of the Watchman's chin, driving the whole blade into his skull.

The room exploded into chaos.

A woman let out a piercing shriek. The Watchman fell backward, gurgling, the hilt of Razz's dagger jutting from his jaw. Razz's men rushed forward, sprinting toward the stairway, unsheathing their blades. Half the tavern patrons hurled themselves out of their way. But the other half lunged forward to meet them, yelling in outrage and anger. A hulking drunk grabbed a wooden chair and smashed it across a mercenary's face. One of the musicians swung her lyre into the back of another's head, and it exploded in a noisy spray. Even Razz got intercepted, tackled to the ground by the tattooed barkeep. The room broke into a full-on brawl.

I guess it's true what they say: never piss off an East Bridgetown bar.

Zell rushed to the balcony's edge and threw one of his daggers. It spiraled through the air and somehow, even on the crowded floor below, caught one of the mercenaries in the side of the head. He dropped like a stone. Another, a tall, thin man with spiked hair, hurled his hand ax back up in our direction. It missed Zell by a foot, but it almost took off Timofei's nose. The apothecary shrieked and fell onto his back, and his flailing hand caught the edge of my shirt and pulled me down with him.

Timofei landed on his back on the balcony, and I landed on top of him. Our faces just a few inches apart, he stared at me in shock, and his eyes went wide with recognition. "You're—you're—you're those fugitives!"

I pressed my elbows into his chest. "The antidote! Give it to me!"

"Take it!" he gasped, and fumbled a hand inside his coat. He pulled out the thin vial, the blue liquid inside sloshing around, and it almost tumbled out of his trembling fingers before I grabbed it. It was in my hand. The antidote was in my hand!

And not a moment too soon. The spiky-haired mercenary had somehow made it to the stairs and was almost at the top, a glistening ax in his right hand. Miles stumbled away, but Zell stepped forward. With one hand, he hurled a goblet of rye into the mercenary's face, and with the other, he grabbed a torch off a nearby wall and threw it toward him. The alcohol-soaked mercenary burst into flame, and he tumbled back over the stairway's railing, plunging toward the brawling crowd below like a flaming comet.

"I'll hold them here!" Zell barked. "Get to the window! Get outside!"

Window? I spun around and then I saw it, a small square pane of glass on the floor's far end. I had no idea where it dropped to, but it had to be safer than staying here. Clutching the antidote tightly against my chest, I shoved myself off Timofei, who scrambled away, and sprinted toward the window. I couldn't see what was happening behind me, but

I could hear it: people fumbling, blades scraping, and men screaming.

I turned just as I reached the window, and smashed into it with my shoulder. The glass shattered easily, and I felt a sharp pain flare down my arm, pain that almost certainly meant I'd been cut. I'd gotten more injuries in the last week than in all of my life. There was a small awning just under the window, and I rolled down its slope and knocked off a few loose shingles, before free-falling a solid story and landing in the dark, wet mud behind the tavern.

I let out a sharp gasp and, not able to stop myself, looked at my arm. I wished I hadn't. My shoulder was slashed open, warm blood trickling down to my elbow, and a thin sliver of glass jutted out. But that didn't matter. Not right now. The vial in my hand was unbroken, and I could see a few horses tied up behind the tavern. I could make a run for it. But I wasn't just going to leave Miles and Zell. Clutching one hand over my bleeding cut, I looked up to the window. There was no sign of them, but there was an awful lot of smoke billowing out, and I could hear, under the sounds of brawling, the crackling of flame. The fire was spreading.

That was when the mercenary stepped around the corner.

He was young, my age, with a soft unshaven face and pretty gray eyes. For some stupid reason, I thought maybe he'd let me go, that because he looked so nice he wouldn't just attack an unarmed girl. Then he drew his sword from the sheath on his back and charged me with a scream.

Maybe it was the adrenaline. Maybe it was Zell's training. But I jerked my shoulder back, perfectly dodging his downward slice. I felt the whoosh of the air as it streaked by me, saw my face reflected in the polished blade. The vial flew out of my hand and rolled away into the mud. The mercenary jerked the blade up, trying to catch me on the backswing, but I dodged that one, too, and when his arm rose up past my head, I shot out a hand and grabbed his wrist. My combat training was mostly limited to dodging and catching, so I acted purely on impulse: I shoved the sword away from myself, smacking the mercenary in the face with the hilt, and then hit him again and again with my spare hand, yelling an incoherent string of syllables. Most of my punches missed, glancing off the side of his incredibly hard skull, but the last one connected. My fist hit his nose, and I felt it break with a way-too-satisfying crack. The mercenary broke free of my grip and staggered back, blood trickling down over his mouth, staring at me in stunned disbelief.

For once in my life, I wasn't thinking. I wasn't planning, either, or analyzing, or any other thing that used my brain. I was all heart, raging, pounding, bleeding, fighting. I wanted to live, and I wanted my friends to live, and in that moment I would have murdered any idiot who dared get in my way. I lunged forward with a guttural roar, hands outstretched for the mercenary's face. . . .

And slipped in the mud, falling flat on my ass.

Now I was thinking again. I was thinking about what an idiot I was. I was thinking about how I was going to die. Why the hell hadn't I just run? The pretty-boy mercenary stepped over me, grinning. He turned his sword over in his hands and raised it high.

How do most warriors die? On their backs.

I closed my eyes. I was terrified of dying. And somehow,

even in the face of that fear, I was disappointed I hadn't done a better job of fighting back.

There was a sudden roar from above, and a person tumbled over the awning's edge and fell right onto the mercenary. Miles. *Holy shit.* It was Miles. He drove the shocked mercenary down into the ground, hard, mud splattering everywhere, the man's sword flying out of his hands. I'm pretty sure I heard something snap. The mercenary let out a pained gurgle, but before he could recover, Miles scrambled to his feet. He was holding something in his hands, a long wooden stick with a broken end. A leg from a chair, maybe? The mercenary fumbled for his sword, and Miles swung the chair leg down like a club, hitting the man right in the center of the forehead. That did the trick. Pretty Boy was knocked clean out, facedown in the mud.

I pushed myself up onto my elbows, gasping, mostly for relief. Miles stared at me, still clutching the chair leg tight in his white-knuckled hands. "I just hit that guy," he said in a daze. "I hit him right in the face."

"Yeah, you did," I whispered, legitimately impressed. "I think you just saved my life."

"I did, didn't I? I did." Miles blinked himself back into the moment. "The vial!"

"I dropped it when I fell. Somewhere in the mud."

Miles dropped to his hands and knees, scrambled around, then held up the mud-caked but mercifully unbroken vial. "Okay. Got the vial. Time to run."

"Run?" I turned back to the flaming tavern. I could still hear the clash of blades, the screams of men. "We can't leave without Zell!"

I stepped forward, and Miles grabbed my shoulder. "Tilla, please! We've got the vial, we've got our lives! Don't throw it all away for—"

A deafening blast sounded from the tavern, blowing out the remaining windows, shaking the ground, and knocking us both back. One of the massive kegs must have gone up. The horses tied to the side broke and ran, neighing into the night. The whole building was full-blown on fire now. Dancing orange flames grasped like hands out through the roof and lit up every shattered window frame. I could hear a frantic commotion from the front of the bar, the patrons running for their lives. Now I couldn't hear any more fighting from inside. Just crackling wood and low, raspy screams.

No.

No!

I struggled to my feet and moved toward the tavern. "Lyriana!" Miles shouted. "The mages! The war!" He got up and grabbed me, actually grabbed me by the hand and pulled me away. "Come on!"

He was right. There was too much at stake. We had to go, and hope Zell would find his way back to us.

Miles and I rushed out around the side of the tavern and stumbled into a huge crowd. Half of it was pushing away from the burning building in terror, and the other half was pushing toward it to get a better look. Almost no one was pushing toward the alley that led to the apothecary's, though, which meant we had a clear run of it. As we ran, I looked back at the burning tavern, which was now just a towering pillar of fire, catching onto the roofs of the neighboring buildings. City Watchmen broke through the crowd behind us, carrying buckets and ladders. I felt a pang of guilt, the same pang I felt whenever I thought of Markos. People were going to die in this fire. People *had* died. Maybe even Zell. And it was only happening because of me.

We rounded the corner of the alley to the empty apothecary, where, thankfully, our horses were still tethered. Miles scrambled onto his, and I climbed onto mine. And as the two of us raced toward the town's exit, a shape, a person, came out of the shadows in front of us. My hand jerked toward my knife before I remembered I didn't have a knife, but it didn't matter because the person staggered into the moonlight and I saw those deep brown eyes.

Zell's hair was a ruffled mess, his face caked with soot, and his pant leg was slit open, revealing a long, bleeding cut along his calf. A huge black bruise blossomed around his left eye. But he was alive, alive and safe. The surge of relief that passed through me was almost painful. I yanked on the reins, and before I'd even stopped he pulled himself onto the horse, sliding up behind me.

"Zell," I breathed. "We had to . . . Lyriana . . ."

He shook his head sharply. "No time. We need to ride. Now."

I swallowed and nodded, spurring my horse along, and as we rode onto the main street, I saw why Zell was in such a hurry. The entire block was crawling with City Watchmen, a sea of bustling blue-and-green uniforms. Luckily, most of them were still preoccupied by the tavern fire they'd just barely started to contain. The rest were distracted by something else, a commotion in a noisy crowd. I leaned over to see what it was and found myself staring, once again, into Razz's eyes.

He was on his knees, surrounded by Watchmen, with his hands bound behind his back. His face was caked with blood, and some still dribbled down his chin. He must have put those fangs to use. The furious Watchmen surrounded him, kicking him into the dirt and pulling him up again, but he barely seemed to care. All of his attention was on me, and his gaze burned with hate.

He could have stopped us so easily there, with one simple shout that we were the fugitives the whole Province was looking for. But he didn't say anything. Of course he didn't. Razz wanted to let us go, just so he could be the one to hunt us down. *See you soon,* he mouthed.

A wave of dread washed over me. Somehow, I knew to take him at his word. This wouldn't be over for him until he dragged my body back to his father, probably in several pieces. I thought of that mother in the cottage. I shuddered.

As we crossed the city entrance and galloped back onto the dirt road, the buildings gave way to the comforting shadows of trees, but I didn't feel safe. My heart was still thundering, my breath still ragged. It felt like every close call was catching up to me in a rush. Timofei almost seeing through our ruse. The pretty-boy mercenary looming over me with his blade. And worst of all, Razz, his nightglass grin looming at me in the dark. I was shaking, gasping. My chest felt like a fist, clenching around my heart.

Zell leaned forward and wrapped an arm around my waist.

My shaking slowed. My breath calmed. And that rush of panic, whatever the hell that was, faded away. Zell's touch made me feel calm, like the first quiet moment after a thunderstorm. I melted into him. Zell, the Zitochi warrior, the hardened killer, the boy whose hands were weapons, was the only thing in the world that made me feel safe.

I leaned back, pressing myself against his chest. He felt warm, firm, and, underneath the scent of smoke and sweat, I could still smell *him*, that earthy smell, leaves crumbling in winter frost. Through my back I felt his heart, pounding in his chest, and mine pounded back. He leaned his head forward, just an inch from mine, his hair just barely touching my cheek, his breath warm on my collarbone.

This was like the moment in the river, that powerful, aching physical tension, but I didn't fight it or fear it now. I leaned into it, embraced it. My mind had been resisting what my body had wanted, but I'd been through way too much hell to give it that power anymore. He held me close and I pressed in closer, and damn if this didn't just feel so, so right.

I had the antidote.

I had my life.

And I had Zell's arm around my waist.

I spurred my horse and rode on, away from Bridgetown and Razz and the City Watch, into the night.

TWENTY

WE DIDN'T BOTHER BEING QUIET ON THE RIDE BACK. THERE was no point: anyone who spotted us would just report us to Bridgetown, and we'd already been seen there. The best thing we could do now was take advantage of every second the chaos had bought us.

We got back to our grotto in just two hours and pushed our way through the big willow tree's canopy. I'd gotten this terrible image in my head that we'd arrive to find Lyriana already dead, our efforts having taken too long, so I felt an incredible surge of relief to see her right where we'd left her, still breathing in Jax's arms. Then I got closer and saw how awful she looked. Her skin was translucent, bloodless, and her open eyes were vacant. Her clothes clung to her, sticky with sweat, and her breath came in short, pained gasps. The Rings on her fingers had been a vibrant green when we'd left, but now they were dull, their light almost extinguished.

"The antidote!" Jax shouted. He looked absolutely terrible,

his hair a wild mess, his clothes soaked with sweat. "Please, please tell me you got the antidote."

"Here!" Miles took the vial out of his jacket and, against anything resembling common sense, tossed it to Jax.

Jax caught it, uncorked it, and pressed it to Lyriana's pale lips. "All of it?"

"All of it."

He tipped the vial and let the blue tonic pour into her mouth. She arched her back and wheezed, but the liquid all went down. When Jax pulled the empty vial away, she collapsed back into his arms and lay there, barely panting. "Well?" Jax asked. "Did it work?"

"This is medicine, not magic," Miles replied. "It takes at least a few hours to counteract the poison. We just have to wait."

"I've been waiting all night," Jax said, his voice pinched and angry. "I thought . . . I was sure she was going to die in my arms!"

Miles shook his head. "Yeah, well, our night hasn't been great, either."

Jax started to reply, then finally took a good look at us. Miles and Zell were ragged and worn, their faces blackened with soot, their clothes ripped and stained. I couldn't imagine what I looked like.

"Holy frozen hell," Jax said. "What happened to you guys?"

I glanced down at my left shoulder, which was caked with dried blood from where I'd cut it hurling myself through the window. The big sliver of glass had fallen out in my scuffle with Pretty Boy, but tiny little fragments still glistened around the wound's dark edges, like diamonds dropped in mud. I'd managed to ignore the pain while we were riding, and even now, it somehow didn't seem that bad, like I was looking at a nasty cut on someone else. Maybe I'd just been hurt so much in the last two weeks that I'd lost all sense of perspective.

That was weird, right? A month ago, I would have woken half the castle if I'd stubbed my toe. Now I felt like someone could tear off my arm, and I'd barely blink an eye.

"We got spotted," I explained to Jax, "by Razz, of all people. Yeah. That's how shitty our luck is."

"So he knows we're here?" Jax wrapped one arm protectively around Lyriana. "Are we in trouble?"

"Not just yet," Miles speculated. "Razz got arrested, and between the fire, the brawl, and the half-dozen dead City Watchmen, I think the good folk of Bridgetown are going to be distracted. At least for a little while."

"I don't even want to know." Jax shook his head. "Just once, it'd be nice for things to go smoothly for us. Would that be too much to ask?"

I started to point out that the most important part was that we had come back with the antidote, when a flickering green light distracted me. Lyriana's Rings. They'd faded more and more the sicker she got, but now, suddenly, they lit up a vibrant emerald, brighter than I'd ever seen before. They throbbed like a candle's flame and cast a warm green glow over the willow's canopy. Lyriana stirred and gasped, just a little, but I swore it sounded like her breath was already a little less raspy.

"Okay. Well. *That* literally is magic," Miles said.

Magic or not, the antidote still took its time to work, so I pushed my way out from under the willow and headed toward the edge of the grotto, where a small inlet of the Markson sat still and dark. I pulled off my mud-caked boots and hunkered down by the water's edge, stretching my feet out so the water lapped at my ankles. It was cold, but the cold felt good right now, soothing even. I closed my eyes and just felt the icy water, the crisp air, the slight breeze blowing through my hair. Exhaustion grabbed me like a clenching fist. I felt like I was going to pass out. How long had I been awake? Had it seriously been a day and a half?

I leaned back on my arms and felt a sharp pain in my shoulder. There it was. *Hello, old friend.* As badly as I wanted to lie back in the dirt and fall into the deepest sleep of my life, I probably had to deal with this first. I scooped a handful of water out of the river, washed away the dried blood, then, with a wince, began pulling out the tiny slivers of glass still poking through my skin.

"That's probably going to need some stitches," Miles's voice called from behind me, and I craned my head back around. Even though he'd been like this for a good six hours, my brain still refused to accept this gaunt, bearded, bald man as Miles. He sat down next to me, holding a small leather bag in his hands, its clasp sealed with a beaded tassel. "I found this in one of the mercenaries' packs. All kinds of surgical supplies."

"Yeah, well, if my stitching is anything like my embroidery, I'm probably better off without it."

Miles smiled. There was something different about him, an air of confidence that hung over him like Lyriana's glowing light. "Believe it or not, I'm actually a fairly proficient medic. I can do it."

I blinked. "You know how to stitch up wounds?"

Miles opened the pack and took out a skin of alcohol, a tightly wound spool, and a pointy black needle. "Mother insisted I be trained in it. She said that if I ever found myself on the battlefield, I'd need something useful to do, and it certainly wouldn't be fighting."

I was starting to think that Miles's mom was a huge bitch, but that wasn't really the point.

Miles scooted over to me and gently took my arm, turning it so he could look directly at the cut. I stretched it out and turned away. I did not need to see this. "I have to warn you, it might sting a bit."

It did.

We sat there for a while in silence, as he sterilized my wound with some alcohol, picked out the last shards, and then delicately sewed it shut. Every now and again I glanced back at him, at his determined expression and his shockingly steady and capable hands. I had to admit, he was actually really good at it. Hell, he was good at a lot of things we never gave him credit for. He'd been the one who knew how to get the antidote. He'd been the one who kept Timofei from blowing our cover. And he'd been the one who saved my life.

I felt bad. Bad for all the ways we'd teased him over the years, bad for all the things we'd said behind his back, even bad for how I'd stormed off when he'd told me about our parents' plan. Yeah, it was wrong of him to have kept the truth from me all these years. That still stung. But did it really matter anymore? Did it matter after everything we'd been through? The people we'd been back at Castle Waverly were strangers now, and their mistakes weren't ours. I might resent the pale, curly-haired boy in the ill-fitting tunic who'd lied to me all those years. But that wasn't who had just finished stitching up my arm.

I needed to say something, anything, to lift that guilt. "Miles." I turned to him. "What you did back in town . . . the way you played Timofei . . . that was incredible."

"I know, right? I couldn't believe it. I've never done anything like that in my life. I didn't even know I could do something like that." His face lit up with a huge grin. "And you want to know the funniest part? I don't even *like* Mercanto!"

"That was all bullshit?"

"Total bullshit!" Miles laughed. "And then later, with the mercenaries, us fighting them in the street, when I knocked that guy out, when I saved your life, I mean . . . I just feel like we've become these completely different people overnight. Like my entire life up until these last few weeks was just a dream I've finally woken up from, and for the first time ever, I felt like myself. Do you know what I mean?"

"Yeah. I do."

Miles turned away. I wondered if I looked as different to him as he did to me. "My whole life, Tilla, I've thought of myself as . . . I don't know. Weak. Soft. Lesser. Guys like Jax and Zell, they were the guys who got to have adventures and be heroes and get the girl. And me, well, I'd sit in my room and read books and maybe be lucky enough to one day help them out." He looked more alive than I'd ever seen him. "But now I think that was all just insecurity and fear. I think . . . I think maybe I could be that guy, Tilla. I think I could go out there in the world and have adventures. I could take risks and face my fears and all that, you know?" His smile was so infectious I couldn't help but smile back. "Do you think I could be that guy?"

"I do," I said.

Then he kissed me.

I didn't jerk away or gasp or anything. But I didn't kiss him back, either. I didn't do anything, couldn't do anything, because I was too stunned and flustered. I just sat there, his lips to mine, his breath against mine, and did absolutely nothing.

He pulled away quietly. "Tilla?"

And what was I supposed to say to him? That as happy as I was to see him come into his own and find his confidence, it didn't change the fact that I just wasn't attracted to him? That I wanted to support him going out and getting the girl, but I wasn't the girl? That even though I'd forgiven him for hiding the truth about our betrothal, it still left an icky aftertaste in my mouth, one that might never go away? That even though I was grateful he'd saved my life, did he feel that entitled him to this, that I'd have to be his out of gratitude? That as much I was coming to like and respect and care about him, I still saw him as just a friend, and probably always would?

That the feeling of his lips against mine didn't make me burn with even a hundredth of the yearning I'd felt with Zell's arm around my waist?

I couldn't say any of that. I just couldn't. Not out here, with our lives still on the line, where we still needed to depend on each other. And not tonight, with him feeling so good. I just couldn't crush him.

So I stalled. Okay, maybe I lied. "Miles, I can't," I said softly. "Not right now. Not here. There's just too much going on right now. We're still in so much danger, I can't . . . I can't be distracted. You understand, right?"

He nodded. "Yeah."

"When we get out of this, when we get to Lightspire . . . we'll come back to this, okay? We'll talk about it. That's a promise."

Miles nodded. And maybe this was just wishful thinking, but he didn't look all that hurt or disappointed. "Okay. You're right. We'll revisit this later. When we're safe." He turned away and cleared his throat. "Ahem. Right. We should probably get some rest while the antidote does its work."

"Those are the best words you could have possibly said." I flopped back into the grass and curled onto my side. It was weird how I used to sleep in beds. "I'll sleep out here. You guys wake me up if you need anything."

Miles smiled, and I could tell just looking at him he was still thinking about the kiss, his heart still fluttering inside his chest. "Good night, Tilla."

"'Night, Miles."

He turned and walked off, pushing back through the canopy of the willow tree. I lay alone on my side, the cool grass against my cheek. Above me, the clouds parted to show a clear sky, lit up by a thousand million stars. I could very faintly hear my friends' voices and could just barely make out Miles volunteering to take the first shift.

I'd done the right thing, hadn't I?

I really hoped so.

TWENTY-ONE

IT TOOK MILES SHAKING ME WITH ALL HIS MIGHT TO SNAP ME awake. "What is it?" I swatted vaguely at his head. "Go away!"

"It's Lyriana." He was out of breath with excitement. "She's awake!"

I pulled myself up from my resting spot on the water's edge, and Miles led me by the hand back to the willow tree. Lyriana was resting against the tree's trunk, still cradled in Jax's lap, while Zell stood protectively overhead, and it was amazing how much better she looked. Her skin no longer had that horrible translucent sheen, and she wasn't shivering or sweating or any of that. Her legs were folded under her, but I could see that most of her veins had gone back to normal. Sure, her hair was a poufy mess and she had bags under her eyes like a ninety-year-old swamp seer. But she looked alive, very much alive, and like she was going to stay that way.

"Tillandra." Her voice wavered, and her eyes glistened with tears.

"Lyriana." I settled down next to her, and I realized I was

kind of tearing up, too. "It is so, so good to see you like this again."

She reached out with a trembling hand and touched the fresh stitches on my shoulder. "They told me what happened. The risk you all took riding out to Bridgetown, how you put your lives on the line for me. . . ." She looked up at Jax and ran a weak hand along his cheek, causing him to actually flinch in surprise. "And you, Jax. Staying back and taking care of me. All by yourself. I . . . I . . ." She couldn't hold back the floodgates anymore and clutched a hand over her mouth, overwhelmed by emotion, full-blown crying. "I owe you all so much. I can't even begin to think how I'll repay you."

"We didn't do it for repayment, silly." Jax wiped away her tears with the back of his hand. "We did it because you're one of us. You're our friend."

"Friend," Lyriana repeated, as if tasting an exotic spice for the first time, then looked up with a weak smile. "Titans' breath, Jax. Can it be for once you have no crude jokes? No lewd remarks?"

"Oh right!" Jax grinned. "Uh, let's see here. Ass, tits, balls, and whores?"

Lyriana laughed, she actually laughed, and Jax laughed with her, and then we were all laughing together like a bunch of idiots. I didn't care. I didn't think I'd ever been more relieved in my entire life. I hugged Lyriana and she rested her head on me, and then Miles hugged me, too, and Jax joined us, and Zell even put his hand on my shoulder. We were together. We were alive. We were going to make it, going to get to Lord Reza, going to be saved by a big damn army of mages and stop the war and go to Lightspire.

We were going to live.

A few minutes later, Jax laid out the map of the Western Province, and we huddled around it, our rough position noted by a round green pebble. When we'd first looked at this map, Lord Reza's castle, the Nest, had been impossibly far away. But now our pebble was more than halfway there, closer to the Nest than to Castle Waverly. It didn't seem far at all.

"What do you think?" Jax asked. "Another ten days, maybe? At the rate we've been going?"

Zell shook his head. "No. We can't keep riding like we have been, now that they know we're here. We need to push as hard as we can if we're going to have any shot at escaping my brother."

I cocked an eyebrow. "Your brother's locked up in a Bridgetown dungeon."

"And if even a single one of his men escaped, he'll be free by nightfall. Your jails can't hold us. Your men should have killed him the second they had him captured."

"That's not really how we do things . . ." Jax tried.

"It's not just Razz," I chimed in. "Timofei, the apothecary, recognized me. If he lived through that fire, it's only a matter of time before he tells the City Watch."

"Or hires his own band of mercenaries to claim us himself, visions of fifty thousand Eagles dancing in his head," Miles grumbled. "Never trust a man who loves Mercanto."

Lyriana didn't even bother responding to that. "So we'll have to ride hastily, then. Our only hope is to outrun them."

"Exactly." Zell turned to Jax. "Riding our hardest. What do you think?"

Jax laid his hand down on the map. "A week. Five days, if we're really pushing it."

"Five days it is," Zell said.

So we rode, and we rode our hardest, driving our way across that last stretch of the Western Province. The forest grew thinner around us, densely clustered trees giving way to wider plots and farmsteads, to rolling fields of grain and hilly pastures dotted with cows and sheep. The land here was more domesticated, broken in, branded with wide roads and dotted with bustling towns. We traveled through the countryside in the early evenings and mornings, and took to the roads at night, riding four abreast, our horses' hooves pounding through the dirt, the wind whistling through our hair. We'd pass other travelers here and there, came within spitting distance of the occasional merchant caravan, but it didn't faze us. The real threat was at our backs now. And our goal was so close we could taste it.

Lyriana recovered quickly. The first day, she was still so weak I had to hold her as we rode. The second day, she was able to hold herself up. And the third day, she was back to her usual self. No, actually she was better than her usual self. Coming back from the brink of death had somehow left her more comfortable and relaxed, more willing to ignore the strict rules of her upbringing, more willing to open up. She and Jax started trading dirty jokes, and she taught me how to braid my hair Lightspire-style. When Zell caught us an incredibly juicy and tender boar, Lyriana even ate a bite, before spitting it out in disgust and using magic to Grow us the biggest, plumpest peaches I'd ever seen.

We camped less and spent more of the day riding, talking and resting less than we had before. Despite that, it felt like we were closer to each other than ever. Sometimes while we tore down those night roads, I'd just take a moment and look around, at Lyriana pressed against me, at Zell boldly leading the way, at Miles riding at my right and Jax riding at my left. And I'd feel safe. We didn't feel like random companions thrown together by fate. We felt like one of those companies of soldiers who had fought a hundred battles together. We felt like friends who'd known each other since we were born. We felt like family.

And with Zell I felt something else. Ever since Bridgetown, there was an easiness between us, a shared, silent understanding. I caught him smiling at me a few times as we rode side by side, and I found myself smiling back.

Four days of hard riding later, we camped out in a small thicketed birch grove, its spindly white trees doing their best to block out the morning's bright sun. As far I could tell, we were on the border of the lands of House Reza. The Frostkiss Mountains loomed, tall and vivid, in front of us, and I could make out dark, forested foothills giving way to stony crags and white-capped peaks. There they were, the borders of the West, the wall that cut off everything I knew from the rest of the world. Beyond those mountains lay the Heartlands and the Eastern Baronies and the Southlands and the Red Wastes. Beyond those mountains lay Lightspire, and mages, and the King. Beyond them lay salvation.

Lyriana and Miles napped while Zell had gone off to hunt, which left me and Jax to gather kindling. We walked together along the muddy banks of some unknown river, orange-and-red leaves crunching under our feet, a chill fall wind making us pull our ramskin cloaks tight. It was nice, actually. Between the hard riding and all my training with Zell, I'd spent barely any time with Jax in the last week. I'd missed him.

"So . . ." he said casually, bending down to scoop up a handful of brittle bone-white twigs. "You hook up with Zell yet?"

Okay, maybe I hadn't missed *all* of him. I shot him a glare. "I don't know what you're talking about."

"Yes, you do." He grinned. "Come on. I can see the way you look at him during those 'training sessions.' You're totally smitten." I hurled a twig in Jax's general direction. "Hey, I'm not judging, sis. I know I said some dumb shit about Zitochi back in Castle Waverly, but I was wrong. Zell's a good guy. I'm rooting for you two."

"Yeah, well, there's nothing to root for, so . . ." I started to reply, and then I saw the look on Jax's face that meant he wasn't going to let this go. I tried to hide my smile. "Look. Okay. Maybe I do feel something for him. Something I . . . I haven't really felt for a guy before."

"Ooooooh," Jax squealed, and he sounded like a little girl who'd just been told she got to play the part of the princess in the Midsummer's Play.

"I just don't know," I continued, and okay, it was kind of a relief to actually be getting this off my chest. "I like him. A lot. And I think . . . I mean, he's pretty tough to read, but I think he's into me, too. There's this tension between us that's getting hard to ignore."

"Oh, I know," Jax said. "Why do you think we all look away awkwardly when you two are grappling with each other in the dirt? The real question is, are you gonna take it to the next level?"

I shook my head. "Not now. Not while we're on the road, with everything going on. I don't want . . . anyone to get distracted." I felt a pang of guilt as I thought of Miles kissing me, his expectant, yearning eyes.

"Well, not now, sure," Jax offered. "But when we get to Lightspire and are kicking back in our fancy manors, drinking sparkly wine and eating honeycakes all day . . ."

I couldn't begin to picture Zell drinking sparkly wine and eating honeycakes, but that wasn't really the point. What I was really picturing was the two of us walking together down along some dazzling Lightspire promenade, his arm around my waist, my face nuzzled into this shoulder. I was picturing us training together, not in the mud, but in some fancy sparring hall, and then retiring together, laughing, to the baths. I was picturing his lips on mine, his hands on me, his breath, his smell. . . .

"When we get to Lightspire," I said, snapping myself out of that thought, "we'll see what happens."

"Yeah, you will." Jax grinned. "Actually, I kinda wanted to ask you about something. Do you think . . . think . . ." He trailed off when he saw something on the riverbank. His eyes went wide, and the blood drained from his face. "Oh shit."

I followed his gaze and saw it, too. There, jutting out of the muddy shore just a few feet from where we were walking, was a human hand, its fingers curled into a grasping claw.

I instinctively whipped out my knife, ready to defend us from who the hell knows what, before my brain processed what I was seeing. It was a hand, all right, but it wasn't fleshy or rotting or even covered in skin. It was hard and gray, stained and cracked. It was stone.

Jax seemed to realize it at the same time. "What in the frozen hell . . . ?" he muttered, and walked over to it carefully, as if it might spring up and grab him. "What am I even looking at?"

I had a sinking feeling in my stomach, but I had to be sure. I walked over to the hand, knelt down on my knees, and clawed away at the mud along the river's edge. The hand led to an arm. The arm led to a shoulder. I was right, much as I didn't want to be. There was something much bigger buried here under the silt, something lying flat on its side. I dug my nails into the mud and scraped off a thick brown layer, only to reveal the stone face of a young man, incredibly detailed and lifelike, trapped in an eternal scream.

"Okay, well, that's pretty much the most horrifying thing I've ever seen," Jax said. "What kind of sick asshole dumps a statue like that in the river? What kind of sick asshole makes a statue like that in the first place?"

"It's not a statue," I said weakly. "It's a person. At least, it was. A victim of the Great War."

"What are you talking about?"

"Headmaiden Morga taught me all about it. During the war, when the mages wanted to punish prisoners, they'd sometimes turn them to stone. It would take days, maybe even weeks. It was one of the most horrible deaths imaginable," I said. "I've seen bodies like this before. They did it to my great-great-uncle Xander Kent and his wife. My father kept them in the crypts, even though the Lightspire priests told him not to." In retrospect, that was a pretty big red flag.

"Shit…" Jax whispered. "You hear about history and war and all that… but it doesn't feel real until you see it up close."

He couldn't look away from that screaming face, and I couldn't, either. Who had he been? A soldier? A spy? Just some poor dumb kid in the wrong place at the wrong time? "I wish it stayed in the history books," I said. I couldn't decide what felt more wrong, leaving that boy's face howling at the sky or covering it back up with mud.

Jax was quiet for a while, and when he finally spoke, he spoke softly, hesitantly, unlike himself. "Tilla . . . do you ever think we're maybe on the wrong side of this thing?"

"What do you mean?"

"I'm just saying." He looked up the river, his gaze distant. "I know we didn't have a choice in how it went down, and we're doing what we have to, to save our skins. But pretend we weren't. Pretend we never went to that beach, and we were still happily living in Castle Waverly when this new war broke out. Wouldn't we think your dad was doing the right thing? Wouldn't we be rooting for the West and our families and our people? Wouldn't we want them to win instead of . . ." He looked back down at the young man's frozen face. "Instead of this?"

It was a hell of a question from Jax. It was too much of a question for me. When we'd been back on the other end of the Province, when the idea of surviving had seemed like a desperate delusion, it had been easy to avoid thinking about the consequences of our actions. But here, this close, those thoughts came flooding in, and I felt my chest tighten with worry. I felt so trapped and powerless, just a little wooden pawn in some giants' game, unable to understand the board, unable to predict anything. We weren't just saving ourselves. If we did this, exposed my father's plan, we'd be making history, and scoring a major win for Lightspire. We'd be giving into the King and his mages. We'd be dooming the dream of a new Western Kingdom, maybe even causing Lightspire to tighten its grip on my Province. We might be adding a lot more "statues" to the Castle Waverly crypts.

And what would I be? A hero in Lightspire, according to Lyriana. But out here? I'd be the girl who destroyed the Kent legacy, who screwed over her family and her Province. I'd be the bastard to end all bastards.

Even after everything my father had done to me, from ignoring me for most of my life to putting a price on my head, that still made me feel so guilty. Why did it have to make me feel so guilty?

Tears burned my eyes, and I looked down. "Hey," Jax said, and he reached out to take my arm. "I'm sorry. That was a totally bullshit question. I . . . I shouldn't have asked it."

"No. It was a good question. That's why I'm upset." I turned to look up at Jax, at his big trusting eyes, his goofy, messy hair, his eager smile. And I remembered why I was out here in the first place. "I don't know if we're on the right side. I don't know if there even is a right side. All I know is, I'm not going to let you or Lyriana or Zell or Miles get hurt. That's all I care about now. That's all I can care about. Everything else . . . we'll just have to figure it out as it comes."

Jax gave me a hug, one of his big bear hugs where he wrapped me up in his brawny arms and pulled me up off my feet. "I love you, sis," he said. "You're right. We just gotta get to Lightspire. And then it's all fluffy beds and carafes of wine and making out in hot springs."

Any other day, that would've made me feel better. But today it just left me cold. "Come on," I said, turning my back on Jax and that terrible frozen, screaming face. "This kindling isn't going to gather itself."

TWENTY-TWO

THERE WAS ONLY ONE THING THAT I KNEW WOULD MAKE ME
feel better, and that was some alone time with Zell. Riding this
hard left less time to practice, and my aching thighs deeply
resented anything resembling movement, but I insisted. I had
to. I left Jax in the camp with Miles and Lyriana, and went off
into the woods with Zell to try to squeeze in one good hour
of training.

The grove we'd settled into didn't have a lot of room to
move around, so we were focused on close-quarters combat.
Zell and I stood between two birches, and again and again, he
threw jabs at my raised forearms while I blocked and dodged
them. Well, most of them, anyway.

"Let me ask you something." I bounced on my feet, my
face slick with sweat, my breath hard and fast. "As fun as it is
getting bruised all day, when do I get to learn how to actually
hit someone?"

Zell punched with his right fist, and I blocked it with

my left forearm. He'd wrapped thick cloth around his night-glass knuckles, dulling their edge, but it still hurt like hell. "The khel zhan is the art of deflection, of using your enemy's strength against him. You are not the river. You merely change where it flows."

Another right hook. Another left block. "So I don't get to hit anyone?"

Zell feigned a third right, but instead threw a left jab. I jerked to the side and felt it streak past me. "If you wanted to learn to hit, you should've studied *kharr fell*," he said. "I'm sure my brother would've loved to train you."

"Something tells me he's not the most gracious teacher," I replied. Zell lunged forward and spun, hurling his elbow at the side of my head, but I wove under it, grabbed his wrist, and pulled his arm up tight behind his back, just like he'd taught me. He grunted, and I jerked him back and held him in place, my chest pressed to his back, my heart pounding against his. We stayed like that longer than we had to, and I think we both knew that we should probably break away, but neither of us did. There was something intoxicating about pinning him in place, about knowing, *knowing*, that he wanted this.

I leaned forward with a grin, my cheek against his, my lips almost touching his ear. "Gotcha," I whispered, and let him go.

He hopped away, flexing his arm. "You learn quickly. I think you're a natural warrior."

"That might just be the sweetest thing anyone's ever said to me." I leaned back against a tree, feeling the warm sun as I craned my head up at the sky. "You think I would've made a good Zitochi?"

"No, actually. Zitochi women are forbidden from being warriors. It is considered too low, too dangerous. They must be scholars, healers, crafters, zhantaren. For a man to teach a woman our ways of fighting is a violation of our oldest laws."

"But you trained me."

"So I did," Zell said, as if he himself was a little surprised by it. "There is a legend. One my mother would tell me often. It is . . . not secret, exactly, but not commonly told. It's about a Zitochi girl, Rallia of Clan Hellgen, who dressed as a man to become a warrior and avenge the death of her father. It was my mother's favorite." He cocked his head to the side. "You remind me of Rallia. Rebellious. Determined. Stubborn."

He smiled, just a little bit, at the thought, and I felt my pulse quicken. There was a sweetness to his smile, an odd rustiness, as though it were something he did very rarely and had forgotten how. I'd been seeing more and more of that smile over the last few days. "That's why you've been training me? Because I remind you of Rallia?"

His smile vanished as quickly as it had come. "No. I'm training you because I don't want to see you dead."

"Oh," I said. Well, that was a conversation-killer. I tried to salvage it. "Will you keep training me when we're safe? When we get to Lightspire, I mean? Because I want to keep learning."

I'd assumed that would be an easy yes, but Zell didn't reply. I looked over to find a serious look on his face. "Tilla," he said softly, "I'm not staying in Lightspire."

"What?"

"I'm not staying," he repeated. "I'm not like you. I'm not some southern castle rat who grew up dreaming of your precious King and his fancy city. I don't belong there."

"Well, none of us do," I said, trying to hide my shock. I knew I was maybe overdoing it with the fantasies of Zell and me as Lightspire's hottest couple. I knew it might not work and then we'd just be friends. But it had never occurred to me that he wouldn't be staying *at all*. That thought hurt me more than every bruise and scrape combined. "It'll be okay. We'll learn. Lyriana will make sure we're taken care of and that we settle in. . . ."

"I don't want to be taken care of. I don't want to settle in. That's not who I am."

"So what will you do?" I demanded, maybe more angrily than I should have.

"There will be a war." His voice was hard, cold, not a hint of emotion. "Once your King learns the truth, he will send his armies after your father . . . and mine."

"So? What do you care?"

"What do I *care*?" Zell asked, his voice stinging with insult. "When my father accepted the mantle of Chief of Clans, he swore a vow to put the good of our people above all. Instead, he has betrayed our people and brought a storm to our lands the likes of which we have never faced. He has sullied the name of Clan Gaul. He has destroyed his honor, and mine."

"And what are you going to do about that?"

"I have heard of mercenary companies that will take anyone, even a Zitochi, provided they can fight. Perhaps they will take me," Zell said. "Perhaps I can still fight and die for my Clan. For my people."

"You would do that?" I couldn't even believe what I was hearing. All this time, we'd been running from our parents, from death and chaos, and Zell would just ride right back into it? He would *choose* to kill? "Why?"

"Why not?" He turned away from me with a shrug, and, holy shit, did that shrug piss me off. "I'm a killer. That's what I do."

"Oh come on!" I practically shouted back, and when he didn't turn around, I stepped up to him and grabbed his shoulder. "Everything we're doing, everything we've done, has been to stop a war, to end the killing! That's what this is all about!"

He stood firm, not even turning enough so that I could see his face. "Maybe for you, Tilla. But you don't know me."

"I know you're not just a killer like your brother. I know you wouldn't hurt innocent people."

That must've struck a nerve, because he spun around, throwing my hand aside, and his eyebrows were furrowed deep with anger. "Don't you talk to me about innocent people," he snapped. "You have no idea—no idea—what I've done, what I've lived, what my mercy and weakness have led to!"

"You're right! I don't know!" I yelled back. "I have no idea what the hell has happened in your life, because you don't share it. But I know you're not just some brutal mercenary who thinks mercy is weakness! I know you could be happy in Lightspire!"

Zell shook his head, livid. "Oh, I could be happy? You really think that little of me, don't you?"

"That little?"

"You think because I showed you some kindness, I'm suddenly some weak-kneed castle-rat poet, ready to spend his life sprawled out on a bed, sucking down wine and ordering around his servants?" He stepped toward me, and I jerked back. "You think I'll just change who I am, throw away my culture and beliefs and my whole way of life, just because yours are so superior?"

"No, I—I . . ." I stammered, still pissed but also a little stung at the truth of his words. "I just mean . . ."

"I'm a Zitochi." He took another step toward me, and I stepped away again, my back now pressed against the rough bark of a tree trunk. "I'm a warrior. I fight for Clan Gaul, for Zhal Korso, for the Twelve and their children and the Grayfather above." He leaned in over me, and his eyes were wide with passion. "This is who I am, Tilla. This is who I will always be. Who I should be. So tell me, tell me, why would I be happy in Lightspire?"

"Because you'd be with me!" I shouted.

He froze. His eyes were still blazing with fury, his breath ragged, but there was a spark of something else as he stared at me. He let out a long, sharp exhale and hung there, his face almost touching mine, so close I could see the pulse fluttering in his throat. "With you," he repeated, tasting the words, tasting the thought.

I reached up with one trembling hand and ran it along his face, down his cheek, and oh Titans above, did it feel good to touch him. "Zell, I—"

"Both of you, freeze!" a voice barked from behind us, and it sure as hell wasn't Jax's. I spun around to see a young man, maybe twenty-five years old, standing in the glade behind us. He had dark skin, like a Heartlander's, and his hair was cut short in neat black curls around his head. He was dressed like a soldier, with brown leather straps binding a silver breast-plate over his chest.

Oh, and he was pointing a crossbow right at us.

Zell froze instantly, any expression vanishing from his face, his eyes narrowing into hard, predatory slits. My mind raced. My fingers twitched. My hand drifted toward the dagger at my hilt.

"Don't even think about it, girl," the soldier said. "And you! Zitochi! Raise your hands over your head!"

Zell didn't say anything but slowly lifted his hands, open-palmed, in the air. It was all happening so fast. Just like that, after everything we'd been through, we'd been made, and so close to safety, too. Also, and this was arguably less impor-tant, I had been *about* to kiss Zell. I looked around for any sign of Jax or Miles or Lyriana, but they must have been back at the camp. *Shit. Shit, shit, shit!* I glanced at Zell for any help. . . .

And in one fluid motion, faster than I could blink, he whipped his sword out of the sheath on his back and hurled it at the soldier. It whistled through the air in a glistening spiral, aimed like a missile at the young man's head. The man jerked his crossbow up just in time, and the blade hit the device right in the middle, knocking it out of his hands in a spray of wooden splinters and twanging string.

Somehow, Zell was already halfway across the glade, bounding over it like a cat. Steel shimmered in his other hand as he drew his dagger from the sheath at his hip. He plunged it at the soldier's neck, but it struck metal instead with a resounding clang. The soldier had whipped his own dagger out, a long, curved blade with a gold lining around the edge and a little dip at the end, like a forked tongue. The two of them moved in a dizzying blur of motion, blades slicing through the air and striking only each other, sparks flashing as they slashed and parried. The soldier's style was different from Zell's, choppier and harder, but it seemed to be working, or at least holding him off. As Zell lunged for a strike, the soldier caught the Zitochi's knife with his, trapping the blade in that little forked tongue. The two slammed against a tree, knives locked together, nostrils flaring, eyes furious, just inches away from the daggers' blades.

"*Stop!*" Lyriana screamed from behind me. "Stop this at once!"

The reaction was immediate. The soldier let go of his knife and dropped down to one knee, so fast that Zell tripped over him. "Your Majesty!" he gasped.

Zell spun around, incredulous, his dagger still drawn. "You know this man?" he demanded.

Lyriana was standing at the edge of the grove, flanked by Miles and Jax. The two boys looked as worried and confused as I felt, but Lyriana was smiling. "Of course," she said. "Rise to your feet, Lord Reza."

If I'd been drinking, I would've done the world's biggest spit take. This was Lord Reza? Lord Galen Reza, the man we'd journeyed across the Province to see?

The man who'd keep us safe?

He rose to his feet, his head bowed low. Now, without his crossbow aimed at my head, I could get a better look at him, or at least look at him without panicking. I'd known Lord Reza was among the youngest Lords in the West, inheriting the title from his father, who died in a hunting accident the year before, though I hadn't expected him to look *quite* so young. Still, I could tell now he wasn't the average soldier, even from the Heartlands. His features were smooth, elegant, aristocratic, with sharp cheekbones and a jaw you could slice an apple with. His eyes lacked the telltale glow of the Volaris family, but they still radiated a cunning intelligence.

"You're alive," he said.

"I am." Lyriana nodded. "It's quite the story."

Jax stepped up alongside Lyriana, blocking her with one protective arm. "So you're the fancy-pants Lord of the border?" he asked. "What are you doing out here alone in the woods?"

"I'd heard reports of a suspicious party entering my lands, so I rode out with a group of scouts to investigate. The rest are combing the woods down by the river." Galen Reza's eyes flitted to Jax, to Zell. "Your Majesty, are these people . . . your captors?"

"What? No!" she exclaimed. "These are my friends. They . . . they . . ." Her voice choked up. "They saved my life. They protected me from Lord Kent. They're the only reason I'm here."

"Then it seems the Kingdom owes them a great debt," Galen said. "Don't worry. They're safe with me." His eyes flitted to Zell, who was still clenching his blade. "Even you, Zitochi-Who-I-Almost-Beat."

"In your wildest dreams," Zell said, but he sheathed his blade.

Safe. Galen had said we'd be safe. I heard the word, but I couldn't believe it. I willed my legs to move, but they held, rooted in place. Was this actually happening? Was our ordeal over? Could we possibly, actually be *safe*?

"Oh wow," Miles said, his voice a thousand miles away. Jax let out a sharp exhale. This felt impossible. My knees were trembling. My head was spinning.

Galen looked us all over, nodding to himself. "I recognize you all. From the Whisper. The Zitochi, the stable hand, Lady Hampstedt's boy . . ." He turned to me. "And you. Lord Kent's bastard."

I bowed my head. "My Lord."

His eyes narrowed even further. "Your father is responsible for this?"

I felt a terrible weight press down on me. "He was," I said. "He is."

Galen's mouth twisted into a hard frown, and his thin eyebrows formed a sharp V. "Then it was all a lie, wasn't it? The poster, the bounty—all of it. He was trying to cover up his crime. He killed the Archmagus, not the Zitochi."

"He did," Jax said, sparing me from having to answer.

"Son of a bitch," Galen whispered. "Titans' breath. That lunatic wants a second Great War."

"But we'll stop him," Lyriana said. "Won't we?"

Galen didn't answer. "We have to go," he said. "Now. I have a carriage a mile from here. Let's hurry there and get you out of sight, away from Kent's eyes."

"Kent's eyes?" I asked.

"His advance scouts," Galen said, then clicked his tongue. "Oh. I see. You don't know, do you?"

"Know what?"

He looked past us, down the road, and I hated to admit it, but he actually looked worried. "Lord Kent rides east, to meet the mages himself. He's two days away, at

243

most. And he brings with him a host of soldiers ten thousand strong."

A cold dread set over me like a familiar cloak. No, we weren't safe.

We weren't safe at all.

TWENTY-THREE

I'D ONLY BEEN IN A CARRIAGE ONCE BEFORE, YEARS AGO, when my father and I had visited Bridgetown and Lord Collinwood had given us a tour of his ample vineyards. That carriage had probably been nicer than Lord Reza's, but I didn't care. At that moment, the padded, cushioned seat was the most amazing thing I'd ever felt. When I first slumped down onto it, my aching thighs had practically melted with relief. I didn't even care that the ride was bumpy or that the whole thing smelled like leather and smoke. I was on a pillow, a real pillow, and I wanted to cry. Who knew you could miss pillows that much?

The carriage was packed tight. Me, Zell, and Jax sat on one bench, crammed shoulder-to-shoulder, with Lyriana, Miles, and Galen opposite us. There was something incredibly awkward about sitting this close to Zell, especially given the total lack of resolution we'd had from our moment in the woods. But I forced those thoughts aside.

Lyriana and Galen did most of the talking. She told him our whole story in possibly too much detail, from how we'd snuck out of the castle to our close call in Bridgetown. Galen listened intently, his grave expression breaking only for an occasional profane mutter under his breath. I tried to remember everything I knew about him. I knew that his family had been some hoity-toity Lightspire nobles who'd been granted the Lands of the Pass as a reward for their actions in the Great War. These Lands weren't particularly vast, but they included the Nest, one of the oldest castles in the Province, and Pioneer's Pass, the narrow valley through the Frostkiss Mountains. The other Lords of the West had distrusted the Rezas as outsiders, and had been sure the new young Lord would be in over his head.

Looking at the serious (and, okay, pretty hot) young man in the carriage opposite me, I realized they were half right. Galen was a Heartlander through and through, with his soft skin and elegant features. He looked nothing like the grizzled, bearded men who'd lined the tables in our Great Hall. But he had an intensity about him, a calculating air, like at any given moment there were a half-dozen schemes cranking about in his head.

"Titans' breath," he grumbled when Lyriana finished, rubbing the bridge of his nose with one hand. "This is one hell of a mess. I've got three companies of the Knights of Lazan riding up from the East. I've got Lord Kent and his entire damn army riding down from the West. And then I've got an entire camp of Sisters of Kaia begging me to come meet with them. . . ."

"What?" Lyriana perked up. "The Sisterhood of Kaia is here?"

Galen nodded, but that clearly made him far less happy than it made her. "A small group camped out near Pioneer's Pass. Forty-five of them, including Archmatron Marlena. Some kind of foolhardy pacifist crusade to try to minimize casualties, should a war erupt."

"Can we meet them?"

"Why would you want to . . . ?" Galen began, and then I could see the exact moment when he figured out the answer to his question. "Ah. Yes. Perhaps. At some point. Once everything's been settled."

No disrespect to Lyriana, but meeting up with her Sisters was the least of my priorities. "Sorry, could we back up a bit?" I chimed in, turning to the others in the carriage. "My father's going to be out here with an army? Why? Wasn't his plan to lure the mages up to Castle Waverly?"

"Because of us," Miles said, and we all turned to stare at him. "Think about it. He wanted to lure them to Castle Waverly by sending them on a mission to Zitochi lands to avenge Rolan and Lyriana. That made sense when no one knew the truth. But with us out here, somewhere in the Province, every day the mages ride is a day we could warn them. Your father needs to ambush them as quickly as he can, as soon as they cross into the Province."

"And he planned to do it in my damned castle," Galen grumbled, as if this were really the worst part. "He sent me a Whisper a week ago, demanding I arrange a banquet for all the highest-ranking mages, so he could personally offer his condolences. I knew from the start he was up to something, but I just assumed he was playing some kind of long game, maybe seeing if he could sow dissent in the ranks or curry favor with a future Archmagus. I never thought he'd be so brazen as to just kill them."

"All the highest-ranking mages in one room," Lyriana muttered. "The perfect place for an ambush."

"My mother has at least twenty mage-killer bombs. More, maybe, if she's been able to capture and torture any more mages with that Zitochi ritual. All she'd have to do is plant the remaining mage-killer bombs in the right places in your hall . . . and boom. The whole command taken out right there. Then Lord Kent attacks in the chaos with his ten thousand men. . . ."

Galen nodded. "Strikes a crippling blow before the war's even started. I don't know what angers me more, the plan's brutality . . . or its brilliance."

"Right, but that's all over now, isn't it?" Jax asked. "I mean, we'll ride out first, meet up with the mages, wave Lyriana at them, and then everything's good?"

"That's out of the question," Galen replied. "I might rule the Lands of the Pass, but many here would slit my throat in a heartbeat if Kent asked them to. His men watch the roads, the passes, even the smugglers' paths. If they see that you're alive and with the mages, they'll know we know. They'll retreat back to safety."

I blinked. I must have missed a step. "Wait, what's wrong with them retreating? Isn't that what we want?"

Galen stared at me like I was a drooling idiot. "No. What we want is to strike first and crush your father's men before they realize what's happened. If we're going to win this war decisively, we need to ambush the ambushers."

Miles looked down uncomfortably, and Zell nodded. I

turned to Lyriana for help. "I don't understand. I thought we were doing this to *prevent* a war."

Galen scoffed. "Lord Kent murdered the King's brother in cold blood. There's no preventing this war. What matters is making sure the right side wins."

That sure as hell wasn't what mattered to me, but I doubt Galen could have cared less. This was all moving fast, too fast. Was that what my role in this really was? The girl who helped Lightspire win? The girl who betrayed the West? In an instant, we'd crossed the point of no return, and I hadn't even realized we'd been at it.

"Lord Kent is an incredibly cunning man," Miles cautioned, as if he were talking about some total stranger and not, you know, my father. "You shouldn't underestimate him."

Lord Reza smiled, and his smile was cold and terrifying. "He shouldn't underestimate *me*."

"Right. Yeah. This all sounds great. Win the war, rah, rah," Jax said. "But what about us? Where are we in all this?"

"Hidden away safely, of course. You are the living proof of Kent's treason. I can't let you come into harm's way." The carriage stopped sharply. Galen laughed, just a little. "And here we are. Couldn't have asked for better timing. Welcome to the Nest."

He sat up and threw open the doors, letting bright sunlight flood in. We all stepped out, hands over our eyes. A cold gust of wind chilled me. The dirt underfoot crackled with frost. We must have been riding uphill, because we were much higher up than we'd been when we'd gotten in the carriage. A dense, untamed forest sprawled out behind us, trees just barely parting for a dirt road. In front of us sprawled a vast and imposing castle, with towering walls of ancient brick and an enormous redwood gate lined with iron beams. Barred windows loomed above the stony parapets, and dozens of watchtowers jutted up like spearheads from the walls.

From a distance, it could have been Castle Waverly's twin. But where Castle Waverly was built on a woody hilltop near the coast, this castle appeared to have been built on the edge of the world itself. Behind the castle was no land or sea but just the open sky, and the sound of the howling wind was almost too loud to talk over. Squinting against the sun, I could barely make sense of where we were: on a high, rocky peak, near the start of the Frostkiss Mountains. The castle was built on the edge of a cliff, with a massive drop to certain and incredibly unpleasant death beyond it. I'd always known the Nest overlooked Pioneer's Pass, but I'd never realized how literally.

Oh. The *Nest*. I got it now.

"Okay, yeah, this place looks pretty safe," Jax said. Miles bounced, giddy, and Zell wouldn't meet my gaze. I needed to get him alone, to figure out what the hell our deal was . . . but this wasn't the time. It was never the time.

"Thank you, Lord Reza," Lyriana said. "Your kindness will be remembered and rewarded."

"The only reward I need is Kent's head on a pike." He glanced at me, and I realized his words were a test, a little prick to see how sharply I'd react. I put on my most stoic face, which probably looked like I had to sneeze.

The heavy gates swung open, and a few men hurried out. Most were armored and armed, castle guard, but one was tall and prim, with a neat beard, a perfectly fitted tunic, and a sour look on his face. A steward if I'd ever seen one. "My Lord?" he asked.

"We have guests, Arramian," Galen said. "Guests of great import. See that the Northeast Wing is cleared out for them, and made hospitable. I want clothes, food, sheets—all of it. Keep it discreet: just Headmaiden Alana, Jezzaline, Kenna. No one else is to go in or out. And get fifteen guardsmen, five on each door. I want no mistakes."

"Of course," the steward said, nodding. "And for you?"

"Prepare the rookeries. I need to dispatch a Whisper to the mages at once."

The steward nodded again. "As you wish."

Galen turned back to us. To Lyriana, really. "Don't worry, Your Majesty. Within an hour, the mages will know full well the threat that awaits them."

"Does my cousin lead them?" Lyriana asked. "Ellarion?"

He nodded. "Indeed. With two days, we'll have more than enough time to prepare a counterambush. This will all be over soon, and you . . . and your friends . . . will be on your way to Lightspire."

"What do we do until then?" I asked.

Galen smiled, and this time, with genuine warmth. "You've had a hell of a journey," he said. "Why don't you go and settle in?"

I settled in.

Oh, holy shit, did I ever settle in.

The Northeast Wing turned out to be a tall, circular tower, packed dense with guest rooms, dining chambers, and luxurious foyers. And you'd better believe the first thing I did was take a bath. At the bottom of the tower was a cavernous bath chamber with a large stone pool, waist-deep and filled with crisp, clear water. It was shockingly, amazingly warm; Galen had had the base lined with special bricks from the Artificers Guild in Lightspire, thick red rocks that trapped the fire of mages and stayed hot for months on end. I floated in that pool for a good hour. I'd never realized just how much of a pleasure there was in getting clean, in scrubbing weeks of travel and grit and pain off myself, out of my hair, out from under my fingernails. Even weirder, I couldn't recognize my own body anymore. It wasn't just the bruises and the stitches. It was the muscle. My thighs were firm from all the hard riding. My arms had biceps, real biceps, like you'd see on those farmer women who came by Castle Waverly to hawk their goods. And my stomach, which had always been a little soft, had become hard and firm, with, for real, abs. It was a stranger's body.

I liked it.

Then I got dressed. In clothes! Real, actual clothes, designed for a girl, and one who was almost my size. Sure, the dress wasn't really my style, a little too frilly on the shoulders and a dark blue I wouldn't normally wear, but who cared? I was just so happy not to be in the same torn, stained breeches that I would've taken a potato sack.

We ate dinner together in the wing's biggest dining room, at a long wooden table, with an actual tablecloth and silverware and everything! The food, though. The food. I'd never eaten Lightspire cuisine, and it turns out, I'd been missing out my whole life. The servants brought heaping trays of a spicy, seasoned chicken stew and roasted potatoes in a creamy broth, and the thickest, juiciest beef I'd ever seen, topping it off with a sweet cream cake that dissolved on my tongue. It was, far and away, the best thing I'd ever eaten, and I wasn't just saying that because I'd been eating lanky rabbit and mushrooms for weeks. We all sat together around the table, and even though Miles warned us that we'd get sick, we all stuffed ourselves until our stomachs hurt. Miles included.

I was nodding off halfway through the meal and barely even standing by the time I got to the bedroom. I collapsed into the bed, with its fur blanket and goose-feather pillows, and was somehow asleep before I even closed my eyes.

I woke up just as night was falling, because my sleep schedule had become fully nocturnal. Jax was hanging out in my doorway wearing his new clothes, which were more formal and fancy than anything I'd ever seen him in: a gray tunic with gold trim on the shoulders, in the Heartlander style with the two rows of vertical buttons down the chest. He looked adorable.

"Tilla!" he whispered, his face lit up by the dim glow of a Sunstone. "Wake up! You gotta get out here!"

"Why? Am I going to miss the masquerade ball?" I pulled myself out of bed and stumbled toward him, rubbing my eyes with the back of my hand. "What's going on?"

"Just follow me." Jax led me away from the bedchambers, through the dining hall, and down the winding staircase to the bottom of the tower. A pair of heavy doors blocked our way to the Great Hall. I could make out the shadows of Galen's guardsmen on the other side. I started to ask what we were doing, but Jax raised a finger to shush me, and then turned his hand around to point at my feet.

"What am I looking at?" I whispered, and then I saw it.

Not my feet. Below them. A wide, hexagonal stone tile. "No way."

Jax just grinned, knelt down, and slowly and carefully lifted it up. Dust wafted out, stale and dry, and even in the dim light, I could see what lay beneath it: a tight, dark tunnel. I couldn't believe it, but I guess it made sense. The same architects had built both castles. Why wouldn't they have built the same secret passages as well?

I looked to Jax, and now I was grinning. "Do the others know?" I whispered.

"Follow me," he replied, and hopped down.

Before I could even consider whether this was a good idea, I was sliding down the hole onto a hard dirt floor. We were in some tunnels, all right—tight, unpleasant corridors lined with spiderwebs, dust, and broken tiles. And yet, amazingly, I felt like I was home.

Jax led wordlessly, and I followed, after sliding the tile above us back into place. Even by the wavering light of the Sunstone, I could tell these tunnels were a little different from the ones back in Castle Waverly. The ones there had been built into the natural caves below the castle, so they were wider, more earthy, with way more jagged roots and scary drops. These ones were clearly man-made, dug by some grizzled ancient Westerners in the days of the Old Kings. They were narrower, lined with bricks, with far fewer dead ends, and actual stone ladders built into walls so you could climb out. While the tunnels in Castle Waverly were a tangled labyrinth, these seemed to closely match the layout of the Nest itself; the narrow passageway under the Northeast Wing gave way to a wide, cavernous space that must have lain right under the

Great Hall. A half-dozen smaller tunnels branched out from it, presumably leading to various parts of the castle.

"That one goes to a creepy dungeon," Jax explained. "That one leads out into the forest through a hidden cave. That one goes right under the kitchens."

"Have you been down here for hours just mapping it?"

Jax ignored my question. "Let me show you my favorite one." He took my hand and pulled me through the tunnel that led due west. We rounded a corner, and all at once, the dark passageway was flooded with moonlight.

"What . . . ?" I said, before I realized where we were. The brick corridor led to an opening in the wall, which led to a natural rocky platform, outside the tunnels, into the fresh air. I stepped onto it carefully, even though the platform was wide and smooth, its edge a good fifteen feet away. We were outside the Nest, I realized, outside and below it, the platform a ledge jutting off of the cliff face. It hung like an outstretched tongue over a sheer, massive drop, but I didn't care because I was transfixed by what lay beyond it. From this ledge, without the castle blocking me, I had an incredible view of the Frostkiss Mountains, their craggy white peaks looming above, seeming close enough to touch. I could see the trees dotting their porous surfaces, and even make out a few distant fuzzy shapes that I thought were mountain goats. But even better than all that was the sky overhead, maybe the single most beautiful night sky I'd ever seen. There wasn't a cloud in sight. The moon was a perfect crescent sliver, and I swear I could see every single star shining above. "Wow," I sighed.

"Tillandra!" Lyriana called out from nearby. I spun around to see her and Miles sprawled out on the platform by the tunnel's exit, with Zell standing on the edge, looking out. I'd gotten so used to seeing us scruffy and worn-out that my eyes had trouble with how clean and well-dressed everyone looked. Miles was back in a Heartlander tunic, the kind he always wore, and for once it looked like it fit him. Zell was wearing a formal tunic like Jax's, but for some reason he had the highest three buttons undone, showing off the top of his chest, the curve of his collarbone. And Lyriana looked like a Princess again, in a blue-and-ivory gown that fit as if it had been custom-tailored for her.

"Looks like I'm late to the party." I walked over to the others and sat down next to them. I'd expected Zell and Miles, but I was comforted by the sight of Lyriana. A part of me had worried that, back in the trappings of a Heartlander castle, we'd lose her—that those old walls between the royals and the bastards would spring back up. But I had no reason to worry. She was one of us. Now and forever.

"Oh, the party's just getting started." Jax grinned, opened his knapsack, and pulled out a few bottles of red wine. "Look what I stole from the cellars!"

"Oh yes, please," I said. I hadn't had any wine since . . . what, the feast at Castle Waverly? A million years ago?

"Not that I wouldn't like some wine, but is this really the best time?" Miles asked. "I mean, I don't want to be a downer, but Lord Kent's army could be just a day away. Maybe we should stay alert, be ready for action, that sort of thing."

Jax groaned, and I shot him a scowl. "Look, Miles," I said, "I'm never going to claim you're some kind of coward, not after that amazing stunt you pulled back in Bridgetown. But there's nothing we can do now. It's out of our hands. In two days, everything changes. In two days, we live with what we've done. In two days, we become . . . whoever it is we become." I craned my head up to the night sky. A warm breeze blew over us, gently ruffling my hair. Was I talking to him? Or to myself? "We have had the hardest, roughest month of our lives. And we've managed to overcome it. I don't know what will happen next, but I do know that tonight might be the only chance we have to just relax and be ourselves. I don't want to think about my father tonight. I don't want to worry about what's going to happen. I don't want to think about the West or Lightspire or the war. I just want to have fun with my friends."

Miles said nothing for a moment, and I could see the gears turning in his head. Then he took the bottle from Jax's hand, pulled out the cork, and took a swig. "What the hell," he said, beaming, his teeth already purple.

"Yeah!" Jax slapped his palms together and uncorked another bottle. "Oh! We should play a game! Drinking Truths? Anyone up for Drinking Truths?"

"I'm in." I scooted to make a circle with the others.

"Dare I even ask what Drinking Truths is?" Lyriana asked.

"It's really simple," I explained. "We sit in a circle. One person asks a question. Then we all have to answer totally honestly, or take a drink."

"But I do not drink alcohol."

"Then you're going to be sharing a lot of truths!" Jax grinned.

Zell walked over and took a seat between me and Jax. He was still acting like nothing had happened between us. Maybe that was for the best. "What if I would like to both share a truth and also have a drink?"

Jax threw his arm around Zell's shoulders. "I love this guy. Have I ever said how much I love this guy?"

There were many truths I wanted Zell to answer. I wanted to know what had happened in his past to make him so guarded. I wanted to know why he'd come all this way, if he was just planning on abandoning us. I wanted to know what he really felt about me.

But looking around at everyone's faces, I knew tonight wasn't about that. This was, just maybe, our last time together as a group, or at the very least, as this specific group. That bond that we'd had by the cottage, as we'd held each other and buried that family, would soon change, become something else, maybe even fade away. Tonight was our chance to celebrate this group. To be the Bastard Table one last time.

"Okay! I'll start us off!" Lyriana said. "What is everyone's favorite food?"

Jax blinked. "That's not really . . . I mean, usually the questions are a little more . . ." He sighed deeply. "Peaches. I really love peaches."

The thing about Drinking Truths is that, even though you're only supposed to drink when you're skipping a question, everyone just sort of drinks the whole time anyway. So by the time we'd gone a full round, learning that Jax had once made out with a thirty-year-old minstrel and that Miles had never been skinny-dipping, I was already feeling a little bit drunk, that soft, gentle wine-warmth glowing through me.

"Okay." Jax took the bottle out of my hands. "We've had our little warm-up round. But it's time for this game to get interesting."

"Uh-oh," Miles murmured.

"My question is . . . how many people have you slept with?"

I fought back a giggle. "How many people have *you* slept with? Or can you not remember?"

"I can remember just fine, I'll have you know," Jax said, but took an obvious minute to count. "Nine. No, ten. Ten. Eleven."

"Eleven?" Lyriana gasped. "Eleven whole people?"

"Well, I'd hope there were no partial people involved," Miles said, and Zell laughed.

"Well, you know, I mean, eleven's not that many," Jax said, oddly bashful. "I know guys who have slept with way more. Eleven's just, you know, a regular number." He handed the bottle to Zell. "How about you? How many beautiful Zitochi girls have you bedded on a cavebear pelt?"

"One," Zell said.

"That's it? No details? No story?" Jax playfully pushed Zell's shoulder. "Come on, man, give us the goods!"

"The question was how many. I've answered that," Zell replied, but he sounded amused, not annoyed. He passed me the bottle, making eye contact for just a second before looking away. "Your turn."

"My turn," I said, and then, unexpectedly, froze up. The answer was zero; I was a virgin, and Jax, at least, knew that. It wasn't a big deal or anything, and it's not like there was some special reason. I just hadn't met the right guy. But, for some reason, I suddenly felt self-conscious about it. Why? Because of Zell?

I didn't know, and I didn't want to go into it, so I just tipped the bottle to my lips and took a big swig. "A lady's got her secrets," I said, and passed it to Miles. "How about you? What's your number?"

Miles glanced down at the bottle. "One."

That surprised me, and then I felt bad for being surprised. Jax obviously didn't. "For real, Boy Genius? Tell me more!"

Miles shrugged. "Her name was Alaine. Daughter of one of the scholars in Port Hammil's university. I'd spend a lot of time in the library there, where the two of us ended up talking. One thing led to another, and we were, well, together, for about six months."

"What happened?" I asked.

Miles shrugged and looked right at me, his gray eyes so big and earnest I had to look away. "She wasn't the one," he said. "Not for me."

Jax thankfully broke up the awkwardness. "Hey! We're talking about sex, not depressing breakups! Pass the bottle to the Princess and let her answer the question!"

Lyriana took the bottle, more symbolically than anything else. "The answer is zero, of course. I've never even kissed a boy."

We all turned to stare at her, even Zell. "Wait, really?" I asked.

"Well, yes," Lyriana said, as if this was totally normal. "The nobility of Lightspire prizes purity, and chastity is a part of that. As the Princess, it is doubly important for me to maintain that purity, to remain untouched and unsullied."

"Come on," Jax said. "You're bullshitting us. You've never hooked up with anyone? Not even Lord Galen Hotpants?"

Lyriana's eyebrow arched so hard it looked like it might pop off her head. "Of course not. House Reza is of far too low a station to marry with the Volaris. Besides . . . I believe Lord Reza prefers the company of men."

"Really?" Miles asked. "That guy? Huh."

"Can we go back to this whole no-kissing thing?" I asked Lyriana. "Is that, like, forever? You never get to be with a guy?"

"No, of course not," she said. "It is simply a vow until marriage. Once I am wed, I may give myself to my husband in every way."

I was still having a hard time wrapping my mind around this. Everyone knew they were more conservative out there in Lightspire, but I had no idea it went so far. "Aren't you worried?" I asked. "What if your husband is a terrible kisser? What if you guys don't match in the bedroom? What if it turns out you like girls? How would you know?"

Lyriana shot me a polite smile, the kind I'm sure she flashed in the court. "I'm reasonably confident I like men, Tillandra," she said. "And I know our customs might seem conservative or strange to you. But you have to understand, they hold real meaning to me. It's not just about my vows, or about securing the best possible suitor. It's . . . it's something I just believe in. For myself."

"How?"

"Think of it this way." She sighed. "When you get married, and you kiss your husband on your wedding day, it'll be just another kiss for you. It will probably be the thousandth time you've kissed him. The only thing different, the only thing special, is the day that you're doing it on." She looked away, and I could tell this was something she'd thought about a lot. "But for me, it'll be different. When I kiss my husband for the first time, it'll be the culmination of years and years of yearning. It'll be a moment I have dreamed about and wanted so badly for my whole life, something I have craved but never experienced, not until then, not until him. And he'll know it and I'll know it, and we'll share that knowledge, and it will make that moment between us so much more special and meaningful. It'll be the greatest gift we can offer each other." She gave a guilty smile. "I'm human, just like you. I want to be kissed, to be touched, to be held. But that's why I keep my vow of purity. For that moment."

I had no way to respond to that. "This guy you'll get married to," Jax said. "He'll probably be some hoity-toity Lightspire noble, right? Not someone you choose on your own?"

"Almost certainly," Lyriana said. Was that a hint of sadness in her voice? "In Lightspire, marriage is a matter of politics and power, not love."

"Have you ever been in love?" I asked.

Lyriana turned to me, and now she had no reply. She sat there for a moment, deliberating what to say, and then, with the most adorably naughty smile, put the bottle to her lips and took a sip.

"Ohhhhhhh!" Jax yelled, and I couldn't help but clap. "This is totally happening! We're getting the Princess drunk!"

"You most certainly are not," Lyriana said, but she was smiling. "Tell anyone of this, anyone at all, and I swear I will take back every nice thing I promised you."

The game went on, and it was great. Lyriana told us about her childhood crush on her father's Captain of the Guard, Miles rambled on about his first kiss with Alaine, and Zell talked about how guys in his Clan often wrestled in the nude (which, okay, come on). Soon enough, we'd forgotten the game entirely and were just drinking and talking and trying to make each other crack up. We polished off most of the bottles and took turns singing: I belted out "Lady Doxley's Garland," Lyriana beautifully serenaded us with "The Cant of the Titans," and we all danced around while Zell drummed on the stones and sang this rousing Zitochi drinking song. When he was done, Lyriana threw her arms around me and Jax, and her cheeks were warm and flushed. "You're my best friends." She giggled, totally tipsy. "My very, very best friends."

As fun as it was, the night eventually wound down. Miles was the first casualty, puking off the cliff face before stumbling back to his room. Lyriana excused herself, leaving for the bathroom and never coming back, and Zell simply vanished at some point. In the end, Jax and I sat alone on the platform's edge, gazing down at the valley below the cliffs, at the beautiful sky above. It reminded me of how we'd sat in Castle Waverly, waiting for the royal procession to arrive, no idea what was in store for us.

"Can I tell you something?" Jax abruptly mumbled. He had that groggy tone, the one he always had when he was half drunk and half sleepy, sentimental and prone to babbling secrets. "I know the truth. I know why you did this. I know why . . . why you're here at all."

"What're you talking about?" I asked, and I actually felt kind of sober, except for the way the whole world was bobbing up and down.

"You could've gone back to your father. You could've been his daughter. You could've had it all." His voice trembled, just a little. I could see tears in his eyes. "You did this for me. Because you knew he'd have me killed no matter what."

"Jax . . ."

He dabbed at his eyes and shook his head, and when he looked back up, he had that same goofy grin he always had, the one I loved so damn much. "It's okay. I'd do the same for you. In a heartbeat."

He turned away, looking out at the glorious vista below. "We never did get to toast Mom's memory, did we?"

"Nope."

He lifted an almost-empty wine bottle to the sky. "Here's to her."

I leaned over and gave him a hug, resting my head on his shoulder. "Here's to us."

He smiled and I smiled, and we sat there like that for a while, before wandering back up to our rooms.

TWENTY-FOUR

I couldn't sleep. Naturally.

Maybe it was the fact that I was still a little drunk. Maybe it was my messed-up sleep schedule. Maybe it was the fact that I couldn't stop thinking about Zell. Either way, I lay in my bed, staring up at the stone ceiling for a good hour before deciding that if I was going to be awake, I might as well make the most of it. I wanted to hit that bath again.

Galen had given each of us a Sunstone, and I used mine on the dimmest setting to light my way as I crept through the Nest. All my friends were asleep. The only people still up were the handful of guards, and they said nothing, standing silently at their posts as I walked by. I nodded at them and went down the long staircase to the bathing chamber's heavy wooden door. I stripped out of my nightgown at the entrance, wrapped myself in a towel, and stepped inside.

Except someone was already there.

I gasped and jerked back, before realizing that even in my

Sunstone's dim light I could make out a familiar toned frame and black hair. Zell was resting just inside the pool, the dark water up to his hips, his arms sprawled out along the pool's edge, and his head craned to the ceiling. He was definitely, totally, completely naked. I couldn't see below the water's edge, but I could see just the top curve of his pubic bone above it. My breath choked up in my throat.

"Tilla." He glanced up at me. He seemed totally unashamed, which made me feel weirdly prudish for having gasped. "Can't sleep, either?"

"Nope."

"I guess it's something we'll always have in common." There was something off about his voice. "You can join me. If you'd like."

The thought of joining a totally naked Zell in a pool was terrifying, but it was also kind of exciting, and I didn't want to back out now. Still, I was keeping my towel on. "Sure," I said, and lowered myself onto the bench next to him. My Sunstone was still very dim, and I kept it that way, letting the dark water hide our bodies. "Been here awhile?"

Zell didn't say anything. I noticed for the first time the empty wine bottle lying on its side behind him. The weirdness in his voice suddenly made sense. He was drunk. But instead of seeming happy and relaxed, he seemed on edge, like he was struggling and failing to keep up his cool front.

"Are you okay?" I asked.

He breathed deeply, his eyes shut. "No," he said quietly. "I'm not."

"What's wrong? I don't understand. It seemed like you were having fun tonight. . . ."

He shook his head. "I was. That's the problem."

"How is that a problem?"

He opened his eyes to look at me, and now I could see that whatever wall he'd been trying to put up between us was crumbling fast. He didn't say anything for a while, then finally his breathing hitched and the words slipped out, like he couldn't bear to hold them in a second longer. "Her name was Kalia."

"Her . . . the girl? The one you slept with?" Was that what this about? Was Zell this broken up over some girl back home? I hated to admit it, but I felt a jealous sting.

"Yes," Zell said. "Kalia Vale. She was the daughter of the Chief of Clan Vale, one of Clan Gaul's greatest allies. And she was betrothed to my brother."

"Oh," I said, and that jealousy turned to something else, a cold, rising dread. "Razz, you mean?"

Zell nodded. "She was beautiful and smart and had a true kindness in her. We'd been friends since childhood. We told each other our secrets, we shared our dreams, we made each other laugh. We were each other's first kiss, first love, all of it. I begged my father to let me marry her, but Razz was the older son, and we needed to secure Clan Vale's alliance. So she was made his." The words were just spilling out now, and there was no stopping them. How long had Zell kept this bottled up? Had he ever talked to anyone about it? "I swallowed my pride, and she swallowed hers. But she deserved so, so much better. I found her one morning outside my room, shivering, naked, wrapped in just a blanket. She'd defied Razz, told him she would leave him if he ever laid hands on her again. And he'd . . . he'd hurt her. Beat her. Used her." Zell's brow furrowed with rage, and hate danced in his eyes. But for once, I felt like there was no barrier between us, that he was speaking to me without holding anything back. It made my heart ache with his pain. And it scared the hell out of me. "I took her in. I swore I'd never let my brother harm her again. So the next day, I challenged him to a *tain rhel lok.*"

"A duel," I guessed.

Zell nodded. "A duel to the death. The highest challenge of a Zitochi warrior, offered before the eyes of the Gods themselves. There was no turning back. And Razz, he just laughed and accepted it. My father gathered all the Chieftains to watch. I swore the last rites. I put on my paint. I met Razz in the Hall of Gods. And when he saw my face, when he saw how angry I was, I think that was the only time he ever looked scared." Zell was starting to choke up a little, his voice scratchy and raw. "I was so angry, so Gods-damned angry. I kept thinking of the bruises on Kalia's neck, the tears in her eyes. I hated Razz so much then. I beat the hell out of him. I knocked him down, kicked his daggers away, and put my sword to his neck." Zell breathed deeply. His eyes glistened. "And I couldn't do it, Tilla. Even with how much I hated him, how much I loved Kalia, I couldn't kill my own brother. I was weak. I was a coward. I spared him." His voice was filled with disgust.

"You showed mercy, Zell," I said softly. "That's not weakness. It's strength."

"It was the greatest shame Clan Gaul had ever experienced," Zell said. "You do not show mercy in a *tain rhel lok.* Not with the Gods watching. Not before the Chieftains of all the clans. My father was furious. He beat me half to death. Broke my arm. Gave me this." He reached down and touched a long, crooked scar on his stomach. "Worse than that, he disowned me. I lost my title, my rank, my home. I became a bastard, to live forever in dishonor, trying to atone for my failure." A tear ran down Zell's cheek. "That night, Kalia told Razz that she loved me. And she would sooner join the *zhindain*, the clanless women, than ever be his wife. So he choked Kalia to death and left her body in the snow just outside my window."

"Zell . . . I—I'm . . ." I stammered. "I'm so sorry."

"He knew, you see. He knew that if anyone found out what he'd done, Clan Gaul would be shamed and sullied in the eyes of the Twelve. Kalia's father would demand all of our hands. My father would never yield. It would be war in the hall of Zhal Korso, clan against clan, bloodshed the likes of which we haven't seen in centuries." Another tear streaked down Zell's face, then another. "So I took her body, and I buried her, far away in the woods, where no one would find her. I told lies about how she was planning to flee to the South and said nothing when others called her a coward, a traitor, a runaway. Razz killed her and left her because he knew, he knew I'd cover it up for him. That was exactly what he wanted." Zell brushed his cheek, then showed me the back of his hand. The nightglass blades growing out of his knuckles sparkled darkly in the Sunstone's light, their tips looking sharper and deadlier than ever. "That's why I got these. Not just as a weapon. But as a reminder. To never show mercy. To never be weak. To never let someone hurt me like that again." He was breathing fast now, his nostrils flaring. "Every day I look at these, and all I can think about is how much I failed her!"

"Zell, please," I tried, but I was crying too, now, because finally, after all this time, he made sense. His coldness, his distance, his insistence on running—all of it was an armored front put on to battle a greater pain than any I had ever known. He had stuck with us, protected us without hesitation, because he knew exactly what would happen if he didn't. He could have left us. Instead, he chose to face his worst nightmare every time Razz got close.

I reached out and took his hand, ran my finger along the knuckle, where cold stone met warm skin. "You kept us safe with these hands," I said. "You saved us a dozen times over, kept us alive, helped us cross an entire Province. If it wasn't for you, we'd all be dead. *I'd* be dead."

"I showed weakness," Zell repeated, like he couldn't bring himself to hear me. "I killed Kalia."

"No. Razz killed Kalia. And he killed her because he's a vicious, evil piece of shit." I clutched his hand tight. "But your mercy, your kindness, isn't weakness. It's strength. It's what guides you to protect others. It's what separates you from Razz. It's the best thing about you." And then the words spilled out, like a surging river through a broken dam, because I just couldn't keep them in anymore. "It's why I love you."

He stared at me, stunned, and I couldn't believe it, but he was actually shaking.

"I'll fail you," he whispered. "I'll let you down. I'll get you killed. I can't . . . I can't . . ."

"Shhh," I whispered, and I couldn't think of anything else to say, not with words, so I lifted his hand to my lips and I kissed it, so softly, like a Lord with a Lady at a courtly dance. I pressed my lips to him, right where nightglass met flesh, and I tasted cold, hard stone and soft, warm skin. Zell inhaled sharply, his bare chest heaving, but he didn't pull away, so I kept kissing him, working my way along his hand, tenderly kissing each blade. He turned his hand around and ran his fingertip along my lips, and my heart was thundering and my cheeks were flushed.

I could feel his breath on my skin, and when I looked up to meet his eyes, they were burning with a certainty I'd never seen before. A rush of heat spread through me. More. I needed more. I lifted my face and found his lips, slow and gentle at first. I felt him ease me onto his lap and my towel slipped into the dark water as I erased the distance between us, and the kisses became deeper, more frantic, as we breathed each other in.

His hands were running through my hair, and I was clutching at the firm muscles of his back. We moved as one, melting together like wax streaking down a candle, and as he whispered my name again and again, my hands tightened around his arms and I pressed my face into the crook of his shoulder, knowing in the deepest part of my being that this moment would always, always be ours.

• • •

Afterward, we lay on the bench inside the pool's edge, my cheek pressed against his bare chest while he cradled me with one strong arm, the water lapping against our hips. We didn't say anything. We didn't have to. We just lay together, and sometimes I'd lean up and kiss him, and sometimes he'd bend down and kiss me, and he held me close and I traced my fingertips along his thigh as I listened to his heart beat in his chest. The water was cold, but he was so, so warm.

And I felt safe, and I felt right, and I felt the happiest I thought I'd ever felt in my entire life.

TWEnTY-FIVE

I WENT BACK TO MY ROOM AN HOUR LATER, BUT NOT BEFORE Zell left me with the best kiss I'd ever had. I'm not saying Lyriana was totally wrong with her special-moment thing. But this kiss was pretty damn special. Still glowing inside, I collapsed in my bed and fell into the deepest and richest sleep of my life.

I woke up hours later, and when I threw open the windows, the sky was the soft pink of sunset. I'd slept through the entire day. Again.

I lay in my bed for a while, just letting the events of last night play out over and over in my head. I had to keep forcing myself to acknowledge it hadn't been a dream.

I might have lay there for another couple of hours, just soaking up the memories, but a commotion from the courtyard roused me from bed. I peeked out the window and saw that the Nest's gates were open, and the Castle's wide, grassy courtyard was covered in a throng of people. Women, by the looks of them, from Lightspire, all wearing faint green robes with gossamer veils over their faces. Were they . . .

"The Sisters of Kaia!" Lyriana cried in my doorway, helpfully answering my question. "They're here! Even Archmatron Marlena! Come on, Tilla! You have to meet them!"

I followed after Lyriana, down the tower's winding staircase, through the sprawling Great Hall that connected all of the Nest's wings, and out the heavy wooden doors to the courtyard. Galen was there, a dour look on his face, and he was talking to one of the Sisters. She was tall, taller than him, and had a confident, refined air that told me she had to be someone in power. She turned to us as we approached, and even through the veil, I could see her emerald eyes glow with excitement.

"Novice Lyriana," she said, her voice matronly and warm. "We had all mourned your passing when the Whispers came. It is a wonder and honor to see you again."

Maybe the Lyriana I'd met back at Castle Waverly would have responded with equal decorum, but the Lyriana who'd tromped her way through the Western Province had no time for that. She ran over and grabbed the woman in a hug. "Archmatron! I am so, so happy to see you again!"

The older woman stepped back, trying to maintain some dignity, but patted Lyriana gently on the back. She had at least three Rings on each finger, green and turquoise and lavender, and they clinked together very lightly as she moved. "Your help will be greatly needed in the coming days. I fear a terrible war is coming, perhaps even more terrible than the last, and its first battle will be fought in these very lands. We must be ready to take care of the wounded, to evacuate civilians, to offer aid and sustenance."

I looked around the courtyard. There were definitely a lot of Sisters there, maybe thirty or forty, all of them standing stiff and composed, waiting, presumably, to be told what to do. If they were curious about us, their posture didn't betray it. Their Rings sparkled in the sun. I wondered how much good they could actually do, how many lives they would be able to save.

Heavy footsteps padded toward us. I turned around to see Jax stumbling into the courtyard, looking green and very, very hungover. And just behind him was Zell. For a second, I was afraid to look at him. What if he looked away? What if last night had just been a drunken mistake for him? What if when I went to kiss him, he pushed me away? What if he still just wanted to leave?

Then his deep dark eyes met mine, and he smiled, and I knew I had nothing to worry about.

"Your mission is truly noble, Archmatron," Galen said. He had this way of making you feel like he was totally sincere and lying through his teeth at the same time. "And I wouldn't dream of interfering with it. But right now I need to prepare my men for Lord Kent's arrival. And you need to go back to your camp."

The older woman turned back to Galen, confusion written all over her face. "I don't understand. Why did you summon us, then?"

Galen blinked. "Why did I what?"

"Why did you summon us?" the Archmatron repeated. "You sent a Whisper telling us to come straight here to make plans for an evacuation."

"No, I didn't," Galen said, every muscle in his body tensing at once. He spun around to the guards standing alongside the hall's door. "Something's wrong. Something's very wro—"

He was cut off by the trumpeting of horns overhead, from the Castle's watchtowers. "No!" Galen gasped, and then I heard it, suddenly deafening, the thunder of hooves, the rearing of horses spurred into action. Outside the Nest's open gates, past the courtyard, the tree line shuddered and then burst apart as a dozen men on horseback raced out, swords glinting in their hands. Their faces were hidden behind black helms, and their armor was red and gold.

Kent colors.

The trumpets overhead blared again, louder, more urgent. The guards at the gate scrambled to slam them shut, but they were too late, too slow. A volley of arrows whistled out from the tree line, and tore through them. A single shaft flew into the courtyard and caught one of the Sisters in the back of the skull.

"No!" I shouted, but I was drowned out by the noise around me, by the yells of men, by the screaming of the Sisters, by the roar of horses. A hand grabbed mine, its knuckles sharp and cold. Zell was by my side. The archers all along the castle ramparts fired back, dropping a few of my father's men, but most of their arrows hit only empty earth. The riders were moving too fast. The front line had already closed half the distance between the tree line and the gate, and more were emerging from the trees, a second row of riders followed by charging footmen.

They were going to take the castle. They were going to take us.

The Sisters around us were panicking, that refined composure lost in a second as they screamed and ran. Archmatron Marlena barked orders at them, demanding they stay calm. Jax sprang forward and grabbed Lyriana's hand. There was no sign of Miles. I looked up at Zell and found his eyes hard, ready.

"Get inside!" Galen yelled. "Run!" And yeah, that was probably a better plan than fighting an entire army on our own. We turned and sprinted as a group, racing across the wide lawn back toward the Great Hall's closed doors. The earth shook underfoot as the horses grew closer. I heard more screaming, the twang of bows, and now the clang of steel on steel. A man shrieked as he plunged off the walls, and his body hit the ground with a wet thump. Everything was so loud, it sounded like the fighting wasn't just behind me but all around me, in the Hall, on the ramparts above. But that didn't make any sense.

I didn't have time to think about it. Leading the pack, with Zell at my side and the others behind me, I lunged up the stone steps to the Great Hall, and pulled open the doors. . . .

And found Razz's grinning face, his nightglass fangs sparkling.

I pulled back with a stifled scream and threw a jab at his face. But Razz was fast, so much faster. He effortlessly grabbed my wrist and twisted it, jamming it hard against my back. I yelped, and then I saw them, the other Zitochi, his entire mercenary band, standing alongside him in the Great Hall. Their nightglass blades were out, dripping crimson. Bodies lay behind them, Galen's guardsmen, throats slit, heads crushed, chests ragged. Something warm and wet oozed over my feet. I didn't look down.

Razz shoved me in front of himself like a shield and spun me around so I was facing my friends, so I could see their faces as they realized just how screwed we were. We were trapped, with my father's men charging up on one side and Razz's thugs on the other. Galen threw up his hands, a despairing look on his face. Jax stepped protectively in front of Lyriana. Behind them, the horsemen breached the gates and rode into the courtyard, circling the Sisters and forcing them to their knees. There was still some scattered fighting, swords clanging on the distant ramparts, but the battle was over. The Lord had surrendered. The castle had been taken.

How? How the hell had this happened? How had they gotten in? How had it all gone so wrong, so fast?

Zell alone didn't surrender. He had his sword in one hand and his dagger in the other, and his eyes burned a hole through me and Razz, as he calculated any possible way to save me.

Razz was having none of it. "Drop the weapon, snow cub," he taunted. "Or your new girlfriend will find out exactly what happens to bitches who get in my way."

Zell's grip on his sword loosened. I struggled with all my might, but Razz was too strong and holding me too well. *Damn it. Damn it!* All that training, all that practice, and it hadn't made any difference.

Razz sighed with annoyance and jerked my head to the side, then pressed his nightglass fangs to my throat. I could smell his sour breath and feel the fangs' sharp prick. "Now!"

"Don't do it," I begged, but it was no use. Zell let his blades fall to the ground.

"Never change, baby brother." Razz laughed. He reared his head back, mouth agape, fangs ready. My heart thundered. I sucked in my breath. I'd failed my friends. I'd failed my brother. I was going to die. I was really going to die.

"Let her go," a stern voice commanded from the court-yard. It was the leader of the riders, a tall armored man, and he took off his helm as he hopped down from his horse. I already knew who he was, though.

I'd recognize my father's voice anywhere.

Time seemed to slow down as he approached us, striding confidently past the rows of kneeling Sisters. I'd never seen my father fully armored before. An ornate metal breastplate guarded his chest, and fine chain mail hung low over his arms. A sword was sheathed along his back, and his daggers hung at his hips. But his face was just how I remembered it, his hair neatly combed, his beard nicely groomed, his eyes as cold and resolute as ever.

He was here. My father was really here. Looking at me. Just fifteen feet away.

Saving my life.

"Let her go," he said again. "Now."

Why was he protecting me? Didn't he want me dead? Was he going to kill me himself? Or did he actually plan on spar-ing me? Was it possible he really did care?

Why the hell was I still thinking like this?

Razz grumbled but shoved me forward, into the ranks of Jax and Zell. I pulled myself behind them, and as I looked at my father I felt way too many emotions at once, relief and fear and gratitude and something else, something I was afraid was still love. "I don't see why we can't just kill them..." Razz said.

"I made a promise," my father replied, and he refused to meet my gaze.

"A promise?" I forced out. I wanted to scream. "A promise to who?"

My father glanced over his shoulder. Two riders emerged from the trees, cantering slowly toward us now that the combat had stopped. One was a woman, and even at this distance, I could tell it was Lady Hampstedt, her hair up in a bun behind her head, her signature arrogant posture. And riding next to her was . . .

No.

No no no no no.

"To Miles Hampstedt," my father said. "Heir to House Hampstedt and as of this morning, newly legitimized son of Lady Robin. He made us swear to spare your lives."

"And in exchange, that soft little nerd told us everything," Razz boasted. "The Sisters. The tunnels. Everything we needed."

Whatever adrenaline I had left drained out of me. I crumpled to my knees. The world throbbed at the edges of my vision. I felt like I was going to pass out. This was too much. It was just too much.

No one spoke as Miles rode into the courtyard, or as he climbed off his horse and walked toward us. I think we just couldn't believe it. He wore a new tunic, all black, and had the golden owl of House Hampstedt pinned to his chest. My brain raced with all the possibilities. Maybe this was all part of his plan. Maybe my father was trying to trick me. Maybe this would all work out.

Then I saw his face. His eyes looked angry and broken,

like something deep inside him had shattered. His mouth was clenched in a furious line, and his eyebrows blazed down in deep, angry furrows.

He'd sold us out.

Miles had actually sold us out.

"You piece of shit!" Jax howled, and lunged forward. Razz kicked him in the back of the leg before he could go anywhere, and Jax went sprawling out into the courtyard, where two of my father's men tackled him to the ground. "You traitorous rat piece of shit!"

"I did what I had to do," Miles said coldly. "For my House. For the West."

How was this happening? I'd trusted Miles. I'd believed in him. After everything we'd done, everything we'd been through, was he seriously selling us all out just so he could get back in his mother's good graces?

Then he walked toward me, his eyes burning, and I realized, no, that wasn't it at all. This wasn't about his House. This was personal. He grabbed me by the chin and jerked my face up, hard, so I was looking right into his livid eyes. "I saw you," he hissed, angrier than I'd ever seen anyone. "With *him*. In the pool. With the savage!"

No. It couldn't be. *That* was what this was about? What Miles was willing to sell us all out for? This was all about his stupid crush?

"Miles," I whispered, "how could you do this to us? We're your friends. We care about you."

"If you cared about me, you wouldn't have screwed Zell!" Miles yelled, and holy shit, something in him *had* completely snapped. He was like a child throwing a tantrum, totally out of control. Had this been in him all along? Had the promise of my love been the only thing keeping him loyal? He shoved me down onto my back and slammed his hands against the wall, howling in fury. "You said this wasn't the right time! That we'd talk later! But all along, you just wanted him! *Him!* How could you do this to me? I saved your life, Tilla! I loved you first! You were supposed to be mine!"

"I was never going to be yours," I whispered back.

Miles glowered at me, breathing hard, then spun around. "You still will be. You'll see."

He stormed away. I tried to pull myself up, but my father flicked his hand in the air, gesturing to his men. "Wait—" I said, and then one of them flipped his sword around and cracked me across the head with its hard wooden pommel, and the darkness swallowed me before I even hit the ground.

TWENTY-SIX

YOU KNOW THAT FEELING WHEN YOU WAKE UP IN A NEW place, and you're confused because you don't know where you are? Imagine that, except you're on a hard floor in a cold room, and your head is throbbing from the blow you took, and, oh yeah, one of your best friends just horribly sold you out.

It's not a great feeling.

I awoke with a start only to immediately be jerked back by a sharp pain in my wrists. Thick iron manacles bound my hands together, and a short chain hooked them into the wall behind me. I was in a small stone room with a single barred door, lit only by a pair of torches mounted in the walls. Through a slit of a window, I could see the night sky, which meant we were in a tower of some kind. Jax and Zell sat on opposite sides of me, both chained to the same wall, and Lyriana was across the room. Her hands looked tiny in the heavy manacles, and then I realized why: all her Rings were gone. She was powerless. We weren't going to magic our way out of this.

"Well, shit," I said.

Jax turned to me. He had a big purple bruise on his jawline and a busted lip. I guessed he'd taken more of a beating than I had. "Yup. That about covers it."

I closed my eyes. I had no idea how long I'd been out. My head hurt. But my heart ached more. "I don't suppose you guys have come up with any great escape plan?"

"Not unless Lyriana can find a way to do magic without any Rings," Jax said.

That seemed like a joke, but Lyriana's eyes darted around, like she was struggling with a secret. "There are some circumstances where that might happen." Lyriana jerked her chained hands, showing that she could barely move them at all. "But even without Rings, I'd still need my hands free to do the forms."

I looked over at Zell, but he didn't look back. He was just staring straight ahead, totally still, his gaze hard and focused on nothing at all. "I failed you," he said softly. "I should have seen this coming. I let my guard down, and I failed you all."

I wanted to reach out and touch him, but the chain was too short. "Zell, no. None of us could have seen this coming." I tried to figure out what had happened. Miles must have walked in on me and Zell in the baths, sometime during the night. And then what? He'd snuck out, gotten on his horse, and rode off into the distance, galloping until he got to my father's camp? Had he spent the whole time thinking about what he was going to say, the best way to betray us?

Was he really willing to throw away everything we'd done just because I dared to sleep with someone else?

It was unthinkable, unbearable, but honestly, it made a horrible kind of sense. Miles had never cared about the mages or the war or even Lyriana. He'd just cared about me. He'd gone along with this whole plan because I'd wanted to, and everything he'd done had been to protect me, to get closer to me. I had been the only thing keeping him from running back to his mother.

And then I'd gone and broken his stupid heart.

"Don't despair," Lyriana said, and even she sounded like she was forcing it. "We've survived worse situations. We'll survive this, too."

I was about to tell her I wished I had her optimism, when a rattling sound came from the prison door. I pulled back against the wall, and next to me Jax jerked up his manacles to wield as weapons. I don't know who we were expecting. A torturer, maybe, or a leather-masked executioner?

The door swung open, and Miles walked in. Worst option of all.

He was still wearing that impeccable black tunic with the obnoxious golden owl pinned to his chest. I suspected it'd be months until he took it off. There was a confidence in his stride that hadn't been there before, almost a bit of a swagger. It pissed me off something awful.

Miles looked around the room, at how far we'd all pulled away from him, even Lyriana. "Come on, guys," he said, and I couldn't believe how betrayed he sounded. "I'm not going to hurt *you*."

I wondered at his weird emphasis, and then he gestured

behind him. Two guards, House Hampstedt men by their winged helms, came in, dragging a third man behind them. Galen. His face was a mess of dried blood and puffy bruises, his eyes so swollen I doubted he could see out of them. I can't say I liked the guy much, but I hated seeing him like this.

He didn't say anything as the guards dragged him across the floor, shoved him against the wall next to Lyriana, and clamped his wrists into the spare set of chains dangling there. I thought he might be unconscious, but I caught a glimpse of his eyes through those narrow, puffy slits. He looked *pissed*.

We all were. "Hey, traitor. I've got a hell of a secret for you," Jax growled. "Why don't you come close and I'll tell you."

Miles sighed. "Look. I'm not happy about how this played out. You probably don't believe me, but it honestly upsets me to see you all like this. I was hoping you'd surrender peacefully. But it is what it is." He gestured again to his guards, sending them out of the room, then turned to look right at me. "Don't worry, though. This is just temporary, I promise. Soon the mages will be taken care of, and this will all be over. You won't have to be in this tower for very long."

I'd been trying to hold back the commentary, but now I just couldn't help myself. "Seriously? What exactly do you think our parents are going to do to us?"

"I've got it all planned out," Miles said. "I made sure my terms of surrender were very clear. None of you are to be harmed. Not even . . . not even the Zitochi."

"And what is to become of me?" Zell asked.

"You'll be returned to the custody of your father so he may do with you as he sees fit," Miles said, unable to hide a certain nasty satisfaction. "Lord Reza and the Princess will be held as high-value hostages, to be ransomed back to Lightspire when the time is right. And Tilla and Jax, you'll be taken to Castle Waverly, where you'll live as Lord Kent's wards. You won't be able to leave the castle, of course, but other than that, things will go back to exactly how they were. And once this war is over, if you've proven your loyalty to the West, you'll be pardoned of your crimes and granted your freedom." He gave a small shrug. "It's a great deal. The best any of us could have hoped for."

"I don't want a great deal," Lyriana scowled. "I want to prevent a war!"

Miles rolled his eyes. "Oh please, Princess. You can bullshit the others, but you can't bullshit me. There was always going to be a war, if not today, then a month from now. We both know it's going to happen. You just want to make sure your side wins. Isn't that right, Lord Reza?"

Galen craned his head up toward Miles and spat out a tooth. It left a long, bloody trail on the floor.

"I rest my case." Miles turned to look at me. "We forgot who we were, Tilla. But I remember now. I'm a Hampstedt. I'm a Westerner. And I'm not going to sell out my family and my people for scraps from the table of some Lightspire King!"

I didn't know which was scarier: the idea that Miles had so quickly embraced his family's ideology, or the possibility he'd just been swallowing it down to woo me. I had to hope it was the first. "Miles, listen to me. It's not too late. Let us out of here. We can still meet up with the mages and try to make this right."

Miles scoffed. "The mages are riding straight into an

ambush. This time tomorrow, they'll be dead, and the West will be on its path toward freedom."

Jax laughed. "Uh, yeah, except the mages know all about the ambush. Lord Reza warned them, remember? No way they're going to fall into your trap."

"You really are dumber than a bag of bricks, aren't you, Jax?" Miles said. "The mages know all about Lord Kent's first plan, ambushing them during the banquet he had Lord Reza set up. Which is why we're going to ambush them when they ride through Pioneer's Pass instead."

The room was silent, and Miles's smug smile was unbearable. "What are you talking about?" I demanded. "How are you going to ambush three companies of mages?"

"With a hundred mage-killer bombs, strapped to arrows, raining down on them as they pass through the valley's narrowest point," Miles casually explained, and in that second, he sounded *exactly* like his mother. "Why do you think we needed to take those Sisters of Kaia alive? Every one of them is a stack of mage-killers just waiting to get made!"

Lyriana gasped. I felt sick. "You piece of shit," I muttered. "You heard your mom explain how they made those things! Those Sisters . . . those poor women . . . You're going to let your mother drug them and torture them to death? All so she can kill *more* people?"

Miles looked away. Was that, maybe, a flicker of guilt? "It's . . . a necessary evil."

"I saw it," Galen said, his voice scratchy and raw. "They've turned the Great Hall into a torture chamber, and they're going through the Sisters one by one. It's unspeakable."

"Wars have casualties," Miles said. "How many Westerners

died last time around? How many more will your mages kill?"

He really was this far gone. "Who the hell are you, Miles? People are dead because of you! Those innocent women are being murdered! How could you do this? How could you betray us like this?"

A vein in Miles's forehead pulsed, and his nostrils flared. I'd struck a nerve. "How could . . . how could I betray you? How could *I* betray *you*?" He walked forward, shaking a finger, and this was the other Miles now, the one who had grabbed me back in the hallway, the one who scared me more than Razz. "You betrayed me, Tilla! You betrayed *me*!"

"How? Because I was promised to you? By our parents?"

Miles's eyes were wild, his voice fast and frantic. "When we kissed, back in that grove, you said we just needed to get to safety, and then we'd talk. There was an implication there that you felt the same way. Don't deny it!"

I glanced away, a little out of guilt but mostly because I couldn't keep looking at him. He wasn't totally wrong. I could have been more honest with him. I could have had the hard talk. And maybe I did let him walk away thinking there was more of a chance than there was. But did that in any way justify this? Was any of this even close to what I, what we, deserved?

"When you told me you needed more time, I listened." Miles jabbed his finger in my face like a dagger. "I respected you. I was a perfect gentleman. And then you . . . you choose Zell? A Zitochi murderer?" Miles turned away, and the bitter resentment just oozed out of his voice. "Why? Because he's so much better looking than I am? Because he's got those dreamy eyes and those perfect abs? Well, what the hell am I supposed to do about that? What can I even begin to do about that? I saved your life, Tilla! I tackled a mercenary for you! I did so much, and still, still . . . *him*?"

I closed my eyes. "I can't deal with this, Miles. Not now. And sure as hell not shackled in a tower. If you wanted to talk to me like a person, like a friend, you could have. But that chance is gone."

"Actually, it isn't." Miles ran his hands along his shaved head, like he had done back when he'd had hair. "When I saw you with Zell, it felt like you'd ripped my heart out through my throat. I've never been more upset. I rode off, no idea what I was doing. I honestly thought about just throwing myself off one of the cliffs."

"Shoulda done that," Jax grumbled.

"And then I realized this just didn't make sense. The Tilla I know, the Tilla I loved, wouldn't hurt me like that. That just wasn't her."

"But it is me, Miles," I pleaded. "The *Tilla that you know* is this weird, elaborate fantasy you've built up over the years, because you thought we'd be getting married." Jax cocked an eyebrow at that. "You don't love me. You love an idea of me. But this is who I am. And Zell is who I really choose."

"No. No. You're wrong. You're confused," Miles said with the creepy reassuring quality of someone talking to themselves. "This whole thing, with your father and what we saw and then the Dolan brothers . . . it's messed you up. Tangled your mind. Made you hysterical. What you're saying, what you're doing, it just doesn't make any sense."

"Sense? What sense is there in betraying your friends?"

Miles acted like he hadn't heard me. "Just think about it.

Use your head. If we ally ourselves with our parents, we'll be better off than we ever could be in Lightspire. Their revolution is going to succeed. The West will be free, your father will be King, and we'll both be nobles sitting on the highest court in the Kingdom. You'd give all that up to be . . . what?" He gestured his hand around the cell, at Zell, at Jax. "Queen of the bastards?"

"I don't want to be the queen of anything," I growled.

"And that's something only a deluded person would say." Miles's face had never looked more punchable. "That's why I'm not mad anymore, Tilla. I forgive you."

And holy shit, wow, I didn't think it'd be possible for Miles to make me angrier with him, but there he went and did it. It was bad enough to paint me as some kind of betrayer. But to act like I was crazy, like my choices weren't my own, like he knew me so much better than I knew myself? "You forgive me? Are you serious?"

"I am," he said. "And when we get back to Castle Waverly, you'll see. You'll remember. Everything will go back to how it was."

"How it . . ." I repeated, and then I understood what he was implying and I actually had to fight back the urge to lunge at him. "No. No way in hell. You don't still expect us to get married, do you?"

Miles turned away. Now he couldn't look at me. "You'll see. You'll remember."

"No, I will not see!" I yelled. Maybe when he'd walked into this room, I'd had a glimmer of pity for him, the tiniest part of me that still felt bad for what he'd been through. Not anymore. All I felt was burning, pulsing, white-hot anger. I wanted to hurt him. I wanted to hurt him so bad. "Let me make one thing crystal clear, Miles. I don't care if you're Lord of House Hampstedt or King of Noveris. If you drag me down the altar, I will kick and spit and scream the whole way. And if you pull me into your bed, I will slit your throat the second you're asleep." I couldn't see his face, but I could see his shoulders shuddering. *Good.* "Listen to me very clearly, Miles. I will never want you. And I will never, ever love you."

Miles stood there for a while, silent, trembling, and I almost wondered if he was going to spin around and hit me or something. But he just took a deep breath and collected himself. "The real Tilla would never say something so horrible," he said firmly, reassuring himself more than talking to me. "You'll remember who you are. You'll see. We'll fix this. We'll fix it all."

He stalked out of the room, and his guardsmen followed, pulling the door shut. The latch slid loudly into place on the other side.

I yelled and thrashed around, kicking my feet out and slamming my manacles onto the ground. It hurt. I didn't care.

"Tilla, it's . . . it's okay," Lyriana tried. "You'll be okay."

"No. I won't," I said. I closed my eyes, took a deep breath, and held it in my lungs for a count of ten. One . . . two . . . I let it out, too angry to keep going. "Shit! If I had just been a little more honest with him, if I had just told him how I really felt, then none of this would have happened!"

"No," Zell said. He stared at the door, a distant look on his face. He was armoring up, putting on that hardened exterior. I wished he wouldn't, but how could I possibly tell him not to? "This isn't your fault. Miles made his choices. He is who he is.

291

Who he always was and will be." He narrowed his gaze. "Lots of men have their hearts broken. Most of them don't betray their friends as a result."

I wanted so badly to be in his arms again, to feel his lips and his warmth. How the hell could Miles take the best moment of my life and turn it into something so shameful and horrible? "What are we going to do?"

"For starters, we're going to escape," Galen said, and we all turned to stare at him. "You. Stable hand. Feel around in the wall behind your right ear. There should be a tiny crack between two of the bricks."

"Uh . . ." Jax said, but he did as he was told. He craned his hand up and rooted around there for a while, and then his eyes went wide. He pulled his hand back, and lying in the center of his big palm was a thin metal pin. A lock pick. "Son of a . . ."

"Here's a tip if you're ever taking a castle," Galen said. "Don't lock a Lord in his own tower. You know how to use that thing, stable hand?"

Jax grinned at me. "Remember when I was twelve and wanted to be a master thief? Lock-picking is pretty much the only useful skill I got out of that."

"I seem to recall you being pretty good at pinching peaches off fruit stands." I smiled back. Even now, Jax somehow had the power to make me feel better. "Didn't you want us to call you the Silky Phantom?"

Jax slid the pin into the keyhole on his manacle and began delicately twisting it around, his tongue poking out in concentration. "It was the Velvet Phantom. And you really didn't have to share that with the group."

Lyriana giggled. I turned to Zell, but he was deep in concentration. "So Jax will free himself, and then us," he thought out loud. "I've been listening to the footfalls outside the door, and my guess is there are two guards, maybe three. We can lure them in by claiming the Princess is ill, and then I can take them. Then what?"

"Got it!" Jax exclaimed, jerking his hands up. His manacles fell to the floor with a metallic clatter. I figured he'd free Zell next, or Galen, but he ran over to Lyriana and gently took her hands in his. "I've got you, Your Majesty. Let's get you out of those things."

Lyriana glanced down. "Thank you."

"Anytime." Jax slid the pin into her manacles. "Just gotta feel around until I find the mechanism. . . ."

"No!" Zell shot up sharply. "Get back now! I hear footsteps!"

Ugh! It had to be Miles, probably coming back to make me even angrier. Jax jumped away in a hurry, leaving the hairpin still in Lyriana's manacles, and scurried back to his part of the room. He slid against the wall and sat down, pulling his hands and his chain underneath him. It looked like an incredibly awkward way to sit, but you couldn't see his free wrists or his opened manacles. I hoped that was good enough.

The latch on the other side of the door rattled and slid aside.

"Miles, I swear, if you've come back to talk to me . . ." I grumbled, and then the door swung open, and my words turned into a gasp.

"Oh, I'm not Miles." Razz stepped into the room and

quietly shut the door behind him. "And I definitely haven't come here to talk." He turned to where Lyriana was lying, and he grinned, poking at his fangs with the tip of his tongue. "I came here to play."

I pressed my back against the wall. Lyriana shrieked and fell onto her side. Zell alone sprang forward, as if trying to break his manacles free from the wall. "Razz! Fight me, you coward! Let's finish this now!"

Razz let out an exaggerated sigh. "You had your chance to finish this with honor. And you blew it at the *tain rhel lok*. Now you get to sit there and watch me have my fun." On the ground, Lyriana had crawled back as far as her chain would let her, but Razz walked toward her, slowly, deliberately, obviously enjoying how scared she was. That sick son of a bitch! I tugged against my manacles, begging them to break, but they held firm. "Back in Zhal Korso, Father promised me I'd get to kill a castle-rat Princess. And you idiots took that away from me."

"She's Lord Kent's most valuable hostage, and he needs her alive!" I tried desperately. "If you kill her, you're ordering your own execution."

"Don't you worry, bastard. I'm not going to kill her." Razz had walked all the way up to Lyriana's gasping, trembling form. He hunkered down in a squat next to her and grabbed her chin in one gloved hand, turning her face around so she was staring right at him. "I won't even leave a mark."

With a roar, Jax lunged up from the ground and charged across the room, his manacles flying away behind him. Razz spun around and for one tiny moment was too surprised to react. That moment was all Jax needed. He barreled into

Razz with his shoulder and slammed him into the hard stone wall. Razz let out a choked wheeze as the impact knocked the breath out of him. Lyriana scrambled away, pulling herself as far in the other direction as she could go.

"Get him, Jax!" I shouted as Jax started punching Razz once, twice, right in the face. On the third punch, though, Razz snapped to his senses and jerked his head aside. Jax's fist swung right into the wall. He hissed in pain and stumbled back, clutching his hand, crimson trickling out between his fingers. Moving fast, way too fast, Razz spun one of his curved daggers out of his sheath and plunged it straight at Jax's heart.

I fought back a scream.

But Jax caught Razz's wrist with one hand, stopping the point of the dagger barely an inch from his chest. Razz growled and shoved harder, pushing the dagger with both hands, but Jax held firm, and the two men stood there, locked, sweating and gritting their teeth. They turned around, still shoving, and now Jax's back was to me and I could barely see what was going on. My heart was thundering. Blood roared in my ears. Razz was a brutal warrior who'd spent his life training for moments just like this.

But Jax was strong as a damn ox.

With a roar of his own, Jax pulled back his head and then smashed it forward, hitting Razz right in the face with a devastating head-butt. Razz's nose shattered with a loud crack. The Zitochi staggered back, blood trickling down his lips, and Jax spun around and hit him with the single hardest uppercut I'd ever seen in my life. Razz was lifted clear off his feet and flew across the room, and the back of his head hit the wall with a wet thump. He crumpled to the ground and lay there, knocked clean out.

Lyriana cried out in relief. I let out a whoop of my own, grinning from ear to ear.

Then Jax turned around slowly, with a stumble, and my joy turned to horror. The front of his tunic was soaked red. Jutting out of his chest, just below his heart, was a dagger's hilt. Razz's second blade. The one he must have drawn when Jax went for the head-butt.

"Shit," Jax whispered, and collapsed to the floor.

"No!" I screamed, and pulled forward, tearing my wrists against the manacles. I looked to Zell for help, but his grim expression said everything I didn't want to hear. "No!"

Lyriana frantically twisted the hairpin around and, with a flick of her wrists, threw off her manacles. She slid forward to where Jax was lying and pulled his head up, resting it in her lap. "Jax," she begged. "Jax, no. Stay with me. Please, please stay with me."

All the color had drained from Jax's face. His eyes were distant, unable to focus. He was going fast. "I . . . I . . ." he tried weakly, his lips barely moving. "I don't want to die. I don't want to die here. Please. I don't want to die." And the fear in his voice was like a fist crushing my heart because he couldn't die, not my big brother. He couldn't die scared and begging and broken on the floor. It couldn't end like this.

"I don't want to die," Jax whispered, already growing faint.

Lyriana cradled him in her lap, stroking his hair, and then she leaned down and kissed him. This wasn't a gentle kiss between friends. This was a kiss of passion, loving, tender, lingering, the kiss she'd saved her whole life, the kind of kiss you never forget. She held him there and she kissed him so deeply, and when she pulled away, his face wasn't scared or pained, but at peace. He looked up into Lyriana's eyes and his mouth gave the slightest hint of a smile, and this was the Jax I knew, the Jax I'd grown up with, the Jax who couldn't imagine a better way to go out than kissing a Princess.

"I love you," she whispered.

"Love," he murmured. He went still, his eyes fixed, staring up at Lyriana. He looked at peace.

And he died.

I clutched my hand over my mouth and made a horrible sound, part scream and part gasp and part retch. I couldn't see because my eyes were burning. The world trembled and shook. My stomach roiled. This couldn't be happening. But it was. My brother. My rock. My best friend.

You know how they say your life flashes before your eyes when you die? Well, mine flashed before my eyes right then. Not the life I'd lived. But the life I wouldn't get to live. The life where Jax and I made it to Lightspire together. The life where we got to settle down and explore the city and joke around, like we always had. The life where he went to my wedding, and I went to his, and our kids played together while we sat back with a glass of wine. The life I'd always taken for granted. It was gone now, just like that, washed away like a chalk drawing in the rain.

Lyriana gave a choked sob. "Tilla, I'm sorry. I'm so sorry."

"You will be," Razz replied.

He was conscious, somehow, back on his feet at the far end of the room. The lower half of his face was a bloody mess, and his nose was bent right in the middle. His right hand held a curved dagger, its razor-sharp tip glinting in the light. All of his sadistic swagger was gone. What was left was murderous rage. "You have no idea how badly you've screwed up. I wasn't going to kill any of you. Just make you beg. But now? Now this is an escape attempt. Now I'd be in the right to do whatever I w—"

He was interrupted by Lyriana, who spun toward him with a howl of utter fury, a howl that turned into a guttural, unearthly roar. The walls buckled. The air crackled electric. The smell of copper and wet earth flooded my nose. Lyriana's hands were free now, and she jerked them up and Razz jerked up with them, Lifting clean off his feet and up into the air. He hung there, legs twitching, arms locked in place, like some kind of ghastly marionette.

"You killed him," Lyriana growled. Her eyes were burning a pure gold, the pupils gone entirely. Rivulets of molten light streaked through her hair. The air around her wavered and twisted, like hot stone on a summer day. "You killed him!"

"How are you doing this, witch?" Razz rasped out. His eyes were wide, his lip trembling. He was actually scared. "We took your Rings!"

"My Rings?" Lyriana laughed, a cruel, hard laugh that shook the walls and sent dust billowing into the air. "Rings are conduits. They channel magic, focus it, turn willpower into action. Common mages need Rings to do anything. But true-blood mages like me? We just wear them so people underestimate the power we hold in our hands." Lyriana twisted both hands in a circle, the gesture I knew meant Grow. "This power."

"Witch!" Razz managed to get out, and there was a strange and horrible crackling sound, and his head jerked backward. Thin black tendrils twisted under his skin, snaking up from his fangs and toward his eyes.

Nightglass was a living metal, after all. That meant it could grow.

And Lyriana was Growing it right into his skull.

"My name is not 'Witch.'" Lyriana twisted her hands again, and the tendrils shot up farther, burrowing into Razz's head. A few sharp thorns broke the skin, pricking out through his cheeks like saplings through dirt. "I am Lyriana Ellaria Volaris! Princess of Noveris and Heir to the Throne! The blood of Titans runs in my veins!" She twisted again, and now I could see the tendrils burrowing up through the whites of Razz's eyes as he gurgled and twitched. "My Rings aren't magic."

She clenched both hands into fists and a massive nightglass tusk burst out the back of Razz's skull.

"*I'm* magic."

Lyriana dropped her hands. The burning golden glow faded from her eyes. The air came back into the room with a rush, and Razz's broken corpse fell to the ground, hitting the stone with a metallic clang.

We all sat in stunned silence, even Zell.

"You broke your vow," I whispered at last.

"To hell with my vow." Lyriana turned around and walked toward us. She wasn't the terrifying glowing being of Heartmagic that had killed Razz, but she wasn't herself, either, the sweet girl who wouldn't even hurt a skarrling. She never would be again.

She knelt down and opened my manacles, then Zell's,

then Galen's. Even though my legs didn't want to move, even though I wanted so badly to pretend it wasn't there, I forced myself to walk to Jax's body. There was no pain on his face, just that tiny smile he'd had when he'd gone. I knelt down next to him and pressed my hand to his cheek, which was already going cold, and I ran my palm along his face and closed his eyes. I wanted to hear his laugh. I wanted to see him grin. I wanted him to make a stupid joke or play some dumb game or grab me up in one of those big hugs that always made me feel so safe.

How could he be dead? How could the world go on without Jax in it?

I couldn't move. I couldn't breathe. My chest was collapsing. My breath was ragged. My hands dug into the ground, nails bleeding. The pain I was feeling was worse than anything I'd ever felt, worse than anything I'd thought I could feel. I didn't even want to escape. I didn't want to live.

A firm hand took my shoulder. Zell. He knelt down by my side and wrapped his arms around me and held me firmly, strongly. I turned and buried my face into his shoulder, and he held me as I cried harder than I'd ever cried.

Maybe a second passed. Maybe an hour. Zell leaned in close, his lips against my ear, and whispered, "We have to go now. We have to move. We have to live." I felt a droplet hit my shoulder, and when I looked up, Zell had tears in his eyes, too. "For Jax."

"For Jax." I took a deep breath and wiped the tears from my eyes. It took every ounce of willpower I had, but I took that pain and I shoved it down, deep down, so deep I couldn't feel it. This pain could wait. It had to wait.

I took Zell's arm and forced myself to my feet. Galen and Lyriana were on the other side of the room. Galen's face was unreadable, in part because it was so mangled, and Lyriana's was all rage. I guess that was what she did with her pain.

"We're at the top of the Eastern Keep," Galen said. "Once we're out, I can get us through the Servants' Quarters to a stockroom that leads to the stables. We can take a back trail and tear down the mountain, and if we're lucky, we'll cut the mages off before they get to the Pass."

I looked down at Jax. I looked at his calm face, at his limp hands, at the slick hole in his chest. And I felt a sudden, powerful, all-encompassing certainty. I felt *willstruck*.

"No," I said to Galen, and everyone turned to stare at me. "You can run if you want. But if we all go, we're leaving those thirty Sisters of Kaia to be tortured to death. And that's not something I can live with. I'm staying, and I'm fighting."

"Me too," Lyriana said, and I got the feeling she was relieved I'd spoken first. "They're my Sisters. I'm not going to leave them to die."

Zell just nodded and took my hand. That was enough.

Galen's mouth opened and shut wordlessly for a moment. "I understand you've been through a lot," he said at last. "But what you're describing is madness. Suicide. I was just down there in the Great Hall. There's at least a dozen Zitochi there, armed to the teeth."

"We can take them," Zell said. "We've got a mage on our side."

"And if you fail?"

"Then we die doing the right thing." I glanced down at Jax. "There's worse fates than that."

Galen rubbed the bridge of his nose between two fingers. "It's not that simple. This isn't just about you or those Sisters. Right now we have the element of surprise. If we can warn the mages in time, we can spring a counterambush, take out your father's men, and—"

"I don't care," I said, and I felt my hand clench into a fist. Galen and my father were exactly the same, obsessed with this game, with winning, unable to see past their crusades to the damage they were doing. I thought of that statue Jax and I had found in the creek, that forever-screaming victim of the *last* war. Jax had wondered if we were on the right side, but what I was just starting to get was that there was no right side. There were just the people in the castles barking orders, and people on the ground getting killed.

"You can't not care," Galen insisted.

"Well, I don't. I'm sick of ambushes and counterambushes and schemes and plots and all of your bullshit. I don't care who wins the war, because at the rate we're going, there'll be another one tomorrow, and another one after that. Here's what I care about. Lyriana. Zell. The thirty innocent women chained up in the Great Hall, waiting to be slaughtered. I'll fight for them. And that's it."

Galen stood there, speechless. I could see the gears in his head whirring as he tried to figure out how to change my mind . . . and I could see the moment when he realized he couldn't. "Titans' breath," he cursed. "You're a lunatic, just like your father. And you're going to get me killed."

"You'll fight with us?" Lyriana asked.

Galen sighed. "You're the Princess of Noveris. I can't well just let you die, can I? Yes. I'll fight with you. And if your father asks, your bastard friends forced me to do it at knifepoint."

"That was my next plan," I said, and turned toward the tower's door. A part of me wanted to kneel back down and touch Jax again, to kiss his cold face one last time. But I knew if I did, it might give the pain strength, might test this resolve. Right now this resolve was the only thing I had. I had to leave him here. I had to say good-bye.

I cracked my knuckles. "Let's go."

Zell took the guards outside the door just as easily as he'd predicted, dropping one with a nightglass jab and the other with a chokehold. We armed ourselves with what they were carrying: Zell took a sword and sheath, slinging it across his back, and Galen and I each took a dagger. Lyriana didn't pick any weapons up, not that she needed any; hell, as it turned out, she didn't even need her Rings. I had a library's worth of questions about that, but they would have to wait. For now, I was just grateful to have her on my side.

We made our way down the tower, creeping along a winding staircase. I'd worried we'd have to fight our way through an army of guards, but the place was emptier than it had been when we'd been hiding out here. Most of my father's men were probably at Pioneer's Pass, preparing their ambush.

Was Miles still here, I wondered, holed up in his room, or had he ridden out after his little tantrum? Just thinking about him got me seeing red. It was his fault all this had happened. It was his fault Jax was dead. And if I saw him again, I'd . . . I'd . . .

Zell reached out and pressed his hand lightly against the small of my back. *Stay calm*, he said without saying it. *Stay focused.*

I did.

We made our way around a corner to the heavy wooden double doors that led to the Great Hall. They were shut, but I could hear sounds through them: padding footsteps, the clink and clank of metal, the crackle of flame . . . and a choked, weak sound that might well have been a muffled scream.

I looked around, at Zell, and Galen, and Lyriana, met their eyes, made sure they all looked ready. Zell and Galen drew their blades. I reached down, wrapped my hand around the hilt of my dagger.

"Let's do this," I said.

Zell threw open the doors.

TWENTY-SEVEN

THE FIRST THING I SAW WAS A SISTER.

She was young, maybe a little older than me, and without her veil I could make out smooth brown skin and a shaved head. She sat strapped to a chair with several tight leather bands, a knotted rope wrapped around her mouth as a gag. Her arms were outstretched, clamped to the chair's armrests, and the Rings on her fingers were pulsing hot with magical energy, flickering stormy purple and sizzling red, just like that fragment in the mage-killer I'd seen back at Whitesand Beach. Her chest was ripped up with long, horizontal cuts, and several fresh burns glistened on her bare shoulders. But what really caught my gaze were her eyes. They were wide and vacant, all white, like they'd been permanently rolled up into her head. The mind-breaking drug, in action. It was way more horrible than I'd imagined, and I'd imagined it pretty damn horrible.

One of Razz's mercenaries stood next to her, an older man with white hair and heavy jowls. He held a poker in one hand, its tip glowing red. Behind him, throughout the hall, were at least ten other mercenaries sharpening weapons and drinking wine out of big clay jugs. The long tables had been stripped of food and were covered in knives, axes, and other sharp, pointy things, as if you'd get bored torturing with just one. At the hall's far end, by the open doors to the courtyard, I could make out the rest of the Sisters, or what was left of them. Fifteen women, maybe twenty, sat on their knees, arms bound behind their backs, gags in their mouths. They looked up in astonishment at the sight of us.

The mercenaries looked up, too, though it wasn't astonishment on their faces. They bolted out of their seats as we entered, fumbling for their weapons. The older one torturing the Sister, his beard stained purple from wine, actually dropped his poker in surprise. I decided I'd go for him first.

"Impressive," a voice boomed across the hall. A hulking figure stepped into the hall from the courtyard, standing two heads taller than any man there. He was shirtless, and his tattooed pecs were bigger than my head. Each massive hand held an enormous ax, their nightglass blades sharpened to a razor tip.

Grezza Gaul. The Chief of Clans. Zell's father.

Of course he was here. Because my luck couldn't get any worse, right?

Grezza didn't look drunk, unlike the others, but he'd probably have to drink a barrel of wine just to get a buzz. He looked right past me and glowered at Zell. "Have you finally decided to face me, boy?" he demanded.

Zell strode forward and leveled his sword at his father. "Drop your axes. Surrender. And we'll let you live."

Grezza laughed, a thunderous boom. "I'll admit this, bastard. You don't give up. If only you had some balls to back it up, maybe you'd be—"

"Razz is dead," Zell said coldly. "You're running out of sons."

Grezza stopped, stunned. Then he let out a bellow that shook the walls, and charged forward, and the room exploded into violence.

Grezza crossed the room in ten gigantic strides and swung his axes down in vertical arcs, like he was hammering a giant nail into the earth. Zell jerked back, just barely dodging the attack, and the axes hit the ground with a shower of sparks. Grezza had the upper hand; Zell would have to get close enough to use his sword, and he couldn't do that when his father had twice the range. I wanted to rush forward to help him, but then the other mercenaries charged at us.

I wasn't scared. Maybe I should have been, but I wasn't. Sure, these were trained killers and they outnumbered us twelve to four. But I had Zell's training. I had Galen and Lyriana at my back. And I really, really wanted to hurt someone.

The Princess jerked her hand up, shooting a gust of Lift that knocked two of the mercenaries off their feet and sent them sprawling out on the stone. Another tried to rush her with his sword, but Lyriana flipped her hand over, Lifted a table off the ground, and smashed it down on him in an explosive spray of splinters. The Sisters screamed. The mercenary went down. I didn't think he was getting back up. A third rushed at Galen, swinging a heavy, two-handed blade. The Lord of the Nest dodged it effortlessly, wove around behind him, and stabbed him in the back over and over again in a dizzying, bloody fury.

I was distracted from that horrible sight by a drunken holler. The older mercenary with the heavy jowls came charging at me and swung a hand ax at my throat in a clumsy swipe. My brain shut down. My body took over. I threw myself back, and his hand ax's chipped blade cut through the air in front of me. He stumbled forward. I whipped my dagger up. I'd been aiming for his chest, I think, but I ended up driving it up to the hilt into the meaty part of his bicep.

The mercenary let out a yelp of pain, his breath reeking of booze. His hand ax flew harmlessly across the room. He staggered forward, my dagger still in his arm, and I wove around him, pressed both hands to the back of his head, and jumped up, putting all my weight on his neck. This wasn't some graceful khel zhan move, more like a clumsy grapple you'd see in a barroom brawl. But it worked. The mercenary fell forward and hit the sharp corner of a table with his chin. There was an audible crack from his neck, and he crumpled to the ground and lay still.

I didn't even have a moment to breathe, because another mercenary was coming at me, a short, husky one with a braided beard. He had a long sword with a subtle curve, like Zell's way back at the feast. He sliced it down at me in a blindingly fast chop. I jerked to the side, just barely, the blade's polished edge scraping the skin off the side of my arm, and then I swung forward, spun around, and hit the mercenary in the back of the head with my elbow.

That was a khel zhan move, executed flawlessly, if I could give myself credit. The mercenary crumpled to the ground, his blade sliding out of his hands. He tried to get up, but I smashed the heel of my boot into his face. He didn't try to get up again.

I took a quick survey of the room. Most of the enemies were down. Galen was in the corner, choking a scrawny mercenary with his knee on the man's neck. Lyriana was holding her own against the remaining three, hurling chairs at them with her magic as they cowered behind a doorway. Zell and Grezza were fighting toward the chamber's entryway. Grezza was still on the offensive, driving Zell farther and farther back. Zell was faster, rolling and dodging his father's strikes, but Grezza was too big and too strong. His broad swings with his axes kept Zell a good yard away, rendering his sword useless. Zell looked desperate, his face slick and his breath fast, but Grezza hadn't even broken a sweat. He was taking his time. All he had to do was get in one hit.

Footsteps pounded toward them. Galen had knocked out his mercenary and was running Zell's way, a dagger in his hand and a clear shot at Grezza's back. While Zell held his father's attention, Galen bounded across the room, leaped onto a bench, onto a table, and then dove at Grezza, knife held high. . . .

But it was like Grezza had eyes in the back of his head. He spun around in a wide arc and hit Galen in midair with the back of his ax. Galen flew across the room like a doll, hit the wall, and crumpled.

I started to run toward him, when Lyriana screamed. "Tilla! Look out!"

I spun around. One of Lyriana's mercenaries had broken away and was rushing at me. It was Pretty Boy, from the alley in Bridgetown, with a bandage on his nose and a furious scowl. His hand darted up from his belt. Something streaked through the air at my face, something glinting and metal and sharp. A throwing knife.

My hand shot up on pure reflex and caught it by the polished metal hilt, stopping it an inch from my face. Just like the rock. Pretty Boy froze, stunned, and he looked as surprised as I felt. Still not thinking, I hurled the knife back. My throw was a lot less graceful, a wobbly horizontal spin, but it did the job. The edge of the knife clipped his throat as it passed by. A thin stream of blood shot out, like wine out of a punctured skin. The mercenary grabbed his throat with a gurgle and fell to his knees. I let out a wild cry and rushed toward him, and grabbed a weapon off the table, a heavy wooden club with nightglass teeth embedded in the head. Pretty Boy looked up at me, and I swung the club in a wide arc that caught him right in the face. I heard bone shatter and flesh tear. He toppled onto his back and lay there.

I don't know if I killed him. But he sure as hell wasn't pretty anymore.

I turned around. Lyriana had handled her last mercenary, ripping the door off its hinges and smashing him to the ground with it. The Sisters were watching her in stunned disbelief, and Archmatron Marlena, who I was happy to see was still alive, had a look that seemed somewhere in between admiration and disgust. I didn't care, though, because in the room's entryway, Zell and Grezza were still fighting, and it was somehow even worse than when I'd last looked. Grezza had lost one of his axes, but Zell had lost his only sword and was bleeding from a cut in his side. His father kept driving him back with wild swings, but there was only so far Zell could go before he hit the hallway wall. He was unarmed and wounded and trapped.

Then I saw his face. And I recognized the look. It was the look he'd had before saving me from Tannyn, the look he'd had taking out the skarrlings, the look he'd had throwing that knife in Bridgetown. It wasn't just determination. It was certainty.

He gritted his teeth and sprinted forward, rushing right at his father. Grezza growled and swung his ax down over his shoulder, like a massive bladed windmill plunging right at Zell's head. I cringed. But right before the blade could hit, Zell swerved in his sprint and jumped to the side, running for three whole strides along the wall itself. Grezza's ax smashed into the ground, and Zell lunged off the wall in an amazingly high leap, as high up as Grezza was tall. Grezza tried to react, but he was too slow and his ax was too heavy. Zell planted one hand on his father's shoulder, flipped over his head, and landed perfectly behind him. . . .

Then he threw out a dozen blindingly fast punches, each one driving the full length of his nightglass blades into his father's back, up and down the length of his spine.

Grezza let out a wheezing rasp and collapsed to his knees. His ax clattered to the floor. He sat there like that, rigid as a stone. His fingertips twitched, but his arms didn't move, dead weight hanging off his shoulders. His massive chest heaved with breath, but he didn't get up and didn't fall down. The thick, veiny muscles in his neck twitched, but his head was still. It was as if he'd been frozen.

Zell hadn't just beaten him. He'd paralyzed him.

Zell staggered away, panting, as if the reality of the fight had just hit him. The room was still and silent, except for the broken moaning of a few wounded mercenaries. Along the far wall, Galen pulled himself up into a slump and watched with great interest as Zell circled Grezza.

A grimace of blinding pain crossed the Zitochi Chief's face, but then it twisted into, unbelievably, a smile. "I underestimated you, son," Grezza choked out, each syllable a labor. "That was my folly."

"You had a lot of follies." Zell knelt down and grabbed his father's ax, lifting it up with both hands. He rested the tip of the blade against the base of Grezza's neck. "Underestimating me was the least of them."

Grezza didn't seem remotely fazed. "It is a father's greatest gift to see his son surpass him. When we meet again, in the halls of *Zhallaran*, I shall treat you better." He closed his eyes. "End this."

Zell breathed hard. I could see so much hatred in his eyes. I could see that killer's rage. So much fury. So much pain. But still, he held the ax straight and didn't swing it.

"Do it!" Grezza barked. "Don't you dare leave me like this! Broken! Dishonored!"

Zell looked up at me, and I could see it now in his eyes, behind the fury and the pain, the kindness he couldn't suppress, the mercy that had spared his brother, the compassion that had driven him to protect us all this time. I didn't say anything, but I didn't have to. Zell looked at me and nodded.

"Being dishonored was the best thing that ever happened to me." He flipped the ax around, so the wooden handle was against his father's neck. "You give it a shot." Then he swung it in a hard arc that cracked Grezza in the back of the head and sent him sprawling, unconscious, onto the chamber's floor.

I let out a long exhale. The Sisters looked relieved, too. Zell dropped the ax to the floor and looked around, nodding in approval. "Nice moves."

"I learned from the best." I smiled. "How are you holding up?"

Zell glanced down at his father's sprawled form. "Good," he said. "Surprisingly good."

Then he collapsed onto the floor.

I crossed the room faster than I've ever moved in my life and dropped down to him. With both hands, I propped him up and eased him against a wall, and my palms came back soaked red. "Oh no," I gasped, and pulled open his shirt, seeing for the first time just how bad the cut in his side was: a jagged rift from his rib cage to just above his hip. Blood, too much blood, was trickling out, running all the way down his side. I pressed my hands to the wound, desperately trying to keep his life in.

"It's okay," he choked out, even as the color was draining from his sweat-slick face. He tried to force a smile, but he just ended up with a grimace. "I've had worse."

"The wound isn't fatal," a woman's voice said from above me. I looked up to see the wizened face of Archmatron Marlena peering over my shoulder. Lyriana must have freed her. "The Sisters can mend this. If we can work our magic, he'll live." She gently pushed me aside and hovered over Zell, laying a strip of cloth from a nearby table onto his wound.

"Of course he'll live," I said, in part because I couldn't

even begin to fathom a world where Zell died, too. "You can save him."

"I'll be fine," Zell repeated, his eyes locked onto mine. "Don't worry. We'll make it through this." His breath got more ragged, and he struggled to keep his head up. "We'll . . . we'll . . ."

"Shhhh," Archmatron Marlena whispered, and eased his head back as he passed out. I clenched my hand over my mouth and turned away. I'd never been religious, never believed in any of it, but in that second, I prayed, to the Titans and the Old Kings and anyone else who would listen, prayed to hell that the Archmatron knew what she was doing.

"We need to get to safety," Lyriana said. "Now."

Oh. Right. The Zitochi were down, but we were still ass-deep in enemy territory. "Yeah. We need to move." I turned to Galen. "Time to go for your escape route. Can you help carry Zell?"

He rubbed at his side where Grezza had hit him. "Pretty sure I've got a broken rib . . . or three. . . ."

"I can Lift most of his weight, if you can guide him," Lyriana said. Her eyes flitted to one of the shattered tables in the room, the one crushing two Zitochi mercenaries. "Believe me, I can still Lift."

By the door to the courtyard, Lyriana was freeing the other Sisters one by one. I'll give them this: I'd thought they might be shell-shocked or rattled. But the second they were free, each one moved with a purpose, rushing to Marlena's side, tending to Zell. A few were even ministering to the wounded Zitochi. Lyriana probably thought that was noble. I thought it was a waste of effort.

The Sister in the chair, the one with the terrible white eyes, must have died during the fight. One of the others gently eased her out of her seat and laid her on the ground, draping a tablecloth over her prone form as she whispered the Cant of Departure.

"Our Rings," Archmatron Marlena said, gesturing toward a table along the wall without looking up. "Get the rest of our Rings."

"On it!" I said, and ran over. Sure enough, there they were on a small round table, a pile of Rings stacked up like treasures in a storybook, shimmering green and blue and turquoise like the surface of a rushing creek. I realized as I got to the table that I had no idea how they actually worked. Did certain Rings go to certain mages? Or could they just sort of trade them around? And what the frozen hell had Lyriana meant back in the tower when she'd said that "true-blood" mages didn't even need them?

A flicker caught my eye, from just by the table's side. A thick cloth sack lay there, and inside, something was pulsing and flickering. My stomach tightened, and the hairs on my neck stood on end. These were the other Rings, the ones from the Sisters the Zitochi had already tortured, the ones they were going to turn into mage-killers. My hand shook a little as I pried open the sack to look inside. There were at least two dozen Rings. While the ones on the table glowed solid colors, these changed and turned, the light inside them throbbing and twisting like trapped lightning storms. Just looking at them felt wrong, dangerous.

"Halt!" a man's voice screamed. Not one of ours. I jerked up, shocked, and through the hall's open door I saw pretty much the worst possible thing I could imagine. A dozen men, Kent men, were racing toward us across the courtyard, cross-bows in hand and leveled our way. They must have heard the commotion and come running.

Leading them, with an expression somewhere between stunned and outraged, was my father.

That was the second time today he'd surprised me on that courtyard. And this time, he looked a lot less inclined to save my life.

Lyriana acted first, and quickly. She threw up her hands and the doors to the courtyard swung shut with a heavy thud. Not a moment too soon. I heard crossbows twang, and the doors shook with the impact of their bolts. Lyriana flicked her hands, again and again, hurling the hall's two remaining big tables across the room. They slammed against the doors, frames cracking, but made a halfway-decent barricade.

Not good enough. "We have to go," Lyriana said. "They'll break through that in a minute." She turned to Galen. "Lord Reza. Can you get us to the stables?"

Galen knelt down, looping an arm under Zell's and lift-ing him to his feet. Zell's face was pale, his eyes lidded. I couldn't bear to look at him. "Yes," Galen grunted. "Yes, I think so. But—"

He was cut off by thundering footsteps. On the other side of the doors, I heard the shouting of men, the banging of fists. And then . . . the crunch of blades on wood.

"Shit," Galen hissed. "They're going to break through that in a second. We're not going to make it in time."

I knew he was right. Fifteen stunned Sisters, Zell barely conscious, Galen limping . . . there was no way we'd be able to run and get seated and riding, not before my father and his men caught up with us. The sound of hacking got louder and louder. The doors buckled and trembled.

I felt fear. . . .

And then I felt *it* again. The same thing I'd felt back in the tower, when I'd committed to save the Sisters in the first place. That certainty. That strength. That resolve. I knew exactly what I had to do.

We hadn't come this far just to give up now. Jax hadn't died for that.

"You all go," I said, and okay, even I was kind of surprised at how calm I sounded. "I'll stay and hold them off."

"What?" Lyriana gaped. "No. We're not leaving you."

"You have to," I said. "Look. I know my father. I know how to stall him." I wasn't sure my plan would work, didn't even know if it was likely, but I had to try. "Go. Get the Sisters to safety. Make this worth it. Make this count."

She stared at me, her eyes glistening, and a single golden tear streaked down her cheek like a shooting star. I could tell she knew what I was thinking and was trying to find a way to talk me out of it, so I grabbed her in a hug instead and held her close. "Go," I whispered. "Go."

She nodded and pulled away, sniffling. "Thank you, Tilla. For everything." She turned to Archmatron Marlena, who was slipping her Rings back onto her fingers. "Lead the Sisters out the northern door. We need to move."

The doors to the courtyard trembled as the first blade cut through them, a glistening ax head smashing through with a spray of splinters. The Sisters rushed out, led by Archmatron Marlena. The last to go was Lyriana, who was twirling her hands delicately to keep a Lift going, raising Zell's prone form just enough so that Galen could ease him onto his shoulder.

"Tilla," he moaned, so softly I could barely hear him. He was hanging on to the ragged edge of consciousness, too weak to do anything but whisper. "No . . ."

The doors buckled now. Dozens of ax heads had chopped through them. They'd be down any second. "It's okay," I told Zell, even though he probably wasn't awake enough to hear me.

"Tilla . . ." he rasped.

I leaned forward and ran my hand along his way-too-cold cheek. "You've protected me this whole journey," I whispered. "Now it's my turn to protect you." Then I leaned in and kissed him, and I felt his lips, and his breath, and his skin against mine, and now it took every ounce of strength *I* had to break it off, like I was ripping away my own skin. "We'll meet again," I said. "And when we do, I'm never leaving your side."

Zell was too weak to respond, too weak to even open his eyes. I was grateful for that. Galen shot me a quick nod and then turned across the room, hurrying after the Sisters with Zell slumped over his shoulder and Lyriana trailing after. They rushed out the back doors, to the Servants' Quarters and the passage to the stables. To freedom.

Alone in the hall, I fought back my tears and choked down my fear. I balled my hands into fists. I needed anger now. I needed grit.

The doors to the courtyard finally shattered, collapsing in with a decisive burst and knocking away the tables. I sprinted forward across the room even as my father's men rushed in, crossbows leveled at me, and I dove for the table with the mage-killers even as a few crossbows twanged.

I hit the ground in a roll and the bolts whizzed over me, collided harmlessly with the wall, and I was right where I wanted to be. My father threw up his hand, stopping his men, maybe because he wanted to spare me, maybe because he wanted to see what I was doing. Right then, I didn't care.

I stood up to face the mob of soldiers and I held out my hand, and my palm burned with the impossible, sizzling heat of a trapped mage's power. One of the Rings from the bag, a big, shiny crimson one, hung in my outstretched fist, its dancing light streaking out from my fingers like sunlight through a row of trees. The men recoiled, startled, as if I were holding a fire-breathing dragon. Even my father looked surprised.

"Yeah." I grinned. "That's right. Put your weapons down now. Or I blow us all to hell."

TWENTY-EIGHT

My father's men looked back and forth at one another and then at him, desperately hoping for an order. But he didn't give one. He just stared at me through his narrow eyes, my eyes, analyzing, considering. It was like he was seeing me for the first time.

"Well, aren't you a brave little bastard," a cold female voice said. Lady Robin Hampstedt pushed her way forward from the back of the crowd, and her scowl was so hateful it had its own scowl. Miles walked behind her, pale, speechless, looking way less confident than he had back in the tower. I shot him a glare that would've made a Titan tremble.

"You can threaten all you want, but you can't actually hurt us," Lady Hampstedt said. "That's just a tainted Ring without a shell. Without a spark, you won't be able to set it off."

I wasn't a scientific genius like her, but even I knew she was full of shit. This Ring in my hand radiated power, pulsed with it. It was scorching hot and freezing cold at the same time.

I felt its energy run through my whole body, like I'd kissed a lightning bolt. My vision throbbed; my bones hummed. A voice whispered in my brain, soft and seductive, in a language I couldn't understand. There was so much power in this Ring, desperate to break free, straining against the gem that trapped it. The case and the spark might have made it a convenient weapon, but they weren't necessary. One good crack, and this thing would go boom.

"You sure about that, Robin?" I shouted back. "Why don't I throw it at your face and we'll test it out?"

Lady Hampstedt actually growled. She ripped a crossbow out of the hands of the baffled soldier next to her and aimed it directly at my face. "How about we do a different test? I'm a crack shot, you know. And you'll have an awful hard time throwing with a bolt through your eye. What do you think is faster . . . your arm? Or my finger?"

"Don't shoot her, Mother!" Miles begged, and I decided I'd throw it at him instead. "You promised you wouldn't hurt her!"

"That was when she was locked safely in a dungeon." Lady Hampstedt squinted one eye. Was she actually enjoying this? "Not threatening me with a mage-killer."

"Please! Don't shoot her!"

"No one's shooting anyone," my father said sternly, like an adult finally tiring of the children's bickering. Every head in the room turned to his. Every head except Lady Hampstedt's, which remained as aimed at me as her crossbow. "I mean it, Robin. Don't pull that trigger."

She shot my father an annoyed look, but nodded. She knew better than to talk back to him. She released her finger off the crossbow's trigger but kept it pointed at me. "If she makes a move, I'll shoot."

"She won't," my father said. He took a step forward, and even in the dim moonlight his eyes were burning right through me. "Will you, Tillandra?"

"I don't know!" I shouted back, and I was trying to make it sound tough, but I honestly didn't know. My brilliant plan had been: step one, threaten them with a Ring; step two, figure out step two. All I could really do was stall for time.

My father knew that. "Come on, Tillandra. Put the Ring down." I thought he'd be angry, but his voice was soft and kind, the voice he'd used when I was a little girl to comfort me over a skinned knee. "I'm amazed you made it this far. Really, truly amazed. But this is over. There's no stopping progress. All that's left is to stand by my side and join me as I return glory and freedom to the West."

Join him? Stand at his side? I shook my head. "It's too late."

"Of course it's not." He took a step forward. "We still have more than enough time to round up your friends and finish making the rest of the bombs. And then . . . Picture it. Picture it! The mages will hasten through Pioneer's Pass tomorrow night. I have a hundred archers hidden in the mountains, each with a mage-killer on the end of his arrow. The mages stop at a checkpoint at the Pass's narrowest point, none the wiser. And then . . ." My father raised one hand and snapped his long fingers. "It'll be over in a heartbeat. The Knights of Lazan, the best and brightest of the warrior mages, wiped out. The Volaris Dynasty's reign of terror will be over. The era of mages will die out in one thunderous burst." The corners of his mouth twitched, hinting at a smile. "And the West will be a free Kingdom once more."

I wasn't smiling. A month ago, I couldn't have fathomed the idea of talking back to my father, but now I couldn't hold back. "You make it sound so good, so important. But what you're really talking about is murder. The murder of hundreds of people!"

Lady Hampstedt rolled her eyes. "Be still my bleeding heart. . . ."

My father shot her a glare that could melt stone. "They are not *people*, Tillandra. They're mages. Knights of Lazan. Brutal killers, every last one. Do you know how they learn their craft, at that sickening Academy in Lightspire? By practicing on prisoners, half of whom are innocent to begin with. They turn men inside out, boil their blood within them, melt their brains so all that's left is a drooling husk. . . ." He shook his head. "Those are not people. They're monsters. And they need to be stopped."

I thought of that boy in the creek, the screaming statue. And then I thought of the Sister in the chair, the one with the hollow, glassy eyes, the one lying under a cloth just a few feet away from me. "It's not just the mages," I said. "What about all the innocent people who'll get caught in the crossfire of the war? What about the Sisters you plan to torture to death? What about the people who've already been killed?"

"Wars have casualties," he said.

"You started this war!" I yelled back. "Maybe we weren't free before, but we had peace. . . . Wasn't that good enough?"

"Peace," my father sneered. "This isn't peace. This is oppression. This is bending down to lick the boots of the men who beat you. You want to talk about innocents killed? Do you know what the mages did in the Great War? Have you heard what happened at Orstulk and New Kendletown? Can you imagine an entire village murdered, their flayed corpses mounted on the roofs of their homes?" His eyes burned with righteous passion. "Do you know what they did to my grandfather?"

"No," I whispered.

That seemed to shake him. His hard expression softened, and a look I'd never seen before crossed his face. "No," he repeated quietly, and stepped back. "No, you wouldn't. Because I never told you."

Never told me what? What the hell did they do to his grandfather? What was happening here?

My father, he of the penetrating stare, actually looked down, ashamed. "I've made many mistakes, Tillandra. There is so much I've done wrong. But there is nothing I regret more than how I treated you. Everything that's happened to you— all of it—is because of my failure as a father."

My mouth went dry, and I felt my hand start to tremble. Even the Ring's power felt distant, diminished. This had to be a ruse, right? But how? Why? "What are you talking about?"

"When I came of age, my father took me into his study and he told me his great secret. On the Day of Surrender, the Kents had yielded to the Volaris in name but not in spirit. Albion Kent had made a promise, a promise that was passed to my grandfather, to my father, to me. A promise to be vigilant, to be dedicated, to watch for the moment when the Volaris were weak, and then strike." My father's voice was distant, reverent. "I made that promise. I swore I would restore our

Kingdom. I spent two decades planning my . . . our revenge. Everything I've done in the last twenty years, every choice I've made, was to bring us to this day."

"Every choice?" I whispered back, and suddenly, this was very, very personal. "What about ignoring me the second you married Lady Evelyn? Was that for your revenge as well?"

"Yes! Of course, yes!" he replied, and I couldn't believe the emotion I was hearing. "I loved your mother, Tillandra. I might have thrown it all away for her, if she hadn't died. And you remind me so much of her, just looking at you makes my heart ache." I had no idea my father was even capable of talking like this. Had he bottled it away so deeply for decades? Was this who he really was? "In another life, I might have just raised you as my real daughter from the start, politics be damned. But I couldn't. I needed House Yrenwood's loyalty, and that could only be bought through marriage, through legitimate heirs. I had to do it. And I had to distance myself from you, lest it cast our alliance into doubt. It killed me inside to do it. But I had to."

And there it was. The words I'd spent almost my entire life dreaming of hearing, the answer I'd so badly hoped for but never really dared to think could be true. Out in the open, just like that. I wanted to be skeptical, to not let it distract me, to focus on the mage-killer in my hand and the crossbow pointed at my face. But I couldn't. There was just too much weight in his words. "Why didn't you say something?" I demanded, and tears stung my eyes. "Fine, you couldn't legitimize me. But you could have told me about your promise! You could have brought me in! You could have let me know!"

"I didn't trust you," my father admitted without a

moment's hesitation. "I thought you were still a child. I thought you wouldn't understand, that you'd slip up and compromise my plan. I thought I could just wait until the mages were dead, and then I could bring you in. I didn't think you needed to know. I was so wrong." Then he looked up at me, eyes shining with pride. "I wish I had, Tillandra. I wish I'd brought you into my study and told you what my father had told me. Had I known what you were capable of, I would have. You fought for what you believed in, even when it meant defying your own House. You traveled through the entire Province, even with those Zitochi mercenaries on your heels. Even now, you somehow broke out of the tower, and what did you do? Did you run for your life? No. You marched straight into the heart of danger itself. Because you have a bold heart and the iron will of a true Kent, straight from the line of the Old Kings. I only wish I had given you the upbringing that would have had you fighting by my side. I can only imagine what we could have accomplished."

"You're proud of me . . . because I defied you?"

"Yes. There's no greater courage than defying your own father, than defying your King. In its way, your rebellion was just as courageous as my own. That's why I'm proud."

It's a trap! my brain screamed. *He's manipulating you! He's just saying what you want to hear!* But my heart refused to listen. "You ordered me dead. You sent mercenaries after me!"

"And it was the most painful decision I've ever made," my father said. "But I had no choice. This is about more than you, more than me. Tonight is about the freedom and future of every citizen of the West. No one life can outweigh that.

Not even yours." He stepped toward me. "But the Old Kings have smiled on us and given us a second chance. You don't have to die, and you don't have to run. Tonight the world changes. And tomorrow you can join me, by my side, as you always should have been. Tomorrow we can live the life we were always meant to." He smiled, he actually smiled, not a smirk or a hint, but a full, genuine, earnest smile, the smile I'd wanted to see my entire life. "Tillandra Kent. You're my true daughter. And one day you will rule all these lands as the rightful Queen of the West."

It felt like I was being swallowed by an endless sea, sinking into a massive, thundering whirlpool. I sucked in my breath and closed my eyes. I wanted to believe it. I wanted to feel it. I wanted so badly to picture that future, to picture him finally embracing me as a daughter, to going home again. To being a Queen. To living that life, that dream. I wanted to see it.

But I couldn't.

Because all I could see was Archmagus Rolan, gurgling in the sand as my father's dagger plunged into his eye. Markos and Tannyn, their corpses turning blue on the floor of their villa. That family murdered in the cottage, bodies strewn around like they were nothing, and that Watchman in Bridgetown, just doing his job before getting a knife to the skull. That Sister in the chair, eyes glassy, streaked with blood.

All I could see was Jax.

Jax, who would never matter. Jax, who my father would never see as family. Jax, who my father would have killed in a heartbeat.

Jax, who lay dead because of my father's war.

And he wanted me to be Queen of the West.

I looked up at my father and met his eyes. "Sorry, Lord Kent," I said. "But I'm just a bastard."

I threw the Ring as hard as I could. Not at my father. Not at Lady Hampstedt. But between us, at the floor of the Great Hall.

Many things happened at once.

"No!" my father screamed.

His men dove and scattered.

Lady Hampstedt fired her crossbow.

The Ring whistled through the air, spinning, spiraling, casting that terrible crimson light in all directions. . . .

And then it hit right where I'd been aiming, dead center on the wide hexagonal tile.

The explosion was deafening, a thunderous boom and a burst of red flame that scorched the walls and sent sizzling shards of ore flying in all directions. I heard screams as they struck my father's men, but I didn't even have time to process it, because the floor of the Great Hall shuddered and shattered, collapsing inward in a gaping maw of a sinkhole. We all fell together, in a shower of brick and dirt, down into the darkness of the tunnels.

I hit the ground, but not as hard as my father and his men, who hadn't expected it. We were in the wide chamber below the Great Hall, the one that connected all the tunnels. I couldn't see my father or his men through the thick, billowing cloud of dust between us, but I could hear them, shouting, coughing, drawing blades.

I had a moment, just a tiny, tiny moment before they realized what had happened, and I wasn't going to waste it. I sprang to my feet and reached for the sack that had been lying next to me, the one with all the other tainted Rings.

"Stop her!" my father bellowed, but they couldn't see me, couldn't tell where I was going. I sprinted as hard as I could, ignoring the pain in my arm, ignoring the voice in my head that knew I was almost certainly about to die. The tunnels should have been pitch-black, but the sack illuminated my way, cutting through the darkness with a blinding rainbow of pulsing reds and blues and greens.

That wasn't a good thing. The other Rings must have been jostled in the fall, because the sack rumbled with their energy. I could feel it shuddering, hear the cracking of gems like panes of glass.

I sprinted even harder through the narrow eastern tunnel, and then I was out in the fresh night air, under the stars, on that narrow rocky platform overlooking the sheer cliffs. A cold wind blew over me. The moon overhead was full and bright. Even as the sack in my hands started to burn, even as I heard my father scream behind me, I had a sudden moment of utter calm.

I saw myself and Jax on the platform's edge, just one night ago, sitting together in loving silence, one last time.

I smiled and wound my arm up and hurled the sack as hard as I could.

It hurtled out of my hand, over the ledge, down into the abyss below. I watched in wonder as it ripped open midair and all the Rings went flying, like a multicolored star-scape, shining out across the night.

And then they blew up.

I heard a boom so loud I felt it in my bones. I heard ice snap and flame roar. I heard voices scream. I heard stone crumble.

I saw an enormous fireball that was every single color at once blast out, tearing through the mountains, lighting up the night sky brighter than the sun. In that fireball, I saw crystal shards and rivulets of lava and dancing bands of emerald light.

I felt myself lift off my feet and fly backward away from the ledge, into the tunnels, and smash incredibly hard into a stone wall. I felt my bones break and blood flood my mouth.

And then I felt nothing.

TWENTY-NINE

Smoke was stinging my eyes and burning my throat.

I coughed and winced, blinking away tears. I was lying on a pile of sharp, jagged stones. I couldn't tell what the hell I was looking at, at first, and then I realized it was the ceiling of the Great Hall, as seen from the tunnels through the hole where the floor used to be. The blast must have thrown me all the way back into the wide chamber.

That wasn't the only damage it had done. Big chunks of the Great Hall's ceiling were missing, having caved in from the blast. Tiny fires smoldered all around. Huge piles of broken stones lay around me, and underneath a few, I could make out the broken forms of crushed men. My father's men. I tried to crane my head to look at them.

That was when I realized I was in the worst pain of my life.

I sucked in my breath and gritted my teeth. My left leg must have been tucked behind me when I hit the wall, because it was shattered now, broken clean in the middle of the shin, bloodied white bone jutting through. My foot was twisted around completely backward, like a doll a kid had played with too roughly. My chest felt like it was on fire, probably from a couple of broken ribs, and every time I coughed, I spat blood.

I was going to die here, wasn't I? Yeah. No way I made it out of this.

And even though a tiny part of me screamed in horror, the rest of me was surprisingly calm. Better to die here than back in the tower, at Razz's hands. Better here than in Bridgetown. Better here than in the skarrling's mine, better here than on the road, better here than on Whitesand Beach. Better to die here than live a lie.

If I died here, I'd die Tilla of the tunnels. I could live with that.

A whimpering from somewhere in the smoke snapped me out of my calm. I squinted and could make out a hunched, sobbing form. It was Miles, his fancy tunic torn, his face caked with soot. Lady Robin Hampstedt lay next to him on her stomach, not moving. There was something weird about her head, and then I realized it wasn't there at all, crushed under a huge stone chunk.

I tried to say something, but then another shape stepped in front of me, tall and thin, clad all in black. A hand grabbed my jaw and slammed my head back into the wall, and then a face leaned right into mine.

"You little bitch," my father snarled. A long cut on his forehead bled into his eyes, and his hair was messy and burned. Any love or pride he'd had was gone. All that was left was hot, raging hate. "You stupid, traitorous little bitch." He pulled a small, slender knife out of a sheath on his boot and jammed its cold tip against my throat. "Do you have any idea what you've done? Any idea what you've cost me?" I felt a sting as its trembling blade punctured my skin. "I should kill you right now. I should cut your ungrateful, selfish little throat. . . ."

And now I wasn't scared at all. Not of him. Not of his knife. I was tired and sore and angry, angry at everything he'd put me through, angry that I'd ever even wanted his worthless love. I looked right into his hateful green eyes, and I forced my cracked lips into a smile. "Then do it," I said.

He stared at me, nostrils flaring, hand shaking. But he couldn't do it. Even after everything I'd done to him, he couldn't hurt me, his first daughter, his true daughter. He turned away with a roar and hurled his knife at the tunnel's wall, where it bounced with a clatter. And I grinned and laughed.

Voices sounded from a distance, people shouting. More Kent men? Or was it Lyriana and Galen?

My father collected himself with a deep breath, then walked over and jerked Miles up to his feet by his collar. "Quit your blubbering," he commanded. "We have to go now."

"My . . . mother . . ." Miles moaned. "She killed my mother. She killed my mother!"

"Yes. She did. Which makes you the Lord of House Hampstedt. You know what that means, don't you?" My father leaned down into Miles's face. "It means we have a war to win."

Miles sniffled but nodded. Without so much as another glance back at me, the two stormed off, leaving me alone, slumped against the wall, mangled, bleeding, choking on smoke, unable to move.

I hoped Zell was okay. I hoped Lyriana was okay. That was all I cared about now.

I smiled and closed my eyes.

The darkness took me.

THIRTY

Daylight.

A beige canopy, swaying gently.

The smell of herbs, and earth, and freshly cut flowers.

Where...?

I blinked awake. I was lying on a stretcher in some kind of a makeshift tent, wrapped up in a thin white sheet. A pair of iron braziers stood on opposite sides of my bed, and there was obviously something weird burning inside them because the smoke coming out was green and smelled like spices and cinnamon. I had no idea how, but my body didn't hurt at all; it felt numb and distant, like I was just a floating soul.

"Hey there," Zell said from somewhere nearby. "Welcome back."

I craned my head to the side, and there he was, the color back in his face, looking just as strong and healthy as he did when I'd met him. He sat on a stool by my bedside, and his eyes lit up as he smiled. He'd made it. He was alive! And so, apparently, was I.

"Zell," I choked out, my throat scratchy and raw. "You're okay!"

"I am. Got a new scar, too." He lifted up his shirt to show me his stomach. Right where his father has slashed him, just left of his abs, was a wide white strip of scar tissue. It was faded, impossibly so, like something from a wound suffered a decade ago.

"How . . . ?"

"The Sisters of Kaia." Zell jerked his head to the side, and I noticed a woman sitting behind him. Her face was hidden behind a golden gossamer veil, but I could make out dark skin and green eyes. She held her Ringed hands together and rocked back and forth slightly, humming softly. "They saved both our lives."

"Well, we saved theirs." I lifted my head, just a little, to check myself out. My leg was splinted and bandaged up, the bone set with a pair of metal rods. My right forearm was wrapped up just as tightly, but there was some kind of weird flowering vine tied around the outside of the bandage, like a string on a present. The vine pulsed and throbbed, just a little, like someone giving my arm a gentle squeeze. I clenched my hand into a fist, and lifted it up and moved it around. It all worked. "Whoa."

Zell reached out and took that hand, gently lacing my fingers with his. Somehow, that touch made this all feel real. I'd actually survived. And there was nothing in the world that felt better than Zell's skin against mine. "My thought as well. What these Sisters can do . . . it's beyond anything I've ever imagined. I see now why they are so powerful, and so feared."

"Lyriana," I asked, suddenly remembering. "Is she okay?"

"She's fine. Better than fine, really. Would you like to go see her?" Zell glanced back at the Sister in the corner of the tent. "May I take Tilla out for a walk?"

The Sister stopped humming, and the vine around my arm stopped throbbing. "That should be fine. Just make sure to come back before sunset. Her wounds are still healing." Even through the veil, I could see her smirk. "Don't do anything *too* physical."

"Too physical? Like what?" Zell asked, and then got it. "Oh . . . I mean . . . We—we wouldn't. Not that we couldn't. . . . I just mean, not now, necessarily, unless, well, unless she wanted to, but . . . we wouldn't—"

I laughed and pressed two fingers to Zell's lips. Him being flustered was maybe the most adorable thing I'd ever seen. "We'll be fine," I said, and Zell gave my fingers the tiniest kiss, and I decided maybe I'd push just how physical we could get after all.

Zell helped me out of the bed and slung a strong arm under my shoulders to help me walk. I leaned into him, maybe a little more than I had to, and we made our way toward the tent's entrance. My legs felt floaty and numb, my feet tingling with each step. "How long was I out?"

"Two days." Zell pushed open the tent's flap, and we stepped out, squinting against the daylight. We were in what appeared to be a makeshift army camp, a cluster of tents stretching out in all directions. Mages bustled by, armored warriors with swords floating at their backs, robed scholars carrying heavy tomes, and veiled Sisters drifting wordlessly from tent to tent. At the edge of the camp, I could see the entrance to Pioneer's Pass. Long black scorch marks ran along the valley's walls, and huge chunks of stone had been blasted away. It looked as scarred as we were.

A battle had been fought here. Galen had gotten his counterambush after all.

"I take it the mages won," I said.

Zell nodded. "They did. That blast you caused was visible for miles away. When the mages saw it, they knew something had gone wrong, so they charged into the Pass in battle formation. Your father's men were still waiting for their orders." He paused. "The battle lasted less than an hour."

"My father?" I asked.

"He escaped, along with Miles. They fled back west, along with what was left of his army."

So he lived. There was that.

Zell led me toward the center of the camp. Obviously, this was where the important people were. The tents were bigger, and the mages looked older, more weathered, more serious. We passed a group of men gathered around a long table, talking in hushed tones. Galen was among them, his face healed. He met my gaze as we passed, and he gave me a quick, knowing nod. I'm pretty sure he was saying thanks.

The biggest tent was right in the middle, nearly five times bigger than the others, with a high ceiling and an ornate gold trim. Two hulking mages stood outside, their faces hidden behind mirrored helms, their hands encased in clawed silver gauntlets. They seemed to recognize Zell, though. One nodded, and the other pulled open the tent's flap.

We stepped inside. This was obviously some kind of war room, lit up by a half-dozen floating balls of Light. Stacks of books and maps lined the tent's walls, and a massive darkwood table took up most of the room. A map rested on top of it, not a flat drawing like I'd always seen, but an actual tiny version of the West, like the world's most detailed dollhouse, complete with snow-tipped mountains and little green forests and even running rivers that flowed impossibly up to the edge of the table. Dozens of little ivory figurines had been set up all over it, toy soldiers with House banners hoisted over them, all the armies of the West laid out.

At any other point in my life, I would have been totally fascinated and probably spent hours just staring at it. But now I was mostly interested in the person standing behind the table. Lyriana had cleaned up and looked amazing. She wore a shimmering black dress and a beaded golden circlet, and her hair was braided in a handful of intricate circling bands. She was talking to a tall man in an ornate robe, but she spun toward me the moment I walked in. "Tilla!" She sprinted toward me, almost knocking the table over. "You're awake!"

She grabbed me in a ferocious hug, and I stumbled backward. Zell had to catch us. "Easy there," he said. "Tilla is still a little weak."

"Sorry," Lyriana said, but she kept hugging me just as tightly. "I'm just so happy to see you again!"

I grinned and hugged her back. "It's good to see you, too."

"So this is the famous Tillandra," the man in the ornate robe said, his voice low and silky. He stepped toward us, and now I could see him clearly in the tent's soft light. He was young, maybe twenty, tall and thin, with skin as dark as Lyriana's and a face that looked uncannily like hers as well. His hair was neatly curled around his head, and a thin, stubbly beard lined his elegant jaw. His eyes burned a furious red, like the brightest roses in Lady Evelyn's garden. He strode across the room, his crimson robe billowing out behind him like a cape, and bowed his head ever so slightly. "It's my honor to meet you."

"My cousin, Ellarion," Lyriana introduced.

I didn't know if I was supposed to bow or offer my hand or what, so I just kind of stood there. Ellarion didn't seem put out. "Lyriana told me everything you did for her. My family owes you a debt beyond words. When you arrive at Lightspire, I shall ensure that you want for nothing."

"All I want now is a hot bath and a cold drink," I replied.

Ellarion smirked. "A girl after my own heart," he said as Lyriana rolled her eyes.

Was he hitting on me? That would be weird, right? I glanced to Zell for help, but he was standing by the war table, head cocked to the side as he studied the pieces. "Kent's men flee to Castle Waverly," he said. "Will you ride after them?"

Ellarion scowled. "As badly as I want to, we must hold and wait for reinforcements, for orders from King Leopold. We came out here prepared for an incursion into Zitochi lands, not a damned Second Great War." He turned to me. "A special caravan will take you three back to Lightspire. I'll ride with you the whole way, just in case. My cousin is heir to the throne. Her safety is paramount." I swear his red eyes actually flickered, like a candle's flame. "But I will return here. Lord Kent will be brought to justice. He'll pay for what he did to my father. I promise you that."

I tried to think of a suitable response to that but came up empty. The truth is, I just didn't care anymore. They could lock my father away in the darkest dungeon or mount his head on the walls of Castle Waverly. It didn't matter. That part of my life was done. I was alive, Lyriana and Zell were alive, and we'd escaped. That was all I cared about.

That, and one other thing. "Jax," I said softly, a cold, hard knot twisting in my stomach. "Did you . . . get him?"

Lyriana nodded. "Come with me. I'll show you."

Lyriana, Zell, and I left Ellarion in the central tent and set back out across the camp. Lyriana led now, Zell and me following close behind. At the sight of the Princess, mages dropped to their knees, heads bowed. She waved at them with the back of her hand, and her fingers sparkled. She'd gotten new Rings to replace her old ones.

There was something else on her arm, too, a black square of charred flesh where she'd been burned. I blinked and then realized. Her tattoo, the flowering sigil of the Sisters of Kaia. It was gone.

Lyriana caught me staring. "They burned it off me this morning," she said. "Don't worry. It doesn't hurt."

"Doesn't hurt? What? Why did they burn it in the first place?"

Lyriana cocked her head to the side, like she was almost amused. "I killed men, Tilla. I used my magic to take lives. I broke my vows. I could not stay among the Sisters, not after that."

"But . . . but . . . but you broke your vows for them!" I stammered. "You did it for a good cause!"

"If we could break our vows whenever a good cause came along, they wouldn't be very good vows, would they?" Lyriana said. "Relax, Tilla. I made my choice. I'm ready to live with it."

"If you're not a Sister of Kaia, then what are you?" Zell asked.

"An apostate. A mage without a school." Lyriana smiled, her eyes sparkling with mischief. "A bastard."

I wanted to press further, but then we'd walked across the camp's western border. I inhaled sharply. Where there had once been a wide grassy plain, there was now a sprawling graveyard, an endless field of burial mounds as far as the eye could see. Each had a single plant growing out of it, a tall green stalk with an orange-and-black flower at the head. An elderbloom. The flower of the Volaris Dynasty, of the Kingdom of Noveris. I guess that's how mages were buried. And I was looking at a whole forest of them.

"How many mages died?" I asked.

"Two hundred and fifty," Lyriana replied.

"And how many of my father's men?"

Lyriana bit her lip. "A thousand."

"A thousand," I repeated. A thousand. A thousand men dead because of me. A thousand sons, brothers, fathers, men of the West. Had I known any of them? Had I seen them training in the barracks or marching by the castle? Had they understood, even remotely, what they were fighting for?

A cold wind blew over us. The elderblooms swayed from side to side. Tears stung my eyes. "Did we do the right thing?" I asked.

Zell wrapped an arm around me and pulled me close. "We didn't do the wrong thing. That might be all we get."

"I think I'm okay with that."

"I am, too."

"Come on," Lyriana said. "I'll show you to Jax."

The graves of the nonmages were at the far end of the field, where the stretch of yellowing grass gave way to forest. The mounds here didn't have elderblooms, of course, but that didn't make them unmarked. Some had swords planted at their heads, others staffs or shields, or a stack of books.

Jax's grave was at the very end of the field, under the shadow of the forest. A tiny tree grew at the head, and I could make out small yellow-orange fruits hidden in its leaves. "A peach tree," I choked out.

"I think he would've been happy with it," Lyriana replied with a sad smile.

"He would have been happy you cared."

I walked over to the grave, my knees trembling, and hunkered down alongside it. Zell and Lyriana stood back, and I ran my hand along the tree, and I smelled that damp earth. I couldn't think about the fact that Jax's body was just beneath me, that he was down there, cold and gray and dead. So I closed my eyes and I just touched the tree's rough bark and I talked to him, as if he were sitting by my side, like he had for so many years.

"Guess I'm going to Lightspire after all," I said. "Can't believe you won't be there to see it with me. Almost makes me not want to go." My eyes burned. I blinked the tears away. Jax wouldn't want me to sit here all weepy. He'd want me to go on, to live life, to get drunk and have adventures and be happy. "Shit, Jax. I'm going to miss you so much. I'm never going to forget you. Not ever." I took a handful of earth up and pressed my hand to my lips, letting it trickle out through my fingers.

Lyriana knelt down by my side and wordlessly reached

out, running her fingers along the tree. Her golden eyes glistened with tears.

"Did you mean what you said back in the tower?" I asked her. "Did you really love Jax?"

"I did." She closed her eyes. "I do."

I wrapped my arm around her shoulders and pulled her close. We had the same aching wound inside us, the same emptiness that would never be filled. Being together, holding each other . . . it didn't make the pain go away. But at least we had someone to share its sting.

"We'll see you again, Jax," Lyriana whispered to the gently swaying tree. "In the stars above, when the Titans take us."

"Just save a little wine for us, okay?" I added, and I could almost hear him laugh.

I stood up and turned away from the grave. I'd done what I had to, and I couldn't stay any longer, not without breaking down in tears. I helped Lyriana to her feet. "When do we leave for Lightspire?"

"Tomorrow morning. And I made sure we'd all be in a carriage together."

I turned to Zell. "So you're coming with us?"

"I am."

I hesitated, terrified to ask the question gnawing at me from within, but I couldn't hold it back. "And then? When we get there?"

Zell chose his words slowly and carefully. "I will not kneel. I will not serve. I am a Zitochi, first and forever, and my loyalty will always be to my people." His eyes shifted toward Lyriana, and she nodded. "But I have had some conversation with Lyriana on this topic. And she has convinced me that I will hold far more influence at her side, speaking to the nobles at Lightspire, than I would dying in the mud with some band of cutthroats."

"So you're saying . . ."

He leaned in and kissed me, long and deep, his arms firm around my waist, his body warm against mine, our hearts beating together. When we pulled away, he pressed his forehead against mine, his eyes looking right into me. "I'm never leaving your side again."

Lyriana grinned. "You two are absolutely adorable. Can I just say that? Because you are."

"I've never been called adorable before," Zell mused.

I threw one arm around his shoulders and one around Lyriana's. "You'd better get used to it."

For one fleeting second, the weight of the moment hit me. My life as I knew it was over. I was going to Lightspire, the greatest city, capital of all of Noveris. What the hell was I going to do there? Where would I live? How would I fit in? Who would I even be, if not a Westerner, if not a bastard?

And just as quickly as it had come, that panic vanished. Who cared if I didn't know where to live or what to do? I'd have Lyriana there, my best friend, my sister, and we'd take care of each other no matter what happened. I'd have Zell, and in his arms I'd never be afraid or lost. We'd crossed a Province, faced skarrlings and mercenaries, and saved innocent lives. What the hell couldn't we do?

The sun was starting to set, its broad orange disk slipping behind the trees to the West. Beyond them lay my father, and Miles, and their war. Beyond them lay Castle Waverly and my past. I turned my back on them, and the three of us walked into camp together, the Princess and the Zitochi and the bastard, holding each other up, not letting each other go. We were family now. More family than I'd ever had. I held Zell and Lyriana close, and we walked as one, to the camp, to the future, to the wide and uncertain East.

ACKNOWLEDGMENTS

Thanks, first and foremost, to my incredible, totally kick-ass agent, Sara Crowe. She believed in this story from the start, and her encouragement and support gave me the fire to keep on writing.

To my incomparable editor, Laura Schreiber, who gave me the most insightful and on-point notes I've ever gotten and helped shape this book into something so much better. It's a hell of a feeling when someone else understands your book better than you do, and working with Laura was a series of endless *Eureka!* moments. Thanks as well to the rest of the team at Hyperion: Mary Mudd, Cassie McGinty, Christine Ma, Levente Szabo, and everyone else on Team Bastard. These guys are the best.

To my generous readers: Kara Loo, Jennifer Young, Eric Dean, Max Doty, Royal McGraw, Kenny Wat, and Oliver Miao. Their feedback and guidance shaped me into a better writer; their support and patience made me a better person.

To all the teachers and mentors who helped me along this journey, who encouraged the weird kid with the gory short stories to keep on writing. Thank you Sharron Mittlestet, Sylvia Harp, Dean Crawford, and Paul Russell.

To my parents, Simon and Ann, who always encouraged me to pursue this dream, who taught me how to appreciate a good story and tell a good joke; to my grandparents Yakov, Yulya, and Marina, for their endless kindness and support, no matter how rambling my anecdotes got; to my brother, Daniel, for always being there to make me laugh, to talk through my ideas, and to distract me with video games when I got stuck.

And finally to Sarah, my muse, my puzzle piece, my forever-first-reader. None of this would have been possible without you, and may I always be your wordslinger.